A PRISONER OF BIRTH

JEFFREY ARCHER, whose novels and short stories include *Not a Penny More, Not a Penny Less*, *Kane & Abel* and *Twist in the Tale* has topped the bestseller lists around the world, with sales of over 130 million copies.

The author has served five years in the House of Commons, fourteen years in the House of Lords and two in Her Majesty's prisons, which spawned three highly acclaimed Prison Diaries.

False Impression, his most recent full-length novel, was an international number one bestseller and remained in the UK bestseller charts for over two months.

The author is married with two children, and lives in London and Cambridge.

JEFFREY ARCHER

A PRISONER OF BIRTH

MACMILLAN

First published 2008 by Macmillan

This edition published 2008 by Macmillan
an imprint of Pan Macmillan Ltd
Pan Macmillan, 20 New Wharf Road, London N1 9RR
Basingstoke and Oxford
Associated companies throughout the world
www.panmacmillan.com

ISBN 978-0-230-70700-9

5 7 9 8 6 4

A CIP catalogue record for this book is available from
the British Library.

Typeset by SetSystems Ltd, Saffron Walden, Essex
Printed and bound in the UK by
CPI Mackays, Chatham ME5 8TD

Visit www.panmacmillan.com to read more about all our books
and to buy them. You will also find features, author interviews and
news of any author events, and you can sign up for e-newsletters
so that you're always first to hear about our new releases.

TO JONATHAN AND MARION

ACKNOWLEDGEMENTS

I would like to thank the following for their invaluable advice
and help with this book:

The Hon Michael Beloff QC, Kevin Robinson, Simon Bainbridge,

Rosie de Courcy, Mari Roberts, Alison Prince and

Billy Little (BX7974, HMP Whitemoor,
LVCM (Hons), BSc (Hons), Soc Sci (Open), Dip SP & C (Open))

PROLOGUE

'YES,' SAID BETH.

She tried to look surprised, but wasn't all that convincing as she had already decided that they were going to be married when they were at secondary school. However, she was amazed when Danny fell on one knee in the middle of the crowded restaurant.

'Yes,' Beth repeated, hoping he'd stand up before everyone in the room stopped eating and turned to stare at them. But he didn't budge. Danny remained on one knee, and like a conjurer, produced a tiny box from nowhere. He opened it to reveal a simple gold band boasting a single diamond that was far larger than Beth had expected – although her brother had already told her that Danny had spent two months' wages on the ring.

When Danny finally got off his knee, he took her by surprise again. He immediately began to tap a number on his mobile. Beth knew only too well who would be on the other end of the line.

'She said yes!' Danny announced triumphantly. Beth smiled as she held the diamond under the light and took a closer look. 'Why don't you join us?' Danny added before she could stop him. 'Great, let's meet at that wine bar off the Fulham Road – the one we went to after the Chelsea game last year. See you there, mate.'

Beth didn't protest; after all, Bernie was not only her brother, but Danny's oldest friend, and he'd probably already asked him to be his best man.

Danny turned off his phone and asked a passing waiter for the bill. The maitre d' bustled across.

'It's on the house,' he said, giving them a warm smile.

It was to be a night of surprises.

—◄o►—

When Beth and Danny strolled into the Dunlop Arms, they found Bernie seated at a corner table with a bottle of champagne and three glasses by his side.

'Fantastic news,' he said even before they had sat down.

'Thanks, mate,' said Danny, shaking hands with his friend.

'I've already phoned Mum and Dad,' said Bernie as he popped the cork and filled the three champagne glasses. 'They didn't seem all that surprised, but then it was the worst-kept secret in Bow.'

'Don't tell me they'll be joining us as well,' said Beth.

'Not a chance,' said Bernie raising his glass, 'you've only got me this time. To long life and West Ham winning the cup.'

'Well, at least one of those is possible,' said Danny.

'I think you'd marry West Ham if you could,' said Beth, smiling at her brother.

'Could do worse,' said Bernie.

Danny laughed. 'I'll be married to both for the rest of my life.'

'Except on Saturday afternoons,' Bernie reminded him.

'And you might even have to sacrifice a few of those once you take over from Dad,' said Beth.

Danny frowned. He had been to see Beth's father during his lunch break and had asked for permission to marry his daughter – some traditions die hard in the East End. Mr Wilson couldn't have been more enthusiastic about Danny becoming his son-in-law, but went on to tell him that he had changed his mind about something Danny thought they'd already agreed on.

'And if you think I'm gonna call you guv when you take over from my old man,' said Bernie, breaking into his thoughts, 'you can forget it.' Danny didn't comment.

'Is that who I think it is?' said Beth.

Danny took a closer look at the four men standing by the bar. 'It certainly looks like 'im.'

'Looks like who?' asked Bernie.

'That actor what plays Dr Beresford in *The Prescription*.'

'Lawrence Davenport,' whispered Beth.

'I could always go and ask him for his autograph,' said Bernie.

'Certainly not,' said Beth. 'Although Mum never misses an episode.'

'I think you fancy him,' said Bernie as he topped up their glasses.

'No, I don't,' said Beth a little too loudly, causing one of the men at the bar to turn round. 'And in any case,' she added smiling at her fiancé, 'Danny's far better looking than Lawrence Davenport.'

'Dream on,' said Bernie. 'Just because Danny boy's shaved and washed his hair for a change, don't think he's gonna make a habit of it, sis. No chance. Just remember that your future 'usband works in the East End, not the City.'

'Danny could be anything he wanted to be,' said Beth, taking his hand.

'What've you got in mind, sis? Tycoon or tosser?' said Bernie, thumping Danny on the arm.

'Danny's got plans for the garage that will make you—'

'Shh,' said Danny, as he refilled his friend's glass.

'He'd better have, 'cause gettin' spliced don't come cheap,' said Bernie. 'To start with, where you goin' to live?'

'There's a basement flat just round the corner that's up for sale,' said Danny.

'But have you got enough readies?' demanded Bernie. ''Cause basement flats don't come cheap, even in the East End.'

'We've saved enough between us to put down a deposit,' said Beth, 'and when Danny takes over from Dad—'

'Let's drink to that,' said Bernie, only to find that the bottle was empty. 'I'd better order another.'

'No,' said Beth firmly. 'I've got to be on time for work tomorrow morning, even if you haven't.'

'To hell with that,' said Bernie. 'It's not every day that my little sister gets engaged to my best mate. Another bottle!' he shouted.

The barman smiled as he removed a second bottle of champagne

3

from the fridge below the counter. One of the men standing at the bar checked the label. 'Pol Roger,' he said, before adding in a voice that carried: 'Wasted on them.'

Bernie jumped up from his place, but Danny immediately pulled him back down.

'Ignore them,' he said, 'they're not worth the space.'

The barman walked quickly across to their table. 'Don't let's be havin' any trouble, lads,' he said as he removed the cork. 'One of them's celebratin' his birthday, and frankly they've had a bit too much to drink.'

Beth took a closer look at the four men while the barman refilled their glasses. One of them was staring at her. He winked, opened his mouth and ran his tongue around his lips. Beth quickly turned back, relieved to find that Danny and her brother were chatting.

'So where you two goin' on honeymoon?'

'Saint Tropez,' said Danny.

'That'll set you back a bob or two.'

'And you're not coming along this time,' said Beth.

'The slut's quite presentable until she opens her mouth,' said a voice from the bar.

Bernie leapt to his feet again, to find two of them staring defiantly at him.

'They're drunk,' said Beth. 'Just ignore them.'

'Oh, I don't know,' said the other man. 'There are times when I quite like a slut's mouth to be open.'

Bernie grabbed the empty bottle, and it took all of Danny's strength to hold him down.

'I want to leave,' said Beth firmly. 'I don't need a bunch of public-school snobs ruining my engagement party.'

Danny immediately jumped up, but Bernie just sat there, drinking his champagne. 'Come on, Bernie, let's get out of here before we do something we regret,' said Danny. Bernie reluctantly stood up and followed his friend, but he never once took his eyes off the four men at the bar. Beth was pleased to see that they had turned their backs on them, and appeared to be deep in conversation.

But the moment Danny opened the back door, one of them swung round. 'Leaving, are we?' he said. He then took out his wallet and added, 'When you've finished with her, my friends and I have just enough left over for a gang bang.'

'You're full of shit,' said Bernie.

'Then why don't we go outside and sort it out?'

'Be my guest, Dickhead,' said Bernie as Danny shoved him through the door and out into the alley before he had the chance to say anything else. Beth slammed the door behind them and began walking down the alley. Danny gripped Bernie by the elbow, but they had only gone a couple of paces before he shook him off. 'Let's go back and sort them.'

'Not tonight,' said Danny, not letting go of Bernie's arm as he continued to lead his friend on down the alley.

When Beth reached the main road she saw the man Bernie described as Dickhead standing there, one hand behind his back. He leered at her and began licking his lips again, just as his friend came rushing round the corner, slightly out of breath. Beth turned to see her brother, legs apart, standing his ground. He was smiling.

'Let's go back inside,' Beth shouted at Danny, only to see that the other two men from the bar were now standing by the door, blocking the path.

'Fuck 'em,' said Bernie. 'It's time to teach the bastards a lesson.'

'No, no,' pleaded Beth as one of the men came charging up the alley towards them.

'You take Dickhead,' said Bernie, 'and I'll deal with the other three.'

Beth looked on in horror as Dickhead threw a punch that caught Danny on the side of the chin and sent him reeling back. He recovered in time to block the next punch, feint, and then land one that took Dickhead by surprise. He fell on one knee, but was quickly back on his feet before taking another swing at Danny.

As the other two men standing by the back door didn't seem to want to join in, Beth assumed the fight would be over fairly quickly. She could only watch as her brother landed an uppercut on the other man, the force of which almost knocked him out. As Bernie waited for him to get back on his feet, he shouted to Beth,

'Do us a favour, sis, grab a cab. This ain't gonna last much longer, and then we need to be out of 'ere.'

Beth turned her attention to Danny to make sure he was getting the better of Dickhead. Dickhead was lying spread-eagled on the ground with Danny on top of him, clearly in control. She gave them both one last look before reluctantly obeying her brother. She ran off down the alley and once she reached the main road, began searching for a taxi. She only had to wait a couple of minutes before she spotted a familiar yellow *FOR HIRE* sign.

Beth flagged down the cabbie as the man Bernie had felled staggered past her and disappeared into the night.

'Where to, luv?' asked the cabbie.

'Bacon Road, Bow,' said Beth. 'And two of my friends will be along in a moment,' she added as she opened the back door.

The cabbie glanced over her shoulder and down the alley. 'I don't think it's a taxi they'll be needing, luv,' he said. 'If they were my friends, I'd be phoning for an ambulance.'

BOOK ONE

THE TRIAL

1

'Not guilty.'

Danny Cartwright could feel his legs trembling as they sometimes did before the first round of a boxing match he knew he was going to lose. The associate recorded the plea on the indictment and, looking up at Danny, said, 'You can sit down.'

Danny collapsed on to the little chair in the centre of the dock, relieved that the first round was over. He looked up at the referee, who was seated on the far side of the courtroom in a high-backed green leather chair that had the appearance of a throne. In front of him was a long oak bench littered with case papers in ring binders, and a notebook opened at a blank page. Mr Justice Sackville looked across at Danny, his expression revealing neither approval nor disapproval. He removed a pair of half-moon spectacles from the end of his nose and said in an authoritative voice, 'Bring in the jury.'

While they all waited for the twelve men and women to appear, Danny tried to take in the unfamiliar sights and sounds of court number four at the Old Bailey. He looked across at the two men who were seated at either end of what he'd been told was counsel's bench. His young advocate, Alex Redmayne, looked up and gave him a friendly smile, but the older man at the other end of the bench, whom Mr Redmayne always referred to as prosecution counsel, never once glanced in his direction.

Danny transferred his gaze up into the public gallery. His parents were seated in the front row. His father's burly tattooed arms were resting on the balcony railing, while his mother's head remained bowed. She raised her eyes occasionally to glance down at her only son.

It had taken several months for the case of The Crown versus Daniel Arthur Cartwright finally to reach the Old Bailey. It seemed to Danny that once the law became involved, everything happened in slow motion. And then suddenly, without warning, the door in the far corner of the courtroom opened and the usher reappeared. He was followed by seven men and five women who had been chosen to decide his fate. They filed into the jury box and sat in their unallocated places – six in the front row, six behind them; strangers with nothing more in common than the lottery of selection.

Once they had settled, the associate rose from his place to address them. 'Members of the jury,' he began, 'the defendant, Daniel Arthur Cartwright, stands before you charged on one count of murder. To that count he has pleaded not guilty. Your charge therefore is to listen to the evidence and decide whether he be guilty or no.'

2

Mr Justice Sackville glanced down at the bench below him. 'Mr Pearson, you may open the case for the Crown.'

A short, rotund man rose slowly from the counsel's bench. Mr Arnold Pearson QC opened the thick file that rested on a lectern in front of him. He touched his well-worn wig, almost as if he were checking to make sure he'd remembered to put it on, then tugged on the lapels of his gown; a routine that hadn't changed for the past thirty years.

'If it please your lordship,' he began in a slow, ponderous manner, 'I appear for the Crown in this case, while my learned friend' – he glanced to check the name on the sheet of paper in front of him – 'Mr Alex Redmayne, appears for the defence. The case before your lordship is one of murder. The cold-blooded and calculated murder of Mr Bernard Henry Wilson.'

In the public gallery, the parents of the victim sat in the far corner of the back row. Mr Wilson looked down at Danny, unable to mask the disappointment in his eyes. Mrs Wilson stared blankly in front of her, white-faced, not unlike a mourner attending a funeral. Although the tragic events surrounding the death of Bernie Wilson had irrevocably changed the lives of two East End families who had been close friends for several generations, it had hardly caused a ripple beyond a dozen streets surrounding Bacon Road in Bow.

'During the course of this trial, you will learn how the defendant' – continued Pearson, waving a hand in the direction of the dock without bothering even to glance at Danny – 'lured Mr Wilson to a public house in Chelsea on the night of Saturday,

September eighteenth 1999, where he carried out this brutal and premeditated murder. He had earlier taken Mr Wilson's sister' – once again he checked the file in front of him – 'Elizabeth, to Lucio's restaurant in Fulham Road. The court will learn that Cartwright made a proposal of marriage to Miss Wilson after she had revealed that she was pregnant. He then called her brother Mr Bernard Wilson on his mobile phone and invited him to join them at the Dunlop Arms, a public house at the back of Hamble-don Terrace, Chelsea, so that they could all celebrate.'

'Miss Wilson has already made a written statement that she had never visited this public house before, although Cartwright clearly knew it well, which the Crown will suggest was because he had selected it for one purpose and one purpose only: its back door opens on to a quiet alleyway, an ideal location for someone with murderous intent; a murder that Cartwright would later blame on a complete stranger who just happened to be a customer at the Dunlop Arms that night.'

Danny stared down at Mr Pearson. How could he possibly know what had happened that night when he wasn't even there? But Danny wasn't too worried. After all, Mr Redmayne had assured him that his side of the story would be presented during the trial and he mustn't be too anxious if everything appeared bleak while the Crown was presenting its case. Despite his barrister's repeated assurances, two things did worry Danny: Alex Redmayne wasn't much older than he was, and had also warned him that this was only his second case as leader.

'But unfortunately for Cartwright,' continued Pearson, 'the other four customers who were in the Dunlop Arms that night tell a different story, a story which has not only proved consistent, but which has also been corroborated by the barman on duty at the time. The Crown will present all five as witnesses, and they will tell you that they overheard a dispute between the two men, who were later seen to leave by the rear entrance of the bar after Cartwright had said, "Then why don't we go outside and sort it out?" All five of them saw Cartwright leave by the back door, followed by Bernard Wilson and his sister Elizabeth, who was clearly in an agitated state. Moments later, a scream was heard.

Mr Spencer Craig, one of the customers, left his companions and ran out into the alley, where he found Cartwright holding Mr Wilson by the throat, while repeatedly thrusting a knife into his chest.

'Mr Craig immediately dialled 999 on his mobile phone. The time of that call, m'lord, and the conversation that took place were logged and recorded at Belgravia police station. A few minutes later, two police officers arrived on the scene and found Cartwright kneeling over Mr Wilson's body, with the knife in his hand – a knife that he must have picked up from the bar, because *Dunlop Arms* is engraved on the handle.'

Alex Redmayne wrote down Pearson's words.

'Members of the jury,' continued Pearson, once again tugging at his lapels, 'every murderer has to have a motive, and in this case we need look no further than the first recorded slaying, of Abel by Cain, to establish that motive: envy, greed and ambition were the sordid ingredients that, when combined, provoked Cartwright to remove the one rival who stood in his path.

'Members of the jury, both Cartwright and Mr Wilson worked at Wilson's garage in Mile End Road. The garage is owned and managed by Mr George Wilson, the deceased's father, who had planned to retire at the end of the year, when he intended to hand over the business to his only son, Bernard. Mr George Wilson has made a written statement to this effect, which has been agreed by the defence, so we shall not be calling him as a witness.

'Members of the jury, you will discover during this trial that the two young men had a long history of rivalry and antagonism which stretched back to their schooldays. But with Bernard Wilson out of the way, Cartwright planned to marry the boss's daughter and take over the thriving business himself.

'However, everything did not go as Cartwright planned, and when he was arrested, he tried to place the blame on an innocent bystander, the same man who had run out into the alley to see what had caused Miss Wilson to scream. But unfortunately for Cartwright, it was not part of his plan that there would be four other people who were present throughout the entire episode.' Pearson smiled at the jury. 'Members of the jury, once you have heard their testimony, you will be left in no doubt that Daniel Cartwright is guilty of the heinous crime of murder.' He turned to the judge. 'That concludes the prosecution opening for the Crown, m'lord.' He tugged his lapels once more before adding, 'With your permission I shall call my first witness.' Mr Justice Sackville nodded, and Pearson said in a firm voice, 'I call Mr Spencer Craig.'

Danny Cartwright looked to his right and watched as an usher at the back of the courtroom opened a door, stepped out into the corridor and bellowed, 'Mr Spencer Craig.' A moment later, a tall man, not much older than Danny, dressed in a blue pinstriped suit, white shirt and mauve tie, entered the courtroom. How different he looked from when they'd first met.

Danny hadn't seen Spencer Craig during the past six months, but not a day had passed when he hadn't visualized him clearly. He stared at the man defiantly, but Craig didn't even glance in Danny's direction – it was as if he didn't exist.

Craig walked across the courtroom like a man who knew exactly where he was going. When he stepped into the witness box, he immediately picked up the Bible and delivered the oath without once looking at the card the usher held up in front of him. Mr Pearson smiled at his principal witness, before glancing down at the questions he had spent the past month preparing.

'Is your name Spencer Craig?'

'Yes, sir,' he replied.

'And do you reside at forty-three Hambledon Terrace, London SW3?'

'I do, sir.'

'And what is your profession?' asked Mr Pearson, as if he didn't know.

'I am a barrister at law.'

'And your chosen field?'

'Criminal justice.'

'So you are well acquainted with the crime of murder?'

'Unfortunately I am, sir.'

'I should now like to take you back to the evening of September eighteenth, last year, when you and a group of friends were enjoying a drink at the Dunlop Arms in Hambledon Terrace.

Perhaps you could take us through exactly what happened that night.'

'My friends and I were celebrating Gerald's thirtieth birth-day—'

'Gerald?' interrupted Pearson.

'Gerald Payne,' said Craig. 'He's an old friend from my days at Cambridge. We were spending a convivial evening together, enjoy-ing a bottle of wine.'

Alex Redmayne made a note – he needed to know how many bottles.

Danny wanted to ask what the word convivial meant.

'But sadly it didn't end up being a convivial evening,' prompted Pearson.

'Far from it,' replied Craig, still not even glancing in Danny's direction.

'Please tell the court what happened next,' said Pearson, looking down at his notes.

Craig turned to face the jury for the first time. 'We were, as I said, enjoying a glass of wine in celebration of Gerald's birth-day, when I became aware of raised voices. I turned and saw a man, who was seated at a table in the far corner of the room with a young lady.'

'Do you see that man in the courtroom now?' asked Pearson.

'Yes,' replied Craig, pointing in the direction of the dock.

'What happened next?'

'He immediately jumped up,' continued Craig, 'and began shouting and jabbing his finger at another man, who remained seated. I heard one of them say: "If you think I'm gonna call you guv when you take over from my old man, you can forget it." The young lady was trying to calm him down. I was about to turn back to my friends – after all, the quarrel was nothing to do with me – when the defendant shouted, "Then why don't we go outside and sort it out?" I assumed they were joking, but then the man who had spoken the words grabbed a knife from the end of the bar—'

'Let me stop you there, Mr Craig. You saw the defendant pick up a knife from the bar?' asked Pearson.

'Yes, I did.'

'And then what happened?'

'He marched off in the direction of the back door, which surprised me.'

'Why did it surprise you?'

'Because the Dunlop Arms is my local, and I had never seen the man before.'

'I'm not sure I'm following you, Mr Craig,' said Pearson, who was following his every word.

'The rear exit is out of sight if you're sitting in that corner of the room, but he seemed to know exactly where he was going.'

'Ah, I understand,' said Pearson. 'Please continue.'

'A moment later the other man got up and chased after the defendant, with the young lady following close behind. I wouldn't have given the matter another thought, but moments later we all heard a scream.'

'A scream?' repeated Pearson. 'What kind of scream?'

'A high-pitched, woman's scream,' replied Craig.

'And what did you do?'

'I immediately left my friends and ran into the alley in case the woman was in any danger.'

'And was she?'

'No, sir. She was screaming at the defendant, begging him to stop.'

'Stop what?' asked Pearson.

'Attacking the other man.'

'They were fighting?'

'Yes, sir. The man I'd earlier seen jabbing a finger and shouting now had the other chap pinned up against the wall, with his forearm pressed against his throat.' Craig turned to the jury and raised his left arm to demonstrate the position.

'And was Mr Wilson trying to defend himself?' asked Pearson.

'As best he could, but the defendant was thrusting a knife into the man's chest, again and again.'

'What did you do next?' asked Pearson quietly.

'I phoned the emergency services, and they assured me that they would send police and an ambulance immediately.'

'Did they say anything else?' asked Pearson, looking down at his notes.

'Yes,' replied Craig. 'They told me under no circumstances to approach the man with the knife, but to return to the bar and wait until the police arrived.' He paused. 'I carried out those instructions to the letter.'

'How did your friends react when you went back into the bar and told them what you had seen?'

'They wanted to go outside and see if they could help, but I told them what the police had advised and that I also thought it might be wise in the circumstances for them to go home.'

'In the circumstances?'

'I was the only person who had witnessed the whole incident and I didn't want them to be in any danger should the man with the knife return to the bar.'

'Very commendable,' said Pearson.

The judge frowned at the prosecuting counsel. Alex Redmayne continued to take notes.

'How long did you have to wait before the police arrived?'

'It was only a matter of moments before I heard a siren, and a few minutes later a plain-clothes detective entered the bar through the back door. He produced his badge and introduced himself as Detective Sergeant Fuller. He informed me that the victim was on his way to the nearest hospital.'

'What happened next?'

'I made a full statement, and then DS Fuller told me I could go home.'

'And did you?'

'Yes, I returned to my house, which is only about a hundred yards from the Dunlop Arms, and went to bed, but I couldn't sleep.'

Alex Redmayne wrote down the words: *about a hundred yards*.

'Understandably,' said Pearson.

The judge frowned a second time.

'So I got up, went to my study and wrote down everything that had taken place earlier that evening.'

'Why did you do that, Mr Craig, when you had already given a statement to the police?'

17

'My experience of standing where you are, Mr Pearson, has made me aware that evidence presented in the witness box is often patchy, even inaccurate, by the time a trial takes place several months after a crime has been committed.'

'Quite so,' said Pearson, turning another page of his file. 'When did you learn that Daniel Cartwright had been charged with the murder of Bernard Wilson?'

'I read the details in the *Evening Standard* the following Monday. It reported that Mr Wilson had died on his way to Chelsea and Westminster Hospital, and that Cartwright had been charged with his murder.'

'And did you regard that as the end of the matter, as far as your personal involvement was concerned?'

'Yes, although I knew that I would be called as a witness in any forthcoming trial, should Cartwright decide to plead not guilty.'

'But then there was a twist that even you, with all your experience of hardened criminals, could not have anticipated.'

'There certainly was,' responded Craig. 'Two police officers visited my chambers the following afternoon to conduct a second interview.'

'But you had already given verbal and written statements to DS Fuller,' said Pearson. 'Why did they need to interview you again?'

'Because Cartwright was now accusing *me* of killing Mr Wilson, and was even claiming that I had picked up the knife from the bar.'

'Had you ever come across Mr Cartwright or Mr Wilson before that night?'

'No, sir,' replied Craig truthfully.

'Thank you, Mr Craig.'

The two men smiled at each other before Pearson turned to the judge and said, 'No more questions, m'lord.'

3

MR JUSTICE SACKVILLE turned his attention to the counsel at the other end of the bench. He was well acquainted with Alex Redmayne's distinguished father, who had recently retired as a high court judge, but his son had never appeared before him.

'Mr Redmayne,' intoned the judge, 'do you wish to cross-examine this witness?'

'I most certainly do,' replied Redmayne as he gathered up his notes.

Danny recalled that not long after he'd been arrested, an officer had advised him to get himself a lawyer. It had not proved easy. He quickly discovered that lawyers, like garage mechanics, charge by the hour and you only get what you can afford. He could afford ten thousand pounds: a sum of money he had saved over the past decade, intending to use it as the deposit on a basement flat in Bow, where Beth, he and the baby would live once they were married. Every penny of it had been swallowed up long before the case had come to court. The solicitor he selected, a Mr Makepeace, had demanded five thousand pounds up front, even before he took the top off his fountain pen, and then another five once he'd briefed Alex Redmayne, the barrister who would represent him in court. Danny couldn't understand why he needed two lawyers to do the same job. When he repaired a car, he didn't ask Bernie to lift the bonnet before he could take a look at the engine, and he certainly wouldn't have demanded a deposit before he picked up his toolkit.

But Danny liked Alex Redmayne from the day he met him, and

not just because he supported West Ham. He had a posh accent and had been to Oxford University, but he never once spoke down to him.

Once Mr Makepeace had read the charge sheet and listened to what Danny had to say, he had advised his client to plead guilty to manslaughter. He was confident that he could strike a deal with the Crown, which would allow Danny to get away with a sentence of six years. Danny turned the offer down.

Alex Redmayne asked Danny and his fiancée to go over what had taken place that night again and again, as he searched for any inconsistencies in his client's story. He found none, and when the money ran out he still agreed to conduct his defence.

'Mr Craig,' began Alex Redmayne, not tugging his lapels or touching his wig, 'I am sure it is unnecessary for me to remind you that you are still under oath, and of the added responsibility that carries for a barrister.'

'Tread carefully, Mr Redmayne,' interjected the judge. 'Remember that it is your client who is on trial, not the witness.'

'We shall see if you still feel that way, m'lord, when the time comes for your summing up.'

'Mr Redmayne,' said the judge sharply, 'it is not your responsibility to remind me of my role in this courtroom. Your job is to question the witnesses, mine to deal with any points of law that arise, and then let us both leave the jury to decide on the verdict.'

'If your lordship pleases,' said Redmayne, turning back to face the witness. 'Mr Craig, what time did you and your friends arrive at the Dunlop Arms that evening?'

'I don't recall the exact time,' Craig replied.

'Then let me try and jog your memory. Was it seven? Seven thirty? Eight o'clock?'

'Nearer eight, I suspect.'

'So you had already been drinking for some three hours by the time my client, his fiancée and his closest friend walked into the bar.'

'As I have already told the court, I did not see them arrive.'

'Quite so,' said Redmayne, mimicking Pearson. 'And how much drink had you consumed by, let's say, eleven o'clock?'

'I've no idea. It was Gerald's thirtieth birthday so no one was counting.'

'Well, as we have established that you had been drinking for over three hours, shall we settle on half a dozen bottles of wine? Or perhaps it was seven, even eight?'

'Five at the most,' retorted Craig, 'which is hardly extravagant for four people.'

'I would normally agree with you, Mr Craig, had not one of your companions said in his written statement that he drank only Diet Coke, while another just had one or two glasses of wine because he was driving.'

'But I didn't have to drive,' said Craig. 'The Dunlop Arms is my local, and I live only a hundred yards away.'

'Only a hundred yards away?' repeated Redmayne. When Craig didn't respond, he continued, 'You told the court that you were not aware of any other customers being in the bar until you heard raised voices.'

'That is correct.'

'When you claim you heard the defendant say: "Then why don't we go outside and sort it out?"'

'That is also correct.'

'But isn't it the truth, Mr Craig, that it was you who started this whole quarrel when you delivered another unforgettable remark to my client as he was leaving – ' he glanced down at his notes – '"When you've finished with her, my friends and I have just enough left over for a gang bang"?' Redmayne waited for Craig to reply, but again he remained silent. 'Can I assume from your failure to respond that I am correct?'

'You can assume nothing of the sort, Mr Redmayne. I simply didn't consider your question worthy of a response,' replied Craig with disdain.

'I do hope that you feel, Mr Craig, that my next question is worthy of a response, because I would suggest that when Mr Wilson told you that you were "full of shit", it was *you* who said: "Then why don't we go outside and sort it out?"'

'I think that sounds more like the kind of language one would expect from your client,' responded Craig.

'Or from a man who had had a little too much to drink and was showing off to his drunken friends in front of a beautiful woman?'

'I must remind you once again, Mr Redmayne,' interjected the judge, 'that it is your client who is on trial in this case, not Mr Craig.'

Redmayne gave a slight bow, but when he raised his eyes, he noticed that the jury was hanging on his every word. 'I suggest, Mr Craig,' he continued, 'that you left by the front door and ran around to the back because you wanted a fight.'

'I only went into the alley after I'd heard the scream.'

'Was that when you picked up a knife from the end of the bar?'

'I did no such thing,' said Craig sharply. 'Your client grabbed the knife when he was on his way out, as I made clear in my statement.'

'Is that the statement you so carefully crafted when you couldn't get to sleep later that night?' asked Redmayne.

Again, Craig didn't respond.

'Perhaps this is another example of something that's unworthy of your consideration?' Redmayne suggested. 'Did any of your friends follow you out into the alley?'

'No, they did not.'

'So they didn't witness the fight you had with Mr Cartwright?'

'How could they, when I did not have a fight with Mr Cartwright.'

'Did you get a Boxing Blue when you were at Cambridge, Mr Craig?'

Craig hesitated. 'Yes, I did.'

'And while at Cambridge, were you rusticated for—'

'Is this relevant?' demanded Mr Justice Sackville.

'I am happy to leave that decision to the jury, m'lord,' said Redmayne. Turning back to Craig, he continued, 'Were you rusticated from Cambridge after being involved in a drunken brawl with some locals whom you later described to the magistrates as a "bunch of yobs"?'

'That was years ago, when I was still an undergraduate.'

'And were you, years later, on the night of September eighteenth 1999, picking another quarrel with another "bunch of yobs"' when you resorted to using the knife you'd picked up from the bar?'

'As I've already told you, it wasn't me who picked up the knife, but I did witness your client stabbing Mr Wilson in the chest.'

'And then you returned to the bar?'

'Yes, I did, when I immediately called the emergency services.'

'Let us try to be a little more accurate, shall we, Mr Craig. You didn't actually call the emergency services. In fact, you phoned a detective sergeant Fuller on his mobile.'

'That's correct, Redmayne, but you seem to forget that I was reporting a crime, and was well aware that Fuller would alert the emergency services. Indeed, if you recall, the ambulance arrived before the detective sergeant.'

'Some minutes before,' emphasized Redmayne. 'However, I'm curious to know how you were so conveniently in possession of a junior police officer's mobile phone number.'

'We had both been recently involved in a major drugs trial that required several lengthy consultations, sometimes at very short notice.'

'So DS Fuller is a friend of yours.'

'I hardly know the man,' said Craig. 'Our relationship is strictly professional.'

'I suggest, Mr Craig, that you knew him well enough to phone and make sure that he heard your side of the story first.'

'Fortunately, there are four other witnesses to verify my side of the story.'

'And I look forward to cross-examining each one of your close friends, Mr Craig, as I'm curious to discover why, after you had returned to the bar, you advised them to go home.'

'They had not witnessed your client stabbing Mr Wilson, and so were not involved in any way,' said Craig. 'And I also considered they might be in some danger if they stayed.'

'But if anyone was in danger, Mr Craig, it would have been the only witness to the murder of Mr Wilson, so why didn't you leave with your friends?'

Craig once again remained silent and this time not because he considered the question unworthy of a reply.

'Perhaps the real reason you told them to leave,' said Red-mayne, 'was because you needed them out of the way so that you could run home and change out of your blood-covered clothes before the police turned up? After all, you only live, as you have admitted, "a hundred yards away".'

'You seem to have forgotten, Mr Redmayne, that Detective Sergeant Fuller arrived only a few minutes after the crime had been committed,' responded Craig scornfully.

'It was seven minutes after you phoned the detective sergeant that he arrived on the scene, and he then spent some considerable time questioning my client before he entered the bar.'

'Do you imagine that I could afford to take such a risk when I knew the police could be turning up at any moment?' Craig spat out.

'Yes, I do,' replied Redmayne, 'if the alternative was to spend the rest of your life in prison.'

A noisy buzz erupted around the court. The jurors' eyes were now fixed on Spencer Craig, but once again he didn't respond to Redmayne's words. Redmayne waited for some time before adding, 'Mr Craig, I repeat that I am looking forward to cross-examining your friends one by one.' Turning to the judge, he said, 'No more questions, m'lord.'

'Mr Pearson?' said the judge. 'You will no doubt wish to re-examine this witness?'

'Yes, m'lord,' said Pearson. 'There is one question I'm keen to have answered.' He smiled at the witness. 'Mr Craig, are you Superman?'

Craig looked puzzled, but, aware that Pearson would be trying to assist him, replied, 'No, sir. Why do you ask?'

'Because only Superman, having witnessed a murder, could have returned to the bar, briefed his friends, flown home, taken a shower, changed his clothes, flown back to the pub and been casually sitting at the bar by the time DS Fuller appeared.' A few members of the jury tried to suppress smiles. 'Or perhaps there was a convenient telephone box near at hand.' The smiles turned to laughter. Pearson waited for them to die down before he added, 'Allow me, Mr Craig, to dispense with Mr Redmayne's fantasy world and ask you one serious question.' It was Pearson's turn to wait until every eye was concentrated on him. 'When Scotland Yard's forensic experts examined the murder weapon, was it your fingerprints they identified on the handle of the knife, or those of the defendant?'

'They certainly weren't mine,' said Craig, 'otherwise it would be me who was seated in the dock.'

'No more questions, m'lord,' said Pearson.

4

THE CELL DOOR opened and an officer handed Danny a plastic tray with several little compartments full of plastic food which he picked at while he waited for the afternoon session to begin.

Alex Redmayne skipped lunch so he could read through his notes. Had he underestimated the amount of time Craig would have had before DS Fuller walked into the bar?

Mr Justice Sackville took lunch along with a dozen other judges, who didn't remove their wigs or discuss each other's cases as they munched through a meal of meat and two veg.

Mr Pearson ate lunch on his own in the Bar Mess on the top floor. He considered that his learned friend had made a bad mistake when questioning Craig about the timing, but it wasn't his duty to point that out. He pushed a pea from one side of the plate to the other while he considered the ramifications.

Once two o'clock struck, the ritual began again. Mr Justice Sackville entered the courtroom and gave the jury the flicker of a smile before taking his place. He looked down at both counsel and said, 'Good afternoon, gentlemen. Mr Pearson, you may call your next witness.'

'Thank you, m'lord,' said Pearson as he rose from his seat. 'I call Mr Gerald Payne.'

Danny watched a man enter the courtroom whom he didn't immediately recognize. He must have been around five feet nine inches tall, prematurely balding, and his well-cut beige suit was unable to disguise the fact that he'd lost a stone since Danny had last seen him. The usher guided him towards the witness box, handed him a copy of the Bible and held up the oath. Although Payne read from the card, he displayed the same self-confidence as Spencer Craig had shown that morning.

'You are Gerald David Payne, and you reside at sixty-two Wellington Mews, London W2?'

'That is correct,' replied Payne in a firm voice.

'And what is your profession?'

'I am a land management consultant.'

Redmayne wrote down the words *estate agent* next to Payne's name.

'And which firm do you work for?' enquired Pearson.

'I am a partner with Baker, Tremlett and Smythe.'

'You are very young to be a partner of such a distinguished firm,' suggested Pearson innocently.

'I am the youngest partner in the firm's history,' replied Payne, delivering a well-rehearsed line.

It was obvious to Redmayne that someone had been tutoring Payne long before he entered the witness box. He knew that for ethical reasons it couldn't have been Pearson, so there was only one other possible candidate.

'My congratulations,' said Pearson.

'Get on with it, Mr Pearson,' said the judge.

'I do apologize, m'lord. I was simply trying to establish the credibility of this witness for the jury.'

'Then you have succeeded,' said Mr Justice Sackville sharply. 'Now get on with it.'

Pearson patiently took Payne through the events of the night in question. Yes, he confirmed, Craig, Mortimer and Davenport had all been present at the Dunlop Arms that evening. No, he had not ventured out into the alley when he heard the scream. Yes, they had gone home when advised to do so by Spencer Craig. No, he had never seen the defendant before in his life.

'Thank you, Mr Payne,' concluded Pearson. 'Please remain there.'

Redmayne rose slowly from his place, and took his time rearranging some papers before he asked his first question – a trick his father had taught him when they had conducted mock trials. 'If you're going to open with a surprise question, my boy,' his father used to say, 'keep the witness guessing.' He waited until the judge, the jury and Pearson were all staring at him. Only a few seconds, but he knew it would seem a lifetime to anyone standing in the box.

'Mr Payne,' said Redmayne finally, looking up at the witness, 'when you were an undergraduate at Cambridge, were you a member of a society known as the Musketeers?'

'Yes,' replied Payne, looking puzzled.

'And was that society's motto: "All for one and one for all"?'

Pearson was up on his feet even before Payne had a chance to reply. 'My lord, I am puzzled to know how the past membership of a university society can have any bearing on the events of September eighteenth last year.'

'I am inclined to agree with you, Mr Pearson,' replied the judge, 'but no doubt Mr Redmayne is about to enlighten us.'

'I am indeed, m'lord,' Redmayne replied, his eyes never leaving Payne. 'Was the Musketeers' motto: "All for one and one for all"?' Redmayne repeated.

'Yes, it was,' replied Payne with a slight edge to his voice.

'What else did the members of that society have in common?' asked Redmayne.

'An appreciation of Dumas, justice and a bottle of fine wine.'

'Or perhaps several bottles of fine wine?' suggested Redmayne as he extracted a small, light blue booklet from the pile of papers in front of him. He began to turn its pages slowly. 'And was one of the society's rules that if any member found himself in danger, it was the duty of all other members to come to his assistance?'

'Yes,' replied Payne. 'I have always considered loyalty to be the benchmark by which you can judge any man.'

'Do you indeed?' said Redmayne. 'Was Mr Spencer Craig by any chance also a member of the Musketeers?'

'He was,' replied Payne. 'In fact, he's a past chairman.'

'And did you and your fellow members come to his assistance on the night of September eighteenth last year?'

'My lord,' said Pearson leaping to his feet once again, 'this is outrageous.'

'What is outrageous, m'lord,' retorted Redmayne, 'is that whenever one of Mr Pearson's witnesses looks as if he might be in some trouble, he leaps to their assistance. Perhaps he is also a member of the Musketeers?'

Several of the jurors smiled.

'Mr Redmayne,' said the judge quietly, 'are you suggesting that the witness is committing perjury just because he was a member of a society while he was at university?'

'If the alternative was life imprisonment for his closest friend, m'lord, then yes, I do think it might have crossed his mind.'

'This is outrageous,' repeated Pearson, still on his feet.

'Not as outrageous as sending a man to jail for the rest of his life,' said Redmayne, 'for a murder he did not commit.'

'No doubt, m'lord,' said Pearson, 'we are about to discover that the barman was also a member of the Musketeers.'

'No, we are not,' responded Redmayne, 'but we will contend that the barman was the only person in the Dunlop Arms that night who did not go out into the alley.'

'I think you have made your point,' said the judge. 'Perhaps it's time to move on to your next question.'

'No more questions, m'lord,' said Redmayne.

'Do you wish to re-examine this witness, Mr Pearson?'

'I do, m'lord,' said Pearson. 'Mr Payne, can you confirm, so that the jury are left in no doubt, that you did not follow Mr Craig out into the alley after you had heard a woman scream?'

'Yes, I can,' said Payne. 'I was in no condition to do so.'

'Quite so. No more questions, m'lord.'

'You are free to leave the court, Mr Payne,' said the judge.

Alex Redmayne couldn't help noticing that Payne didn't look quite as self-assured as he walked out of the courtroom as he had done when he'd swaggered in.

'Do you wish to call your next witness, Mr Pearson?' asked the judge.

'I had intended to call Mr Davenport, m'lord, but you might feel it would be wise to begin his cross-examination tomorrow morning.'

The judge didn't notice that most of the women in the court-room seemed to be willing him to call Lawrence Davenport without further delay. He looked at his watch, hesitated, then said, 'Perhaps it would be better if we were to call Mr Davenport first thing tomorrow morning.'

'As your lordship pleases,' said Pearson, delighted with the effect the prospect of his next witness's appearance had already had on the five women on the jury. He only hoped that young Redmayne would be foolish enough to attack Davenport in the same way he had Gerald Payne.

5

THE FOLLOWING MORNING a buzz of expectation swept around the courtroom even before Lawrence Davenport made his entrance. When the usher called out his name, he did so in a hushed voice.

Lawrence Davenport entered the court stage right, and followed the usher to the witness box. He was about six foot, but so slim he appeared taller. He wore a tailored navy blue suit and a cream shirt that looked as if it had been unwrapped that morning. He had spent a considerable time debating whether he should wear a tie, and in the end had accepted Spencer's advice that it gave the wrong impression if you looked too casual in court. 'Let them go on thinking you're a doctor, not an actor,' Spencer had said. Davenport had selected a striped tie that he would never have considered wearing unless he was in front of a camera. But it was not his outer garments that caused women to turn their heads. It was the piercing blue eyes, thick wavy fair hair and helpless look that made so many of them want to mother him. Well, the older ones. The younger ones had other fantasies.

Lawrence Davenport had built his reputation playing a heart surgeon in *The Prescription*. For an hour every Saturday evening, he seduced an audience of over nine million. His fans didn't seem to care that he spent more time flirting with the nurses than performing coronary artery bypass grafts.

After Davenport had stepped into the witness box, the usher handed him a Bible and held up a cue card so that he could deliver his opening lines. As Davenport recited the oath, he turned court number four into his private theatre. Alex Redmayne couldn't help noticing that all five women on the jury were smiling at the witness. Davenport returned their smiles, as if he were taking a curtain call.

Mr Pearson rose slowly from his place. He intended to keep Davenport in the witness box for as long as he could, while he milked his audience of twelve.

Alex Redmayne sat back as he waited for the curtain to rise, and recalled another piece of advice his father had given him.

Danny felt more isolated in the dock than ever as he stared across at the man he recalled so clearly seeing in the bar that night.

'You are Lawrence Andrew Davenport?' said Pearson, beaming at the witness.

'I am, sir.'

Pearson turned to the judge. 'I wonder, m'lord, if you would allow me to avoid having to ask Mr Davenport to reveal his home address.' He paused. 'For obvious reasons.'

'I have no problem with that,' replied Mr Justice Sackville, 'but I will require the witness to confirm that he has resided at the same address for the past five years.'

'That is the case, my lord,' said Davenport, turning his attention to the director and giving a slight bow.

'Can you also confirm,' said Pearson, 'that you were at the Dunlop Arms on the evening of September eighteenth 1999.'

'Yes, I was,' replied Davenport. 'I joined a few friends to celebrate Gerald Payne's thirtieth birthday. We were all up at Cambridge together,' he added in a languid drawl that he had last resorted to when playing Heathcliff on tour.

'And did you see the defendant that night,' asked Pearson, pointing towards the dock, 'sitting on the other side of the room?'

'No, sir. I was unaware of him at that time,' said Davenport addressing the jury as if they were a matinee audience.

'Later that night, did your friend Spencer Craig jump up and run out of the back door of the public house?'

'Yes, he did.'

'And that was following a girl's scream?'

'That is correct, sir.'

Pearson hesitated, half expecting Redmayne to leap up and protest at such an obvious leading question, but he remained unmoved. Emboldened, Pearson continued, 'And Mr Craig returned to the bar a few moments later?'

'He did,' replied Davenport.

'And he advised you and your other two companions to go home,' said Pearson, continuing to lead the witness – but still Alex Redmayne didn't move a muscle.

'That's right,' said Davenport.

'Did Mr Craig explain why he felt you should leave the premises?'

'Yes. He told us that there were two men fighting in the alley, and that one of them had a knife.'

'What was your reaction when Mr Craig told you this?'

Davenport hesitated, not quite sure how he should reply to this question, as it wasn't part of his prepared text.

'Perhaps you felt you should go and see if the young lady was in any danger?' prompted Pearson helpfully from the wings.

'Yes, yes,' responded Davenport, who was beginning to feel that he wasn't coming over quite so well without an autocue to assist him.

'But despite that, you followed Mr Craig's advice,' said Pearson, 'and left the premises?'

'Yes, yes, that's right,' said Davenport. 'I followed Spencer's advice, but then he is' – he paused for effect – 'learned in the law. I believe that is the correct expression.'

Word-perfect, thought Alex, aware that Davenport was now safely back on his crib sheet.

'You never went into the alley yourself?'

'No, sir, not after Spencer had advised that we should not under any circumstances approach the man with the knife.'

Alex remained in his place.

'Quite so,' said Pearson as he turned the next page of his file and stared at a blank sheet of paper. He had come to the end of his questions far sooner than he'd anticipated. He couldn't understand why his opponent hadn't attempted to interrupt him while he so blatantly led this witness. He reluctantly snapped the file closed. 'Please remain in the witness box, Mr Davenport,' he said, 'as I'm sure my learned friend will wish to cross-examine you.'

Alex Redmayne didn't even glance in Lawrence Davenport's direction as the actor ran a hand through his long fair hair and continued to smile at the jury.

'Do you wish to cross-examine this witness, Mr Redmayne?' the judge asked, sounding as if he was looking forward to the encounter.

'No thank you, m'lord,' replied Redmayne, barely shifting in his place.

Few of those present in the court were able to hide their disappointment.

Alex remained unmoved, recalling his father's advice never to cross-examine a witness the jury likes, especially when they want to believe everything they have to say. Get them out of the witness box as quickly as possible, in the hope that by the time the jury come to consider the verdict, the memory of their performance – and indeed it had been a performance – might have faded.

'You may leave the witness box, Mr Davenport,' said Mr Justice Sackville somewhat reluctantly.

Davenport stepped down. He took his time, trying to make the best of his short exit across the courtroom and out into the wings. Once he was in the crowded corridor, he headed straight for the staircase that led to the ground floor, at a pace that wouldn't allow any startled fan time to work out that it really was Dr Beresford and ask for an autograph.

Davenport was happy to be out of that building. He had not enjoyed the experience, and was grateful that it was over far more quickly than he had anticipated; more like an audition than a performance. He hadn't relaxed for a moment, and wondered if it had been obvious that he hadn't slept the previous night. As Davenport jogged down the steps and on to the road, he checked his watch; he was going to be early for his twelve o'clock appointment with Spencer Craig. He turned right and began to walk in the direction of Inner Temple, confident that Spencer would be pleased to learn that Redmayne hadn't bothered to cross-examine him. He had feared that the young barrister might have pressed him on the subject of his sexual preferences, which, had he told the truth, would have been the only headline in tomorrow's tabloids – unless of course he'd told the whole truth.

6

TOBY MORTIMER did not acknowledge Lawrence Davenport as he strode past him. Spencer Craig had warned them that they should not be seen in public together until the trial was over. He had phoned all three of them the moment he got home that night to tell them that DS Fuller would be in touch the following day to clear up a few points. What had begun as a birthday celebration for Gerald had ended as a nightmare for all four of them.

Mortimer bowed his head as Davenport passed by. He had been dreading his spell in the witness box for weeks, despite Spencer's constant reassurance that even if Redmayne found out about his drug problem, he would never refer to it.

The Musketeers had remained loyal, but none of them pretended that their relationship could ever be the same again. And what had taken place that night had only made Mortimer's craving even stronger. Before the birthday celebration, he was known among dealers as a weekend junkie, but as the trial drew nearer, he had come to need two fixes a day – every day.

'Don't even think about shooting up before you go into the witness box,' Spencer had warned him. But how could Spencer begin to understand what he was going through when he had never experienced the craving: a few hours of sheer bliss until the high began to wear off, followed by the sweating, then the shakes, and finally the ritual of preparation so he could once again depart from this world – inserting the needle into an unused vein, the plunge as the liquid found its way into the bloodstream, quickly making contact with the brain, then finally, blessed release – until the cycle began again. Mortimer was already sweating. How long before the shakes would begin? As long as he was called next, a surge of adrenalin should get him through.

The courtroom door opened and the usher reappeared. Mortimer jumped up in anticipation. He dug his nails into the palms of his hands, determined not to let the side down.

'Reginald Jackson!' bellowed the usher, ignoring the tall, thin man who had risen the moment he appeared.

The manager of the Dunlop Arms followed the usher back into the courtroom. Another man Mortimer hadn't spoken to for the past six months.

'Leave him to me,' Spencer had said, but then, even at Cambridge, Spencer had always taken care of Mortimer's little problems.

Mortimer sank back on to the bench and gripped the edge of the seat as he felt the shakes coming on. He wasn't sure how much longer he could last – the fear of Spencer Craig was being rapidly overtaken by the need to feed his addiction. By the time the barman re-emerged from the courtroom, Mortimer's shirt, pants and socks were soaked in sweat despite its being a cold March morning. *Pull yourself together*, he could hear Spencer saying, even though he was a mile away sitting in his chambers, probably chatting to Lawrence about how well the trial had gone so far. They would be waiting for him to join them. The last piece in the jigsaw.

Mortimer rose and began pacing up and down the corridor as he waited for the usher to reappear. He checked his watch, praying that there would be time for another witness to be called before lunch. He smiled hopefully at the usher as he stepped back into the corridor.

'Detective Sergeant Fuller!' he bellowed. Mortimer collapsed back on to the bench.

He was now shaking uncontrollably. He needed his next fix just as a baby needs the milk from its mother's breast. He stood up and headed unsteadily off in the direction of the washroom. He was relieved to find the white tiled room was empty. He selected the farthest cubicle and locked himself inside. The gap at the top and bottom of the door made him anxious: someone in authority could easily discover that he was breaking the law – in the Central Criminal Court. But his craving had reached the point where common sense was rapidly replaced by necessity, whatever the risk.

Mortimer unbuttoned his jacket and extracted a small canvas pouch from an inside pocket: the kit. He unfolded it and laid it out on the top of the lavatory seat. Part of the excitement was in the preparation. He picked up a small 1mg phial of liquid, cost £250. It was clear, high-quality stuff. He wondered how much longer he'd be able to afford such expensive gear before the small inheritance his father had bequeathed him finally ran out. He stabbed the needle into the phial and drew back the plunger until the little plastic tube was full. He didn't check to see if the liquid was flowing freely because he couldn't afford to waste even a drop.

He paused for a moment, sweat pouring off his forehead, when he heard the door at the far end of the room open. He didn't move, waiting for the stranger to carry out a ritual for which the lavatory had been originally intended.

Once he heard the door close again, he took off his old school tie, pulled up a trouser leg and began to search for a vein: a task that was becoming more difficult by the day. He wrapped the tie around his left leg and pulled it tighter and tighter until at last a blue vein protruded. He held the tie firmly with one hand and the needle in the other. He then inserted the needle into the vein before slowly pressing the plunger down until every last drop of liquid had entered his bloodstream. He breathed a deep sigh of relief as he drifted into another world – a world not inhabited by Spencer Craig.

◄o►

'I am not willing to discuss the subject any longer,' Beth's father had said earlier that day as he took his seat at the table and his wife put a plate of eggs and bacon in front of him. The same breakfast she had cooked for him every morning since the day they were married.

'But, Dad, you can't seriously believe that Danny would kill Bernie. They were best friends since their first day at Clem Attlee.'

'I've seen Danny lose his temper.'

'When?' demanded Beth.

'In the boxing ring, against Bernie.'

'Which is why Bernie always beat him.'

'Perhaps Danny won this time because he had a knife in his hand.' Beth was so stunned by her father's accusation that she didn't reply. 'And have you forgotten,' he continued, 'what happened in the playground all those years ago?'

'No, I haven't,' said Beth. 'But Danny was coming to Bernie's rescue at the time.'

'When the headmaster turned up and found a knife in his hand.'

'Have *you* forgotten,' said Beth's mother, 'that Bernie confirmed Danny's story when he was later questioned by the police?'

'When once again, a knife was found in Danny's hand. Quite a coincidence.'

'But I've told you a hundred times—'

'That a complete stranger stabbed your brother to death.'

'Yes, he did,' said Beth.

'And Danny did nothing to provoke him, or make him lose his temper.'

'No, he didn't,' said Beth, trying to remain calm.

'And I believe her,' said Mrs Wilson as she poured her daughter another coffee.

'You always do.'

'With good reason,' Mrs Wilson responded. 'I've never known Beth to lie.'

Mr Wilson remained silent, as his untouched meal went cold. 'And you still expect me to believe that everyone else is lying?' he eventually said.

'Yes, I do,' said Beth. 'You seem to forget that I was there, so I know Danny is innocent.'

'It's four to one against,' said Mr Wilson.

'Dad, this isn't a dog race we're discussing. It's Danny's life.'

'No, it's my son's life we're discussing,' said Mr Wilson, his voice rising with every word.

'He was my son as well,' said Beth's mother, 'just in case you've forgotten.'

'And have you also forgotten,' said Beth, 'that Danny was the man you were so keen for me to marry, and who you asked to take over the garage when you retired? So what's suddenly stopped you believing in him?'

'There's something I haven't told you,' said Beth's father. Mrs Wilson bowed her head. 'When Danny came to see me that morning, to tell me he was going to ask you to marry him, I thought it was only fair to let him know that I'd changed my mind.'

'Changed your mind about what?' asked Beth.

'Who would be taking over the garage when I retired.'

7

'NO MORE QUESTIONS, my lord,' said Alex Redmayne.

The judge thanked Detective Sergeant Fuller, and told him he was free to leave the court.

It had not been a good day for Alex. Lawrence Davenport had mesmerized the jury with his charm and good looks. DS Fuller had come across as a decent, conscientious officer who reported exactly what he'd seen that night, and the only interpretation he could put on it, and when Alex pressed him on his relationship with Craig, he simply repeated the word 'professional'. Later, when Pearson asked him how long it was between Craig making the 999 call and Fuller entering the bar, Fuller had said he couldn't be sure, but he thought it would have been around fifteen minutes.

As for the barman, Reg Jackson, he just repeated parrot-like that he was only getting on with his job and hadn't seen or heard a thing.

Redmayne accepted that if he was to find a chink in the armour of the four musketeers, his only hope now rested with Toby Mortimer. Redmayne knew all about the man's drug habit, although he had no intention of referring to it in court. He knew that nothing else would be on Mortimer's mind while he was being cross-examined. Redmayne felt that Mortimer was the one Crown witness who might buckle under pressure, which was why he was pleased he'd been kept waiting in the corridor all day.

'I think we have just enough time for one more witness,' said Mr Justice Sackville as he glanced at his watch.

Mr Pearson didn't appear quite as enthusiastic to call the Crown's last witness. After reading the detailed police report, he had even considered not calling Toby Mortimer at all, but he knew that if he failed to do so, Redmayne would become suspicious and might even subpoena him. Pearson rose slowly from his place. 'I call Mr Toby Mortimer,' he said.

The usher stepped into the corridor and roared, 'Toby Mortimer!' He was surprised to find that the man was no longer seated in his place. He'd seemed so keen to be called earlier. The usher checked carefully up and down the benches, but there was no sign of him. He shouted the name even louder a second time, but still there was no response.

A pregnant young woman looked up from the front row, unsure if she was allowed to address the usher. The usher's eyes settled on her. 'Have you seen Mr Mortimer, madam?' he asked in a softer tone.

'Yes,' she replied, 'he went off to the toilets some time ago, but he hasn't returned.'

'Thank you, madam.' The usher disappeared back into the courtroom. He walked quickly over to the associate, who listened carefully before briefing the judge.

'We'll give him a few more minutes,' said Mr Justice Sackville.

Redmayne kept glancing at his watch, becoming more anxious as each minute slipped by. It didn't take that long to go to the lavatory – unless . . . Pearson leaned across, smiled, and helpfully suggested, 'Perhaps we should leave this witness until first thing in the morning?'

'No, thank you,' Redmayne replied firmly. 'I'm happy to wait.' He went over his questions again, underlining relevant words so that he wouldn't have to keep glancing down at his crib sheet. He looked up the moment the usher came back into court.

The usher hurried across the courtroom and whispered to the associate, who passed the information on to the judge. Mr Justice Sackville nodded. 'Mr Pearson,' he said. The prosecution counsel rose to his feet. 'It appears that your final witness has been taken ill, and is now on his way to hospital.' He didn't add, with a needle sticking out of a vein in his left leg. 'I therefore intend to close proceedings for the day. I would like to see both counsel in my chambers immediately.'

Alex Redmayne didn't need to attend chambers to be told that his trump card had been removed from the pack. As he closed the file marked *Crown Witnesses*, he accepted that the fate of Danny Cartwright now rested in the hands of his fiancée, Beth Wilson. And he still couldn't be sure if she was telling the truth.

8

THE FIRST WEEK of the trial was over and the four main protagonists spent their weekends in very different ways.

Alex Redmayne drove down to Somerset to spend a couple of days with his parents in Bath. His father began quizzing him about the trial even before he'd closed the front door, while his mother seemed more interested in finding out about his latest girl-friend.

'Some hope,' he said to both parental enquiries.

By the time Alex left for London on Sunday afternoon, he had rehearsed the questions he intended to put to Beth Wilson the following day, with his father acting as the judge. Not a difficult task for the old man. After all, that was exactly what he had done for the past twenty years before retiring.

'Sackville tells me you're holding your own,' his father reported, 'but he feels you sometimes take unnecessary risks.'

'That may be the only way I can find out if Cartwright is innocent.'

'That's not your job,' responded his father. 'That's for the jury to decide.'

'Now *you're* sounding like Mr Justice Sackville,' Alex said with a laugh.

'It's your job,' continued his father, ignoring the comment, 'to present the best possible defence for your client, whether he is guilty or not.'

His father had clearly forgotten that he'd first proffered this piece of advice when Alex was seven years old, and had repeated it countless times since. By the time Alex went up to Oxford as an undergraduate, he was ready to sit his law degree.

'And Beth Wilson, what sort of witness do you imagine she'll make?' his father asked.

'A distinguished silk once told me,' replied Alex, tugging the lapels of his jacket pompously, 'that you can never anticipate how a witness will turn out until they enter the box.'

Alex's mother burst out laughing. 'Touché,' she said as she cleared the plates and disappeared into the kitchen.

'And don't underestimate Pearson,' said his father, ignoring his wife's interruption. 'He's at his best when it comes to cross-examining a defence witness.'

'Is it possible to underestimate Mr Arnold Pearson QC?' asked Alex, smiling.

'Oh yes, I did so to my cost on two occasions.'

'So were two innocent men convicted of crimes they didn't commit?' asked Alex.

'Certainly not,' replied his father. 'Both of them were as guilty as sin, but I still should have got them off. Just remember, if Pearson spots a weakness in your defence he'll return to it again and again, until he's sure that it's the one point the jury remember when they retire.'

'Can I interrupt learned counsel, to ask how Susan is?' asked his mother as she poured Alex a coffee.

'Susan?' said Alex, snapping back into the real world.

'That charming girl you brought down to meet us a couple of months ago.'

'Susan Rennick? I've no idea. I'm afraid we've lost touch. I don't think the Bar is compatible with having a personal life. Heaven knows how you two ever got together.'

'Your mother fed me every night during the Carbarshi trial. If I hadn't married her, I would have died of starvation.'

'That easy?' said Alex, grinning at his mother.

'Not quite that easy,' she replied. 'After all, the trial lasted for over two years – and he lost.'

'No I didn't,' said his father, placing an arm round his wife's waist. 'Just be warned, my boy, Pearson's not married, so he'll be spending his entire weekend preparing devilish questions for Beth Wilson.'

◄○►

They hadn't granted him bail.

Danny had spent the past six months locked up in Belmarsh high-security prison in south-east London. He languished for twenty-two hours a day in a cell eight foot by six, the sole furnishings a single bed, a formica table, a plastic chair, a small steel washbasin and a steel lavatory. A tiny barred window high above his head was his only view of the outside world. Every afternoon they allowed him out of the cell for forty-five minutes, when he would jog around the perimeter of a barren yard – a concrete acre surrounded by a sixteen-foot wall topped with razor wire.

'I'm innocent,' he repeated whenever anyone asked, to which the prison staff and his fellow inmates inevitably responded, 'That's what they all say.'

As Danny jogged around the yard that morning, he tried not to think about how the first week of the trial had gone, but it proved impossible. Despite looking carefully at each member of the jury, he had no way of knowing what they were thinking. It might not have been a good first week, but at least Beth would now be able to tell her side of the story. Would the jury believe her, or would they accept Spencer Craig's version of what had happened? Danny's father never stopped reminding him that British justice was the best in the world – innocent men just don't end up in prison. If that was true, he would be free in a week's time. He tried not to consider the alternative.

◄○►

Arnold Pearson QC had also spent his weekend in the country, at his cottage in the Cotswolds with its four-and-a-half-acre garden – his pride and joy. After tending the roses he attempted to read a well-reviewed novel, which he ended up putting to one side before deciding to go for a walk. As he strolled through the village he tried to clear his mind of everything that had been taking place in

London that week, although in truth the case rarely strayed from his thoughts.

He felt that the first week of the trial had gone well, despite the fact that Redmayne had proved to be a far doughtier opponent than he had expected. Certain familiar phrases, obvious hereditary traits and a rare gift of timing brought back memories of Redmayne's father, who in Arnold's opinion was the finest advocate he had ever come up against.

But thank heavens, the boy was still green. He should have made far more of the time issue when Craig was in the witness box. Arnold would have counted the paving stones between the Dunlop Arms and the front door of Craig's mews house, with a stopwatch as his only companion. He would then have returned to his own home, undressed, showered and changed into a new set of clothes while once again timing the entire exercise. Arnold suspected that the combined times would amount to less than twenty minutes – certainly no more than thirty.

After he had picked up a few groceries and a local paper from the village store, Pearson set off on the return journey. He stopped by the village green for a moment, and smiled as he recalled the 57 he had scored against Brocklehurst some twenty years before – or was it thirty? All that he loved about England was embodied in the village. He looked at his watch, and sighed as he accepted that it was time to return home and prepare for the morrow.

After tea, he went to his study, sat down at his desk and ran an eye over the questions he had prepared for Beth Wilson. He would have the advantage of hearing Redmayne examine her before he had to ask his first question. Like a cat ready to pounce, he would sit silently at his end of the bench waiting patiently for her to make some tiny mistake. The guilty always make mistakes.

Arnold smiled as he turned his attention to the *Bethnal Green and Bow Gazette*, confident that Redmayne would not have come across the article that had appeared on the front page some fifteen years ago. Arnold Pearson may have lacked Mr Justice Redmayne's elegance and style, but he made up for it with the hours of patient research, which had already uncovered two further pieces of evidence that would surely leave the jury in no doubt of Cartwright's guilt. But he would save both of them for the defendant, whom he was looking forward to cross-examining later in the week.

◄o►

On the day Alex was bantering with his parents over lunch in Bath, Danny was running round the exercise yard at Belmarsh prison and Arnold Pearson was visiting the village store, Beth Wilson had an appointment with her local GP.

'Just a routine check,' the doctor assured her with a smile. But then the smile turned to a frown. 'Have you been under any unusual stress since I last saw you?' he asked.

Beth didn't burden him with an account of how she had spent the past week. It didn't help that her father remained convinced Danny was guilty, and would no longer allow his name to be mentioned in the house, even though her mother had always accepted Beth's version of what had taken place that night. But was the jury made up of people like her mother, or her father?

Every Sunday afternoon for the past six months, Beth had visited Danny in Belmarsh prison, but not this Sunday. Mr Redmayne had told her that she would not be allowed to have any further contact with him until the trial was over. But there was so much she wanted to ask him, so much she needed to tell him.

The baby was due in six weeks' time, but long before then he would be free, and this terrible ordeal would finally be over. Once the jury had reached their verdict, surely even her father would accept that Danny was innocent.

On Monday morning, Mr Wilson drove his daughter to the Old Bailey and dropped her outside the main entrance to the courts. He only uttered three words as she stepped out of the car: 'Tell the truth.'

9

HE FELT SICK when their eyes met. Spencer Craig glared down at him from the public gallery. Danny returned the stare as if he was standing in the middle of the ring waiting for the bell to sound for the first round.

When Beth entered the courtroom, it was the first time he'd seen her for two weeks. He was relieved that she would have her back to Craig while she was in the witness box. Beth gave Danny a warm smile before taking the oath.

'Is your name Elizabeth Wilson?' enquired Alex Redmayne.

'Yes,' she replied, resting her hands on her stomach, 'but I'm known as Beth.'

'And you live at number twenty-seven Bacon Road in Bow, East London.'

'Yes, I do.'

'And Bernie Wilson, the deceased, was your brother?'

'Yes, he was,' said Beth.

'And are you currently the personal assistant to the chairman of Drake's Marine Insurance Company in the City of London?'

'Yes, I am.'

'When is the baby due?' asked Redmayne. Pearson frowned, but he knew he dare not intervene.

'In six weeks,' Beth said, bowing her head.

Mr Justice Sackville leant forward and, smiling down at Beth, said, 'Would you please speak up, Miss Wilson. The jury will need to hear every word you have to say.' She raised her head and nodded. 'And perhaps you'd prefer to be seated,' the judge added helpfully. 'Being in a strange place can sometimes be a little disconcerting.'

'Thank you,' said Beth. She sank on to the wooden chair in the witness box, and almost disappeared out of sight.

'Damn,' muttered Alex Redmayne under his breath. The jury could now barely see her shoulders, and would no longer be continually reminded that she was seven months pregnant, a vision he wanted implanted in the minds of the only twelve people who mattered. He should have anticipated the gallant Mr Justice Sackville and advised Beth to decline the offer of a seat. If she'd collapsed, the image would have lingered in the jury's minds.

'Miss Wilson,' continued Redmayne, 'would you tell the court what your relationship is with the accused.'

'Danny and I are going to be married next week,' she replied. A gasp could be heard around the courtroom.

'Next week?' repeated Redmayne, trying to sound surprised.

'Yes, the final banns were read yesterday by Father Michael, our parish priest at St Mary's.'

'But if your fiancé were to be convicted—'

'You can't be convicted for a crime you didn't commit,' responded Beth sharply.

Alex Redmayne smiled. Word-perfect, and she had even turned to face the jury.

'How long have you known the defendant?'

'As long as I can remember,' replied Beth. 'His family have always lived across the road from us. We went to the same school.'

'Clement Attlee comprehensive?' said Redmayne, looking down at his open file.

'That's right,' confirmed Beth.

'So you were childhood sweethearts?'

'If we were,' said Beth, 'Danny wasn't aware of it, because he hardly ever spoke to me while we were at school.'

Danny smiled for the first time that day, remembering the little girl with pigtails who was always hanging around her brother.

'But did you try to speak to him?'

'No, I wouldn't have dared. But I always stood on the touchline and watched whenever he played football.'

'Were your brother and Danny in the same team?'

'Right through school,' replied Beth. 'Danny was captain and my brother was the goalkeeper.'

'Was Danny always captain?'

'Oh, yes. His mates used to call him Captain Cartwright. He captained all the school teams – football, cricket, even boxing.'

Alex noticed that one or two of the jury were smiling. 'And did your brother get on well with Danny?'

'Danny was his best friend,' said Beth.

'Did they regularly quarrel, as my learned friend has suggested?' asked Redmayne, glancing in the direction of the Crown prosecutor.

'Only about West Ham, or Bernie's latest girlfriend.' A member of the jury just managed to stifle a laugh.

'But didn't your brother knock Danny out in the first round of the Bow Street Boys' Club boxing championship last year?'

'Yes, he did. But Bernie was always the better boxer, and Danny knew it. Danny once told me that he'd be lucky to make the second round if they met in the final.'

'So there was no bad feeling between them, as has been suggested by my learned friend, Mr Pearson.'

'How could *he* know?' asked Beth. 'He never met either of them.' Danny smiled again.

'Miss Wilson,' said the judge, not quite so gently, 'please concentrate on answering the questions.'

'What was the question?' asked Beth, sounding a little flummoxed.

The judge glanced down at his notebook. 'Was there any bad feeling between your brother and the defendant?'

'No,' said Beth. 'I've already told you, they were best mates.'

'You also told the court, Miss Wilson,' said Redmayne, trying to steer her back on to the script, 'that Danny never spoke to you while you were at school. Yet you ended up engaged to be married.'

'That's right,' said Beth, looking up at Danny.

'What caused this change of heart?'

'When Danny and my brother left Clem Attlee, they both went

to work in my dad's garage. I stayed on at school for another year before going on to sixth-form college and then Exeter University.'

'From where you graduated with an honours degree in English?'

'Yes, I did,' replied Beth.

'And what was your first job after leaving university?'

'I became a secretary at Drake's Marine Insurance Company in the City.'

'Surely you could have obtained a far better position than that, remembering your qualifications?'

'Perhaps I could have,' admitted Beth, 'but Drake's head office is in the City and I didn't want to be too far from home.'

'I understand. And how many years have you worked for the company?'

'Five,' replied Beth.

'And during that time you have risen from being a secretary to the chairman's personal assistant.'

'Yes.'

'How many secretaries are employed at Drake's Insurance?' asked Redmayne.

'I'm not sure of the exact number,' Beth replied, 'but there must be over a hundred.'

'But it was you who ended up with the top job?' Beth didn't reply. 'After you returned from university to live in London again, when did you next see Danny?'

'Soon after I'd started working in the City,' said Beth. 'My mother asked me to drop off my dad's lunchbox at the garage one Saturday morning. Danny was there, with his head under a car bonnet. To begin with, I thought he hadn't noticed me, because he could only have seen my legs, but then he looked up and banged his head on the bonnet.'

'And was that when he asked you out for the first time?'

Pearson leapt to his feet. 'M'lord, is this witness to be prompted, line by line, as if she were in a dress rehearsal for an amateur dramatic society production?'

Not bad, thought Alex. The judge might have agreed with him

if he hadn't heard Pearson deliver the same line several times during the past decade. However, he still leant forward to chastise counsel. 'Mr Redmayne, in future, please stick to asking the witness questions and don't resort to giving answers that you hope, or expect, Miss Wilson will agree with.'

'I apologize, m'lord,' said Redmayne. 'I will try not to displease your lordship again.'

Mr Justice Sackville frowned, recalling Redmayne's father delivering that line with the same lack of sincerity.

'When did you next see the defendant?' Redmayne asked Beth.

'That same evening. He invited me to go to the Hammersmith Palais,' said Beth. 'He and my brother used to go to the Palais every Saturday night – more birds per acre than you'll find in the fens, Bernie used to say.'

'How often did you see each other following that first date?' enquired Redmayne.

'Almost every day.' She paused. 'Until they locked him up.'

'I'm now going to take you back to the evening of September eighteenth last year,' said Redmayne. Beth nodded. 'I want you to tell the jury in your own words exactly what took place that night.'

'It was Danny's idea,' Beth began looking up at the defendant and smiling, 'that we should go for dinner in the West End as it was a special occasion.'

'A special occasion?' prompted Redmayne.

'Yes. Danny was going to propose.'

'How could you be so sure of that?'

'I heard my brother telling Mum that Danny had spent two months' wages on the ring.' She held up her left hand so that the jury could admire the single diamond on a gold band.

Alex waited for the murmurs to die down before he asked, 'And did he ask you to be his wife?'

'Yes, he did,' replied Beth. 'He even got down on one knee.'

'And you accepted?'

'Of course I did,' said Beth. 'I knew we were going to be married the first day I met him.'

Pearson noted her first mistake.

'What happened next?'

'Before we left the restaurant Danny called Bernie to tell him the news. He agreed to join us later so we could all celebrate.'

'And where did you arrange to meet up for this celebration?'

'The Dunlop Arms on Hambledon Terrace in Chelsea.'

'Why did you choose that particular venue?'

'Danny had been there once before, after watching West Ham play Chelsea at Stamford Bridge. He told me it was very classy and he thought I'd like it.'

'What time did you arrive?'

'I'm not sure,' said Beth, 'but it can't have been before ten.'

'And your brother was already there waiting for you?'

'He's at it again, m'lord,' objected Pearson.

'I do apologize, m'lord,' said Redmayne. He turned back to Beth. 'When did your brother arrive?'

'He was already there,' said Beth.

'Did you notice anyone else in the room?'

'Yes,' said Beth, 'I saw the actor, Lawrence Davenport – Dr Beresford – standing at the bar with three other men.'

'Do you know Mr Davenport?'

'Of course not,' said Beth. 'I'd only ever seen him on the TV.'

'So you must have been quite excited to see a television star on the night you became engaged?'

'No, I wasn't that impressed. I remember thinking that he wasn't as good-looking as Danny.' Several members of the jury took a closer look at the unshaven man with short spiky hair who was wearing a West Ham T-shirt that looked as if it hadn't been ironed recently. Alex feared that not many of the jurors would agree with Beth's judgement.

'What happened next?'

'We drank a bottle of champagne, and then I thought we ought to go home.'

'And did you go home?'

'No, Bernie ordered a second bottle, and when the barman took the empty one away, I heard someone say, "Wasted on them".'

'How did Danny and Bernie react to that?'

'They didn't hear it, but I saw one of the men at the bar staring

at me. He winked, then opened his mouth and started circling his tongue round his lips.'

'Which of the four men did that?'

'Mr Craig.'

Danny looked up into the gallery to see Craig scowling down at Beth, but fortunately she couldn't see him.

'Did you tell Danny?'

'No, the man was obviously drunk. Besides, you hear worse than that if you've been brought up in the East End. And I knew only too well how Danny would react if I told him.' Pearson didn't stop writing.

'So you ignored him?'

'Yes,' said Beth. 'But then the same man turned to his friends and said, "The slut's quite presentable until she opens her mouth." Bernie did hear that. Then one of the other men said, "I don't know, there are times when I quite like a slut's mouth to be open," and they all began laughing.' She paused. 'Except for Mr Davenport, who looked embarrassed.'

'Did Bernie and Danny also laugh?'

'No. Bernie grabbed the champagne bottle and stood up to face him.' Pearson wrote down her exact words, as she added: 'But Danny pulled him back down and told him to ignore them.'

'And did he?'

'Yes, but only because I said I wanted to go home. As we were on our way out, I noticed that one of the men was still staring at me. He said, "Leaving, are we?" in a loud whisper, then, "When you're finished with her, my friends and I have just enough left over for a gang bang."'

'A gang bang?' repeated Mr Justice Sackville, looking bemused.

'Yes, m'lord. It's when a group of men have sex with the same woman,' said Redmayne. 'Sometimes for money.' He paused while the judge wrote down the words. Alex looked across at the jury, none of whom appeared to require any further explanation.

'Can you be sure those were his exact words?' asked Redmayne.

'It's not something I'm likely to forget,' said Beth sharply.

'And was it the same man who said this?'

'Yes,' said Beth, 'Mr Craig.'

'How did Danny react this time?'

'He continued to ignore them – after all, the man was drunk – but my brother was the problem, and it didn't help when Mr Craig added, "Then why don't we go outside and sort it out?"'

'Why don't we go outside,' repeated Redmayne, 'and sort it *out*.'

'Yes,' said Beth, not quite sure why he was repeating her words.

'And *did* Mr Craig join you outside?'

'No, but only because Danny pushed my brother into the alley before he could retaliate, and I quickly closed the door behind us.'

Pearson picked up a red pen and underlined the words *pushed him out into the alley*.

'So Danny managed to get your brother out of the bar without any further trouble?'

'Yes,' said Beth. 'But Bernie still wanted to go back and sort him.'

'And sort him?'

'Yes,' said Beth.

'But you walked on down the alley?'

'Yes, I did, but just before I reached the road I found one of the men from the bar was standing in my way.'

'Which one?'

'Mr Craig.'

'What did you do?'

'I ran back to join Danny and my brother. I begged them to return to the bar. That was when I noticed the other two men – one of them was Mr Davenport – were standing by the back door. I turned round to see that the first man had been joined by his mate at the far end of the alley, and they were now walking towards us.'

'What happened next?' asked Redmayne.

'Bernie said, "You take Dickhead and I'll deal with the other three," but before Danny could reply, the one my brother called Dickhead came running towards him and threw a punch that caught Danny on the chin. After that an almighty fight broke out.'

'Did all four of the men join in?'

'No,' said Beth. 'Mr Davenport remained by the back door and one of the others, a tall, skinny guy, hung back, and when my

brother nearly knocked out the only other man willing to fight, Bernie told me to go and get a taxi as he was confident it would be all over fairly quickly.'

'And did you?'

'Yes, but not until I was sure that Danny was getting the better of Craig.'

'And was he?'

'No contest,' said Beth.

'How long did it take you to find a taxi?'

'Only a few minutes,' said Beth, 'but when the cabbie drew up, to my surprise he said, "I don't think it's a taxi you'll be needing, luv. If they were my friends, I'd be phoning for an ambulance," and without another word he shot off.'

'Has any attempt been made to locate the taxi driver concerned?' asked the judge.

'Yes, m'lord,' replied Redmayne, 'but so far no one has come forward.'

'So how did you react when you heard the taxi driver's words?' Redmayne asked, turning back to Beth.

'I swung round to see my brother lying on the ground. He appeared to be unconscious. Danny was holding Bernie's head in his arms. I ran back down the alley to join them.'

Pearson made another note.

'And did Danny give an explanation as to what had happened?'

'Yes. He said that they had been taken by surprise when Craig produced a knife. He had tried to wrestle it from him when he was stabbing Bernie.'

'And did Bernie confirm this?'

'Yes, he did.'

'So what did you do next?'

'I phoned the emergency services.'

'Please take your time, Miss Wilson, before you answer my next question. Who turned up first? The police or an ambulance?'

'Two paramedics,' said Beth without hesitation.

'And how long was it before they arrived?'

'Seven, perhaps eight minutes.'

'How can you be so sure?'

'I never stopped looking at my watch.'

'And how many more minutes passed before the police arrived?'

'I can't be certain,' said Beth, 'but it must have been at least another five.'

'And how long did Detective Sergeant Fuller remain with you in the alley before he went into the bar to interview Mr Craig?'

'At least ten minutes,' said Beth. 'But it might have been longer.'

'But quite long enough for Mr Spencer Craig to leave, return home, a mere hundred yards away, change his clothes and be back in time to give his version of what had taken place before the detective sergeant went into the bar?'

'M'lord,' said Pearson leaping up from his place, 'this is an outrageous slur on a man who was doing no more than carrying out his public duty.'

'I agree with you,' said the judge. 'Members of the jury, you will ignore Mr Redmayne's last comments. Never forget that it is not Mr Craig who is on trial.' He glared down at Redmayne, but the lawyer didn't flinch, well aware that the jury would not forget the exchange, and that it might even sow some doubt in their minds. 'I do apologize, m'lord,' he said in a contrite voice. 'It won't happen again.'

'Be sure that it doesn't,' said the judge sharply.

'Miss Wilson, while you were waiting for the police to arrive, did the paramedics put your brother on a stretcher and take him to the nearest hospital?'

'Yes, they did everything they could to help,' said Beth, 'but I knew it was too late. He'd already lost so much blood.'

'Did you and Danny accompany your brother to the hospital?'

'No, I went on my own because Detective Sergeant Fuller wanted to ask Danny some more questions.'

'Did that worry you?'

'Yes, because Danny had also been wounded. He'd been—'

'That's not what I meant,' said Redmayne, not wanting her to finish the sentence. 'Were you anxious that the police might consider Danny to be a suspect?'

'No,' said Beth. 'It never crossed my mind. I had already told the police what happened. In any case, he always had me to back up his story.'

If Alex had looked across at Pearson, he would have seen the rare flicker of a smile appear on the prosecutor's face.

'Sadly your brother died on the way to Chelsea and Westminster Hospital?'

Beth began to sob. 'Yes, I rang my parents, who came immediately, but it was too late.' Alex made no attempt to ask his next question until she had composed herself.

'Did Danny join you at the hospital later?'

'No, he didn't.'

'Why not?'

'Because the police were still questioning him.'

'When did you next see him?'

'The following morning, at Chelsea police station.'

'Chelsea police station?' repeated Redmayne, feigning surprise.

'Yes. The police came round to my house first thing in the morning. They told me they'd arrested Danny and charged him with Bernie's murder.'

'That must have come as a terrible shock.' Mr Pearson leapt up. 'How did you react to this piece of news?' asked Redmayne quickly.

'In total disbelief. I repeated exactly what had happened, but I could see they didn't believe me.'

'Thank you, Miss Wilson. No more questions, m'lord.'

Danny breathed a sigh of relief as Beth stepped down from the witness box. What a diamond. She smiled anxiously up at him as she passed the dock.

'Miss Wilson,' said the judge before she had reached the door. She turned back to face him. 'Would you be kind enough to return to the witness box? I have a feeling Mr Pearson may have one or two questions for you.'

59

10

BETH WALKED SLOWLY back to the witness box. She looked up at her parents in the public gallery – and then she saw him, glaring down at her. She wanted to protest, but realized that it would serve no purpose, and nothing would please Spencer Craig more than to know the effect his presence had on her.

She stepped back into the witness box, more determined than ever to defeat him. She remained standing, and stared defiantly at Mr Pearson, who was still seated in his place. Perhaps he wasn't going to ask her any questions after all.

The old prosecutor rose slowly from his seat. Without glancing at Beth, he began to rearrange some papers. He then took a sip of water before finally looking across at her.

'Miss Wilson, what did you have for breakfast this morning?'

Beth hesitated for a moment, while everyone in the court stared at her. Alex Redmayne cursed. He should have realized that Pearson would try to throw her off guard with his first question. Only Mr Justice Sackville didn't look surprised.

'I had a cup of tea and a boiled egg,' Beth eventually managed.

'Nothing else, Miss Wilson?'

'Oh, yes, some toast.'

'How many cups of tea?'

'One. No, two,' said Beth.

'Or was it three?'

'No, no, it was two.'

'And how many slices of toast?'

She hesitated again. 'I can't remember.'

'You can't remember what you had for breakfast *this morning*, and yet you can recall in great detail every sentence you heard six months ago.' Beth bowed her head again. 'Not only can you recall every word Mr Spencer Craig uttered that night, but you can even remember such details as him winking at you and rolling his tongue round his lips.'

'Yes, I can,' insisted Beth. 'Because he did.'

'Then let's go back and test your memory even further, Miss Wilson. When the barman picked up the empty bottle of champagne, Mr Craig said, "Wasted on them".'

'Yes, that's right.'

'But who was it who said' – Pearson leant forward to check his notes – '"There are times when I quite like a slut's mouth to be open"?'

'I'm not sure if that was Mr Craig or one of the other men.'

'You're "not sure". "One of the other men". Do you mean the defendant, Cartwright?'

'No, one of the men at the bar.'

'You told my learned friend that you didn't react, because you'd heard worse in the East End.'

'Yes, I have.'

'In fact, that's where you heard the phrase in the first place, isn't it, Miss Wilson,' said Pearson, tugging the lapels of his black gown.

'What are you getting at?'

'Simply that you never heard Mr Craig deliver those words in a bar in Chelsea, Miss Wilson, but you have heard Cartwright say them back in the East End many times, because that's the sort of language he would use.'

'No, it was Mr Craig who said those words.'

'You also told the court that you left the Dunlop Arms by the back door.'

'Yes.'

'Why didn't you leave by the front door, Miss Wilson?'

'I wanted to slip out quietly and not cause any more trouble.'

'So you had already caused *some* trouble?'

'No, *we* hadn't caused any trouble.'

'Then why didn't you leave by the front door, Miss Wilson? If you had, you would have found yourself on a crowded street, and could have slipped away, to use your words, without causing any more trouble.'

Beth remained silent.

'Then perhaps you can also explain what your brother meant,' said Pearson checking his notes, 'when he said to Cartwright, "If you think I'm gonna call you guv, you can forget it".'

'He was joking,' said Beth.

Pearson stared at his file for some time before saying, 'Forgive me, Miss Wilson, but I can't see anything humorous in that remark.'

'That's because you don't come from the East End,' said Beth.

'Neither does Mr Craig,' responded Pearson, before quickly adding, 'and then Cartwright pushes Mr Wilson towards the back door. Was that when Mr Craig heard your brother say, "Then why don't I join you and we can sort it"?'

'It was Mr Craig who said: "Then why don't I join you and we can sort it *out*," because that's the kind of language they use in the West End.'

Bright woman, thought Alex, delighted that she'd picked up his point and rammed it home.

'And when you were outside,' said Pearson quickly, 'you found Mr Craig waiting for you at the other end of the alley?'

'Yes, I did.'

'How long was it before you saw him standing there?'

'I don't remember,' replied Beth.

'This time you *don't* remember.'

'It wasn't that long,' said Beth.

'It wasn't that long,' repeated Pearson. 'Less than a minute?'

'I can't be sure. But he was standing there.'

'Miss Wilson, if you were to leave the Dunlop Arms by the front door, make your way through a crowded street, then down a long lane, before finally reaching the end of the alley, you'd find it's a distance of two hundred and eleven yards. Are you suggesting that Mr Craig covered that distance in under a minute?'

'He must have done.'

'And his friend joined him a few moments later,' said Pearson.

'Yes, he did,' said Beth.

'And when you turned round, the other two men, Mr Davenport and Mr Mortimer, were already positioned by the back door.'

'Yes, they were.'

'And this all took place in under a minute, Miss Wilson?' He paused. 'When do you imagine the four of them found time to plan such a detailed operation?'

'I don't understand what you mean,' said Beth, gripping the rail of the witness box.

'I think you understand only too well, Miss Wilson, but for the benefit of the jury, two men leave the bar by the front door, go around to the rear of the building while the other two station themselves by the back door, all in under a minute.'

'It could have been more than a minute.'

'But you were keen to get away,' Pearson reminded her. 'So if it had been more than a minute you would have had time to reach the main road and disappear long before they could have got there.'

'Now I remember,' said Beth. 'Danny was trying to calm Bernie down, but my brother wanted to go back to the bar and sort Craig, so it must have been more than a minute.'

'Or was it Mr Cartwright he wanted to sort out,' asked Pearson, 'and leave him in no doubt who was going to be the boss once his father retired?'

'If Bernie had wanted to do that,' said Beth, 'he could have flattened him with one punch.'

'Not if Mr Cartwright had a knife,' responded Pearson.

'It was Craig who had the knife, and it was Craig who stabbed Bernie.'

'How can you be so sure, Miss Wilson, when you didn't witness the stabbing?'

'Because Bernie told me that's what happened.'

'Are you sure it was Bernie who told you, and not Danny?'

'Yes, I am.'

'You'll forgive the cliché, Miss Wilson, but *that's my story and I'm sticking to it.*'

'I am, because it's the truth,' said Beth.

'Is it also true that you feared your brother was dying, Miss Wilson?'

'Yes, he was losing so much blood I didn't think he could survive,' replied Beth as she began sobbing.

'Then why didn't you call for an ambulance, Miss Wilson?' This had always puzzled Alex, and he wondered how she would respond. She didn't, which allowed Pearson to add, 'After all, your brother had been stabbed again and again, to quote you.'

'I didn't have a phone!' she blurted.

'But your fiancé did,' Pearson reminded her, 'because he had called your brother earlier, inviting him to join you both at the pub.'

'But an ambulance arrived a few minutes later,' replied Beth.

'And we all know who phoned the emergency services, don't we, Miss Wilson,' said Pearson, staring at the jury.

Beth bowed her head.

'Miss Wilson, allow me to remind you of some of the other half-truths you told my learned friend.' Beth pursed her lips. 'You said, "I knew we were going to be married the first day I met him."'

'Yes, that's what I said and that's what I meant,' said Beth defiantly.

Pearson looked down at his notes. 'You also said that in your opinion Mr Davenport "wasn't as good-looking as" Mr Cartwright.'

'And he isn't,' said Beth.

'And that if anything went wrong, "he always had me to back up his story".'

'Yes, he did.'

'Whatever that story was.'

'I didn't say that,' protested Beth.

'No, I did,' said Pearson. 'Because I suggest you'd say anything to protect your husband.'

'But he isn't my husband.'

'But he will be, if he is acquitted.'

'Yes, he will.'

'How long has it been since the night your brother was murdered?'

'Just over six months.'

'And how often have you seen Mr Cartwright during that period?'

'I've visited him every Sunday afternoon,' said Beth proudly.

'How long do those visits last?'

'About two hours.'

Pearson looked up at the ceiling. 'So you've spent roughly,' he calculated, 'fifty hours together during the past six months.'

'I've never thought of it that way,' said Beth.

'But now you have, wouldn't you agree that it would be quite long enough for the two of you to go over your story again and again, making sure that it was word-perfect by the time you appeared in court.'

'No, that's not true.'

'Miss Wilson, when you visited Mr Cartwright in prison' – he paused – 'for fifty hours, did you ever discuss this case?'

Beth hesitated. 'I suppose we must have.'

'Of course you did,' said Pearson. 'Because if you didn't, perhaps you can explain how you recall every detail of what happened that night, and every sentence delivered by anyone involved, while you can't remember what you had for breakfast this morning.'

'Of course I remember what happened on the night my brother was murdered, Mr Pearson. How could I ever forget? In any case, Craig and his friends would have had even more time to prepare their stories because they had no visiting hours or any restrictions on when or where they could meet.'

'Bravo,' said Alex, loud enough for Pearson to hear.

'Let us return to the alley and test your memory one more time, Miss Wilson,' said Pearson, quickly changing the subject. 'Mr Craig and Mr Payne, having arrived in the alley in under a minute, began walking towards your brother, and without any provocation started a fight.'

'Yes, they did,' said Beth.

'With two men they'd never seen before that night.'

'Yes.'

'And when things began to go badly, Mr Craig pulls a knife out of thin air and stabs your brother in the chest.'

'It wasn't out of thin air. He must have picked it up from the bar.'

'So it wasn't Danny who picked up the knife from the bar?'

'No, I would have seen it, if it had been Danny.'

'But you didn't see Mr Craig pick up the knife from the bar?'

'No, I didn't.'

'But you did see him, one minute later, standing at the other end of the alley.'

'Yes, I did.'

'Did he have a knife in his hand at that time?' Pearson leant back and waited for Beth to reply.

'I don't remember.'

'Then perhaps you can remember who had the knife in his hand when you ran back to join your brother.'

'Yes, it was Danny, but he explained that he had to get hold of it when Craig was stabbing my brother.'

'But you didn't witness that either.'

'No, I didn't.'

'And your fiancé was covered in blood?'

'Of course he was,' said Beth. 'Danny was holding my brother in his arms.'

'So if it was Mr Craig who stabbed your brother, he must also have been covered in blood.'

'How could I know? He'd disappeared by then.'

'Into thin air?' said Pearson. 'So how do you explain that when the police arrived a few minutes later, Mr Craig was sitting at the bar, waiting for the detective, and there was not a sign of blood anywhere.' This time Beth didn't have a reply. 'And may I remind you,' continued Pearson, 'who it was that called for the police in the first place? Not you, Miss Wilson, but Mr Craig. A strange thing to do moments after you've stabbed someone, and your clothes are covered in blood.' He paused to allow the image to settle in the jury's mind, and waited for some time before he asked his next question.

'Miss Wilson, was this the first time your fiancé had been involved in a knife fight and you had come to his rescue?'

'What are you getting at?' said Beth.

Redmayne stared at Beth, wondering if there was something she hadn't told him.

'Perhaps the time has come to test your remarkable memory once again,' said Pearson.

The judge, the jury and Redmayne were now all staring at Pearson, who didn't seem to be in any hurry to reveal his trump card.

'Miss Wilson, do you by any chance recall what took place in the playground of the Clement Attlee comprehensive school on February twelfth 1986?'

'But that's nearly fifteen years ago,' protested Beth.

'Indeed it is, but I think it's unlikely that you would forget a day when the man you always knew you were going to marry ended up on the front page of your local paper.' Pearson leant back and his junior passed him a photocopy of the *Bethnal Green and Bow Gazette*, dated February 13th 1986. He asked the usher to hand a copy to the witness.

'Do you also have copies for the jury?' asked Mr Justice Sackville, as he peered over his half-moon spectacles at Pearson.

'I do indeed, m'lord,' Pearson replied as his junior passed across a large bundle to the court usher, who in turn handed one up to the judge before distributing a dozen copies to the jury and giving the final one to Danny, who shook his head. Pearson looked surprised, and even wondered if Cartwright couldn't read. Something he'd follow up once he had him in the witness box.

'As you see, Miss Wilson, this is a copy of the *Bethnal Green and Bow Gazette*, in which there is a report of a knife fight that took place in the playground of Clement Attlee comprehensive on February twelfth 1986, after which Daniel Cartwright was questioned by the police.'

'He was only trying to help,' said Beth.

'Getting to be a bit of a habit, isn't it?' suggested Pearson.

'What do you mean?' demanded Beth.

'Mr Cartwright being involved in a knife fight, and then you saying he was "only trying to help".'

'But the other boy ended up in Borstal.'

'And no doubt you hope that in this case it will be the other man who ends up in prison, rather than the person you are hoping to marry?'

'Yes, I do.'

'I'm glad we have at least established that,' said Pearson. 'Perhaps you would be kind enough to read out to the court the third paragraph on the front page of the newspaper, the one that begins, "Beth Wilson later told the police . . ."'

Beth looked down at the paper. *'Beth Wilson later told the police that Danny Cartwright had not been involved in the fight, but came to the aid of a classmate and probably saved his life.'*

'Would you agree that that also sounds a little familiar, Miss Wilson?'

'But Danny wasn't involved in the fight.'

'Then why was he expelled from the school?'

'He wasn't. He was sent home while an inquiry was carried out.'

'In the course of which you gave a statement which cleared his name, and resulted in another boy being sent to Borstal.' Beth once again lowered her head. 'Let's return to the latest knife fight, when once again you were so conveniently on hand to come to your would-be boyfriend's rescue. Is it true,' said Pearson, before Beth could respond, 'that Cartwright was hoping to become the manager of Wilson's garage when your father retired?'

'Yes, my dad had already told Danny that he was being lined up for the job.'

'But didn't you later discover that your father had changed his mind and told Cartwright that he intended to put your brother in charge of the garage?'

'Yes, I did,' said Beth, 'but Bernie never wanted the job in the first place. He always accepted that Danny was the natural leader.'

'Possibly, but as it was the family business, wouldn't it have been understandable for your brother to feel resentful at being passed over?'

'No, Bernie never wanted to be in charge of anything.'

'Then why did your brother say that night: "And if you think I'm going to call you guv if you take over from my old man, you can forget it"?'

'He didn't say *if*, Mr Pearson, he said *when*. There's a world of difference.'

Alex Redmayne smiled.

'Sadly, we only have your word for that, Miss Wilson, while there are three other witnesses who tell a completely different story.'

'They're all lying,' said Beth, her voice rising.

'And you're the only one who's telling the truth,' responded Pearson.

'Yes, I am.'

'Who does your father believe is telling the truth?' asked Pearson, suddenly changing tack.

'M'lord,' said Alex Redmayne, jumping to his feet, 'such evidence would not only be hearsay but also can have no bearing on the case.'

'I agree with my learned friend,' replied Pearson before the judge could respond. 'But as Miss Wilson and her father live in the same house, I felt that perhaps the witness might at some time have been made aware of her father's feelings on the subject.'

'That may well be the case,' said Mr Justice Sackville, 'but it is still hearsay and I therefore rule it to be inadmissible.' He turned to Beth and said, 'Miss Wilson, you don't have to answer that question.'

Beth looked up at the judge. 'My father doesn't believe me,' she said in between sobs. 'He's still convinced Danny killed my brother.'

Suddenly everyone in the court seemed to be chattering. The judge had to call for order several times before Pearson could resume.

'Do you want to add anything else that might assist the jury, Miss Wilson?' asked Pearson hopefully.

'Yes,' replied Beth. 'My father wasn't there. I was.'

'And so was your fiancé,' interjected Pearson. 'I suggest that what started out as just another in a long line of quarrels ended in tragedy when Cartwright fatally stabbed your brother.'

'It was Craig who stabbed my brother.'

'While you were at the other end of the alley, trying to hail a taxi.'

'Yes, that's right,' said Beth.

'And when the police arrived, they found Cartwright's clothes were covered in blood, and the only fingerprints they could identify on the knife were your fiancé's?'

'I have already explained how that happened,' said Beth.

'Then perhaps you can also explain why, when the police interviewed Mr Craig a few minutes later, there was not a single drop of blood on his spotless suit, shirt or tie.'

'He would've had at least twenty minutes to run home and get changed,' said Beth.

'Even thirty,' added Redmayne.

'So you endorse the Superman theory, do you?' said Pearson.

'And he admitted he was in the alley,' added Beth, ignoring the comment.

'Yes, he did, Miss Wilson, but only after he'd heard you scream, when he left his friends in the bar to find out if you were in any danger.'

'No, he was already in the alley when Bernie was stabbed.'

'But stabbed by whom?' asked Pearson.

'Craig, Craig, Craig!' shouted Beth. 'How many times do I have to tell you?'

'Who managed to reach the alley in less than a minute? And then somehow found time to phone the police, return to the bar, ask his companions to leave, go home, change out of his blood-covered clothes, shower, return to the bar and still be sitting around waiting for the police to arrive? He was then able to give a coherent account of exactly what took place, one which every witness who was in the bar that night was later able to verify?'

'But they weren't telling the truth,' said Beth.

'I see,' said Pearson. 'So all the other witnesses were willing to lie under oath.'

'Yes, they were all protecting him.'

'And you're not protecting your fiancé?'

'No, I'm telling the truth.'

'The truth as you see it,' said Pearson, 'because you didn't actually witness what took place.'

'I didn't need to,' said Beth, 'because Bernie told me exactly what happened.'

'Are you sure it was Bernie, and not Danny?'

'No, it was Bernie,' she repeated.

'Just before he died?'

'Yes!' shouted Beth.

'How convenient,' said Pearson.

'And once Danny is in the witness box, he'll confirm my story.'

'After seeing each other every Sunday for the past six months, Miss Wilson, I have no doubt he will,' said Pearson. 'No more questions, m'lord.'

11

'WHAT DID YOU have for breakfast this morning?' said Alex.

'Not that hoary old chestnut,' said his father, his voice booming down the phone.

'What's so funny?'

'I should have warned you. Pearson has only two openings when it comes to cross-examining a defence witness; as a young barrister he worked out that only the judge will have heard them before, but to any unsuspecting witness, not to mention a jury, they will always come as a complete surprise.'

'And what's the other one?' asked Alex.

'What's the name of the street second on the left when you come out of your front door to go to work in the morning? Few witnesses manage to answer that one correctly, as I know to my cost. And I suspect that Pearson walks the streets around the defendant's home on the evening before he opens a cross-examination. I bet you'd find him prowling around the East End right now.'

Alex sank back in his chair. 'Well, you did warn me not to underestimate the man.'

Sir Matthew didn't reply immediately. When he did eventually speak, he raised a subject Alex hadn't even considered. 'Are you going to put Cartwright in the witness box?'

'Of course,' said Alex. 'Why wouldn't I?'

'Because it's the one element of surprise you have left. Pearson will be expecting Cartwright to be in the witness box for the rest of the week, but if you were to close your case tomorrow morning without any warning, he'd be on the back foot. He's assuming that he'll be cross-examining Cartwright some time towards the end of the week, perhaps even next week, not to be asked to sum up for the prosecution first thing tomorrow.'

'But if Cartwright doesn't give evidence, surely the jury will assume the worst.'

'The law is quite clear on that point,' replied Alex's father. 'The judge will spell out that it is the prerogative of the defendant to decide if he wishes to enter the witness box, and that the jury should not jump to conclusions based on that decision.'

'But they invariably do, as you've warned me so many times in the past.'

'Perhaps, but one or two of the jury will have noticed that he wasn't able to read that article in the *Bethnal Green and Bow Gazette* and assume you've advised him not to face Pearson, especially after the grilling he gave his fiancée.'

'Cartwright is every bit as bright as Pearson,' said Alex. 'He just isn't as well educated.'

'But you mentioned that he has a short fuse.'

'Only when someone attacks Beth.'

'Then you can be sure that once Cartwright's in the witness box, Pearson will go on attacking Beth until he lights that fuse.'

'But Cartwright doesn't have a criminal record, he's been in work since the day he left school, and he was about to get married to his long-term girlfriend who just happens to be pregnant.'

'So now we know four subjects Pearson won't mention in cross-examination. But you can be sure he'll question Cartwright about the playground incident in his youth, continually reminding the jury that a knife was involved, and that his girlfriend conveniently came to his rescue.'

'Well, if that's my only problem—' began Alex.

'It won't be, I can promise you,' replied his father, 'because now that Pearson has raised the knife fight in the playground with Beth Wilson, you can be pretty confident that he has one or two other surprises in store for Danny Cartwright.'

'Like what?'

'I've no idea,' said Sir Matthew, 'but if you put him in the

73

witness box, no doubt you'll find out.' Alex frowned as he considered his father's words. 'Something's worrying you,' said the judge when Alex didn't reply.

'Pearson knows that Beth's father told Cartwright he had changed his mind about appointing him as manager of the garage.'

'And intended to offer the job to his son instead?'

'Yes,' said Alex.

'Not helpful when it comes to motive.'

'True, but perhaps I've also got one or two surprises for Pearson to worry about,' said Alex.

'Such as?'

'Craig stabbed Danny in the leg, and he's got the scar to prove it.'

'Pearson will say it's an old wound.'

'But we have a doctor's report to show it isn't.'

'Pearson will blame it on Bernie Wilson.'

'So you are advising me *not* to put Cartwright in the box?'

'Not an easy question to answer, my boy, because I wasn't in court, so I don't know how the jury responded to Beth Wilson's testimony.'

Alex was silent for a few moments. 'One or two of them appeared sympathetic, and she certainly came across as an honest person. But then, they might well conclude that, even if she is telling the truth, she didn't see what happened and is taking Cartwright's word for it.'

'Well, you only need three jurors to be convinced that she was telling the truth, and you could end up with a hung jury and at worst a retrial. And if that turned out to be the result, the CPS might even feel that another trial was not in the public interest.'

'I should have spent more time pressing Craig on the time discrepancy, shouldn't I?' said Alex, hoping his father would disagree.

'Too late to worry about that,' responded his father. 'Your most important decision now is whether you should put Cartwright in the witness box.'

'I agree but if I make the wrong decision, Danny could end up in prison for the next twenty years.'

12

ALEX ARRIVED AT the Old Bailey only moments after the night porter had unlocked the front door. Following a long consultation with Danny in the cells below, he went to the robing room and changed into his legal garb, before making his way across to court number four. He entered the empty courtroom, took his seat on the end of the bench and placed three files marked *Cartwright* on the table in front of him. He opened the first file and began to go over the seven questions he'd written out so neatly the night before. He glanced up at the clock on the wall. It was 9.35 a.m.

At ten minutes to the hour, Arnold Pearson and his junior strolled in and took their places at the other end of the bench. They didn't interrupt Alex as he appeared to be preoccupied.

Danny Cartwright was the next to appear, accompanied by two policemen. He sat on a wooden chair in the centre of the dock and waited for the judge to make his entrance.

On the stroke of ten, the door at the back of the court opened and Mr Justice Sackville entered his domain. Everyone in the well of the court rose and bowed. The judge returned the compliment, before taking his place in the centre chair. 'Bring in the jury,' he said. While he waited for them to appear, he put on his half-moon spectacles, opened the cover of a fresh notebook and removed the top from his fountain pen. He wrote down the words: *Daniel Cartwright examination by Mr Redmayne*.

Once the jury members were settled in their places, the judge turned his attention to defence counsel. 'Are you ready to call your next witness, Mr Redmayne?' he asked.

Alex rose from his place, poured himself a glass of water and took a sip. He glanced towards Danny and smiled. He then looked down at the questions in front of him before turning the page to reveal a blank sheet of paper. He smiled back up at the judge and said, 'I have no further witnesses, m'lord.'

An anxious look crossed Pearson's face. He swung quickly round to consult his junior, who appeared equally bemused. Alex savoured the moment, while he waited for the whispering to die down. The judge smiled down at Redmayne, who thought for a moment he might even wink.

Once Alex had milked every moment he felt he could get away with, he said, 'My lord, that concludes the case for the defence.'

Mr Justice Sackville looked across at Pearson, who now resembled a startled rabbit caught in the headlamps of an advancing lorry.

'Mr Pearson,' he said as if nothing untoward had taken place, 'you may begin your closing speech for the Crown.'

Pearson rose slowly from his place. 'I wonder, m'lord,' he spluttered, 'given these unusual circumstances, if your lordship would allow me a little more time to prepare my closing remarks. May I suggest that we adjourn proceedings until this afternoon in order that—'

'No, Mr Pearson,' interrupted the judge, 'I will not adjourn proceedings. No one knows better than you that it is a defendant's right to choose not to give evidence. The jury and the court officials are all in place, and I need not remind you how crowded the court calendar is. Please proceed with your closing remarks.'

Pearson's junior extracted a file from the bottom of the pile and passed it across to his leader. Pearson opened it, aware that he had barely glanced at its contents during the past few days.

He stared down at the first page. 'Members of the jury . . .' he began slowly. It soon became evident that Pearson was a man who relied on being well prepared, and that thinking on his feet was not his strong suit. He stumbled from paragraph to paragraph as he read from his script, until even his junior began to look exasperated.

Alex sat silently at the other end of the bench, concentrating his attention on the jury. Even the ones who were usually fully alert looked bored; one or two occasionally stifling a yawn as their glazed eyes blinked open and closed. By the time Pearson came to the last page, two hours later, even Alex was dozing off.

When Pearson finally slumped back on to the bench, Mr Justice Sackville suggested that perhaps this might be a convenient time to take the lunch break. Once the judge had left the court, Alex glanced across at Pearson, who could barely disguise his anger. He was only too aware that he had given an out-of-town matinee performance to an opening-night audience in the West End.

Alex grabbed one of his thick files and hurried out of the courtroom. He ran down the corridor and up the stone steps to a small room on the second floor that he had booked earlier that morning. Inside were just a table and chair, not even a print on the wall. Alex opened his file and began to go over his summing up. Key sentences were rehearsed again and again, until he was confident that the salient points would remain lodged in the jury's mind.

As Alex had spent most of the night, as well as the early hours of the morning, crafting and honing each and every phrase, he felt well prepared by the time he returned to court number four an hour and a half later. He was back in his place only moments before the judge reappeared. Once the court had settled, Mr Justice Sackville asked if he was ready to make his closing submission.

'I am indeed, m'lord,' Alex replied, and poured himself another glass of water. He opened his file, looked up and took a sip.

'Members of the jury,' he began, 'you have now heard . . .'

Alex did not take as long as Mr Pearson to present his closing argument, but then, for him it was not a dress rehearsal. He had no way of knowing how his most important points were playing with the jury, but at least none of them was nodding off, and several were making notes. When Alex sat down an hour and a half later, he felt he could reply yes should his father ask if he had served his client to the best of his ability.

'Thank you, Mr Redmayne,' said the judge, who then turned to the jury. 'I think that will be enough for today,' he said. Pearson checked his watch. It was only three thirty. He had assumed the judge would spend at least an hour addressing the jury before they rose for the day, but it was clear that he too had been taken by surprise with Alex Redmayne's morning ambush.

The judge rose from his place, bowed and left the courtroom without another word. Alex turned to chat with his opposite number as an usher handed Pearson a slip of paper. After Pearson had read it, he jumped up and hurried out of the courtroom, followed closely by his junior. Alex turned to smile at the defendant in the dock, but Danny Cartwright had already been escorted back down the stairwell to be locked in the cells below. Alex couldn't help wondering which door his client would leave by tomorrow. But then he had no idea why Pearson had left the courtroom in such a hurry.

13

Mr Pearson's clerk phoned Mr Justice Sackville's clerk at one minute past nine the following morning. Mr Justice Sackville's clerk said he would pass on Mr Pearson's request and come straight back to him. A few minutes later, Mr Justice Sackville's clerk phoned back to inform Mr Pearson's clerk that the judge would be happy to see Mr Pearson in chambers at 9.30, and he assumed, given the circumstances, that Mr Redmayne would also need to be present.

'He'll be my next call, Bill,' replied Mr Pearson's clerk, before putting the phone down.

Mr Pearson's clerk then called Mr Redmayne's clerk and asked if Mr Redmayne would be free at 9.30 to see the judge in chambers to discuss a matter of the utmost urgency.

'So what's this all about, Jim?' Mr Redmayne's clerk asked.

'No idea, Ted. Pearson never confides in me.'

Mr Redmayne's clerk called Mr Redmayne on his mobile and caught him just as he was about to disappear below ground into Pimlico tube station.

'Did Pearson give any reason why he wants a meeting with the judge?' asked Alex.

'He never does, Mr Redmayne,' replied Ted.

◄○►

Alex knocked quietly on the door before entering Mr Justice Sackville's chambers. He found Pearson lounging in a comfortable chair chatting to the judge about his roses. Mr Justice Sackville would never have considered broaching the relevant subject until both counsel were present.

'Good morning, Alex,' said the judge, waving him to an old leather armchair next to Pearson.

'Good morning, judge,' replied Alex.

'As we are due to sit in less than thirty minutes,' said the judge, 'perhaps, Arnold, you could brief us on why you requested this meeting.'

'Certainly, judge,' said Pearson. 'At the request of the CPS, I attended a meeting at their offices yesterday evening.' Alex held his breath. 'After a lengthy discussion with my masters, I can report that they are willing to consider a change of plea in this case.'

Alex tried not to show any reaction, although he wanted to leap up and punch the air, but this was judge's chambers, and not the terraces at Upton Park.

'What do they have in mind?' asked the judge.

'They felt that if Cartwright was able to plead guilty to man-slaughter . . .'

'How do you feel your client might respond to such an offer?' asked the judge, turning his attention to Redmayne.

'I have no idea,' admitted Alex. 'He's an intelligent man, but he's also as stubborn as a mule. He's stuck rigidly to the same story for the past six months and has never once stopped protesting his innocence.'

'Despite that, are you of a mind to advise him to accept the CPS's offer?' asked Pearson.

Alex was silent for some time before he said, 'Yes, but how does the CPS suggest I dress it up?'

Pearson frowned at Redmayne's choice of phrase. 'If your client were to admit that he and Wilson did go into the alley for the purpose of sorting out their differences . . .'

'And a knife ended up in Wilson's chest?' asked the judge, trying not to sound too cynical.

'Self-defence, mitigating circumstances – I'll leave Redmayne to fill in the details. That's hardly my responsibility.'

The judge nodded. 'I will instruct my clerk to inform the court officials and the jury that I do not intend to sit –' he glanced at his watch – 'until eleven a.m. Alex, will that give you enough time to instruct your client and then return to my chambers with his decision?'

'Yes, I feel sure that will be quite enough time,' replied Alex.

'If the man's guilty,' said Pearson, 'you'll be back in two minutes.'

14

AS ALEX REDMAYNE left the judge a few moments later and made his way slowly across to the other side of the building, he tried to marshal his thoughts. Within two hundred paces, he exchanged the peaceful serenity of a judge's chambers for cold bleak cells only occupied by prisoners.

He came to a halt at the heavy black door that blocked his way to the cells below. He knocked twice before it was opened by a silent policeman who accompanied him down a narrow flight of stone steps to a yellow corridor known by the old lags as the yellow brick road. By the time they reached cell number 17, Alex felt he was well prepared, although he still had no idea how Danny would react to the offer. The officer selected a key from a large ring and unlocked the cell door.

'Do you require an officer to be present during the interview?' he asked politely.

'That won't be necessary,' Alex replied.

The officer pulled open the two-inch-thick steel door. 'Do you want the door left open or closed, sir?'

'Closed,' replied Alex as he walked into a tiny cell that boasted two plastic chairs and a small formica table in the middle of the room, graffiti the only decoration on the walls.

Danny rose as Alex entered the room. 'Good morning, Mr Redmayne,' he said.

'Good morning, Danny,' replied Alex, taking the seat opposite him. He knew it would be pointless to ask his client once again to call him by his first name. Alex opened a file that contained a single sheet of paper. 'I have some good news,' he declared. 'Or at least, I hope you'll feel it's good news.' Danny showed no emotion. He rarely spoke unless he had something worthwhile to say. 'If you felt able to change your plea to one of guilty of manslaughter,' continued Alex, 'I think the judge would only sentence you to five years, and as you've already served six months, with good behaviour you could be out in a couple of years.'

Danny stared across the table at Alex, looked him straight in the eye and said, 'Tell 'im to fuck off.'

Alex was almost as shocked by Danny's language as he was by his instant decision. He'd never heard his client swear once during the past six months.

'But, Danny, please give the offer a little more consideration,' pleaded Alex. 'If the jury finds you guilty of murder you could end up serving a life sentence, with a tariff of twenty years, perhaps more. That would mean you wouldn't be released from prison until you're nearly fifty. But if you accept their offer, you could begin your life with Beth in two years' time.'

'What kind of life?' asked Danny coldly. 'One where everyone thinks I murdered my best mate and got away with it? No, Mr Redmayne. I didn't kill Bernie, and if it takes me twenty years to prove it . . .'

'But, Danny, why risk the whims of a jury when you can so easily accept this compromise?'

'I don't know what the word compromise means, Mr Redmayne, but I do know that I'm innocent and once the jury 'ears about this offer—'

'They'll never hear about it, Danny. If you turn the offer down, they won't be told why proceedings are being held up this morning, and the judge will make no reference to it in his summing up. The trial will just continue as if nothing has happened.'

'So be it,' said Danny.

'Perhaps you'd like a little more time to think about it,' said Alex, refusing to give up. 'You could talk to Beth. Or your parents. I'm sure I could get the judge to hold things up until tomorrow morning, which would at least give you time to reconsider your position.'

''ave you thought about what you're asking me to do?' said Danny.

'I'm not sure I understand,' said Alex.

'If I admit to manslaughter that would mean that everything Beth said while she was in the witness box was a lie. She didn't lie, Mr Redmayne. She told the jury exactly what 'appened that night.'

'Danny, you could spend the next twenty years regretting this decision.'

'I could spend the next twenty years living a lie, and if it takes me that long to prove I'm innocent, that 'as to be better than the world believing I killed my best mate.'

'But the world would quickly forget.'

'I wouldn't,' said Danny, 'and neither would my mates in the East End.'

Alex would like to have given it one last go, but he knew it was pointless to try to change the mind of this proud man. He rose wearily from his place. 'I'll let them know your decision,' he said before banging his fist on the cell door.

A key turned in the lock and moments later the heavy steel door was pulled open.

'Mr Redmayne,' said Danny quietly. Alex turned to face his client. 'You're a diamond, and I'm proud to 'ave been represented by you and not that Mr Pearson.'

The door was slammed shut.

15

NEVER BECOME emotionally involved in a case, his father had often warned him. Although Alex hadn't slept the previous night, he still paid rapt attention to every word the judge had to say in his four-hour summing up.

Mr Justice Sackville's summary was masterful. He first went over any points of law as they applied to the case. He then proceeded to help the jury sift through the evidence, point by point, trying to make the case coherent, logical and easy for them to follow. He never once exaggerated or showed any bias, only offering a balanced view for the seven men and five women to consider.

He suggested they should take seriously the testimony of three witnesses who had stated unequivocally that only Mr Craig had left the bar to go out into the alley, and only then after he'd heard a woman scream. Craig had stated on oath that he had seen the defendant stab Wilson several times, and had then immediately returned to the bar and called the police.

Miss Wilson, on the other hand, told a different story, claiming that it was Mr Craig who had drawn her companions into a fight, and it was he who must have stabbed Wilson. However, she did not witness the murder, but explained it was her brother who told her what had happened before he died. If you accept this version of events, the judge said, you might ask yourselves why Mr Craig contacted the police, and perhaps more important, when DS Fuller interviewed him in the bar some twenty minutes later, why there was no sign of blood on any of the clothes he was wearing.

Alex cursed under his breath.

'Members of the jury,' Mr Justice Sackville continued, 'there is nothing in Miss Wilson's past to suggest that she is other than an honest and decent citizen. However, you may feel that her evidence is somewhat coloured by her devotion and long-held loyalty to Cartwright, whom she intends to marry should he be found not guilty. But that must not influence you in your decision. You must put aside any natural sympathy you might feel because Miss Wilson is pregnant. Your responsibility is to weigh up the evidence in this case and ignore any irrelevant side issues.'

The judge went on to emphasize that Cartwright had no previous criminal record, and that for the past eleven years he had been employed by the same company. He warned the jury not to read too much into the fact that Cartwright had not given evidence. That was his prerogative, he explained, although the jury might be puzzled by the decision, if he had nothing to hide.

Again, Alex cursed his inexperience. What had been an advantage when he took Pearson by surprise, and had even caused the CPS to come up with their offer to accept a guilty plea to a lesser charge, might now be working against him.

The judge ended his summing up by advising the jury to take their time. After all, he emphasized, a man's future was in the balance. However, they should not forget that another man had lost his life, and if Danny Cartwright did not kill Bernie Wilson, they might well ask, who else could possibly have committed the crime?

At twelve minutes past two, the jury filed out of the court to begin their deliberations. For the next two hours, Alex tried not to remonstrate with himself for having failed to put Danny in the witness box. Did Pearson, as his father had suggested, really have other damning material that would have taken them both by surprise? Would Danny have been able to convince the jury that he didn't murder his closest friend? Pointless questions that Alex nevertheless continued to mull over as he waited for the jury to return.

It was just after five o'clock when the seven men and five women returned to the court and took their places in the jury box.

Alex couldn't interpret the blank looks on their faces. Mr Justice Sackville looked down from the bench and asked, 'Members of the jury, have you reached a verdict?'

The foreman rose from his new place at the end of the front row. 'No, m'lord,' he responded, reading from a prepared script. 'We are still sifting through the evidence, and will need more time before we can come to a decision.'

The judge nodded, and thanked the jury for their diligence. 'I'm going to send you home now, so that you can rest before you continue your deliberations tomorrow morning. But be aware,' he added, 'that once you leave this courtroom, you should not discuss the case with anyone, including your families.'

Alex returned home to his little flat in Pimlico and spent a second sleepless night.

16

ALEX WAS BACK in court and seated in his place by five minutes to ten the following morning. Pearson greeted him with a warm smile. Had the old codger forgiven him for his ambush, or was he simply confident of the outcome? As the two of them waited for the jury to return, they chatted about roses, cricket, even who was most likely to be the first Mayor of London, but never once referred to the proceedings that had occupied every waking minute for the past two weeks.

The minutes turned into hours. As there was no sign of the jury returning by one o'clock, the judge released everyone for an hour's lunch break. While Pearson went off for a meal in the Bar Mess on the top floor, Alex spent his time pacing up and down the corridor outside court number four. Juries in a murder trial rarely take less than four hours to reach a verdict, his father had told him over the phone that morning, for fear that it might be suggested that they had not taken their responsibilities seriously.

At eight minutes past four, the jury filed back into their places and this time Alex noted that their expressions had changed from blank to bemused. Mr Justice Sackville had no choice but to send them home for a second night.

◄o►

The following morning, Alex had only been pacing up and down the marble corridors for just over an hour before an usher emerged from the courtroom and shouted, 'The jury are returning to court number four.'

Once again, the foreman read from a prepared statement. 'My lord,' he began, his eyes never rising from the sheet of paper he was holding, his hand trembling slightly. 'Despite many hours of deliberation, we are unable to come to a unanimous decision and wish to seek your guidance on how we should proceed.'

'I sympathize with your problem,' responded the judge, 'but I must ask you to try one more time to reach a unanimous decision. I am loath to call a retrial only for the court to be put through the whole procedure a second time.'

Alex bowed his head. He would have settled for a retrial. If they gave him a second chance, he wasn't in any doubt that . . . The jury filed back out without another word and didn't reappear again that morning.

◄○►

Alex sat alone in a corner of the restaurant on the third floor. He allowed his soup to go cold, and shifted his salad around the plate, before he returned to the corridor and continued his ritual pacing.

At twelve minutes past three, an announcement came over the tannoy. 'All those involved in the Cartwright case, please make their way back in to court number four, as the jury is returning.'

Alex joined a stream of interested parties as they walked quickly down the corridor and filed back into the courtroom. Once they were settled, the judge reappeared and instructed the usher to summon the jury. As they entered the court, Alex couldn't help noticing that one or two of them looked distressed.

The judge leant forward and asked the foreman, 'Have you been able to reach a unanimous verdict?'

'No, m'lord,' came back the immediate reply.

'Do you think that you might reach a unanimous verdict if I were to allow you a little more time?'

'No, m'lord.'

'Would it help if I were to consider a majority verdict, and by that I mean one where at least ten of you are in agreement?'

'That might solve the problem, m'lord,' the foreman replied.

'Then I'll ask you to reconvene and see if you can finally come to a verdict.' The judge nodded to the usher, who led the jury back out of court.

Alex was about to rise and continue his perambulations, when Pearson leant across and said, 'Stay still, dear boy. I have a feeling they'll be back shortly.' Alex settled down on his corner of the bench.

Just as Pearson had predicted, the jury were back in their places a few minutes later. Alex turned to Pearson, but before he could speak, the elderly QC said, 'Don't even ask, dear boy. I've never been able to fathom the machinations of a jury despite almost thirty years at the Bar.' Alex was shaking as the usher stood and said, 'Would the foreman please rise.'

'Have you reached a verdict?' the judge asked.

'We have, m'lord,' replied the foreman.

'And is it a majority of you?'

'Yes, m'lord, a majority of ten to two.'

The judge nodded in the direction of the usher, who bowed. 'Members of the jury,' he said, 'do you find the prisoner at the bar, Daniel Arthur Cartwright, guilty or not guilty of murder?' What seemed like an eternity to Alex before the foreman responded was in fact no more than a few seconds.

'Guilty,' the foreman pronounced.

A gasp went up around the court. Alex's first reaction was to turn and look at Danny. He showed no sign of emotion. Above him in the public gallery came cries of 'No!' and the sound of sobbing.

Once the courtroom had come to order, the judge delivered a long preamble before passing sentence. The only words that would remain indelibly fixed in Alex's mind were *twenty-two years*.

His father had told him never to allow a verdict to affect him. After all, only one defendant in a hundred was wrongly convicted.

Alex was in no doubt that Danny Cartwright was one in a hundred.

BOOK TWO

PRISON

17

'WELCOME BACK, Cartwright.' Danny glanced at the officer seated behind the desk in reception, but didn't respond. The man looked down at the charge sheet. 'Twenty-two years,' Mr Jenkins said with a sigh. He paused. 'I know how you must feel, because that's just about the length of time I've been in the service.' Danny had always thought of Mr Jenkins as old. Is that how I'll look in twenty-two years, he wondered. 'I'm sorry, lad,' the officer said – not a sentiment he often expressed.

'Thanks, Mr Jenkins,' Danny said quietly.

'Now you're no longer on remand,' said Jenkins, 'you're not entitled to a single cell.' He opened a file, which he studied for some time. Nothing moves quickly in prison. He ran his finger down a long column of names, stopping at an empty box. 'I'm going to put you in block three, cell number one-two-nine.' He checked the names of the present occupants. 'They should make interesting company,' he added without explanation, before nodding to the young officer standing behind him.

'Look sharp, Cartwright, and follow me,' said the officer Danny had never seen before.

Danny followed the officer down a long brick corridor that was painted in a shade of mauve no other establishment would have considered purchasing in bulk. They came to a halt at a double-barred gate. The officer selected a large key from the chain that hung round his waist, unlocked the first gate and ushered Danny through. He joined him before locking them both in, then unlocking the second gate. They now stepped into a corridor whose walls were painted green – a sign that they had reached a secure area. Everything in prison is colour-coded.

The officer accompanied Danny until they reached a second double-barred gate. This process was repeated four more times before Danny arrived at block three. It wasn't hard to see why no one had ever escaped from Belmarsh. The colour of the walls had turned from mauve to green to blue by the time Danny's keeper handed him over to a unit officer who wore the same blue uniform, the same white shirt, the same black tie, and had the inevitable shaven head to prove that he was just as hard as any of the inmates.

'Right, Cartwright,' said his new minder casually, 'this is going to be your home for at least the next eight years, so you'd better settle down and get used to it. If you don't give us any trouble, we won't give you any. Understood?'

'Understood, guv,' repeated Danny, using the title every con gives a screw whose name he doesn't know.

As Danny climbed the iron staircase to the first floor he didn't come across another inmate. They were all locked up – as they nearly always were, sometimes for twenty-two hours a day. The new officer checked Danny's name on the call sheet and chuckled when he saw which cell he had been allocated. 'Mr Jenkins obviously has a sense of humour,' he said as they came to a halt outside cell number 129.

Yet another key was selected from yet another ring, this time one heavy enough to open the lock of a two-inch-thick iron door. Danny stepped inside, and the heavy door slammed shut behind him. He looked suspiciously at the two inmates who already occupied the cell.

A heavily built man was lying half-asleep on a single bed, facing the wall. He didn't even glance up at the new arrival. The other man was seated at the small table, writing. He put down his pen, rose from his place and thrust out a hand, which took Danny by surprise.

'Nick Moncrieff,' he said, sounding more like an officer than an inmate. 'Welcome to your new abode,' he added with a smile.

'Danny Cartwright,' Danny replied, shaking his hand. He looked across at the unoccupied bunk.

'As you're last in, you get the top bunk,' said Moncrieff. 'You'll have the bottom one in two years' time. By the way,' he said, pointing to the giant who lay on the other bed, 'that's Big Al.' Danny's other cellmate looked a few years older than Nick. Big Al grunted, but still didn't bother to turn round to find out who'd joined them. 'Big Al doesn't say a lot, but once you get to know him, he's just fine,' said Moncrieff. 'It took me about six months, but perhaps you'll be more successful.'

Danny heard the key turning in the lock, and the heavy door was pulled open once again.

'Follow me, Cartwright,' said a voice. Danny stepped back out of the cell and followed another officer he'd never seen before. Had the authorities already decided to put him in a different cell, he wondered, as the screw led him back down the iron staircase, along another corridor, and through a further set of double-barred gates before coming to a halt outside a door marked STORES. The officer gave a firm rap on the little double doors, and a moment later they were pulled open from the inside.

'CK4802 Cartwright,' said the officer, checking his charge sheet.

'Strip off,' said the stores manager. 'You won't be wearing any of those clothes again' – he looked down at the charge sheet – 'until 2022.' He laughed at a joke he cracked about five times a day. Only the year changed.

Once Danny had stripped, he was handed two pairs of boxer shorts (red and white stripes), two shirts (blue and white stripes), one pair of jeans (blue), two T-shirts (white), one pullover (grey), one donkey jacket (black), two pairs of socks (grey), one pair of shorts (blue gym), two singlets (white gym), two sheets (nylon, green), one blanket (grey), one pillow case (green) and one pillow (circular, solid); the one item he was allowed to keep were his trainers – a prisoner's only opportunity to make a fashion statement.

The stores manager gathered up all of Danny's clothes and dropped them in a large plastic bag, filled in the name Cartwright CK4802 on a little tag, and sealed up the bag. He then handed Danny a smaller plastic bag which contained a bar of soap, a toothbrush, a plastic disposable razor, one flannel (green), one hand towel (green), one plastic plate (grey), one plastic knife, one plastic fork and one plastic spoon. He ticked several boxes on a green form before swivelling it round, pointing to a line with his forefinger and handing Danny a well-bitten biro that was attached to the desk by a chain. Danny scrawled an illegible squiggle.

'You report back to the stores every Thursday afternoon between three and five,' said the stores manager, 'when you'll be given a change of clothes. Any damage and you'll have the requisite sum deducted from your weekly wage. And I decide how much that will be,' he added before slamming the doors closed.

Danny picked up the two plastic bags and followed the officer back down the corridor to his cell. He was locked up moments later, without a single word having passed between them. Big Al didn't seem to have stirred in his absence, and Nick was still seated at the tiny table, writing.

Danny climbed up on to the top bunk and lay flat on the lumpy mattress. While he'd been on remand for the past six months, he'd been allowed to wear his own clothes, roam around the ground floor chatting to his fellow inmates, watch television, play table tennis, even buy a Coke and sandwich from a vending machine – but no longer. Now he was a lifer, and for the first time he was finding out what losing your freedom really meant.

Danny decided to make up his bed. He took his time, as he was beginning to discover just how many hours there are in each day, how many minutes in each hour and how many seconds in each minute when you're locked up in a cell twelve foot by eight, with two strangers to share your space – one of them large.

Once he'd made the bed, Danny climbed back on to it, settled down and stared up at the white ceiling. One of the few advantages of being on the top bunk is that your head is opposite the tiny barred window: the only proof that there is an outside world. Danny looked through the iron bars at the other three blocks that made up the spur, the exercise yard and several high walls topped with razor wire that stretched as far as the eye could see. Danny stared back up at the ceiling. His thoughts turned to Beth. He hadn't even been allowed to say goodbye to her.

Next week, and for the next thousand weeks, he'd be locked up in this hellhole. His only chance of escape was an appeal. Mr Redmayne had warned him that that might not be heard for at least a year. The court lists were overcrowded, and the longer your sentence, the longer you had to wait before they got around to your appeal. Surely a year would be more than enough time for Mr Redmayne to gather all the evidence he needed to prove that Danny was innocent?

—◦—

Moments after Mr Justice Sackville had passed sentence, Alex Redmayne left the courtroom and walked down a carpeted, wall-papered corridor that was littered with pictures of former judges. He knocked on the door of another judge's chambers, walked in, slumped on a comfortable chair in front of his father's desk and said simply, 'Guilty.'

Mr Justice Redmayne walked across to the drinks cabinet. 'You may as well get used to it,' he said as he drew out the cork from the bottle he'd selected that morning, win or lose, 'because I can tell you that since the abolition of capital punishment, far more prisoners charged with murder have been convicted, and, almost without exception, the jury gets it right.' He poured two glasses of wine and handed one to his son. 'Will you continue to represent Cartwright when his case comes up for appeal?' he asked before taking a sip from his own glass.

'Yes, of course I will,' said Alex, surprised by his father's question.

The old man frowned. 'Then all I can say is good luck, because if Cartwright didn't do it, who did?'

'Spencer Craig,' said Alex without hesitation.

18

AT FIVE O'CLOCK the heavy iron door was pulled open once again, accompanied by a raucous bellow of 'ASSOCIATION' from a man whose previous occupation could only have been as a Guards sergeant major.

For the next forty-five minutes all the prisoners were released from their cells. They were given two choices as to how they might spend their time. They could, as Big Al always did, go down to the spacious area on the ground floor. There he slumped in front of the television in a large leather chair that no other inmate would have considered occupying, while others played dominoes, with tobacco as the only stake. If, on the other hand, you were willing to brave the elements, you could venture out into the exercise yard.

Danny was thoroughly searched before he stepped out of the block into the yard. Belmarsh, like every other prison, was awash with drugs and dealers who would hurriedly ply their trade during the only time in the day that prisoners from all four blocks came into contact with each other. The system of payment was simple and accepted by all the addicts. If you wanted a fix – hash, cocaine, crack cocaine or heroin – you let the wing dealer know your requirements, and the name of the person on the outside who would settle up with his contact; once the money had changed hands, the goods would appear a day or two later. With a hundred remand prisoners being driven in and out of the jail to attend court every morning, there were a hundred different opportunities to bring the gear back in. Some were caught red-handed, which resulted in time being added to their sentence, but the financial rewards were so high that there were always enough donkeys who considered it a risk worth taking.

Danny had never shown any interest in drugs; he didn't even smoke. His boxing coach had warned him that he would never be allowed in the ring again if he were caught taking drugs.

He began to stride around the perimeter of the yard, a patch of grass about the size of a football pitch. He kept up a fast pace, as he knew that this would be his only chance of getting any exercise, other than a twice-weekly visit to an overcrowded gym during the day. He glanced up at the thirty-foot wall that circled the exercise yard. Although it was topped with razor wire, that didn't stop him thinking about escape. How else would he be able to seek revenge on the four bastards who were responsible for stealing his freedom?

He passed several other prisoners who were walking at a more leisurely pace. No one overtook him. He noticed a lone figure striding out in front of him who was keeping roughly the same speed. It was some time before he realized that it was Nick Moncrieff, his new cellmate, who was clearly as fit as he was. What could a guy like him have done to end up behind bars, Danny wondered. He recalled the old prison rule that you never ask another con what he's in for; always wait for him to volunteer the information himself.

Danny glanced to his right to see a small group of black prisoners lying bare-chested on the grass, sunbathing as if they were on a package holiday in Spain. He and Beth had spent a fortnight last summer in Weston-super-Mare, where they made love for the first time. Bernie had come along too, and every evening he seemed to end up with a different girl, who had vanished by the light of day. Danny hadn't looked at another woman since the day he had seen Beth at the garage.

When Beth had told him she was pregnant, Danny had been surprised and delighted at the news. He'd even thought about suggesting going straight to the nearest register office and taking out a marriage licence. But he knew Beth wouldn't hear of it, and neither would her mother. After all, they were both Roman

Catholics, and therefore they must be married in St Mary's, just as both of their parents had been. Father Michael would have expected nothing less.

For the first time, Danny wondered if he should offer to break off the engagement. After all, no girl could be expected to wait for twenty-two years. He decided not to make a decision until after his appeal had been heard.

◄o►

Beth hadn't stopped crying since the foreman had delivered the jury's verdict. They didn't even allow her to kiss Danny goodbye before he was taken down to the cells by two officers. Her mother tried to comfort her on the way home, but her father said nothing.

'This nightmare will finally be over once the appeal is heard,' her mother said.

'Don't count on it,' said Mr Wilson, as he swung the car into Bacon Road.

◄o►

A klaxon proclaimed that the forty-five minutes set aside for Association was over. The prisoners were quickly herded back into their cells block by block.

Big Al was already slumbering on his bunk by the time Danny walked back into the cell. Nick followed a moment later, the door slamming behind him. It wouldn't be opened again until tea – another four hours.

Danny climbed back on to the top bunk, while Nick returned to the plastic chair behind the formica table. He was just about to start writing again, when Danny asked, 'What are you scribblin'?'

'I keep a diary,' replied Nick, 'of everything that goes on while I'm in prison.'

'Why would you want to be reminded of this dump?'

'It whiles away the time. And as I want to be a teacher when I'm released, it's important to keep my mind alert.'

'Will they let you teach after you've done a stretch in 'ere?' asked Danny.

'You must have read about the teacher shortage?' said Nick with a grin.

'I don't read a lot,' admitted Danny.

'Perhaps this is a good chance to start,' said Nick, putting his pen down.

'Can't see the point,' said Danny, ''specially if I'm going to be banged up in 'ere for the next twenty-two years.'

'But at least you'd be able to read your solicitor's letters, which would give you a better chance of preparing your defence when the case comes up for appeal.'

'Ur yous ever gonnae stop talkin'?' asked Big Al in a thick Glaswegian accent that Danny could barely translate.

'Not much else to do,' replied Nick with a laugh.

Big Al sat up and removed a pouch of tobacco from a pocket in his jeans. 'So whit you in fur, Cartwright?' he asked, breaking one of prison's golden rules.

'Murder,' said Danny. He paused. 'But I was stitched up.'

'Aye, that's whit they aw say.' Big Al took out a packet of cigarette papers from his other pocket, extracted one and laid a pinch of tobacco on top of it.

'Maybe,' said Danny, 'but I still didn't do it.' He didn't notice that Nick was writing down his every word. 'What about you?' he asked.

'Me, I'm a fuckin' bank robber,' said Big Al, licking the edge of the paper. 'Sometimes I pull it aff and get rich, other times I dinnae. The judge gied me fourteen years this fuckin' time.'

'So how long have you been banged up in Belmarsh?' asked Danny.

'Two years. They transferred me tae an open prison for a while, but I decided tae abscond, so they'll no be takin' that risk again. Huv yous no got a light?'

'I don't smoke,' said Danny.

'And neither do I, as you well know,' added Nick, continuing to write his journal.

'What a pair of numpties,' said Big Al. 'Noo I'll no be able to huv a drag till efter tea.'

'So you'll never be moved out of Belmarsh?' asked Danny in disbelief.

'Not until mah release date,' said Big Al. 'Wance ye've absconded fae a cat D, they send you back tae a high-security nick. Cannae say I blame the fuckers. If they transferred me I'd only try it again.' He placed the cigarette in his mouth. 'Still, I've only got three years tae go,' he said as he lay back down and turned to face the wall.

'What about you?' Danny asked Nick. 'How much longer have you got?'

'Two years, four months and eleven days. And you?'

'Twenty-two years,' said Danny. 'Unless I win my appeal.'

'Naeb'dy wins their appeal,' said Big Al. 'Wance they've got ye banged to rights, they're no going tae let you oot, so ye'd better get used tae it.' He removed the cigarette from his lips before adding, 'Or top yersel.'

◄○►

Beth was also lying on her bed staring up at the ceiling. She would wait for Danny however long it took. She had no doubt that he would win his appeal, and that her father would finally come round to realizing that both of them had been telling the truth.

Mr Redmayne assured her that he would continue to represent Danny at the appeal and that she shouldn't worry about the cost. Danny was right. Mr Redmayne was a real diamond. Beth had already spent all her savings and forgone her annual holiday so that she could attend every day of the trial. What was the point of a holiday if she couldn't spend it with Danny? Her boss could not have been more understanding and told her not to report back until the trial was over. If Danny was found not guilty, Mr Thomas had told her she could take another fortnight off for the honeymoon.

But Beth would be back at her desk on Monday morning, and the honeymoon would have to be postponed for at least a year. Although she had spent her life savings on Danny's defence, she still intended to send him some cash every month, as his prison wages would be only twelve pounds a week.

'Do you want a cup of tea, luv?' her mother shouted up from the kitchen.

---◄o►---

'Tea!' hollered a voice as the door was unlocked for the second time that day. Danny picked up his plastic plate and mug and followed a stream of prisoners as they made their way downstairs to join the queue at the hotplate.

An officer was standing at the front of the queue, allowing six prisoners up to the hotplate at any one time.

'More fights break out over food than anything else,' explained Nick as they waited in line.

'Other than in the gym,' said Big Al.

Eventually Danny and Nick were told to join four others at the hotplate. Standing behind the counter were five prisoners dressed in white overalls and white hats, wearing thin latex gloves. 'What's the choice tonight?' asked Nick, handing over his plate.

'You can 'ave sausages with beans, beef with beans or spam fritters with beans. Take your choice, squire,' said one of the inmates who was serving behind the counter.

'I'll have spam fritters without beans, thank you,' said Nick.

'I'll 'ave the same, but with beans,' said Danny.

'And who are you?' asked the server. 'His fuckin' brother?'

Danny and Nick both laughed. Although they were the same height, around the same age, and in prison uniform they didn't look unalike, neither of them had noticed the similarity. After all, Nick was always clean-shaven with every hair neatly in place, while Danny only shaved once a week and his hair, in Big Al's words, 'looked like a bog brush'.

'How do you get a job workin' in the kitchen?' asked Danny as they made their way slowly back up the spiral staircase to the first floor. Danny was quickly discovering that whenever you're out of your cell, you walk slowly.

'You have to be enhanced.'

'And how do you get enhanced?'

'Just make sure you're never put on report,' said Nick.

''ow do you manage that?'

'Don't swear at an officer, always turn up to work on time, and never get involved in a fight. If you can manage all three, in about a year's time you'll be enhanced, but you still won't get a job in the kitchen.'

'Why not?'

'Because there ur a thousand other fuckin' cons in this prison,' said Big Al, following behind, 'and nine hundred of thum want tae work in the kitchen. Yur oot of yer cell for most of the day, and ye get the best choice of grub. So ye can forget it, Danny boy.'

In the cell, Danny ate his meal in silence, and thought about how he could become enhanced more quickly. As soon as Big Al had forked the last piece of sausage into his mouth, he stood up, walked across the cell, pulled down his jeans and sat on the lavatory. Danny stopped eating and Nick looked away until Big Al had pulled the flush. Big Al then stood up, zipped his jeans, slumped back down on the end of his bunk and began rolling another cigarette.

Danny checked his watch: ten to six. He usually went round to Beth's place around six. He looked down at the unfinished scraps on his plate. Beth's mum made the best sausage and mash in Bow.

'What other jobs are goin'?' asked Danny.

'Are yous still talking?' demanded Big Al.

Nick laughed again as Big Al lit his cigarette.

'You could get a job in the stores,' said Nick, 'or become a wing cleaner or a gardener, but most likely you'll end up on the chain gang.'

'The chain gang?' asked Danny. 'What's that?'

'You'll find out soon enough,' replied Nick.

'What about the gym?' asked Danny.

'Ye have tae be enhanced for that,' said Big Al, inhaling.

'So what job 'ave you got?' asked Danny.

'You ask too many questions,' replied Big Al as he exhaled, filling the cell with smoke.

'Big Al is the hospital orderly,' said Nick.

'That sounds like a cushy number,' said Danny.

'I huv tae polish the floors, empty the midgies, prepare the morning rota and make tea fur every screw that visits matron. I niver stop moving,' said Big Al. 'I'm enhanced, aren't I?'

'Very responsible job, that,' said Nick smiling. 'You have to have an unblemished record when it comes to drugs, and Big Al doesn't approve of junkies.'

'Too fuckin' right I don't,' said Big Al. 'And I'll thump anyone who tries tae steal any drugs fae the hospital.'

'Is there any other job worth considerin'?' asked Danny desperately.

'Education,' said Nick. 'If you decided to join me, you could improve your reading and writing. And at the same time you get paid for it.'

'True, but only eight quid a week,' chipped in Big Al. 'Ye get twelve fur every other job. No many of us like the squire here cin turn oor noses up at an extra four quid a week baccy money.'

Danny placed his head back on the rock-hard pillow and stared out of the tiny curtain-less window. He could hear rap blaring from a nearby cell, and wondered if he'd be able to get to sleep on the first night of his twenty-two-year sentence.

19

A KEY TURNED in the lock and the heavy iron door was pulled open.

'Cartwright, you're on the chain gang. Report to the duty officer immediately.'

'But—' began Danny.

'No point arguing,' said Nick as the officer disappeared. 'Stick with me, and I'll show you the drill.'

Nick and Danny joined a stream of silent prisoners who were all heading in the same direction. When they reached the end of the corridor, Nick said, 'This is where you report at eight o'clock every morning and sign up for your work detail.'

'What the hell is that?' asked Danny, staring up at a large hexagonal glass cubicle that dominated the area.

'That's the bubble,' said Nick. 'The screws can always keep an eye on us, but we can't see them.'

'There's screws in there?' said Danny.

'Sure are,' replied Nick. 'About forty, I'm told. They have a clear view of everything going on in all four blocks, so if a riot or any disturbance breaks out, they can move in and deal with the problem within minutes.'

'Ever been involved in a riot?' asked Danny.

'Only once,' replied Nick, 'and it wasn't a pretty sight. This is where we part company. I'm off to education, and the chain gang is in the opposite direction. If you carry on down the green corridor, you'll end up in the right place.'

Danny nodded and followed a group of prisoners who clearly

knew where they were going, although their sullen looks and the speed at which they were moving suggested that they could think of better ways of spending a Saturday morning.

When Danny reached the end of the corridor, an officer carrying the inevitable clipboard ushered all the prisoners into a large rectangular room, about the size of a basketball court. Inside were six long formica tables, with about twenty plastic chairs lined up on each side of them. The chairs quickly filled up with inmates, until almost every one was taken.

'Where do I sit?' asked Danny.

'Wherever you like,' said an officer. 'It won't make any difference.'

Danny found a vacant seat and remained silent as he watched what was going on around him.

'You're new,' said the man seated on his left.

'How do you know that?'

'Because I've been on the chain gang for the past eight years.'

Danny took a closer look at the short, wiry man, whose skin was as white as a sheet. He had watery blue eyes and cropped fair hair. 'Liam,' he announced.

'Danny.'

'You Irish?' asked Liam.

'No, I'm a cockney, born a few miles away from 'ere, but my grandfather was Irish.'

'That's good enough for me,' said Liam with a grin.

'So what happens next?' asked Danny.

'You see those cons standing at the end of each table?' said Liam. 'They're the suppliers. They'll put a bucket in front of us. You see that stack of plastic bags at the other end of the table? They'll be passed down the middle. We drop whatever's in our bucket into each one and pass it on.'

As Liam was speaking, a klaxon sounded. Brown plastic buckets were placed in front of each prisoner by inmates with yellow armbands. Danny's bucket was full of teabags. He glanced across at Liam's, which contained sachets of butter. The plastic bags made their slow progress along the table from prisoner to prisoner, and a packet of Rice Krispies, a sachet of butter, a teabag, and tiny containers of salt, pepper and jam were dropped into each one. When they reached the end of the table, another prisoner stacked them on to a tray and carried them into an adjoining room.

'They'll be sent off to another prison,' Liam explained, 'and end up as some con's breakfast about this time next week.'

Danny was bored within a few minutes, and would have been suicidal by the end of the morning if Liam hadn't provided an endless commentary on everything from how to get yourself enhanced to how to end up in solitary, which kept all those within earshot in fits of laughter.

'Have I told you about the time the screws found a bottle of Guinness in my cell?' he asked.

'No,' replied Danny dutifully.

'Of course I was put on report, but in the end they couldn't charge me.'

'Why not?' asked Danny, and although everyone else at the table had heard the tale many times, they still paid rapt attention.

'I told the guv'nor a screw planted the bottle in my cell because he had it in for me.'

'Because you're Irish?' suggested Danny.

'No, I'd tried that line once too often, so I had to come up with something a little more original.'

'Like what?' said Danny.

'I said the screw had it in for me because I knew that he was gay and he fancied me, but I'd always turned him down.'

'And was he gay?' asked Danny. Several prisoners burst out laughing.

'Of course not, you muppet,' said Liam. 'But the last thing a guv'nor needs is a full investigation into the sexual orientation of one of his screws. It only means mountains of paperwork, while the screw's suspended on full pay. It's all spelt out in prison regu-lations.'

'So what happened?' asked Danny, dropping another teabag into another plastic bag.

'The number-one guv'nor dismissed the charge and that screw hasn't been seen on my block since.'

Danny laughed for the first time since he had been in prison.

'Don't look up,' whispered Liam as a fresh bucket of teabags was placed in front of Danny. Liam waited until the prisoner wearing a yellow armband had removed their empty buckets before he added, 'If you ever come across that bastard, make yourself scarce.'

'Why?' asked Danny, glancing across to see a thin-faced man with a shaven head and arms covered in tattoos leave the room carrying a stack of empty buckets.

'His name's Kevin Leach. Avoid him at all costs,' said Liam. 'He's trouble – big trouble.'

'What kind of trouble?' asked Danny as Leach returned to the far end of the table and started stacking again.

'He came home early from work one afternoon and caught his wife in bed with his best mate. After he'd knocked 'em both out, he tied 'em to the bed posts and waited for 'em to come round, then he stabbed 'em with a kitchen knife – once every ten minutes. He started at their ankles, and moved slowly up the body till he reached the 'eart. They reckon it must have been six or seven hours before they died. He told the judge he was only tryin' to make the bitch realize how much he loved 'er.' Danny felt sick. 'The judge gave him life, with the recommendation that he should never be released. He won't see the outside of this place until they carry 'im out feet first.' Liam paused. 'I'm ashamed to say he's Irish. So be careful. They can't add another day to 'is sentence, so he doesn't care who he cuts up.'

—◦—

Spencer Craig was not a man who suffered from self-doubt or who panicked under pressure, but the same could not be said of Lawrence Davenport or Toby Mortimer.

Craig was aware of the rumours circulating around the corridors of the Old Bailey concerning the evidence he had given during the Cartwright trial; they were only whispers at the moment, but he could not afford for those whispers to become legend.

He was confident that Davenport wouldn't cause any trouble as long as he was playing Dr Beresford in *The Prescription*. After all, he adored being adored by millions of fans who watched him every Saturday evening at nine o'clock, not to mention an income that allowed him a lifestyle that neither of his parents, a car-park attendant and a lollipop lady from Grimsby, had ever experienced. The fact that the alternative could well be a spell in jail for perjury concentrated the mind somewhat. If it didn't, Craig wouldn't hesitate to remind him what he could look forward to once his fellow cons discovered he was gay.

Toby Mortimer presented a different sort of problem. He'd reached the point where he would do almost anything to get his next fix. Craig was in no doubt that when Toby's inheritance finally dried up, he would be the first person his fellow Musketeer would turn to.

Only Gerald Payne remained resolute. After all, he still hoped to become a Member of Parliament. But the truth was it would be a long time before the Musketeers had the same relationship they had enjoyed before Gerald's thirtieth birthday.

◄○►

Beth waited on the pavement until she was certain there was no one left on the premises. She looked up and down the street before she slipped into the shop. Beth was surprised at how dark the little room was, and it took her a few moments before she recognized a familiar figure seated behind the grille.

'What a pleasant surprise,' said Mr Isaacs as Beth walked up to the counter. 'What can I do for you?'

'I need to pawn something, but I want to be sure that I can buy it back.'

'I'm not allowed to sell any item for at least six months,' said Mr Isaacs, 'and if you needed a little more time, that wouldn't be a problem.'

Beth hesitated for a moment, before she slipped the ring off her finger and pushed it under the grille.

'Are you sure about this?' asked the pawnbroker.

'I don't have much choice,' said Beth. 'Danny's appeal is coming up and I need—'

'I could always advance you—'

'No,' said Beth, 'that wouldn't be right.'

Mr Isaacs sighed. He picked up an eyeglass and studied the ring for some time before he offered an opinion. 'It's a fine piece,' he said, 'but how much were you expecting to borrow against it?'

'Five thousand pounds,' said Beth hopefully.

Mr Isaacs continued to make a pretence of studying the stone carefully, although he had sold the ring to Danny for four thousand pounds less than a year ago.

'Yes,' said Mr Isaacs after further consideration, 'that seems to me to be a fair price.' He placed the ring under the counter and took out his chequebook.

'Can I ask a favour, Mr Isaacs, before you sign the cheque?'

'Yes, of course,' said the pawnbroker.

'Will you allow me to borrow the ring on the first Sunday of every month?'

◄○►

'That bad?' said Nick.

'Worse. If it hadn't been for Liam the tealeaf, I would have fallen asleep and ended up on report.'

'Interesting case, Liam,' said Big Al, stirring slightly but not bothering to turn round. 'His whole family are tealeaves. He's got six brothers and three sisters, an' wance, five o' the brothers and two o' the sisters wur aw inside at the same time. His fucking family must already have cost the taxpayer over a million quid.'

Danny laughed, then asked Big Al, 'What do you know about Kevin Leach?'

Big Al sat bolt upright. 'Don't ever mention that name ootside o' this cell. He's a nutter. He'd cut yur throat fur a Mars Bar, and if ye ever cross him . . .' He hesitated. 'They hud tae shift him oot of Garside nick just because another con gave him a V sign.'

'Sounds a bit extreme,' said Nick, writing down Big Al's every word.

'No efter Leach cut aff the two fingers.'

'That's what the French did to the English longbowmen at the battle of Agincourt,' said Nick, looking up.

'How interesting,' said Big Al.

The klaxon sounded, and the cell doors were opened to allow

JEFFREY ARCHER

them to go down and fetch their supper. As Nick closed his diary and pushed his chair back, Danny noticed for the first time that he was wearing a silver chain round his neck.

—◦—

There's a rumour circulating the corridors of the Old Bailey,' said Mr Justice Redmayne, 'that Spencer Craig might not have been entirely forthcoming when he gave evidence in the Cartwright case. I hope it's not you who's fanning that particular flame.'

'I don't have to,' Alex replied. 'That man has more than enough enemies willing to pump the bellows.'

'Nevertheless, as you are still involved in the case, it would be unwise for you to let your views be known among our colleagues at the Bar.'

'Even if he's guilty?'

'Even if he's the devil incarnate.'

—◦—

Beth wrote her first letter to Danny at the end of his first week, hoping he'd be able to find someone to read it to him. She slipped in a ten-pound note before sealing the envelope. She planned to write once a week, as well as visiting him on the first Sunday of every month. Mr Redmayne had explained that lifers can only have one visit a month during their first ten years.

The following morning she dropped the envelope in the post box at the end of Bacon Road before catching the number 25 into the City. Danny's name was never mentioned in the Wilson household, because it only caused her dad to fly off the handle. Beth touched her stomach, and wondered what future a child could possibly hope for who only came into contact with its father once a month while he was in prison. She prayed that it would be a girl.

—◦—

'You need a haircut,' said Big Al.

'What do you expect me to do about it?' said Danny. 'Ask Mr

Pascoe if I can take next Saturday morning off so I can drop into Sammy's on Mile End Road and have my usual?'

'No necessary,' said Big Al. 'Jist book yersel in wi' Louis.'

'And who's Louis?' asked Danny.

'Prison barber,' said Big Al. 'He usually gets through about five cons in forty minutes during Association, but he's so popular ye might huv tae wait for a month before he cin dae ye. As yer no going anywhere fur the next twenty-two years, that shouldnae be a problem. But if ye want tae jump the queue, he charges three fags for a bullet hied, five for a short back and sides. And the squire here,' he said, pointing to Nick who was propped up against a pillow on his bunk reading a book, 'has tae hand over ten fags on account of the fact that he still wishes tae look like an officer and a gentleman.'

'A short back and sides will suit me just fine,' said Danny. 'But what does he use? I don't fancy having my hair cut with a plastic knife and fork.'

Nick put down his book. 'Louis has all the usual equipment – scissors, clippers, even a razor.'

'How does he get away with that?' asked Danny.

'He disnae,' said Big Al. 'A screw hands over the stuff at the beginning of Association then collects it before we go back tae oor cells. An before ye ask, if anything went missing, Louis would lose his job and every cell wid be searched till the screws found it.'

'Is he any good?' asked Danny.

'Before he ended up in here,' said Big Al, 'he used tae work in Mayfair, charging the likes of the squire here fifty quid a hied.'

'So how does someone like that end up in the nick?' asked Danny.

'Burglary,' said Nick.

'Burglary, my arse,' said Big Al. 'Buggery mer like it. Caught wi' his troosers doon on Hampstead Heath, and he wasnae pishin' when the polis turned up.'

'But if the cons know he's gay,' said Danny, 'how does he survive in a place like this?'

'Good question,' said Big Al. 'In maist nicks, when a queer

takes a shower the cons take turns to bugger um, then tear um apart limb fae fucking limb.'

'So what stops them?' asked Danny.

'Good barbers aren't that easy to come by,' said Nick.

'The squire's right,' said Big Al. 'Oor last barber was in fur grievous, and the cons couldnae afford tae relax while he hud a razor in his hand. In fact, one or two of um ended up wi' very long hair.'

20

'Two letters for you, Cartwright,' Mr Pascoe, the wing officer, said as he passed a couple of envelopes across to Danny. 'By the way,' he continued, 'we found a ten-pound note attached to one of the letters. The money's been paid into your canteen account, but tell your girlfriend that in future she should send a postal order to the governor's office and they'll put the money straight into your account.'

The heavy door slammed shut.

'They've opened my letters,' said Danny, looking at the torn envelopes.

'They always do,' said Big Al. 'They also listen in on your phone conversations.'

'Why?' asked Danny.

'Hoping to catch anyone involved in a drugs drop. And last week they caught some stupid bastard planning a robbery for the day after he was due to be released.'

Danny extracted the letter from the smaller of the two envelopes. As it was handwritten, he assumed it had to be from Beth. The second letter was typed, but this time he couldn't be sure who had sent it. He lay silently on his bunk considering the problem for some time before he finally gave in.

'Nick, can you read my letters to me?' he asked quietly.

'I can and I will,' replied Nick.

Danny passed across the two letters. Nick put down his pen, unfolded the handwritten letter first, and checked the signature on the bottom of the page. 'This one's from Beth,' he said. Danny nodded.

'Dear Danny,' Nick read, 'it's only been a week, but I already miss you so much. How could the jury have made such a terrible mistake? Why didn't they believe me? I've filled in the necessary forms and will come and visit you next Sunday afternoon, which will be the last chance I have to see you before our baby is born. I spoke to a woman officer on the phone yesterday and she couldn't have been more helpful. Your mum and dad are both well and send their love, and so does my mother. I'm sure Dad will come round given time, especially after you win the appeal. I miss you so much. I love you, I love you, I love you. See you on Sunday, Beth xxx.'

Nick glanced up to see Danny staring at the ceiling. 'Would you like me to read it again?'

'No.'

Nick unfolded the second letter. 'It's from Alex Redmayne,' he said. 'Most unusual.'

'What do you mean?' asked Danny, sitting up.

'Barristers don't usually write direct to their clients. They leave it to the instructing solicitors. It's marked private and confidential. Are you sure you want me to know the contents of this letter?'

'Read it,' said Danny.

'Dear Danny, just a line to bring you up to date on your appeal. I have completed all the necessary applications and today received a letter from the Lord Chancellor's office confirming that your name has been entered on the list. However, there is no way of knowing how long the process will take, and I must warn you that it could be anything up to two years. I am still following up all leads in the hope that they might produce some fresh evidence, and will write again when I have something more tangible to report. Yours sincerely, Alex Redmayne.'

Nick put the two letters back in their envelopes and returned them to Danny. He picked up his pen and said, 'Would you like me to reply to either of them?'

'No,' said Danny firmly. 'I'd like you to teach me to read and write.'

—◦—

Spencer Craig was beginning to think it had been unwise to choose the Dunlop Arms for the Musketeers' monthly get-together. He had persuaded his fellow members that it would show they had nothing to hide. He was already regretting his decision.

Lawrence Davenport had made some lame excuse for not attending, claiming he had to be at an awards ceremony because he'd been nominated for best actor in a soap.

Craig wasn't surprised that Toby Mortimer hadn't shown up – he was probably lying in a gutter somewhere with a needle sticking out of his arm.

At least Gerald Payne made an appearance, even if he had turned up late. If there had been an agenda for this meeting, disbanding the Musketeers would probably have been item number one.

Craig emptied the remainder of the first bottle of Chablis into Payne's glass and ordered another one. 'Cheers,' he said, raising his glass. Payne nodded, less than enthusiastically. Neither spoke for some time.

'Do you have any idea when Cartwright's appeal is coming up?' said Payne eventually.

'No,' replied Craig. 'I keep an eye on the lists, but I can't risk calling the Criminal Appeal Office, for obvious reasons. The moment I hear anything, you'll be the first to know.'

'Are you worried about Toby?' asked Payne.

'No, he's the least of our problems. Whenever the appeal does come up, you can be sure he'll be in no state to give evidence. Our only problem is Larry. He gets flakier by the day. But the prospect of a spell in jail should keep him in line.'

'But what about his sister?' said Payne.

'Sarah?' said Craig. 'What's she got to do with it?'

'Nothing, but if she ever found out what actually happened that night, she might try to persuade Larry that it was his duty to give evidence at the appeal telling them what really took place. She is a solicitor, after all.' Payne took a sip of his wine. 'Didn't you two have a fling at Cambridge?'

'I wouldn't call it a fling,' said Craig. 'She's not really my type – too uptight.'

'That's not what I heard,' said Payne, trying to make light of it.

'What did you hear?' asked Craig defensively.

'That she gave you up because you had some rather strange habits in the bedroom.'

Craig didn't comment as he emptied what remained of the second bottle. 'Another bottle, barman,' he said.

'The 'ninety-five, Mr Craig?'

'Of course,' said Craig. 'Nothing but the best for my friend.'

'No need to waste your money on me, old fellow,' said Payne.

Craig didn't bother to tell him that it hardly mattered what was on the label, because the barman had already decided how much he was going to charge for 'keeping shtum', as he put it.

◄O►

Big Al was snoring, which Nick had once described in his diary as sounding like a cross between an elephant drinking and a ship's foghorn. Nick somehow managed to sleep through any amount of rap music emanating from the nearby cells, but he still hadn't come to terms with Big Al's snoring.

He lay awake and thought about Danny's decision to give up the chain gang and join him at education. It hadn't taken him long to realize that while Danny may not have had much of a formal education, he was brighter than anyone he'd taught during the past two years.

Danny was rapacious about his new challenge, without having any idea what the word meant. He didn't waste a moment, always asking questions, rarely satisfied with the answers. Nick had read about teachers who discovered that their pupils were cleverer than they were, but he hadn't expected to come across that problem while he was in prison. And it wasn't as if Danny allowed him to relax at the end of the day. No sooner had the cell door been slammed for the night than he was perched on the end of Nick's bunk, demanding that even more questions were answered. And on two subjects, maths and sport, Nick quickly found out that Danny already knew far more than he did. He had an encyclopedic memory that made it quite unnecessary for Nick to look up anything in *Wisden* or the *FA Handbook*, and if you mentioned West Ham or Essex, Danny *was* the handbook. Although he may not have been literate, he was clearly numerate, and had a grasp for figures that Nick knew he could never equal.

'Are you awake?' asked Danny, breaking into Nick's thoughts.

'Big Al's probably preventing anyone in the next three cells from sleeping,' said Nick.

'I was just thinkin' that since I signed up for education, I've told you a lot about me, but I still know almost nothin' about you.'

'I was just *thinking*, and while I know almost *nothing* about you. You're still dropping the g.'

'Thinking. Nothing,' said Danny.

'What do you want to know?' asked Nick.

'For a start, how did someone like you end up in prison?' Nick didn't immediately respond. 'Don't tell me if you don't want to,' Danny added.

'I was court-martialled while my regiment was serving with the NATO forces in Kosovo.'

'Did you kill someone?'

'No, but an Albanian died and another was injured because of an error of judgement on my part.' It was Danny's turn to remain silent. 'My platoon was ordered to protect a group of Serbs who had been charged with ethnic cleansing. During my watch, a band of Albanian guerrillas drove past the compound firing their Kalashnikovs in the air, to celebrate the Serbs' capture. When a car full of them came dangerously close to the compound, I warned their leader to stop firing. He ignored me, so my staff sergeant fired a few warning shots, which resulted in two of them ending up with gunshot wounds. Later one of them died in hospital.'

'So you didn't kill anyone?' said Danny.

'No. But I was the officer in charge.'

'And you got eight years for that?' Nick didn't comment. 'I once thought about going into the army,' said Danny.

'You'd have made a damn good soldier.'

'But Beth was against it.' Nick smiled. 'Said she didn't like the idea of my being overseas half the time when she'd be worrying herself sick about my safety. Ironic really.'

'Good use of the word ironic,' said Nick.

'How come you don't get no letters?'

'*Any* letters. I don't receive *any* letters.'

'Why don't you receive any letters?' repeated Danny.

'How do you spell *receive*?'

'R E C I E V E.'

'No,' said Nick. 'Try to remember, i before e except after c – R E C E I V E. There are some exceptions to that rule, but I won't bother you with them tonight.' There was another long silence, before Nick eventually replied to Danny's question. 'I've made no attempt to stay in contact with my family since the court martial, and they've made no effort to get in touch with me.'

'Even your mum and dad?' said Danny.

'My mother died giving birth to me.'

'I'm sorry. Is your father still alive?'

'As far as I know, yes, but he was colonel of the same regiment I served in. He hasn't spoken to me since the court martial.'

'That's a bit rough.'

'Not really. The regiment is his whole life. I was meant to follow in his footsteps and end up as the commanding officer, not being court-martialled.'

'Any brothers or sisters?'

'No.'

'Aunts and uncles?'

'One uncle, two aunts. My father's younger brother and his wife, who live in Scotland, and another aunt in Canada, but I've never met her.'

'No other relations?'

'*Relatives* is a better word. Relations has a double meaning.'

'Relatives.'

'No. The only person I've ever really cared for was my grandfather, but he died a few years ago.'

'And was your grandfather an army officer too?'

'No,' said Nick, laughing. 'He was a pirate.'

Danny didn't laugh. 'What sort of pirate?'

'He sold armaments to the Americans during the Second World War; made a fortune – enough to retire on, buy a large estate in Scotland and set himself up as a laird.'

'A laird?'

'Clan leader, master of all he surveys.'

'Does that mean you're rich?'

'Unfortunately not,' Nick replied. 'My father somehow managed to squander most of his inheritance while he was colonel of the regiment – "Must keep up appearances, old boy," he used to say. Whatever was left over went on the upkeep of the estate.'

'So you're penniless? You're like me?'

'No,' said Nick, 'I'm not like you. You're more like my grandfather. And you wouldn't have made the same mistake as I did.'

'But I ended up in 'ere with a twenty-two-year sentence.'

'In *here*. Don't drop the *h*.'

'In here,' repeated Danny.

'But unlike me, you shouldn't be in here,' said Nick quietly.

'Do you believe that?' said Danny, unable to hide his surprise.

'I didn't until I read Beth's letter, and clearly Mr Redmayne also thinks the jury made the wrong decision.'

'What's hanging from the chain round your neck?' asked Danny.

Big Al woke with a start, grunted, climbed out of bed, pulled down his boxer shorts and plonked himself on the lavatory. Once he'd pulled the flush, Danny and Nick tried to get to sleep before he started snoring again.

◄○►

Beth was on a bus when she first felt the pains. The baby wasn't due for another three weeks, but she knew at once that she would have to get to the nearest hospital somehow if she didn't want her first child to be born on the number 25.

'Help,' she moaned when the next wave of pain hit her. She

tried to stand when the bus came to a halt at a traffic light. Two older women seated in front of her turned round. 'Is that what I think it is?' said the first one.

'No doubt about it,' said the second. 'You ring the bell, and I'll get her off the bus.'

―◄○►―

Nick handed Louis ten cigarettes after he'd finished brushing off the hair from his shoulders.

'Thank you, Louis,' said Nick, as if he were addressing his regular barber at Trumper's in Curzon Street.

'Always a pleasure, squire,' said Louis as he threw a sheet around his next customer. 'So what's your pleasure, young man?' he asked, running his fingers through Danny's thick, short hair.

'You can cut that out for a start,' said Danny, pushing Louis's hand away. 'All I want is a short back and sides.'

'Suit yourself,' said Louis, picking up his clippers and studying Danny's hair more closely.

Eight minutes later Louis put down his scissors and held up a mirror so Danny could see the back of his head.

'Not bad,' Danny admitted as a voice shouted out: 'Back to your cells. Association's over.'

Danny slipped Louis five cigarettes as an officer hurried across and joined them.

'So what's it to be then, guv? Short back and sides?' Danny asked looking at Mr Hagen's bald head.

'Don't get lippy with me, Cartwright. Back to your cell, and be smart about it or you might just find yourself on report.' Mr Hagen placed the scissors, razor, clippers, brush and an assortment of combs into a box, which he then locked and took away.

'See you in a month's time,' said Louis as Danny hurried back to his cell.

21

'ROMANS AND C OF E!' bellowed a voice that could be heard from one side of the block to the other.

Danny and Nick stood waiting by the door, while Big Al happily snored away, abiding by his long-held belief that while you're asleep you're not in prison. The heavy key turned in the lock and the door swung open. Danny and Nick joined a stream of prisoners making their way towards the prison chapel.

'Do you believe in God?' asked Danny as they walked down the spiral staircase to the ground floor.

'No,' said Nick. 'I'm an agnostic.'

'What's that?'

'Someone who believes we can't know if there's a God, as opposed to an atheist, who is certain there isn't one. But it's still a good excuse to be out of the cell for an hour every Sunday morning, and in any case, I enjoy singing. Not to mention the fact that the padre gives a damn good sermon – even if he does seem to spend an inordinate amount of time on remorse.'

'Padre?'

'Army term for a priest,' explained Nick.

'Inordinate?'

'Excessive, longer than necessary. What about you? Do you believe in God?'

'Used to, before all this 'appened.'

'Happened,' said Nick.

'Happened,' repeated Danny. 'Beth and me are Roman Catholics.'

'Beth and *I* are Roman Catholics; you can't say me is a Roman Catholic.'

'Beth and I are Roman Catholics, so we know the Bible almost off by heart, even though I wasn't able read it.'

'Is Beth still coming this afternoon?'

'Of course,' said Danny, a smile appearing on his face. 'I can't wait to see 'er.'

'*Her*,' said Nick.

'Her,' said Danny dutifully.

'Don't you ever get fed up with me continually correcting you?'

'Yes,' admitted Danny, 'but I know it will please Beth, because she always wanted me to better myself. Still, I'm lookin' forward to the day when I can correct you.'

'*Looking* forward.'

'Looking forward,' repeated Danny as they reached the entrance to the chapel, where they waited in line as each prisoner was given a body search before being allowed to enter.

'Why bother to search us before we go in?' asked Danny.

'Because it's one of the few occasions when prisoners from all four blocks can congregate in one place, and have a chance to exchange drugs or information.'

'Congregate?'

'Get together. A church has a congregation.'

'Spell it,' demanded Danny.

They reached the front of the line, where two officers were carrying out searches – a short woman who was over forty and must have survived on a diet of prison food, and a young man who looked as if he spent a lot of time bench-pressing. Most of the prisoners seemed to want to be searched by the woman officer.

Danny and Nick strolled into the chapel, another large rectangular room but this time filled with long wooden benches that faced an altar displaying a silver cross. On the brick wall behind the altar was a huge mural depicting The Last Supper. Nick told Danny it had been painted by a murderer, and that the models for the disciples had all been inmates at the time.

'It's not bad,' said Danny.

'Just because you're a murderer doesn't mean you can't have other talents,' said Nick. 'Don't forget Caravaggio.'

'I don't think I've met him,' admitted Danny.

'Turn to page 127 in your hymn books,' announced the chaplain, 'and we'll all sing, "He Who Would Valiant Be".'

'I'll introduce you to Caravaggio as soon as we're back in the cell,' promised Nick as the little organ struck up the opening chord.

As they sang, Nick couldn't be sure if Danny was reading the words or knew them off by heart after years of attending his local church.

Nick looked around the chapel. He wasn't surprised that the benches were as packed as a football stand on a Saturday afternoon. A group of prisoners huddled together in the back row were deep in conversation, not even bothering to open their hymn books as they exchanged details of which new arrivals needed drugs; they'd already dismissed Danny as 'no man's land'. Even when they fell on their knees they made no pretence of mouthing the Lord's Prayer; redemption wasn't on their minds.

The only time they fell silent was when the chaplain delivered his sermon. Dave, whose name was printed in bold letters on a lapel badge pinned to his cassock, turned out to be a good old-fashioned fire and brimstone priest, who had chosen murder as his text for the day. This drew loud cries of 'Hallelujah!' from the first three rows, mainly populated by boisterous Afro-Caribbeans who seemed to know a thing or two about the subject.

Dave invited his captive audience to pick up their Bibles and turn to the book of Genesis, then informed them that Cain was the first murderer. 'Cain was envious of his brother's success,' he explained, 'so decided to do away with him.' Dave then turned to Moses, who he claimed killed an Egyptian and thought he'd got away with it, but he hadn't, because God had seen him, so he was punished for the rest of his life.

'I don't remember that bit,' said Danny.

'Nor do I,' admitted Nick. 'I thought Moses died peacefully in his bed at the age of one hundred and thirty.'

'Now I want you all to turn to the second book of Samuel,' continued Dave, 'where you'll find a king who was a murderer.'

'Hallelujah,' cried the first three rows, if not in unison.

'Yes, King David was a murderer,' said Dave. 'He bumped off Uriah the Hittite, because he fancied his wife, Bathsheba. But King David was very cunning, because he didn't want to be seen to be responsible for another man's death, so he placed Uriah in the front line of the next battle to make sure that he was killed. But God saw what he was up to and punished him, because God sees every murder and will always punish anyone who breaks His commandments.'

'Hallelujah,' chorused the first three rows.

Dave ended the service with closing prayers in which the words 'understanding' and 'forgiveness' were repeated again and again. He finally blessed his congregation, probably one of the largest in London that morning.

As they filed out of the chapel, Danny commented, 'There's a big difference between this service and the one I go to at St Mary's.' Nick raised an eyebrow. 'This lot don't take a collection.'

They were all searched again on the way out, and this time three prisoners were pulled over to one side before being marched off down the purple corridor.

'What's that all about?' asked Danny.

'They're off to segregation,' explained Nick. 'Possession of drugs. They'll get at least seven days in solitary.'

'It can't be worth it,' said Danny.

'They must think so,' said Nick, 'because you can be sure they'll be dealing again the moment they're released.'

◄○►

Danny was becoming more excited by the minute at the thought of seeing Beth for the first time in weeks.

At two o'clock, an hour before visits were due to take place, Danny was pacing up and down the cell. He had washed and ironed his shirt, pressed his jeans, and spent a long time in the shower washing his hair. He wondered what Beth would be wearing. It was as if he were taking her out on a first date.

'How do I look?' he asked. Nick frowned. 'That bad?'

'It's just that . . .'

'Just what?' demanded Danny.

'I think Beth might have expected you to shave.'

Danny looked at himself in the little steel mirror above the washbasin. He quickly checked his watch.

22

ANOTHER ROUTE MARCH down another corridor, but this time the line of prisoners was moving a little quicker. No inmate wants to miss one second of a visit. At the end of this corridor was a large waiting room with a wooden bench fixed to the wall. There followed another long wait before prisoners' names began to be called out. Danny spent the time trying to read the notices pinned to the wall; there were several about drugs and the consequences – applying to both prisoners and visitors – of trying to pass anything over during visits. Another concerned prison policy on bullying, and a third was about discrimination – a word Danny wrestled with, and certainly didn't know the meaning of. He would have to ask Nick when he got back to the cell after the visit.

It was nearly an hour before the name 'Cartwright' was announced over the tannoy. Danny leapt to his feet and followed a screw into a tiny box room, where he was told to stand on a small wooden platform, legs apart. Another screw – *officer* – he had never seen before gave him a body search that was far more rigorous than any he'd experienced since being banged up – *imprisoned*. Big Al had warned him that the search would be even more thorough than usual because visitors often tried to transfer drugs, money, blades, knives and even guns to prisoners during visits.

Once the search was over, the officer placed a yellow sash round Danny's shoulder to identify him as a prisoner, not unlike the fluorescent one his mother made him wear when he first learnt to ride a bicycle. He was then led into the largest room he'd been in since arriving at Belmarsh. He reported to a desk that was raised on a platform about three feet above the floor. Another officer checked another list, and said, 'Your visitor is waiting at E9.'

Seven lines of tables and chairs were set out in long rows, marked A to G. The prisoners had to sit on red chairs that were bolted to the floor. Their visitors sat on the other side of a table on green chairs, also bolted to the floor, making it easier for the security staff to carry out surveillance, assisted by several CCTV cameras whirring above them. As Danny walked down the rows, he noticed officers were keeping a close eye on both prisoners and visitors from a balcony above. He came to a halt when he reached row E and searched for Beth. At last he saw her, sitting on one of the green chairs. Despite having her photo sellotaped to the cell wall, he had forgotten quite how beautiful she was. She was carrying a parcel in her arms, which surprised him, as visitors are not allowed to bring in gifts for prisoners.

She leapt up the moment she saw him. Danny quickened his pace, although he had been warned several times not to run. He threw his arms around her, and the parcel let out a cry. Danny stepped back to see his daughter for the first time.

'She's beautiful,' he said as he took Christy in his arms. He looked up at Beth. 'I'm going to get out of here before she ever finds out her father was in jail.'

'How are—'

'When did—' They both began to speak at once.

'Sorry,' said Danny, 'you go first.'

Beth looked surprised. 'Why are you speaking so slowly?'

Danny sat down on the red chair and began to tell Beth about his cellmates as he tucked into a Mars Bar and drained a can of Diet Coke which Beth had purchased from the canteen – luxuries he hadn't experienced since he'd been locked up in Belmarsh.

'Nick is teaching me to read and write,' he told her. 'And Big Al is showing me how to survive in prison.' He waited to see how Beth would react.

'How lucky you were to end up in that cell.'

Danny hadn't thought about that before, and suddenly realized he ought to thank Mr Jenkins. 'So what's happening back in Bacon Road?' he asked, touching Beth's thigh.

'Some of the locals are collecting signatures for a petition to have you released, and *Danny Cartwright is innocent* has been sprayed on the wall outside Bow Road tube station. No one's tried to remove it, not even the council.'

Danny listened to all of Beth's news while he munched his way through three Mars Bars and drank two more Diet Cokes, aware that he wouldn't be allowed to take anything back to his cell once the visit was over.

He wanted to hold Christy, but she'd fallen asleep in Beth's arms. The sight of his child only made him more determined to learn to read and write. He wanted to be able to answer all of Mr Redmayne's questions so that he would be ready for his appeal and to surprise Beth by replying to her letters.

'All visitors must now leave,' announced a voice over the tannoy.

Danny wondered where the shortest hour in his life had gone as he looked up to check the clock on the wall. He rose slowly from his seat and took Beth in his arms, kissing her gently. He couldn't help remembering that this was the most common way for visitors to pass drugs to their partners, and that the security staff would be watching them closely. Some prisoners even swallowed the drugs so they wouldn't be discovered when they were searched before returning to their cells.

'Goodbye, my darling,' said Beth when he eventually released her.

'Goodbye,' said Danny, sounding desperate. 'Oh, I nearly forgot,' he added, pulling a piece of paper out of a pocket in his jeans. No sooner had he passed the message to her than an officer appeared by his side and grabbed it.

'You can't exchange anything while you're on a visit, Cartwright.'

'But it's only—' began Danny.

'No buts. It's time for you to leave, Miss.'

Danny stood watching as Beth walked away, carrying his

daughter. His eyes never left them until they had disappeared out of sight.

'I must get out of here,' he said out loud.

The officer unfolded the note and read the first words Danny Cartwright had ever written to Beth. 'It won't be long before we're together again.' The officer looked worried.

◄o►

'Short back and sides?' asked Louis as the next customer took his place in the barber's chair.

'No,' whispered Danny. 'I want you to make my hair look more like your last customer's.'

'It'll cost you,' said Louis.

'How much?'

'Same as Nick, ten fags a month.'

Danny removed a packet of unopened Marlboro from his jeans. 'Today, and a month in advance,' said Danny, 'if you do the job properly.'

The barber smiled as Danny placed the cigarettes back in his pocket.

Louis walked slowly around the chair, occasionally stopping to take a closer look before he offered an opinion. 'First thing you'll have to do is let your hair grow and wash it two or three times a week,' he said. 'Nick never has a hair out of place, and his curls slightly at the nape of his neck,' he added, as he came to a halt behind him. 'You'll also need to shave every day. And cut your sideboards a lot higher if you want to look like a gent.' After another perambulation, he added, 'Nick parts his hair on the left, not the right, so that's the first change I'll have to make. And his hair's a shade lighter than yours, but nothing a little lemon juice won't take care of.'

'How long will all this take?' asked Danny.

'Six months, no longer. But I'll need to see you at least once a month,' he added.

'I'm not going anywhere,' said Danny. 'So book me in for the first Monday of every month, because the job has to be finished by the time my appeal comes up. My lawyer seems to think that it matters what you look like when you're in the dock, and I want to look like an officer, not a criminal.'

'Shrewd fellow, your lawyer,' said Louis, throwing a green sheet round Danny before picking up his clippers. Twenty minutes later an almost imperceptible change had begun to take place. 'Don't forget,' said Louis as he held up the mirror for his valued customer before brushing a few hairs from his shoulders. 'You'll need to shave every morning. And shampoo your hair at least twice a week if you hope to pass muster, to use one of Nick's expressions.'

'Back to your cells,' shouted Mr Hagen. The officer looked surprised when he saw an unopened packet of twenty cigarettes pass between the two prisoners. 'Found another customer for the alternative service you offer, have you, Louis?' he asked with a grin.

Danny and Louis remained silent.

'Funny that, Cartwright,' said Hagen. 'I'd never have put you down for a queer.'

23

MINUTES TURNED INTO HOURS, hours became days, days ended up being weeks in the longest year of Danny's life. Though, as Beth regularly reminded him, it hadn't been entirely wasted. In a couple of months' time Danny would take – sit, Nick's word – six GCSEs, and his mentor seemed confident that he would pass them all with flying colours. Beth had asked him which A levels he had signed up for.

'I'll have been released long before then,' he promised her.

'But I still want you to take them,' she insisted.

Beth and Christy had visited Danny on the first Sunday of every month, and lately she could talk of little else but his upcoming appeal, even though a date hadn't yet been posted in the court calendar. Mr Redmayne was still searching for fresh evidence, because without it, he admitted, they didn't stand much of a chance. Danny had recently read a Home Office report which said that 97 per cent of lifers' appeals were rejected, and the remaining 3 per cent ended up with no more than a minor reduction in their sentence. He tried not to think about the consequences of failing to win his appeal. What would happen to Beth and Christy if he had to serve another twenty-one years? Beth never raised the subject, but Danny had already accepted that he couldn't expect all three of them to serve a life sentence.

In Danny's experience, lifers fell into two categories: those who completely cut themselves off from the outside world – no letters, no calls, no visits – and those who, like a bedridden invalid, remain a burden to their families for the rest of their lives. He had already decided which course he would take if his appeal was turned down.

◄○►

Dr Beresford killed in car accident read the headline on the front page of the *Mail on Sunday*. The article went on to tell its readers that Lawrence Davenport's star was on the wane, and the producers of *The Prescription* had decided to write him out of the script. Davenport was to be killed off in a tragic car accident involving a drunk-driver. He would be rushed to his own hospital where Nurse Petal, whom he had recently ditched when he discovered she was pregnant, would try to save his life, but would be unable . . . The phone rang in Spencer Craig's study. He wasn't surprised to find it was Gerald Payne on the other end of the line.

'Have you seen the papers?' Payne asked.

'Yes,' said Craig. 'Frankly I'm not surprised. The show's ratings have been going west for the past year, so they're obviously looking for some gimmick to give them a boost.'

'But if they ditch Larry,' said Payne, 'he's not going to find it that easy to get another part. We certainly don't want him going back on the bottle.'

'I don't think we should be discussing this over the phone, Gerald. Let's meet up soon.'

Craig opened his diary, to find several days were blank. He didn't seem to be getting quite as many briefs as he had in the past.

◄○►

The arresting officer placed the prisoner's few possessions on the counter, while the desk sergeant made a note of them in his log book: one needle, one small packet containing a white substance, one match box, one spoon, one tie and one five-pound note.

'Do we have a name, or any ID?' asked the desk sergeant.

'No,' replied the young constable, glancing at the helpless figure slumped on the bench in front of him. 'Poor bastard,' he said, 'what's the point of sending him to prison?'

'The law's the law, my lad. Our job is to carry it out, not to question our masters.'

'Poor bastard,' the constable repeated.

◄o►

During the long, sleepless nights running up to the appeal, Mr Redmayne's advice during the original trial was never far from Danny's thoughts: if you plead guilty to manslaughter, you'll only have to serve two years. If Danny had taken his advice, he would be free in twelve months' time.

He tried to concentrate on the essay he was writing on *The Count of Monte Cristo* – his GCSE set text. Perhaps, like Edmond Dantès, he would escape. But you can't build a tunnel when your cell is on the first floor, and he couldn't throw himself into the sea, because Belmarsh wasn't on an island. So, unlike Dantès, unless he won his appeal, he had little hope of gaining revenge on his four enemies. After Nick had read his last essay, he had given Danny a mark of 73 per cent, with the comment, 'Unlike Edmond Dantès, you won't need to escape, because they'll have to release you.'

How well the two of them had come to know each other during the past year. In truth they had spent more hours together than he and Bernie had ever done. Some of the new prisoners even assumed they were brothers, until Danny opened his mouth. *That* was going to take a little longer.

'You're every bit as bright as I am,' Nick kept telling him, 'and when it comes to maths, you've become the teacher.'

Danny looked up from his essay when he heard the key turning in the lock. Mr Pascoe pulled the door open to allow Big Al to stroll in, regular as clockwork – you must stop using clichés, even in your thoughts, Nick had told him – and slumped down on the bed without a word. Danny continued writing.

'Got some news fur ye, Danny boy,' said Big Al once the door had been slammed shut.

Danny put down his pen; it was a rare event for Big Al to initiate a conversation, unless it was to ask for a match.

'Ever come across a fucker called Mortimer?'

Danny's heart began to race. 'Yes,' he eventually managed. 'He was in the bar the night Bernie was murdered, but he never showed up in court.'

'Well, he's shown up here,' said Big Al.

'What do you mean?'

'Exactly whit I said, Danny boy. He reported tae the hospital this efternoon. Needed some medication.' Danny had learnt not to interrupt Big Al when he was in full flow, otherwise he might not speak again for a week. 'Checked his file. Possession of a class-A drug. Two years. So I've got a feeling he's gonnae be a regular visitor tae the hospital.' Danny still didn't interrupt. His heartbeat was, if anything, even faster. 'Now I'm no as clever as you or Nick, but it's jist possible he might be able tae supply that new evidence you and yer lawyer have been looking fur.'

'You're a diamond,' Danny said.

'A rougher stone, perhaps,' said Big Al, 'but wake me up when yer mate gets back, 'cause I have a feeling it may be me has got something tae teach you two fur a change.'

—◦—

Spencer Craig sat alone nursing a glass of whisky as he watched Lawrence Davenport's final episode of *The Prescription*. Nine million viewers joined him as Dr Beresford, with Nurse Petal clutching on to his hand, gasped out his final line, 'You deserve better.' The episode won the show's largest audience share for over a decade. It ended with Dr Beresford's coffin being lowered into the ground as Nurse Petal sobbed at the graveside. The producers had left no chance of a miraculous recovery, whatever the demands of Davenport's adoring fans.

It had been a bad week for Craig: Toby being sent to the same prison as Cartwright, Larry out of work, and that morning the date for Cartwright's appeal had been posted on the court calendar. It was still several months away, but what would Larry's state of mind be by then? Especially if Toby cracked and in return for a fix was willing to tell anyone who would listen what had really happened that night.

Craig rose from his desk, walked across to a filing cabinet he rarely opened and thumbed through an archive of his past cases. He extracted the files of seven former clients who had ended up at Belmarsh. He studied their case histories for over an hour, but for the job he had in mind there was only one obvious candidate.

—◦—

'He's beginning tae blab,' said Big Al.

'Has he mentioned that night in the Dunlop Arms?' asked Danny.

'No yet, but it's early days. He wull, given time.'

'What makes you so confident?' asked Nick.

'Because I have something he needs, and fair exchange is nae robbery.'

'What have you got that he needs that badly?' asked Danny.

'Never ask a question that you don't need to know the answer to,' said Nick, jumping in.

'Canny man, yer friend Nick,' said Big Al.

—◦—

'So what can I do for you, Mr Craig?'

'I believe you'll find it's what I can do for you.'

'I don't think so, Mr Craig. I've been banged up in this shit-hole for the past eight years and during that time I haven't heard a dicky bird out of you, so don't fuck me about. You know I couldn't afford even an hour of your time. Why don't you just come to the point and tell me what you're doin' here?'

Craig had carefully checked the interview room for any bugs before Kevin Leach had been allowed to join him for a legal visit. Client confidentiality is sacred in English law, and if it were ever breached, any evidence would automatically be ruled inadmissible in court. Despite that fact, Craig still knew he was taking a risk – but the prospect of a long spell in prison locked up with the likes of Leach was an even less attractive proposition.

'Got everything you need, have you?' asked Craig, who had rehearsed each line he intended to deliver as if he was in court cross-examining a key witness.

'I get by,' said Leach. 'Don't need a lot.'

'On twelve pounds a week as a stacker on the chain gang?'

'As I said. I get by.'

'But no one is sending you in any little extras,' said Craig. 'And you haven't had a visit for over four years.'

'I see you are as well informed as ever, Mr Craig.'

'In fact, you haven't even made a phone call during the past two years – not since your Aunt Maisie died.'

'Where's all this leading, Mr Craig?'

'There's just a possibility that Aunt Maisie might have left you something in her will.'

'Now why would she bother to do that?'

'Because she's got a friend who you're in a position to help.'

'What kind of help?'

'Her friend has a problem – a craving, not to put too fine a point on it, and not for chocolate.'

'Let me guess. Heroin, crack or cocaine?'

'Right first time,' said Craig. 'And he's in need of a regular supply.'

'How regular?'

'Daily.'

'And how much has Aunt Maisie left me to cover this considerable outlay, not to mention the risk of being caught?'

'Five thousand pounds,' said Craig. 'But just before she died, she added a codicil to her will.'

'Let me guess. That it wasn't to be paid all at once.'

'Just in case you decided to spend it all at once.'

'I'm still listenin'.'

'She hoped that fifty pounds a week would be enough to make sure her friend wouldn't need to look elsewhere.'

'Tell her if she makes it a hundred, I might just think about it.'

'I think I can say on her behalf that she accepts your terms.'

'So what's the name of Aunt Maisie's friend?'

'Toby Mortimer.'

—◇—

'Always from the outside in,' said Nick. 'It's a simple rule to follow.'

Danny picked up the plastic spoon and began to scoop up the water that Nick had poured into his breakfast bowl.

'No,' said Nick. 'You always tilt a soup bowl away from you, and push the spoon in the same direction.' He demonstrated the movement. 'And never slurp. I don't want to hear a sound while you're drinking your soup.'

'Beth always complained about that,' said Danny.

'Me tae,' said Big Al, not stirring from his bunk.

'And Beth is right,' said Nick. 'In some countries it's considered a compliment to slurp, but not in England.' He removed the bowl and replaced it with a plastic plate on which he had put a thick slice of bread and a helping of baked beans. 'Now, I want you to think of the bread as a lamb chop, and the baked beans as peas.'

'Whit are ye using fur gravy?' asked Big Al, not stirring from his bunk.

'Cold Bovril,' said Nick. Danny picked up his plastic knife and fork, holding them firmly, with the blade and the prongs pointing towards the ceiling. 'Try to remember,' said Nick, 'that your knife and fork are not rockets on a launch pad waiting to blast off. And unlike rockets, they are going to need to refuel whenever they return to earth.' Nick picked up the knife and fork on his side of the table and demonstrated how Danny should hold them.

'It's not natural,' was Danny's immediate response.

'You'll soon get used to it,' said Nick. 'And don't forget that your forefinger should rest along the top. Don't let the handle stick out between your thumb and forefinger – you're holding a knife, not a pen.' Danny adjusted the grip on his knife and fork in imitation of Nick, but still found the whole experience awkward. 'Now I want you to eat the piece of bread as if it was a lamb chop.'

'How wid ye like it, sir?' grunted Big Al. 'Medium or rare?'

'You will only be asked that question,' said Nick, 'if you order a steak, never for a lamb chop.'

Danny dug into his slice of bread. 'No,' said Nick. 'Cut your meat, don't tear it apart, and only a small piece at a time.' Danny once again carried out his instructions, but then started to cut a second piece of bread while still chewing the first. 'No,' said Nick firmly. 'While you're eating, place your knife and fork on the plate, and don't pick them up again until you've finished the mouthful.' Once Danny had swallowed the piece of bread, he scooped up some beans on the end of his fork. 'No, no, no,' said Nick. 'A fork isn't a shovel. Just pierce a few peas at a time.'

'But it will take for ever if I carry on this way,' said Danny.

'And don't speak with your mouth full,' replied Nick.

Big Al grunted again, but Danny ignored him and cut himself another piece of bread, put it in his mouth, then placed his knife and fork back on the plate.

'Good, but chew your meat for longer before you swallow it,' said Nick. 'Try to remember you're a human being, not an animal' – a comment that elicited a loud burp from Big Al. Once Danny had finished another piece of bread, he tried to pierce a couple of beans but they kept escaping. He gave up. 'Don't lick your knife,' was all Nick had to say.

'But if ye'd like tae, Danny boy,' said Big Al, 'you cin lick ma arse.'

It was some time before Danny was able to finish his meagre meal and finally put his knife and fork down on an empty plate.

'Once you've finished your meal,' said Nick, 'place your knife and fork together.'

'Why?' asked Danny.

'Because when you're eating in a restaurant, the waiter will need to know that you've finished your meal.'

'I don't eat in restaurants that often,' admitted Danny.

'Then I shall have to be the first person to invite you and Beth out for a meal as soon as you've been released.'

'And what about me?' asked Big Al. 'Don't I get invited?'

Nick ignored him. 'Now it's time to move on to dessert.'

'Pudding?' asked Danny.

'No, not pudding, dessert,' repeated Nick. 'If you *are* in a restaurant, you only ever order the starter and the main course, and not until you have finished them do you ask to see the dessert menu.'

'Two menus in one restaurant?' said Danny.

Nick smiled as he placed a thinner slice of bread on Danny's plate. 'That is an apricot tart,' he said.

'An I'm in bed wi' Cameron Diaz,' said Big Al.

This time Danny and Nick did laugh.

'For dessert,' said Nick, 'you use the small fork. However, if you order a crème brûlée or ice cream, you pick up the small spoon.'

Big Al suddenly sat bolt upright on his bunk. 'Whit's the fucking point of aw this?' he demanded. 'This isnae a restaurant, it's a prison. The only thing Danny boy's gonnae be eating for the next twenty years is cold turkey.'

'And tomorrow,' said Nick, ignoring him, 'I'll show you how to taste wine after the waiter has poured a small amount into your glass . . .'

'An the day efter that,' said Big Al, accompanied by a long fart, 'I shall allow you to sip a sample of ma piss, a rare vintage that wull remind ye yur in prison and no in the fuckin' Ritz.'

24

THE HEAVY DOOR of his single cell swung open. 'You've got a parcel, Leach. Follow me and look sharp about it.'

Leach climbed slowly off his bed, strolled out on to the landing and joined the waiting officer. 'Thanks for fixin' the single cell,' he grunted as they walked down the corridor.

'You scratch my back and I'll scratch yours,' said Hagen. He didn't speak again until they reached the stores, when he banged loudly on the double doors. The stores manager pulled them open and said, 'Name?'

'Brad Pitt.'

'Don't try it on with me, Leach, or I might have to put you on report.'

'Leach, 6241.'

'You've got a parcel.' The stores manager turned round, took a box from the shelf behind him and placed it on the counter.

'I see you've already opened it, Mr Webster.'

'You know the regulations, Leach.'

'Yes, I do,' said Leach. 'You are required to open any parcel in my presence, so that I can be sure nothing has been removed or planted inside.'

'Get on with it,' said Webster.

Leach removed the lid from the box to reveal the latest Adidas tracksuit. 'Smart piece of gear, that,' said Webster. 'Must have set someone back a few quid.' Leach didn't comment as Webster began to unzip the pockets one by one to check for any drugs contraband or cash. He found nothing, not even the usual five-pound note. 'You can take it away, Leach,' he said reluct-antly.

Leach picked up the tracksuit and began to walk off. He'd only managed a couple of paces before the word 'Leach' was bellowed after him. He turned round.

'And the box, muppet,' Webster added.

Leach returned to the counter, placed the tracksuit back in the box and tucked it under his arm.

'That will be quite an improvement on your present gear,' remarked Hagen as he accompanied Leach back to his cell. 'Perhaps I ought to take a closer look, since you've never been seen in the gym. But on the other hand, perhaps I could turn a blind eye.'

Leach smiled. 'I'll leave your cut in the usual place, Mr Hagen,' he said as the cell door closed behind him.

◄○►

'I can't go on living a lie,' said Davenport theatrically. 'Don't you understand that we've been responsible for sending an innocent man to jail for the rest of his life?'

Once Davenport had been written out of his soap opera, Craig had assumed that it wouldn't be too long before he felt the need for some dramatic gesture. After all, he had little else to think about while he was 'resting'.

'So what do you intend to do about it?' asked Payne as he lit a cigarette, trying to appear unconcerned.

'Tell the truth,' said Davenport, sounding a little over-rehearsed. 'I intend to give evidence at Cartwright's appeal and tell them what really happened that night. They may not believe me, but at least my conscience will be clear.'

'If you do that,' said Craig, 'all three of us could end up in prison.' He paused. 'For the rest of our lives. Are you sure that's what you want?'

'No, but it's the lesser of two evils.'

'And it doesn't concern you that you might end up in a shower being buggered by a couple of eighteen-stone lorry drivers?' said Craig. Davenport didn't respond.

'Not to mention the disgrace it will bring on your family,' added Payne. 'You may be out of work now, but let me assure you, Larry, if you decide to make an appearance in court, it will be your final performance.'

'I've had a lot of time to consider the consequences,' Davenport replied haughtily, 'and I've made up my mind.'

'Have you thought about Sarah, and the effect this would have on her career?' asked Craig.

'Yes, I have, and when I next see her I intend to tell her exactly what happened that night, and I feel confident she will approve of my decision.'

'Could you do me one small favour, Larry?' asked Craig. 'For old times' sake?'

'What's that?' asked Davenport suspiciously.

'Just give it a week before you tell your sister.'

Davenport hesitated. 'All right, a week. But not a day longer.'

◄○►

Leach waited until lights out at ten o'clock before he climbed off his bunk. He picked up a plastic fork from the table and walked across to the lavatory in the corner of the cell – the one place the screws can't see you through the spyhole when they make their hourly rounds to check if you are safely tucked up in bed.

He pulled off his new tracksuit bottoms and sat on the lavatory lid. He gripped the plastic fork firmly in his right hand and began to pick away at the stitching on the middle one of the three white stripes that ran down the length of the leg, a laborious process that took forty minutes. Finally, he was able to extract a long, wafer-thin cellophane packet. Inside was enough fine white powder to satisfy an addict for about a month. He smiled – a rare occurrence – at the thought that there were still another five stripes to unpick: they would guarantee his profit, as well as Hagen's cut.

◄○►

'Mortimer has to be getting the gear from somewhere,' said Big Al.

'What makes you say that?' asked Danny.

'He used tae turn up at the hospital every morning without fail.

144

Doc even got him started on a detox programme. Then one day he's nowhere to be seen.'

'Which can only mean he's found another source,' concurred Nick.

'Not one of the regular suppliers, I can tell that,' said Big Al. 'I've asked around, and come up with nothing.' Danny slumped back down on his bunk, succumbing to lifers' syndrome. 'Dinnae give up on me, Danny boy. He'll be back. They always come back.'

'Visits!' hollered the familiar voice, and a moment later the door swung open to allow Danny to join those prisoners who had been looking forward to a visit all morning.

He had hoped to tell Beth that he'd come up with the fresh evidence Mr Redmayne so desperately needed to win the appeal. Now all he had to hope for was Big Al's belief that Mortimer would be back in the prison hospital before too long.

In prison, a lifer clings on to hope as a drowning sailor clings on to a drifting log. Danny clenched his fist as he made his way towards the visits area, determined that Beth would not suspect even for a moment that anything might be wrong. Whenever he was with her, he never let his guard down; despite all he was going through, he always needed Beth to believe that there was still hope.

◄○►

He was surprised when he heard the key turning in the lock, because he never had a visitor. Three officers charged into the cell. Two of them grabbed him by the shoulders and pulled him off the bed. As he fell, he grabbed at one of the officers' ties. It came off in his hand; he'd forgotten that screws wear clip-on ties so they can't be strangled. One of them thrust his arms behind his back while another kicked him sharply behind the knee, which allowed the third to cuff him. As he collapsed on to the stone floor, the first screw grabbed him by the hair and yanked his head back. In less than thirty seconds he was bound and trussed before being dragged out of his cell and on to the landing.

'What are you fuckin' bastards up to?' he demanded once he'd caught his breath.

'You're on your way to segregation, Leach,' said the first officer. 'You won't be seeing daylight for another thirty days,' he added as they dragged him down the spiral staircase, his knees banging on every step.

'What's the charge?'

'Supplying,' said the second officer as they marched him, almost at a jog, along a purple corridor no prisoner ever wants to see.

'I've never touched drugs, guv, and you know it,' protested Leach.

'That's not what supplying means,' said the third officer once they reached the basement, 'and you know it.'

The four of them came to a halt outside a cell that had no number. One of the officers selected a rarely used key while the other two held firmly on to Leach's arms. Once the door was open, he was hurled head first into a cell that made his upstairs accommodation seem like a motel. A thin, horse-hair mattress lay in the middle of the stone floor; there was a steel washbasin bolted to the wall, a steel lavatory without a flush, one sheet, one blanket, no pillow and no mirror.

'By the time you get out, Leach, you'll find your monthly income has dried up. No one on the top floor believes you've got an aunt Maisie.'

The door slammed shut.

◄○►

'Congratulations,' was Beth's first word when Danny took her in his arms. He looked puzzled. 'Your six GCSEs, silly,' she added. 'You passed them all with flying colours, just as Nick predicted.' Danny smiled. That all seemed such a long time ago, although it couldn't have been more than a month – an eternity in prison – and in any case, he'd already kept his promise to Beth and signed up for three A levels. 'Which subjects did you settle on?' she asked, as if she could read his mind.

'English, maths and business studies,' Danny replied. 'But I've come up against a problem.' Beth looked anxious. 'I'm already better at maths than Nick, so they've had to bring in an outside teacher, but she can only see me once a week.'

'She?' said Beth suspiciously.

Danny laughed. 'Miss Lovett is over sixty and retired, but she knows her stuff. She says if I stick at it, she'll recommend me for a place with the Open University. Mind you, if I win my appeal, I just won't have time . . .'

'*When* you win your appeal,' said Beth, 'you must continue with your A levels, otherwise Miss Lovett and Nick will have wasted their time.'

'But I'll be running the garage all day, and I've already come up with some ideas for making it more profitable.' Beth went silent. 'What's the matter?'

Beth hesitated. Her father had told her not to raise the subject. 'The garage isn't doing that well at the moment,' she finally admitted. 'In fact, it's barely breaking even.'

'Why?' asked Danny.

'Without you and Bernie, we've started losing business to Monty Hughes across the road.'

'Don't worry, love,' said Danny. 'All that will change once I'm out of here. In fact, I even have plans to take over Monty Hughes's place – he must be sixty-five if he's a day.'

Beth smiled at Danny's optimism. 'Does that mean you've come up with the fresh evidence Mr Redmayne is looking for?'

'Possibly, although I can't say too much at the moment,' said Danny, glancing up at the CCTV cameras above their heads. 'But one of Craig's friends who was in the bar that night has turned up in here.' He looked up at the officers on the balcony, who Big Al had warned him could lip-read. 'I won't mention his name.'

'What's he in for?' asked Beth.

'I can't say. You'll just have to trust me.'

'Have you told Mr Redmayne?'

'I wrote to him last week. I was guarded because the screws open your letters and read every word. Officers,' he said correcting himself.

'Officers?' said Beth.

'Nick says I mustn't get into the habit of using prison slang if I'm going to start a new life once I'm out of here.'

'So Nick obviously believes you're innocent?' said Beth.

'Yes, he does. So does Big Al, and even some of the officers. We're not alone any more, Beth,' he said, taking her hand.

'When's Nick due to be released?' asked Beth.

'In five or six months' time.'

'Will you keep in touch with him?'

'I'll try to, but he's off to Scotland to teach.'

'I'd like to meet him,' said Beth, placing her other hand on Danny's cheek. 'He's turned out to be a real mate.'

'Friend,' Danny said. 'And he's already invited us out to dinner.'

Christy tumbled to the ground after trying to take a step towards her father. She began crying, and Danny swept her up in his arms. 'We've been ignoring you, haven't we, little one?' he said, but she didn't stop crying.

'Pass her over,' Beth said. 'We seem to have found something Nick hasn't been able to teach you.'

◄◦►

'No whit I'd call a coincidence,' said Big Al, who was glad to have a private word with the captain while Danny was taking a shower.

Nick stopped writing. '*Not* a coincidence?'

'Leach ends up in segregation and the next morning Mortimer's back, desperate tae see the doctor.'

'You think Leach was his supplier?'

'Like I said, no whit I'd call a coincidence.' Nick put down his pen. 'He has the shakes,' continued Big Al, 'but that always happens when ye start a detox. Doc seems tae think this time he really wants tae come aff the stuff. Anyway, we'll soon find oot if Leach is involved.'

'How?' asked Nick.

'He gets oot of solitary in a couple of weeks. If Mortimer stops turning up tae the hospital fur treatment the moment Leach is back on the block, we'll know who the supplier is.'

'So we've only got another fortnight to gather the evidence we need,' said Nick.

'Unless it *is* a coincidence.'

'That's not a risk we can take,' said Nick. 'Borrow Danny's tape recorder and set up an interview as soon as possible.'

'Yes, sir,' said Big Al, standing to attention by the side of his bed. 'Dae I tell Danny aboot this, or keep ma mooth shut?'

'You tell him everything, so he can pass on the information to his barrister. In any case, three brains are better than two.'

'Jist how clever is he?' asked Big Al as he sat back down on his bunk.

'He's brighter than me,' admitted Nick. 'But don't tell him I said so, because with a bit of luck I'll be out of this place before he works it out for himself.'

'Perhaps it's time we told him the truth about us?'

'Not yet,' said Nick firmly.

◄O►

'Letters,' said the officer. 'Two for Cartwright, and one for you, Moncrieff.' He passed the single letter to Danny, who checked the name on the envelope.

'No, I'm Cartwright,' said Danny. 'He's Moncrieff.'

The officer frowned, and handed the single letter to Nick and the other two to Danny.

'An I'm Big Al,' said Big Al.

'Fuck off,' said the officer, slamming the door behind him.

Danny began to laugh, but then he looked at Nick and saw that he had turned ashen. He was holding the envelope in his hand, and was shaking. Danny couldn't remember when Nick had last received a letter. 'Do you want me to read it first?' he asked.

Nick shook his head, unfolded the letter and began to read. Big Al sat up, but didn't speak. The unusual doesn't happen that often in prison. As Nick read, his eyes began to water. He brushed a shirtsleeve across his face, then passed the letter across to Danny.

Dear Sir Nicholas,

I am sorry to have to inform you that your father has passed away. He died from heart failure yesterday morning, but the doctor assures me that he suffered little or no pain. I will, with your permission, make an application for compassionate leave in order that you can attend the funeral.

    Yours sincerely,

      Fraser Munro, Solicitor

Danny looked up to see Big Al holding Nick in his arms. 'His dad's died, hasn't he?' was all Big Al said.

25

'CAN YOU TAKE CARE of this while I'm away?' asked Nick, unfastening the silver chain from round his neck and handing it to Danny.

'Sure,' said Danny, as he studied what looked like a key attached to the chain. 'But why not take it with you?'

'Let's just say I trust you more than most of the people I'm going to meet up with later today.'

'I'm flattered,' said Danny, putting the chain round his neck.

'No need to be,' said Nick with a smile.

He looked at his reflection in the small steel mirror that was screwed into the wall above the washbasin. His personal possessions had been returned to him at five o'clock that morning, in a large plastic bag that hadn't been unsealed for four years. He would have to leave by six if he was to be in Scotland in time for the funeral.

'I can't wait,' said Danny, staring at him.

'For what?' asked Nick as he straightened his tie.

'Just to be allowed to wear my own clothes again.'

'You'll be allowed to do that at your appeal, and once they overturn the verdict you'll never have to put on prison clothes again. In fact, you'll be able to walk straight out of the courtroom a free man.'

'Especially after they hear ma tape,' chipped in Big Al with a grin. 'I think today's the day.' He was about to explain what he meant when they heard a key turning in the lock. It was the first time they had ever seen Pascoe and Jenkins dressed in civilian clothes.

'Follow me, Moncrieff,' said Pascoe. 'The governor wants a word with you before we set off for Edinburgh.'

'Do give him my best wishes,' said Danny, 'and ask him if he'd like to pop in for afternoon tea some time.'

Nick laughed at Danny's imitation of his accent. 'If you think you can pass yourself off as me, why don't you try taking my class this morning?'

'Are ye talking to me?' asked Big Al.

—◦—

Davenport's phone was ringing, but it was some time before he emerged from under the sheets to answer it. 'Who the hell is this?' he mumbled.

'Gibson,' announced the familiar voice of his agent.

Davenport was suddenly awake. Gibson Graham only rang when it meant work. Davenport prayed it would be a film, another television role, or perhaps an advertisement – they paid so well, even for a voiceover. Surely his fans would still recognize the dulcet tones of Dr Beresford.

'I've had an availability enquiry,' said Gibson, trying to make it sound as if it was a regular occurrence. Davenport sat up and held his breath. 'It's a revival of *The Importance of Being Earnest*, and they want you to play Jack. Eve Best's signed up to play Gwendolen. Four weeks on the road before it opens in the West End. The pay's not great, but it will remind all those producers out there that you're still alive.' Delicately put, thought Davenport, although he didn't warm to the idea. He remembered only too well what it was like to spend weeks on the road followed by night after night in the West End, not forgetting the half-empty matinees. Although he had to admit that it was his first serious offer for nearly four months.

'I'll think about it,' he said.

'Don't take too long,' said Gibson. 'I know they've already put a call in to Nigel Havers' agent to check his availability.'

'I'll think about it,' Davenport repeated, and put the phone down. He checked his bedside clock. It was ten past ten. He groaned, and slid back under the sheets.

◄○►

Pascoe rapped gently on the door, before he and Jenkins escorted Nick into the office.

'Good morning, Moncrieff,' said the governor, looking up from behind his desk.

'Good morning, Mr Barton,' Nick replied.

'You realize,' said Barton, 'that although you have been granted compassionate leave in order to attend your father's funeral, you remain a category-A prisoner, which means that two officers must accompany you until you return tonight. The regulations also state that you should be handcuffed at all times. However, given the circumstances, and in view of the fact that for the past two years you have been an enhanced prisoner, and that it's only a few months before you are due to be released, I'm going to exercise my prerogative and allow you to be uncuffed once you cross the border. That is, unless either Mr Pascoe or Mr Jenkins has reason to believe you might attempt to escape or commit an offence. I'm sure I don't have to remind you, Moncrieff, that if you were foolish enough to try to take advantage of my decision, I would have no choice but to recommend to the Parole Board that you should not be considered for early release on – ' he checked Nick's file – 'July seventeenth, but that you should serve your full sentence, another four years. Is that fully understood, Moncrieff?'

'Yes, thank you, governor,' said Nick.

'Then there is nothing more for me to say other than to offer my condolences for the loss of your father, and to wish you a peaceful day.' Michael Barton rose from behind his desk and added, 'May I say that I am only sorry this sad event did not take place after you had been released.'

'Thank you, governor.'

Barton nodded, and Pascoe and Jenkins led their charge out.

The governor frowned when he saw the name of the next

prisoner who was due to come in front of him. He wasn't looking forward to the encounter.

◄○►

During the morning break, Danny took over Nick's duties as the prison librarian, re-shelving recently returned books and date-stamping those that prisoners wished to take out. After completing these tasks, he picked up a copy of *The Times* from the newspaper shelf and sat down to read it. Papers were delivered to the prison every morning but could only be read in the library: six copies of the *Sun*, four of the *Mirror*, two of the *Daily Mail* and a single copy of *The Times* – which Danny felt was a fair reflection of the prisoners' preferences.

Danny had read *The Times* every day for the past year, and was now familiar with its layout. Unlike Nick, he still couldn't complete the crossword, although he spent as much time reading the business section as he did the sports pages. But today would be different. He leafed through the paper until he came to a section that he had not troubled himself with in the past.

The obituary of Sir Angus Moncrieff Bt MC OBE warranted half a page, even if it was the bottom half. Danny read the details of Sir Angus's life from his days at Loretto School, followed by Sandhurst, from where he graduated and took up a commission as a second lieutenant with the Cameron Highlanders. After winning the MC in Korea, Sir Angus had gone on to become Colonel of the Regiment in 1994, when he was awarded the OBE. The final paragraph reported that his wife had died in 1970, and that the title now passed to their only son, Nicholas Alexander Moncrieff. Danny picked up the Concise Oxford Dictionary that was never far from his side and turned to the back to look up the meaning of the letters Bt, MC and OBE. He smiled at the thought of telling Big Al that they were now sharing a cell with an hereditary knight, Sir Nicholas Moncrieff Bt. Big Al already knew.

'See you later, Nick,' said a voice, but the prisoner had already left the library before Danny could correct his mistake.

Danny played with the key on the end of the silver chain, wishing, like Malvolio, that he could be someone he wasn't. It reminded him that his essay on *Twelfth Night* had to be handed in by the end of the week. He thought about the mistake his fellow prisoner had made, and wondered if he could get away with it when he came face to face with Nick's class. He folded *The Times* and placed it back on the shelf, then crossed the corridor to the education department.

Nick's group were already sitting behind their desks waiting for him, and clearly none of them had been told that their usual teacher was on his way to Scotland to attend his father's funeral. Danny marched boldly into the room and smiled at the dozen expectant faces. He unbuttoned his blue and white striped shirt, to ensure that the silver chain was even more prominent.

'Open your books to page nine,' Danny said, hoping he sounded like Nick. 'You'll see a set of animal pictures on one side of the page, and a list of names on the other. All I want you to do is to match up the pictures with the names. You have two minutes.'

'I can't find page nine,' said one of the prisoners. Danny walked across to help him just as an officer strolled into the room. A puzzled expression appeared on his face.

'Moncrieff?'

Danny looked up.

'I thought you were on compassionate leave?' he said, checking his clipboard.

'You're quite right, Mr Roberts,' said Danny. 'Nick's at his father's funeral in Scotland, and he asked me to take over his reading class this morning.'

Roberts looked even more puzzled. 'Are you taking the piss, Cartwright?'

'No, Mr Roberts.'

'Then get yourself back to the library before I put you on report.'

Danny quickly left the room and returned to his desk in the library. He tried not to laugh, but it was some time before he could concentrate enough to continue his essay on his favourite Shakespeare comedy.

—<o>—

Nick's train pulled into Waverley station a few minutes after twelve. A police car was waiting to drive them the fifty miles from Edinburgh to Dunbroath. As they pulled away from the kerb, Pascoe checked his watch. 'We should have plenty of time. The service doesn't start until two.'

Nick looked out of the car window as the city gave way to open country. He felt a freedom he hadn't experienced in years. He had forgotten how beautiful Scotland was, with its harsh greens and browns and almost purple sky. Nearly four years in Belmarsh with only a view of high brick walls topped with razor wire tends to dim the memory.

He tried to compose his thoughts before they reached the parish church in which he'd been christened and his father would be buried. Pascoe had agreed that after the service was over he could spend an hour with Fraser Munro, the family solicitor, who had made the application for his compassionate leave, and who Nick suspected had also put in a plea for minimum security, and certainly no handcuffs, once they had crossed the border.

The police car drew up outside the church fifteen minutes before the service was due to begin. An elderly gentleman, whom Nick remembered from his youth, stepped forward as the policeman opened the back door. He wore a black tailcoat, wing collar and a black silk tie. He looked more like an undertaker than a solicitor. He raised his hat and gave a slight bow. Nick shook hands with him and smiled. 'Good afternoon, Mr Munro,' he said. 'It's nice to see you again.'

'Good afternoon, Sir Nicholas,' he replied. 'Welcome home.'

◄○►

'Leach, although you have been provisionally released from segregation, let me remind you that it is only provisional,' said the governor. 'Should you cause even the slightest disruption now that you're back on the wing, I don't want you to be in any doubt that you will be returned to closed conditions without recourse to me.'

'Recourse to you?' sneered Leach, as he stood in front of the governor's desk with an officer on either side of him.

'Are you questioning my authority?' asked the governor, 'because if you are . . .'

'No, I am not, sir,' said Leach sarcastically. 'Just your knowledge of the 1999 Prison Act. I was thrown into segregation before being placed on report.'

'A governor is allowed to carry out such an action without resorting to report if he has reason to believe that there is a prima facie case of—'

'I want to put in an immediate request to see my lawyer,' said Leach coolly.

'I'll note your request,' responded Barton, trying to remain composed. 'And who is your lawyer?'

'Mr Spencer Craig,' Leach replied. Barton wrote the name down on the pad in front of him. 'I will be requesting that he makes a formal complaint against you and three members of your staff.'

'Are you threatening me, Leach?'

'No, sir. Just making sure it's on the record that I have made a formal complaint.'

Barton could no longer hide his exasperation, and nodded curtly, his sign that the officers should remove the prisoner from his sight immediately.

◄○►

Danny wanted to tell Nick the good news, but he knew that he wouldn't return from Scotland until after midnight.

Alex Redmayne had written to confirm that the date of his appeal had been set for May 31st, only two weeks away. Mr Redmayne also wanted to know if Danny wished to attend the hearing, remembering that he had not given evidence in his original trial. He'd written back immediately confirming that he wanted to be present.

He had also written to Beth. He would have liked her to be the first to learn that Mortimer had made a full confession, and Big Al had recorded every word of it on Danny's tape recorder. The tape was now secreted inside his mattress, and he would hand it over to Mr Redmayne during his next legal visit. Danny wanted to let Beth know they now had the evidence they needed, but he couldn't risk putting anything in writing.

Big Al didn't try to hide the fact that he was pleased with himself, and even offered to appear as a witness. It looked as if Nick had been right. Danny was going to be released before he was.

26

THE CHURCH WARDEN was waiting for Sir Nicholas in the vestry. He gave a slight bow before accompanying the new head of the family down the aisle to the front pew on the right-hand side. Pascoe and Jenkins took their places in the row behind.

Nick turned to his left, where the rest of the family were seated in the first three rows on the other side of the aisle. Not one of them even glanced in his direction; they were all clearly under his uncle Hugo's instructions to ignore him. That didn't stop Mr Munro joining Nick in the front row. The organ struck up, and the local parish priest, accompanied by the regimental chaplain, led the choir down the aisle to the words of 'The Lord is My Shepherd'.

The trebles filed into the front row of the choir stalls, followed by the tenors and basses. A few moments later a coffin was borne in on the shoulders of six squaddies from the Cameron High-landers, then placed gently on a bier in front of the altar. All the colonel's favourite hymns were sung lustily during the service, ending with 'The Day Thou Gavest Lord is Ended'. Nick bowed his head in prayer for a man who did believe in God, Queen and country.

When the vicar delivered his eulogy, Nick recalled one of his father's expressions, which he invariably repeated whenever they had attended a regimental funeral in the past – 'The padre did him proud.'

Once the chaplain had offered closing prayers and the priest had administered the final blessing, the congregation of family, friends, representatives of the regiment and locals gathered in the churchyard to witness the burial.

For the first time, Nick noticed the massive figure of a man who must have weighed more than twenty-five stone, and who didn't look at home in Scotland. He smiled. Nick returned his smile and tried to recall when they had last met. Then he remembered: Washington DC; the opening of an exhibition at the Smithsonian to celebrate his grandfather's eightieth birthday, when his fabled stamp collection had been put on display to the public. But Nick still couldn't recall the man's name.

After the coffin had been lowered into the grave and the final rites administered, the Moncrieff clan departed, without a single member offering their condolences to the deceased's son and heir. One or two of the locals whose livelihoods did not depend on his uncle Hugo walked across and shook hands with Nick, while the senior officer representing the regiment stood to attention and saluted. Nick raised his hat in acknowledgement.

As he turned to leave the graveside, Nick saw Fraser Munro talking to Jenkins and Pascoe. Munro came across to him. 'They've agreed that you can spend an hour with me to discuss family matters, but they'll not allow you to accompany me back to the office in my car.'

'I understand.' Nick thanked the chaplain and then climbed into the back of the police car. A moment later Pascoe and Jenkins took their places on either side of him.

As the car moved off, Nick looked out of the window to see the large man lighting a cigar.

'Hunsacker,' said Nick out loud. 'Gene Hunsacker.'

◄○►

'Why did you want to see me?' demanded Craig.

'I've run out of gear,' said Leach.

'But I supplied you with enough to last six months.'

'Not after a bent screw's taken his cut.'

'Then you'd better visit the library.'

'Why would I go to the library, Mr Craig?'

'Take out the latest copy of the *Law Review*, the leather-bound edition, and you'll find everything you need taped to the inside of the spine.' Craig closed his briefcase, stood up and headed towards the door.

'It won't be a moment too soon,' said Leach, not moving from his seat.

'What do you mean?' asked Craig as he touched the door handle.

'Aunt Maisie's friend has signed up for a detox programme.'

'Then you'll have to wean him off it, won't you.'

'That may not solve your problem,' said Leach calmly.

Craig walked slowly back to the table, but didn't sit down. 'What are you getting at?'

'A little bird tells me that Aunt Maisie's friend has started singing like a canary.'

'Then shut him up,' spat out Craig.

'It may be too late for that.'

'Stop playing games, Leach, and tell me what you're getting at.'

'I'm told there's a tape.'

Craig collapsed into the chair and stared across the table. 'And what's on this tape?' he asked quietly.

'A full confession . . . with names, dates and places.' Leach paused, aware that he now had Craig's undivided attention. 'It was when I was told the names that I felt I ought to consult my lawyer.'

Craig didn't speak for some time. 'Do you think you can get your hands on the tape?' he eventually asked.

'At a cost.'

'How much?'

'Ten grand.'

'That's a bit steep.'

'Bent screws don't come cheap,' said Leach. 'In any case, I bet Aunt Maisie doesn't have a plan B, so she hasn't got much choice.'

Craig nodded. 'All right. But there's a time limit. If it's not in my possession before May thirty-first, you won't get paid.'

'No prizes for guessing whose appeal will be coming up that day,' said Leach with a smirk.

◄○►

'Your father made a will, which this firm executed,' said Munro, tapping his fingers on the desk. 'It was witnessed by a Justice of the Peace, and I have to advise you that however you feel about its contents, you would be unwise to dispute it.'

'It would not have crossed my mind to oppose my father's wishes,' said Nick.

'I think that is a sensible decision, Sir Nicholas, if I may say so. However, you are entitled to know the details of the will. As time is against us, allow me to paraphrase.' He coughed. 'The bulk of your father's estate has been left to his brother, Mr Hugo Moncrieff, with smaller gifts and annuities to be distributed among other members of the family, the regiment and some local charities. He has left nothing to you except the title, which of course was not his to dispose of.'

'Be assured, Mr Munro, this does not come as a surprise.'

'I'm relieved to hear that, Sir Nicholas. However, your grandfather, a shrewd and practical man, who incidentally my father had the privilege of representing, made certain provisions in his will of which you are now the sole beneficiary. Your father made an application to have that will rescinded, but the courts rejected his claim.'

Munro smiled as he rummaged around among the papers on his desk until he found what he wanted. He held it up in triumph and declared, 'Your grandfather's will. I will only acquaint you with the relevant clause.' He turned over several pages. 'Ah, here's what I'm looking for.' He placed a pair of half-moon spectacles on the end of his nose and read slowly. 'I leave my estate in Scotland, known as Dunbroathy Hall, as well as my London residence in The Boltons, to my grandson Nicholas Alexander Moncrieff, presently serving with his regiment in Kosovo. However, my son Angus will be allowed full and free use of both of these properties until his demise, when they will come into the possession of the aforementioned grandson.' Munro placed the will back on his desk. 'In normal circumstances,' he said, 'this would have guaranteed you a vast inheritance, but unfortunately I have to inform you that your father took advantage of the words *full and free use*, and borrowed heavily against both properties up until a few months before his death.

'In the case of the Dunbroathy estate, he secured a sum of – ' once again Munro put on his half-moon spectacles in order that he could check the figure – 'one million pounds, and for The Boltons, a little over a million. In accordance with your father's will, once probate has been agreed, that money will pass directly to your uncle Hugo.'

'So despite my grandfather's best intentions,' said Nick, 'I've still ended up with nothing.'

'Not necessarily,' said Munro, 'because I believe you have a legitimate case against your uncle to retrieve the money he procured by this little subterfuge.'

'Nevertheless, if those were my father's wishes, I will not go against them,' said Nick.

'I think you should reconsider your position, Sir Nicholas,' said Munro, once again tapping his fingers on the desk. 'After all, a large sum of money is at stake and I'm confident—'

'You may well be right, Mr Munro, but I will not call my father's judgement into question.'

Munro removed his glasses and reluctantly said, 'So be it. I also have to report,' he continued, 'that I have been in correspondence with your uncle, Hugo Moncrieff, who is well aware of your present circumstances, and has offered to take both properties off your hands, and with them the responsibility for both mortgages. He has also agreed to cover any expenses, including legal costs, associated with the transactions.'

'Do you represent my uncle Hugo?' Nick asked.

'No, I do not,' said Munro firmly. 'I advised your father against taking out a mortgage on either of the two properties. In fact, I told him that I considered it to be against the spirit of the law, if not the letter, to conduct such transactions without your prior knowledge or approval.' Munro coughed. 'He did not heed my advice, and indeed decided to take his custom elsewhere.'

'In that case, Mr Munro, may I enquire if you would be willing to represent me?'

'I am flattered that you should ask, Sir Nicholas, and let me assure you that this firm would be proud to continue its long association with the Moncrieff family.'

'Remembering *all* my circumstances, Mr Munro, how would you advise me to proceed?'

Munro gave a slight bow. 'Anticipating the possibility that you might seek my counsel, I have on your behalf set in motion a train of enquiries.' Nick smiled as the glasses returned to the nose of the ageing advocate. 'I am advised that the price of a house in The Boltons is currently around three million pounds, and my brother, who is a local councillor, tells me that your uncle Hugo has recently made enquiries at the town hall as to whether planning permission might be granted for a development on the Dunbroathy estate, despite the fact that I believe your grandfather hoped you would eventually hand over the estate to the National Trust for Scotland.'

'Yes, he said as much to me,' said Nick. 'I made a note of the conversation in my diary at the time.'

'That will not prevent your uncle from going ahead with his plans, and with that in mind, I enquired of a cousin who is a partner in a local estate agent what the council's attitude might be to such a planning application. He informs me that under the latest planning provisions in the 1997 Local Government Act, any part of the estate that currently has buildings on it, including the house, any barns, outbuildings or stables, would be likely to receive provisional planning permission. He tells me that this could amount to as much as twelve acres. He also informed me that the council are looking for land on which to build affordable flats or a retirement home, and they might even consider an application for an hotel.' Munro removed his glasses. 'You could have discovered all this information by reading the minutes of the council's planning committee, which are lodged in the local library on the last day of every month.'

'Was your cousin able to put a value on the estate?' asked Nick.

'Not officially, but he said that similar pockets of land are currently trading at around two hundred and fifty thousand pounds per acre.'

'Making the estate worth around three million,' suggested Nick.

'I suspect nearer four and a half if you include the twelve thousand acres of rural land. But, and there is always a *but* when your uncle Hugo is involved, you must not forget that the estate and the London property are now encumbered with large mortgages which have to be serviced every quarter day.' Nick anticipated the opening of another file and he wasn't disappointed. 'The house in The Boltons has outgoings, including rates, service charge and mortgage, of around three thousand four hundred pounds a month, and there are another two thousand nine hundred pounds a month on the Dunbroathy estate, making in all an outlay of approximately seventy-five thousand pounds a year. It is my duty to warn you, Sir Nicholas, that should either of these payments fall in arrears by more than three months, the mortgage companies concerned are entitled to place the properties on the market for immediate disposal. Were that to happen, I am sure they would find a willing buyer in your uncle.'

'And I must tell you, Mr Munro, that my current income as a prison librarian is twelve pounds a week.'

'Is that so?' said Munro, making a note. 'Such a sum would not make a very large dent in seventy-five thousand pounds,' he suggested, revealing a rare flash of humour.

'Perhaps in the circumstances we might resort to another of your cousins,' suggested Nick, unable to mask a smile.

'Sadly not,' replied Munro. 'However, my sister is married to the manager of the local branch of the Royal Bank of Scotland, and he has assured me that he can see no problem in servicing the payments if you were willing to lodge a second charge on both properties with the bank.'

'You have been most solicitous on my behalf,' said Nick, 'and I am indeed grateful.'

'I must confess,' said Munro, 'and you will understand that what I am about to say is off the record, that although I had great admiration, indeed affection, for your grandfather, and was happy to represent your father, I have never felt quite the same confidence when it came to your uncle Hugo, who is—' There was a knock on the door. 'Come in,' said Munro.

Pascoe put his head round the door. 'I apologize for interrupting you, Mr Munro, but we have to leave in a few minutes if we're to catch the train back to London.'

'Thank you,' said Munro. 'I shall be as expeditious as possible.' He did not speak again until Pascoe had closed the door behind him. 'I fear that despite our brief acquaintance, Sir Nicholas, you are going to have to trust me,' said Munro, placing several documents on the table in front of him. 'I will have to ask you to sign these agreements, although you do not have the time to consider them in detail. However, if I am to proceed while you complete . . .' He coughed.

'My sentence,' said Nick.

'Quite so, Sir Nicholas,' said the solicitor as he removed a fountain pen from his pocket and passed it to his client.

'I also have a document of my own that I wish you to witness,' said Nick. He took out several pieces of lined prison paper from an inside pocket and passed them across to his solicitor.

27

LAWRENCE DAVENPORT took three curtain calls on the night *The Importance of Being Earnest* opened at the Theatre Royal in Brighton. He didn't seem to notice that the rest of the cast were on stage with him.

During rehearsals, he had phoned his sister and invited her to join him for dinner after the show.

'How's it going?' Sarah had asked.

'Just fine,' he replied, 'but that's not the real reason I want you to come down. I need to discuss an important decision I've come to that will affect you, indeed the whole family.'

By the time he put the phone down he was even more determined. He was going to stand up to Spencer Craig for the first time in his life, whatever the consequences. He knew he wouldn't be able to go through with it without Sarah's support, especially remembering her past relationship with Craig.

Rehearsals had been tiresome. In a play there's no second or third take should you forget a line or walk on stage at the wrong time. Davenport even began to wonder how he could hope to shine playing alongside actors who regularly appeared in the West End. But the moment the curtain rose on the first night it was clear that the theatre was full of Dr Beresford's fans, who hung on Lawrence's every word, laughed at his least amusing lines, and applauded every bit of business in which he was involved.

When Sarah dropped into his dressing room to wish him luck before the curtain went up, he reminded her that he had something of great importance to discuss over dinner. She thought he looked pale and a little tired, but put it down to first-night nerves.

'See you after the show,' she said. 'Break a leg.'

When the curtain finally fell, Davenport knew he couldn't go through with it. He felt that he was back where he belonged. He tried to convince himself that he had a duty to take other people into consideration, not least his sister. After all, why should her career be harmed because of Spencer Craig?

Davenport returned to his dressing room to find it full of friends and admirers toasting his good health – always the first sign of a hit. He basked in the praise heaped upon him and tried to forget all about Danny Cartwright, who was, after all, nothing more than an East End thug who was probably best locked up in any case.

Sarah sat in the corner of the room, delighted by her brother's success, but wondering what he needed to discuss with her that was of such great importance.

◄○►

Nick was surprised to find Danny still awake when the cell door was opened by Pascoe just after midnight. Although he was exhausted after the day's events and his long journey back to London, he was pleased to have someone to share his news with.

Danny listened attentively to all that had taken place in Scotland. Big Al lay facing the wall, and didn't speak.

'You would have been so much better at handling Munro than I was,' said Nick. 'To begin with, I doubt if you would have allowed my uncle to get away with stealing all that money.' He was about to go into more detail about the meeting with his solicitor when he suddenly stopped and asked, 'What are you looking so pleased about?'

Danny climbed off the bunk, slipped a hand under his pillow and extracted a small cassette tape. He put it in his cassette player and pressed *play*.

'Whit's yer name,' enquired a man with a thick Glaswegian accent.

'Toby, Toby Mortimer,' responded a voice that had clearly been raised in a different environment.

'So how did ye end up in here?'

'Possession.'

'Class A?'

'The worst. Heroin. I used to need the stuff twice a day.'

'Then ye must be pleased we got ye on a detox programme.'

'It's not proving that easy,' said Toby.

'And whit aboot that load of shite ye told me yesterday? Wis I expected tae believe aw that?'

'It's all true, every word. I just needed you to understand why I dropped out of the programme. I saw my friend stab a man, and I should have told the police.'

'Why didn't ye?'

'Because Spencer told me to keep my mouth shut.'

'Spencer?'

'My friend, Spencer Craig. He's a barrister.'

'An you expect me tae believe that a barrister knifed someone he'd never met before?'

'It wasn't as simple as that.'

'I bet the polis thought it wis as simple as that.'

'Yes, they did. All they had to do was choose between a lad from the East End and a barrister who had three witnesses to say he wasn't even there.' The tape was silent for several seconds before the same voice said, 'But I was there.'

'So whit really happened?'

'It was Gerald's thirtieth birthday and we'd all had a bit too much to drink. That's when the three of them walked in.'

'Three of them?'

'Two men and a girl. It was the girl who was the problem.'

'Wis it the girl who started the fight?

'No, no. Craig fancied the girl the moment he set eyes on her, but she wasn't interested, which really pissed him off.'

'So hur boyfriend started the fight?'

'No, the girl made it obvious that she wanted to leave, so they slipped out the back door.'

'Intae an alley?'

'How did you know that?' asked a surprised-sounding voice.

'Ye told me yesterday,' said Big Al, recovering from his mistake.

'Oh, yes.' Another long silence. 'Spencer and Gerald ran round to the back of the pub the moment they left, so Larry and I went along for the ride. But then it got out of control.'

'Who wis tae blame fur that?'

'Spencer and Gerald. They wanted to pick a fight with the two yobs and assumed we'd back them up, but I was too spaced out to be of any use, and Larry doesn't go in for that sort of thing.'

'Larry?'

'Larry Davenport.'

'The soap star?' said Big Al, trying to sound surprised.

'Yes. But he and I just stood around and watched when the fight broke out.'

'So it wis yer friend Spencer who wis looking fur a fight?'

'Yes. He's always fancied himself as a boxer, got a blue at Cambridge, but those two lads were in a different class. That was until Spencer pulled out the knife.'

'Spencer had a knife?'

'Yes, he picked it up from the bar before he went into the alley. I remember him saying, "Just in case".'

'An he'd nae seen the two men or the girl before?'

'No, but he still fancied his chances with the girl, until Cartwright got the better of him. That's when Spencer lost his temper and stabbed him in the leg.'

'But he didnae kill him?'

'No, just stabbed him in the leg, and while Cartwright was nursing his wound, Spencer stabbed the other guy in the chest.' It was some time before the voice said, 'And killed him.'

'Did ye call the polis?'

'No, Spencer must have done that later, after he told us all to go home. He said that if anyone asked any questions, we were to say we'd never left the bar, and didn't see anything.'

'And did anyone ask any questions?'

'The police came round to my place the next morning. I hadn't slept, but I didn't let on. I think I was more frightened of Craig than the police, but it didn't matter anyway, because the detective in charge of the investigation was convinced he'd arrested the right man.'

The tape ran for several more seconds before Mortimer's voice added, 'That was over two years ago, and not a day goes by when I don't think about that lad. I've already warned Spencer that as soon as I'm fit enough to give evidence . . .' The tape went dead.

'Well done!' exclaimed Nick, but Big Al only grunted. He had stuck to the script Danny had written for him, which covered all the points Mr Redmayne needed for the appeal.

'I still have to get the tape to Mr Redmayne somehow,' said Danny as he removed it from the cassette player and tucked it under his pillow.

'That shouldn't prove too difficult,' said Nick. 'Send it in a sealed envelope marked "legal". No officer would dare to open it unless they were convinced the lawyer was dealing in money or drugs directly with an inmate, and no barrister would be stupid enough to take that sort of risk.'

'Unless that inmate hud a screw working on the inside,' said Big Al, 'who jist happened tae find oot aboot the tape.'

'But that's not possible,' said Danny, 'not while we're the only three who know about it.'

'Don't forget Mortimer,' said Big Al, finally deciding it was time to sit up. 'An he's no capable of keeping his mooth shut, especially when he needs a hit.'

'So what should I do with the tape?' said Danny. 'Because I have no chance of winning my appeal without it.'

'Dinnae risk sending it by post,' said Big Al. 'Make an appointment tae see Redmayne, and then hand it over in person. 'Cause who dae ye think jist happened to huv a meeting wi' *his* lawyer yisterday?'

Nick and Danny didn't speak as they waited for Big Al to answer his own question.

'That bastard Leach,' he eventually said.

'That could just be a coincidence,' said Nick.

'No when that lawyer is Spencer Craig.'

'How can you be so sure it was Spencer Craig?' asked Danny, gripping the railing on the side of his bunk.

'Screws drop in and oot of the hospital to huv a chat wi' sister, and I'm the wan who his tae brew their cuppa.'

'If a bent screw were to find out about that tape,' said Nick, 'there would be no prizes for guessing whose desk it would end up on.'

'So what am I meant to do about that?' said Danny, sounding desperate.

'Make sure it does end up on his desk,' said Nick.

◄o►

'Are you booked in for a consultation?'

'Not exactly.'

'So are you here to seek legal advice?'

'Not exactly.'

'Then what are you here for, exactly?' asked Spencer Craig.

'I require aid, but not of the legal variety.'

'What kind of aid do you have in mind?' asked Craig.

'I've spotted a rare opportunity to get my hands on a large shipment of wine, but there's a problem.'

'A problem?' repeated Craig.

'They require a down payment.'

'How much?'

'Ten thousand pounds.'

'I'll need a few days to think about it.'

'I'm sure you will, Mr Craig, but don't take too long, because I have another interested party, who's hoping I'll be able to answer a few questions this time around.' The barman of the Dunlop Arms paused before adding, 'I promised to let him know before May the thirty-first.'

◄o►

They all heard the key turning in the lock, which took them by surprise, as it was still another hour before Association.

When the cell door was pulled open, Hagen was standing in the doorway. 'Cell search,' he said. 'You three, in the corridor.'

Nick, Danny and Big Al made their way out on to the landing and were even more surprised when Hagen marched into their cell and pulled the door closed behind him. The surprise was not that a screw was carrying out a pad search. They were common enough – officers were always on the lookout for drugs, drink, knives and even guns. But whenever a cell search had taken place in the past, there were always three officers present, and the cell door was left wide open so that prisoners couldn't claim something had been planted.

A few moments later the door swung open and Hagen reappeared, unable to hide the grin on his face. 'OK, lads,' he said, 'you're clean.'

◄◦►

Danny was surprised to see Leach in the library, because he'd never taken out a book before. Perhaps he wanted to read a paper. He was roaming up and down the shelves, looking lost.

'Can I help?' ventured Danny.

'I want the latest copy of the *Law Review*.'

'You're in luck,' said Danny. 'We only had an out-of-date one until a few days ago when someone donated several books to the library, including the latest edition of the *Law Review*.'

'So hand it over,' Leach demanded.

Danny walked across to the legal section, removed a thick leather-bound book from the shelf and brought it back to the counter. 'Name and number?'

'I don't have to tell you nothin'.'

'You'll have to tell me your name if you want to take out a book, because otherwise I can't make out a library card.'

'Leach, 6241,' he snarled.

Danny made out a new library card. He hoped Leach hadn't noticed his hand was trembling. 'Sign on the bottom line.'

Leach put a cross on the place where Danny was pointing.

'You'll have to return the book within three days,' Danny explained.

'Who do you think you are, a fuckin' screw? I'll bring it back when I feel like it.'

Danny watched as Leach grabbed the book and walked out of the library without saying another word. He was puzzled. If Leach couldn't sign his name . . .

28

CRAIG LEFT HIS black Porsche in the visitors' car park, an hour before they were due to see Toby. He had already warned Gerald that it was almost as difficult to get into Belmarsh prison as it was to get out: an endless rat-run of barred gates, double-checking of credentials and thorough body searches, and that was before you even reached the reception area.

Once they had given their names in at the desk, Craig and Payne were handed a numbered key and told to place any valuables, including watches, rings, necklaces and any notes or loose change, in a locker. If they wished to buy any items from the canteen on behalf of a prisoner, they had to hand over the correct amount of money in exchange for small plastic tokens marked £1, 50p, 20p, 10p, so that cash could not be passed to an inmate. Each visitor's name was called separately, and before being allowed to enter the secure area, they were subjected to a further search, on this occasion by an officer assisted by a sniffer dog.

'Numbers one and two,' said a voice over the tannoy.

Craig and Payne sat in a corner of the waiting room with only copies of *Prison News* and *Lock and Key* to help while away the time as they waited for their numbers to be called.

'Numbers seventeen and eighteen,' said the voice some forty minutes later.

Craig and Payne rose from their places and made their way through another set of barred gates to face an even more rigorous security search before they were allowed to enter the visits area, where they were told to take their seats in row G, numbers 11 and 12.

Craig sat down on a green chair that was bolted to the floor, while Payne went off to the canteen to buy three cups of tea and a couple of Mars Bars in exchange for his prison tokens. When he rejoined Craig, he placed the tray on a table that was also bolted to the floor and sat down on another immovable seat.

'How much longer will we have to wait?' he asked.

'Some time yet, I suspect,' replied Craig. 'The prisoners are only let in one by one and I expect they're being searched even more thoroughly than we were.'

'Don't look round,' whispered Beth, 'but Craig and Payne are sitting three or four rows behind you. They must be visiting someone.'

Danny began to shiver, but resisted looking round. 'It has to be Mortimer,' he said. 'But they're too late.'

'Too late for what?' asked Beth.

Danny took her hand. 'I can't say too much at the moment, but Alex will be able to brief you when you next see him.'

'It's Alex now, is it?' said Beth, smiling. 'So are you two on first-name terms?'

Danny laughed. 'Only behind his back.'

'You're such a coward,' said Beth. 'Mr Redmayne always refers to you as Danny, and he even told me how pleased he was that you'd started shaving regularly, and grown your hair longer. He thinks it just might make a difference when it comes to the appeal.'

'How's the garage coming along?' asked Danny, changing the subject.

'Dad's slowing down a bit,' said Beth. 'I wish I could convince him to give up smoking. He never stops coughing, but he won't listen to anything Mum or I have to say on the subject.'

'So who has he made manager?'

'Trevor Sutton.'

'Trevor Sutton? He couldn't run a whelk stall.'

'No one else seemed to want the job,' said Beth.

'Then you'd better keep a close eye on the books,' said Danny.

'Why? You don't think Trevor is on the fiddle?'

'No, but only because he can't add up.'

'But what can I do about it?' said Beth. 'Dad never confides in me, and frankly I'm pretty overworked myself at the moment.'

'Mr Thomas driving you hard, is he?' asked Danny with a grin.

Beth laughed. 'Mr Thomas is a terrific boss, and you know it. Don't forget how kind he was during the trial. And he's just given me another pay rise.'

'I don't doubt he's a good chap,' said Danny, 'but—'

'A *good chap*?' laughed Beth.

'Blame Nick,' said Danny, unconsciously running a hand through his hair.

'If you go on like this,' said Beth, 'you won't be able to mix with your old mates when you've released.'

'But you do realize,' said Danny, ignoring her comment, 'that Mr Thomas fancies you.'

'You must be joking,' said Beth. 'He always behaves like the perfect gentleman.'

'That doesn't stop him fancying you.'

◄○►

'How does anyone ever manage to get drugs into a place as well protected as this?' asked Payne, looking up at the CCTV cameras and the prison officers on the balcony peering down at them through binoculars.

'The carriers are getting more and more sophisticated,' said Craig. 'Children's nappies, wigs – some even put the gear in condoms and then stuff them up their backside, knowing not many officers enjoy searching around in there, while others even swallow the stuff, they're so desperate.'

'And if the packet breaks open inside them?'

'They can die a horrible death. I once had a client who could swallow a small packet of heroin, hold it in his throat, and then cough it up when he got back to his cell. You might consider that one hell of a risk, but imagine being on twelve pounds a week, when you can sell a packet like that for five hundred pounds – they obviously think it's worth it. The only reason why we were put through such a rigorous search is because of what Toby's in for.'

'If Toby takes much longer our time will be up before he even makes an appearance,' said Payne, looking down at a cup of tea that had gone cold.

'Sorry to disturb you, sir.' An officer was standing by Craig's side. 'I'm afraid Mortimer has been taken ill, and won't be able to join you this afternoon.'

'Bloody inconsiderate,' said Craig as he rose from his place. 'The least he could have done was to let us know. Typical.'

◄○►

'Bang up! Everyone back in your cells immediately, and I mean immediately!' bellowed a voice. Whistles were blowing, klaxons were blaring and officers appeared from every corridor and began herding any stray prisoners back into their cells.

'But I have to report to education,' protested Danny as the cell door was slammed in his face.

'No today, Danny boy,' said Big Al, lighting a cigarette.

'What was that all about?' asked Nick.

'It could be wan ay many things,' said Big Al, inhaling deeply.

'Like what?' asked Danny.

'A fight couldae broken oot on another wing, which the screws think might spread. Someone could even huv attacked a screw – God help the bastard. Or a dealer might have been caught handin' over some gear, or a prisoner couldae torched his cell. Ma bet,' he offered, but not before he'd exhaled a large cloud of smoke, 'is that someone's gone and topped himself.' He flicked the ash from the end of his cigarette on to the floor. 'Ye cin take yer choice, because only wan thing's fur certain – we willnae be opened up again fur at least another twenty-four hours, until it's been sorted.'

Big Al turned out to be right: it was twenty-seven hours before they heard a key turning in the lock.

'What was that all about?' Nick asked the officer who opened their cell door.

'No idea,' came back the regulation response.

'Someone's topped himself,' said a voice from the next cell.

'Poor bastard, must have discovered it was the only way out of this place.'

'Anyone we know?' asked another.

'A druggie,' said another voice, 'only been with us for a few weeks.'

—◄○►—

Gerald Payne asked the man at the porter's lodge in Inner Temple to direct him to Mr Spencer Craig's chambers.

'Far corner of the square, sir. Number six,' came back the reply. 'You'll find his office on the top floor.'

Payne hurried across the square, keeping to the path, obeying the notices that firmly announced, *Keep off the grass*. He had left his office in Mayfair as soon as Craig had phoned to say, 'If you come to my chambers around four, you won't be suffering any more sleepless nights.'

When Payne reached the other side of the square, he climbed the stone steps and pushed open a door. He stepped into a cold, musty corridor with stark white walls adorned with old prints of even older judges. At the far end of the corridor was a wooden staircase, and attached to the wall was a shiny black board on which was painted boldly in white a list of names indicating the members of chambers. As the porter had told him, Mr Spencer Craig's chambers was on the top floor. The long climb up the creaking wooden staircase reminded Payne how badly out of shape he'd become – he was breathing heavily long before he reached the second floor.

'Mr Payne?' enquired a young woman who was waiting on the top step. 'I'm Mr Craig's secretary. He's just phoned to say that he's left the Old Bailey and should be with you in a few minutes. Perhaps you'd care to wait in his office?' She led him down the corridor, opened a door and ushered him in.

'Thank you,' said Payne as he stepped into a large room, sparsely furnished with a partner's desk and two high-backed leather chairs, one on either side.

'Would you care for a cup of tea, Mr Payne, or perhaps a coffee?'

'No, thank you,' said Payne, as he looked out of a window overlooking the square.

She closed the door behind her, and Payne sat down facing

Craig's desk; it was almost bare, as if no one worked there – no photos, no flowers, no mementoes, just a large blotting pad, a tape recorder and a bulky, unopened envelope addressed to *Mr S. Craig* and marked 'Private'.

A few minutes later Craig came bursting into the room, closely followed by his secretary. Payne rose and shook hands with him, as if he was a client rather than an old friend.

'Have a seat, old boy,' said Craig. 'Miss Russell, can you make sure we're not disturbed?'

'Of course, Mr Craig,' she replied, and left, closing the door behind her.

'Is that what I think it is?' asked Payne, pointing at the envelope on Craig's desk.

'We're about to find out,' said Craig. 'It arrived in the morning post while I was in court.' He ripped the envelope open and tipped its contents on to the blotting pad – a small cassette tape.

'How did you get hold of it?' asked Payne.

'Better not to ask,' said Craig. 'Let's just say I've got friends in low places.' He smiled, picked up the tape and slotted it in the cassette player. 'We are about to find out what Toby was so keen to share with the rest of the world.' He pressed the play button. Craig leant back in his chair while Payne remained on the edge of his seat, his elbows on the desk. It was several seconds before they heard someone speak.

'I can't be sure which one of you will be listening to this tape.' Craig didn't recognize the voice immediately. 'It could be Lawrence Davenport – but that seems unlikely. Gerald Payne is a possibility.' Payne felt a chill shiver dart through his body. 'But I suspect it's most likely to be Spencer Craig.' Craig showed no emotion. 'Whichever one of you it is, I want to leave you in no doubt that if it takes me the rest of my life, I'm going to make sure that all three of you end up in jail for the murder of Bernie Wilson, not to mention my own unlawful incarceration. If you still hope to get your hands on the tape you were really looking for, let me assure you that it's somewhere you'll never find it, until you're locked up in here.'

29

DANNY LOOKED AT himself in a full-length mirror for the first time in months, and was surprised by his reaction. Nick's influence must have gone further than even he had realized, because he suddenly felt uncomfortably aware that a pair of designer jeans and a West Ham shirt might not be the most appropriate apparel for an appearance at the Royal Courts. He was already regretting having turned down Nick's offer of a sober suit, shirt and tie, which would have been more in keeping with the gravity of the occasion (Nick's words), as the disparity in their size was negligible (two words Danny no longer had to look up).

Danny took his place in the dock and waited for the three judges to appear. He had been driven out of Belmarsh at 7 a.m. in a large white prison van along with twelve other prisoners who were all due to appear at the appeal court that morning. How many of them would be returning that night? On arrival he'd been locked up in a cell and told to wait. It gave him time to think. Not that he would be allowed to say anything in court. Mr Redmayne had gone through the appeal procedure with him in great detail, and had explained that it was very different from a trial.

Three judges would have trawled through all the original evidence, as well as the transcript of the trial, and would have to be persuaded that there was fresh evidence that the judge and jury had not been privy to before they would consider overturning the original verdict.

Once he had heard the tape, Alex Redmayne was confident that doubt would be planted in their lordships' minds, although he didn't intend to dwell for too long on why Toby Mortimer was unable to appear as a witness.

It was some time before the door of Danny's cell was unlocked, and Alex joined him. After their last consultation, he had insisted that Danny call him by his Christian name. He still refused, as it just didn't feel right, despite the fact that his counsel had always treated him as an equal. Alex began to go over all the new evidence in great detail. Despite Mortimer taking his own life, they were still in possession of the tape, which Alex described as their trump card.

'One should always try to avoid clichés, Mr Redmayne,' Danny said with a grin.

Alex smiled. 'Another year and you'll be conducting your own defence.'

'Let's hope that won't be necessary.'

◄o►

Danny looked up to where Beth and her mother were seated in the front row of a gallery that was packed with the good citizens of Bow, who were in no doubt that he would be released later that day. He was only sorry that Beth's father was not among them.

What Danny didn't realize was how many more people were standing on the pavement outside the Royal Courts, chanting and holding up placards demanding his release. He glanced down at the press benches where a young man from the *Bethnal Green and Bow Gazette* sat with his notepad open and his pen poised. Would he have an exclusive for tomorrow's paper? The tape might not prove to be enough in itself, Alex had warned Danny, but once it had been played in court, its contents could be reported in any newspaper in the land, and after that . . .

Danny was no longer alone. Alex, Nick, Big Al and of course Beth were the generals in what was fast becoming a small army. Alex had admitted that he was still hopeful a second witness might come forward to confirm Mortimer's story. If Toby Mortimer had been willing to confess, wasn't it possible that either Gerald Payne or Lawrence Davenport might, after more than two years of having had to live with their consciences, want to set the record straight?

'Why don't you go and see them?' Danny had asked. 'They might just listen to you.'

Alex had explained why that wasn't possible, and went on to point out that even if he bumped into one of them socially he could be forced to withdraw from the case, or face a charge of unprofessional conduct.

'Couldn't you send someone else in your place, and have them get hold of the evidence we need, the way Big Al did?'

'No,' said Alex firmly. 'If such an action were traced back to me, you'd be looking for a new barrister and I'd be looking for another job.'

'What about the barman?' Danny asked.

Alex told him that they'd already carried out a background check on Reg Jackson, the barman of the Dunlop Arms, to find out if he had any previous convictions.

'And?'

'Nothing,' said Alex. 'He's been arrested twice in the past five years for handling stolen goods, but the police didn't have enough evidence to be sure of a conviction, so the charges were dropped.'

'What about Beth?' Danny asked. 'Will they give her a second chance to testify?'

'No,' replied Alex. 'The judges will have read her written testimony as well as the transcript of the trial and they're not interested in repeat performances.' He also warned Danny that he couldn't find anything in the judge's summing up which suggested sufficient prejudice to seek a retrial. 'The truth is, everything rests on the tape.'

'What about Big Al?'

Alex told him that he had considered calling Albert Crann as a witness, but had decided that it might do more harm than good.

'But he's a loyal friend,' said Danny.

'With a criminal record.'

◄o►

As ten o'clock struck, the three judges trooped into the courtroom. The court officials rose, bowed to their lordships and then waited for them to take their places on the bench. To Danny, the two men and one woman who held the rest of his life in their hands appeared somewhat shadowy figures, their heads covered in short wigs and their everyday clothes masked by full-length black gowns.

Alex Redmayne placed a file on a small lectern in front of him. He had explained to Danny that he would be alone on the front bench, as prosecuting counsel didn't have to be present at appeals. Danny felt he wouldn't miss Mr Arnold Pearson QC.

Once the court had settled, the senior judge, Lord Justice Browne, invited Mr Redmayne to begin his summation.

Alex opened by reminding the court of the background to the case, trying once again to sow doubt in their lordships' minds, but from the looks on their faces he clearly wasn't making much of an impression. In fact, Lord Justice Browne interrupted him on more than one occasion to enquire if there was going to be any new evidence presented in this case, as he stressed that all three judges had studied the court transcripts of the original trial.

After an hour, Alex finally gave in. 'Be assured, m'lord, that I do indeed intend to present important new evidence for your consideration.'

'Be assured, Mr Redmayne, that we are looking forward to hearing it,' was Lord Justice Browne's response.

Alex steadied himself and turned another page of his file. 'My lords, I am in possession of a tape recording that I should like you to consider. It is a conversation with a Mr Toby Mortimer, a fellow Musketeer who was present at the Dunlop Arms on the night in question, but was unable to give evidence at the original trial as he was indisposed.' Danny held his breath as Alex picked up the tape and placed it in a cassette player on the table in front of him. He was just about to press the play button, when Lord Justice Browne leant forward and said, 'One moment please, Mr Redmayne.'

Danny felt a shiver go through his body as the three judges whispered among themselves. It was some time before Lord Justice Browne asked a question to which Alex had no doubt he already knew the answer.

'Will Mr Mortimer be appearing as a witness?' he asked.

'No, m'lord, but the tape will show—'

'Why will he not be appearing before us, Mr Redmayne? Is he still indisposed?'

'Unfortunately, m'lord, he died quite recently.'

'May I enquire what was the cause of death?'

Alex cursed. He knew that Lord Justice Browne was well aware of the reason Mortimer couldn't be in court, but was making sure that every detail was on the record. 'He committed suicide, m'lord, after taking an overdose of heroin.'

'Was he a registered heroin addict?' continued Lord Justice Browne relentlessly.

'Yes, m'lord, but fortunately this recording was made during a period of remission.'

'No doubt a doctor will appear before us to confirm this?'

'Unfortunately not, m'lord.'

'Am I to understand that a doctor was not present when the tape recording was made?'

'Yes, m'lord.'

'I see. And where was the tape recording made?'

'In Belmarsh prison, m'lord.'

'Were you present at the time?'

'No, m'lord.'

'Perhaps an officer of the prison was on hand to witness the circumstances in which this tape recording was made?'

'No, m'lord.'

'Then I am curious to know, Mr Redmayne, exactly who was present on the occasion.'

'A Mr Albert Crann.'

'And if he is not a doctor or a member of the prison staff, what was his position at the time?'

'He is a prisoner.'

'Is he, indeed? I am bound to ask, Mr Redmayne, if you have any proof that this recording was made without Mr Mortimer being coerced or threatened.'

Alex hesitated. 'No, m'lord. But I'm confident that you will be able to make such a judgement concerning Mr Mortimer's state of mind once you have listened to the tape.'

'But how can we be sure that Mr Crann wasn't holding a knife to his throat, Mr Redmayne? Indeed, perhaps his very presence would have been enough to put the fear of God into Mr Mortimer.'

'As I have suggested, m'lord, you might feel better able to form an opinion once you have heard the tape.'

'Allow me a moment to consult with my colleagues, Mr Redmayne.'

Once again the three judges whispered among themselves.

After a short time, Lord Justice Browne turned his attention back to defence counsel. 'Mr Redmayne, we are all of the opinion that we cannot allow you to play the tape, as it is clearly inadmissible.'

'But, my lord, may I refer you to a recent European Commission directive—'

'European directives do not yet constitute law in my court,' said Lord Justice Browne, but quickly corrected himself, ' – in this country. Let me warn you that if the contents of this tape were ever to become public, I would be obliged to refer the matter to the CPS.'

The one journalist on the press benches put down his pen. For a moment he had thought he had an exclusive, as Mr Redmayne would surely pass over the tape at the conclusion of the hearing so that he could decide if his readers might be interested, even if their lordships were not. But that would no longer be possible. If the paper published one word of the tape following the judge's directive, it would be in contempt of court – something even the most robust editors draw the line at.

Alex shuffled some papers around, but he knew that he wouldn't be troubling Lord Justice Browne again.

'Please carry on with your submission, Mr Redmayne,' the judge offered helpfully.

Alex continued defiantly with the little new evidence he had left at his disposal, but he could no longer call on anything that caused Lord Justice Browne even to raise an eyebrow. When Alex finally resumed his place, he cursed himself under his breath. He should have released the tape to the press the day before the appeal was due to be heard, and then the judge would have had no choice but to consider the conversation to be admissible as fresh evidence. But Lord Justice Browne proved too wily a customer to allow Alex even to press the play button.

His father had later pointed out that if their lordships had heard so much as one sentence, they would have had no choice but to listen to the whole tape. They hadn't heard one word, let alone a sentence.

The three judges retired at twelve thirty-seven, and it was only a short time before they returned with a unanimous verdict. Alex lowered his head when Lord Justice Browne uttered the words, 'Appeal dismissed.'

He looked across at Danny, who had just been condemned to spend the next twenty years of his life in jail for a crime Alex was now certain he did not commit.

30

SEVERAL OF THE GUESTS were on their third or fourth glass of champagne by the time Lawrence Davenport appeared on the staircase of the crowded ballroom. He didn't move from the top step until he was satisfied that most of them had turned to gaze in his direction. A smattering of applause broke out. He smiled and waved a hand in acknowledgement. A glass of champagne was thrust into his other hand with the words, 'You were magnificent, darling.'

When the curtain fell, the first-nighters had given the cast a standing ovation, but that would not have come as a surprise to any regular theatregoers because they always do. After all, the first eight rows are usually filled with the cast's family, friends and agents and the next six with comps and hangers-on. Only a seasoned critic would fail to rise the moment the curtain fell, unless it was to leave quickly so that they could file their piece in time to catch the first edition the following morning.

Davenport slowly looked around the room. His eyes settled on his sister Sarah, who was chatting to Gibson Graham.

'How do you think the critics will react?' Sarah asked Larry's agent.

'They'll be sniffy,' said Gibson, puffing away on his cigar. 'They always are when a soap star appears in the West End. But as we've got an advance of nearly three hundred thousand pounds and it's only a fourteen-week run, we're critic-proof. It's bums on seats that matter, Sarah, not the critics.'

'Has Larry got anything else lined up?'

'Not at the moment,' Gibson admitted. 'But I'm confident that after tonight there will be no shortage of enquiries.'

'Larry, well done,' said Sarah as her brother walked over to join them.

'What a triumph,' added Gibson, raising his glass.

'Do you really think so?' asked Davenport.

'Oh yes,' said Sarah, who understood her brother's insecurities better than anyone. 'In any case, Gibson tells me that you're almost booked out for the entire run.'

'True, but I still worry about the critics,' said Davenport. 'They've never been kind to me in the past.'

'Don't give them a thought,' said Gibson. 'It doesn't matter what they say – the show's going to be a sell-out.'

Davenport scanned the room to see who he wanted to talk to next. His eyes rested on Spencer Craig and Gerald Payne, who were standing in the far corner, deep in conversation.

◄○►

'It looks as if our little investment will pay off,' said Craig. 'Doubly.'

'Doubly?' said Payne.

'Not only did Larry clam up the moment he was offered the chance to appear in the West End, but with an advance of three hundred thousand, we're certain to get our money back, and possibly even show a small profit. And now that Cartwright has lost his appeal, we won't have to worry about him for at least another twenty years,' Craig added with a chuckle.

'I'm still worried about the tape,' said Payne. 'I'd be far more relaxed if I knew it no longer existed.'

'It's no longer relevant,' said Craig.

'But what if the papers got hold of it?' said Payne.

'The papers won't dare to go anywhere near it.'

'But that wouldn't stop it being published on the internet, which could be every bit as damaging for both of us.'

'You keep worrying yourself unnecessarily,' said Craig.

'Not a night goes by when I don't worry about it,' said Payne. 'I wake up every morning wondering if my face will be plastered across the front pages.'

'I don't think it would be *your* face that ended up on the front pages,' said Craig as Davenport appeared by his side. 'Congratulations, Larry. You were quite brilliant.'

'My agent tells me that you both invested in the show,' said Davenport.

'You bet we did,' said Craig. 'We know a winner when we see one. In fact, we're going to spend part of the profits on the Musketeers' annual bash.'

Two young men came up to Davenport, happy to confirm his own opinion of himself, which gave Craig the opportunity to slip away.

As he circulated around the room, he caught a glimpse of Sarah Davenport talking to a short, balding, overweight man who was smoking a cigar. She was even more beautiful than he remembered. He wondered if the man puffing away on the cigar was her partner. When she turned in his direction, Craig smiled at her, but she didn't respond. Perhaps she hadn't seen him. In his opinion she had always been better looking than Larry and after their one night together . . . He walked across to join her. He would know in a moment if Larry had confided in her.

'Hello, Spencer,' she said. Craig bent down to kiss her on both cheeks. 'Gibson,' said Sarah, 'this is Spencer Craig, an old friend of Larry's from university days. Spencer, this is Gibson Graham, Larry's agent.'

'You invested in the show, didn't you?' said Gibson.

'A modest amount,' admitted Craig.

'I never thought of you as an angel,' said Sarah.

'I've always backed Larry,' said Craig, 'but then I never doubted he was going to be a star.'

'You've become something of a star yourself,' said Sarah with a smile.

'Then I'm bound to ask,' said Craig, 'if you feel that way, why you never brief me?'

'I don't deal with criminals.'

'I hope that won't stop you having dinner with me some time, because I'd like—'

'The first editions of the papers have arrived,' interrupted

Gibson. 'Excuse me while I find out if we've got a hit, or just a winner.'

Gibson Graham made his way quickly across the ballroom, barging anyone aside who was foolish enough to stand in his path. He grabbed a copy of the *Daily Telegraph* and turned to the review section. He smiled when he saw the headline: *Oscar Wilde is still at home in the West End*. But the smile turned to a frown by the time he reached the second paragraph:

> Lawrence Davenport gave us his usual stock performance, this time as Jack, but it didn't seem to matter as the audience was littered with Dr Beresford fans. In contrast, Eve Best, playing Gwendolen Fairfax, sparkled from her first entrance . . .

Gibson looked across at Davenport, pleased to see that he was deep in conversation with a young actor who had been resting for some time.

31

By the time they reached his cell, the damage had been done. The table had been smashed to pieces, the mattresses torn apart, the sheets ripped to shreds and the little steel mirror wrenched from the wall. As Mr Hagen heaved open the door, he found Danny trying to pull the washbasin from its stand. Three officers came charging towards him, and he took a swing at Hagen. If the punch had landed it would have felled a middleweight champion, but Hagen ducked just in time. The second officer grabbed Danny's arm, while the third kicked him sharply in the back of the knee, which gave Hagen enough time to recover and cuff his arms and legs while his colleagues held him down.

They dragged him out of his cell and bounced him down the iron staircase, keeping him on the move until they reached the purple corridor that led to the segregation unit. They came to a numberless cell. Hagen opened the door and the other two threw him in.

Danny lay still on the cold stone floor for some considerable time. Had there been a mirror in the cell, he would have been able to admire his black eye and the patchwork quilt of bruises that was woven across his body. He didn't care; you don't, when you've lost hope and have another twenty years to think about it.

─◄○►─

'My name is Malcolm Hurst,' said the representative from the Parole Board. 'Please have a seat, Mr Moncrieff.'

Hurst had given some thought to how he should address the

prisoner. 'You have applied for parole, Mr Moncrieff,' he began, 'and it is my responsibility to write a report for the board's consideration. Of course I have read your case history, which gives a full account of how you have conducted yourself while you've been in prison, and your wing officer, Mr Pascoe, has described your behaviour as exemplary.' Nick remained silent.

'I have also noted that you are an enhanced prisoner, who works in the library as well as assisting the prison teaching staff in both English and History. You seem to have had remarkable success with some of your fellow prisoners, who have gone on to be awarded GCSEs, and one in particular, who is currently pre-paring to take three A levels.'

Nick nodded sadly. Pascoe had tipped him off that Danny had lost his appeal and was on his way back from the Old Bailey. He had wanted to be waiting in the cell when Danny arrived, but unfortunately the Parole Board had scheduled the interview some weeks ago.

Nick had already resolved to be in touch with Alex Redmayne as soon as he was released, and to offer to assist in any way possible. He couldn't understand why the judge hadn't allowed the tape to be played. No doubt Danny would tell him the reason once he returned to his cell. He tried to concentrate on what the representative from the Parole Board was saying.

'I see that during your time in prison, Mr Moncrieff, you have taken an Open University degree in English, gaining a two-two.' Nick nodded. 'While your record in prison is highly commend-able, I'm sure you'll understand that I still have to ask you some questions before I can complete my report.'

Nick had already taken advice from Pascoe on what those questions might be. 'Of course,' he replied.

'You were convicted by an army board of being reckless and negligent during the course of duty, to which you pleaded guilty. The board stripped you of your commission, and sentenced you to eight years in prison. Is that a fair assessment?'

'Yes it is, Mr Hurst.'

Hurst placed a tick in the first box. 'Your platoon was guarding a group of Serbian prisoners when a band of Albanian militia drove up to the compound firing their Kalashnikovs in the air.'

'That's correct.'

'Your staff sergeant retaliated.'

'Warning shots,' said Nick, 'after I had given the insurgents a clear order to stop firing.'

'But two United Nations observers who witnessed the whole incident gave evidence at your trial suggesting that the Albanians were only firing their guns in the air at the time.' Nick made no attempt to defend himself. 'And although you did not fire a shot yourself, you were the watch commander on that occasion.'

'I was.'

'And you accept that your sentence was just.'

'Yes.'

Hurst made a further note before asking, 'And were the board to recommend that you should be released having served only half of your sentence, what plans do you have for the immediate future?'

'I intend to return to Scotland, where I would take up a teaching post in any school that will employ me.'

Hurst put another tick in another box before moving on to his next question. 'Do you have any financial problems that might prevent you taking up a teaching post?'

'No,' said Nick, 'on the contrary. My grandfather has left me sufficiently well off to ensure that I need not work again.'

Hurst ticked another box. 'Are you married, Mr Moncrieff?'

'No,' said Nick.

'Do you have any children, or other dependants?'

'No.'

'Are you currently on any medication?'

'No.'

'If you were to be released, do you have a home to go to?'

'Yes, I have a house in London and another in Scotland.'

'Do you have any family to assist you were you to be released?'

'No,' said Nick. Hurst looked up; this was the first box not to be ticked. 'Both my parents are dead, and I have no brothers or sisters.'

'Aunts or uncles?'

'One uncle and aunt who live in Scotland, whom I have never been close to, and another aunt on my mother's side, who lives in Canada, and whom I have corresponded with but never met.'

'I understand,' said Hurst. 'One final question, Mr Moncrieff. It may seem a little strange given your circumstances, but nevertheless I have to ask it. Can you think of any reason why you might consider committing the same crime again?'

'As I am unable to resume my career in the army, and indeed have no desire to do so, the answer to your question has to be no.'

'I fully understand,' said Hurst, placing a tick in the last box. 'Finally, do you have any questions for me?'

'Only to ask when I'll be informed of the board's decision.'

'It will take me a few days to write my report before I submit it to the board,' said Hurst, 'but once they've received it, it should be no more than a couple of weeks before they're in touch with you.'

'Thank you, Mr Hurst.'

'Thank you, Sir Nicholas.'

—◦—

'We didn't have any choice, sir,' said Pascoe.

'I'm sure that's right, Ray,' said the governor, 'but I do think a little common sense is called for with this particular prisoner.'

'What do you have in mind, sir?' asked Pascoe. 'After all, he did trash his cell.'

'I'm aware of that, Ray, but we all know how lifers can react if their appeal is turned down: they either become silent loners, or tear the place apart.'

'A few days in the slammer will bring Cartwright to his senses,' said Pascoe.

'Let's hope so,' said Barton, 'because I'd like to get him back on an even keel as quickly as possible. He's a bright lad. I'd hoped he'd be Moncrieff's natural successor.'

'The obvious choice, although he'll automatically lose his enhanced status and have to return to basic.'

'That need only be for a month,' said the governor.

'In the meantime,' said Pascoe, 'what do I do about his work category? Do I take him off education and put him back on the chain gang?'

'Heaven forbid,' said Barton. 'That would be more of a punishment for us than it would be for him.'

'What about his canteen rights?'

'No pay and no canteen for four weeks.'

'Right, sir,' said Pascoe.

'And have a word with Moncrieff. He's Cartwright's closest friend. See if he can knock some sense into him, as well as supporting him over the next few weeks.'

'Will do, sir.'

'Who's next?'

'Leach, sir.'

'What's the charge this time?'

'Failure to return a library book.'

'Can't you deal with something as minor as that without involving me?' asked the governor.

'In normal circumstances yes, sir, but in this case it was a valuable leather-bound copy of the *Law Review*, which Leach failed to return despite several verbal and written warnings.'

'I still don't see why he needs to come in front of me,' said Barton.

'Because when we eventually found the book in a rubbish skip at the back of the block, it had been torn apart.'

'Why would he do that?'

'I have my suspicions, sir, but no proof.'

'Another way of getting drugs in?'

'As I said, sir, I have no proof. But Leach is back in segregation for another month, just in case he takes it upon himself to tear the whole library apart.' Pascoe hesitated. 'We have another problem.'

'Namely?'

'One of my informers tells me he overheard Leach saying he was going to get even with Cartwright, if it was the last thing he did.'

'Because he's the librarian?'

'No, something to do with a tape,' replied Pascoe, 'but I can't get to the bottom of it.'

'That's all I need,' said the governor. 'You'd better keep a twenty-four-hour watch on both of them.'

'We're pretty short-staffed at the moment,' said Pascoe.

'Then do the best you can. I don't want a repeat of what happened to the poor bastard at Garside – and all he did was give Leach a V sign.'

32

DANNY LAY ON the top bunk composing a letter which he'd given a great deal of thought to. Nick had tried to talk him out of it, but he had made his decision and there was nothing that would change his mind.

Nick was taking a shower and Big Al was over at the hospital helping sister with the evening surgery, so Danny had the cell to himself. He climbed down from his bunk and took a seat at the small formica table. He stared at a blank sheet of paper. It was some time before he managed to write the first sentence.

> Dear Beth,
>
> This will be the last time I write to you. I have given a great deal of thought to this letter and have come to the conclusion that I cannot condemn you to the same life sentence that has been imposed on me.

He glanced at the photograph of Beth that was sellotaped to the wall in front of him.

> As you know, I am not due to be released until I'm fifty and with that in mind, I want you to start a new life without me. If you write to me again, I will not open your letters; if you try to visit, I will remain in my cell; I will not contact you, and will not respond to any attempt you make to contact me. On this I am adamant, and nothing will change my mind.
>
> Do not imagine even for a moment that I don't love you and Christy, because I do, and I will for the rest of my life.

But I am in no doubt that this course of action will be best for both of us in the long run.
Goodbye, my love
Danny

He folded the letter and placed it in an envelope which he addressed to Beth Wilson, 27 Bacon Road, Bow, London E3.

Danny was still staring at the photograph of Beth when the cell door swung open.

'Letters,' said an officer standing in the doorway. 'One for Moncrieff, and one for . . .' he spotted the watch on Danny's wrist and the silver chain round his neck and hesitated.

'Nick's taking a shower,' Danny explained.

'Right,' said the officer. 'There's one for you, and one for Moncrieff.'

Danny immediately recognized Beth's neat handwriting. He didn't open the envelope, just tore it up, dropped the pieces into the lavatory and pulled the flush. He placed the other envelope on Nick's pillow.

Printed in bold letters in the top left-hand corner were the words 'Parole Board'.

—◦—

'How many times have I written to him?' asked Alex Redmayne.

'This will be the fourth letter you've sent in the past month,' replied his secretary.

Alex looked out of the window. Several gowned figures were rushing to and fro across the square. 'Lifer's syndrome,' he said.

'Lifer's syndrome?'

'You either cut yourself off from the outside world, or carry on as if nothing has happened. He's obviously decided to cut himself off.'

'So is there any point in writing to him again?'

'Oh yes,' replied Alex. 'I want him to be left in no doubt that I haven't forgotten him.'

—◦—

When Nick came back from the shower room, Danny was still at the table going over some financial forecasts that were part of his A level in business studies, while Big Al remained slumped on his bed. Nick strolled into the cell with a thin wet towel round his waist, his flip-flops making water marks on the stone floor. Danny stopped writing and handed him back his watch, ring and silver chain.

'Thanks,' said Nick. He then spotted the thin brown envelope on his pillow. For a moment he just stared at it. Danny and Big Al said nothing as they waited to see Nick's reaction. Finally he grabbed a plastic knife and slit open an envelope that the prison authorities were not allowed to tamper with.

> Dear Mr Moncrieff,
>   I am directed by the Parole Board to inform you that your request for early release has been granted. Your sentence will therefore be terminated on July 17th 2002. The full details of your release and your parole conditions will be sent to you at a later date, along with the name of your probation officer and the office you will be expected to report to.
>   Yours sincerely,
>   T. L. Williams

Nick looked up at his two cellmates, but he didn't need to tell them that he would soon be a free man.

◄○►

'Visits!' hollered a voice that could be heard from one side of the block to the other. A few moments later the cell door swung open and an officer checked his clipboard. 'You've got a visitor, Cartwright. Same young lady as last week.' Danny turned another page of *Bleak House* and just shook his head.

'Suit yourself,' said the officer, and slammed the cell door closed.

Nick and Big Al didn't comment. They had both given up trying to make him change his mind.

33

HE HAD CHOSEN the day carefully, even the hour, but what he couldn't have planned was that the minute would fall so neatly into place.

The governor had decided the day, and the senior officer had backed his judgement. On this occasion an exception would be made. The prisoners would be allowed out of their cells to watch the World Cup match between England and Argentina.

At five minutes to twelve, the doors were unlocked and the prisoners flooded out of their cells, all heading in one direction. Big Al, as a patriotic Scot, gruffly declined the opportunity to watch the old enemy in action and remained supine on his bunk.

Danny was among those seated at the front, staring attentively at an ancient square box, waiting for the referee to blow his whistle and start the game. All the prisoners were clapping and shouting long before the kick-off, with one exception, who was standing silently at the back of the group. He wasn't looking at the television, but up at an open cell door on the first floor. He didn't move. Officers don't notice prisoners who don't move. He was beginning to wonder if the man had broken his usual routine because of the match. But he wasn't watching the match. His mate was sitting on a bench at the front, so he must still be in his cell.

After thirty minutes, with the score nil–nil, there was still no sign of him.

Then, just before the referee blew his whistle for half-time, an English player was brought down in the Argentine penalty area. The crowd surrounding the TV seemed to make almost as much noise as the thirty-five thousand spectators in the stadium, and even some of the officers joined in. Background noise was all part of his plan. His eyes remained fixed on the open door when suddenly, without warning, the rabbit came out of his hutch. He was wearing boxer shorts and flip-flops with a towel draped over his shoulder. He didn't look down; he clearly had no interest in football.

He walked backwards for a few paces until he had detached himself from the group, but nobody noticed. He turned and walked slowly to the far end of the block, then climbed stealthily up the spiral staircase to the first floor. No one looked round as the referee pointed to the penalty spot.

When he reached the top step he checked to see if anyone had noticed him leave. No one even glanced in his direction. The Argentine players were surrounding the referee and protesting, while the England captain picked up the ball and walked calmly into the penalty box.

He came to a halt outside the shower room, and peered inside to discover it was steamed up; all part of his plan. He stepped inside, relieved to find that only one person was taking a shower. He padded silently over to the wooden bench on the far side of the room, where a single towel lay neatly folded in the corner. He picked it up and carefully twisted it into a noose. The prisoner standing under the shower rubbed some shampoo into his hair.

Everyone on the ground floor had gone silent. There was not a murmur as David Beckham placed the ball on the penalty spot. Some even held their breath as he took a few paces back.

The man in the shower room took a few paces forward as Beckham's right foot connected with the ball. The roar that followed sounded like a prison riot, with all the officers joining in.

The prisoner who was rinsing his hair under the shower opened his eyes when he heard the roar, and immediately had to place a hand across his forehead to stop more lather running into his eyes. He was just about to step out of the shower and grab his towel from the bench when a knee landed in his groin with such force that Beckham would have been impressed, followed by a clenched fist into the middle of his ribs which propelled him against the tiled wall. He tried to retaliate, but a forearm was rammed into his throat, and another hand grabbed his hair and jerked his head back. One swift movement, and although no one heard the bone snap, when he was released his body sank to the ground like a puppet whose strings had been cut.

His attacker bent down and carefully placed the noose round his neck, then with all the strength he possessed lifted the dead man up and held him against the wall while he tied the other end of the towel to the shower rail. He slowly lowered the body into place and stood back for a moment to admire his handiwork. He returned to the entrance of the shower room and poked his head round the doorway to check what was going on down below. The celebrations were now out of control, and any officers were fully occupied making sure that the prisoners didn't start breaking up the furniture.

He moved like a ferret, making his way swiftly and silently back down the spiral staircase, ignoring the dripping water that would have dried long before the match came to an end. He was back in his cell in less than a minute. Laid out on his bed were a towel, a clean T-shirt and a pair of jeans, a fresh pair of socks and his Adidas trainers. He quickly stripped off his wet gear, dried himself and put on the clean clothes. He then checked his hair in the little steel mirror on the wall before slipping back out of the cell.

The prisoners were now impatiently waiting for the second half to begin. He joined his fellow inmates unnoticed, and slowly, a pace here, a sideways move there, made his way to the centre of the melee. For most of the second half the crowd were urging the referee to whistle for full time so that England could leave the pitch as one–nil winners.

When the final whistle eventually blew, there was another eruption of noise. Several officers shouted, 'Back to your cells,' but the response was not immediate.

He turned and walked purposefully towards one particular officer, knocking against his elbow as he passed by.

'Look where you're going, Leach,' said Pascoe.

'Sorry, guv,' said Leach, and continued on his way.

◄○►

Danny made his way back upstairs. He knew that Big Al would have already reported to surgery, but he was surprised that Nick wasn't in the cell. He sat down at the table and stared at the photo of Beth still sellotaped to the wall. It brought back memories of Bernie. They would have been at their local watching the match together, if . . . Danny tried to concentrate on the essay that had to be handed in by tomorrow, but he just went on looking at the photo, trying to convince himself that he didn't miss her.

Suddenly the shriek of a klaxon echoed around the block, accompanied by the sound of officers screaming 'Back to your cells!' Moments later the cell door was pulled open and an officer stuck his head in. 'Moncrieff, where's Big Al?'

Danny didn't bother to correct him – after all, he was still wearing Nick's watch, ring and silver chain, which had been given to him for safekeeping – and simply said, 'He'll be at work in the hospital.'

When the door slammed shut, Danny wondered why he hadn't asked where *he* was. It was impossible to concentrate on his essay with so much noise going on all around him. He assumed some overexuberant prisoner was being carted off to seg-regation in the aftermath of the English victory. A few minutes later the door was pulled opened again by the same officer, and Big Al ambled in.

'Hello, Nick,' he said in a loud voice before the door was slammed shut.

'What's your game?' asked Danny.

Big Al placed a finger on his lips, walked across to the lavatory and sat down on it.

'They cannae see me while I'm sitting here, so look like yur working and don't turn roon.'

'But why—'

'And don't open yer mooth, just listen.' Danny picked up his pen and pretended to be concentrating on his essay. 'Nick's topped himself.'

Danny thought he was going to be sick. 'But why—' he repeated.

'I said don't speak. They found him hangin' in the showers.'

Danny began to pound the table with his fist. 'It can't be true.'

'Shut up, ya stupid fucker, and listen. I wis in surgery when two screws came rushing in – one of them said, "Sister, come quickly, Cartwright's topped himself." I knew that wis balls, 'cause I'd seen ye at the football a few minutes before. It hud tae be Nick. He always uses the shower when he's least likely tae be disturbed.'

'But why—'

'Don't worry about why, Danny boy,' Big Al said firmly. 'The screws and the sister ran off, so I was left on ma own fur a few minutes. Then another screw turns up and marches mi back here.' Danny was now listening intently. 'He told me it wis you who'd committed suicide.'

'But they'll find out it wasn't me as soon as—'

'No, they won't,' said Big Al, 'because I hud enough time tae switch the names on yer two files.'

'You did what?' said Danny in disbelief.

'You heard me.'

'But I thought you told me the files are always locked up?'

'They are, but no during surgery, in case sister needs tae check on someone's medication. And she left in a hurry.' Big Al stopped talking when he heard someone in the corridor outside. 'Keep writing,' he said, and stood up, returned to his bed and lay down. An eye peered through the spyhole then moved on to the next cell.

'But why did you do that?' Danny asked.

'Wance they check his fingerprints and his blood group, they're gonnae go on thinkin it's you who topped himself because ye couldnae face another twenty years in this shite-hole.'

'But Nick had no reason to hang himself.'

'I know,' said Big Al. 'But as long as they think it wis you on the end ay that rope, there's no gonnae be an inquiry.'

'But that doesn't explain why you switched . . .' began Danny. He went silent for some time, before adding, 'So I can walk out of here a free man in six weeks' time.'

'Ye catch on fast, Danny boy.'

The blood drained from Danny's face as the consequences of Big Al's impetuous action began to sink in. He stared at the photo of Beth. He still wouldn't be able to see her, even if he did manage to escape. He'd have to spend the rest of his life pretending to be Nick Moncrieff. 'You didn't think of asking me first?' he said.

'If I hud, it would've been too late. Don't forget, there are only aboot half a dozen people in this place who cin tell ye apart, and wance they've checked the files, even they're gonnae be programmed tae thinking yur died.'

'But what if we're caught?'

'Ye'll carry on serving a life sentence, an I'll lose ma job in the hospital and go back tae being a wing cleaner. Big deal.'

Danny was silent again for some time. Eventually he said, 'I'm not sure I can pull it off, but if, and I mean if—'

'Nae time for ifs, Danny boy. Ye've probably got twenty-four hours before that cell door opens again, by which time ye'll huv tae decide if yer Danny Cartwright, serving another twenty years for a crime ye didnae commit, or Sir Nicholas Moncrieff, due for release in six weeks' time. And let's face it, ye'll huv a far better chance of clearing yer name wance you're on the ootside – not tae mention getting those bastards who murdered yer mate.'

'I need time to think,' said Danny as he began to climb up on to the top bunk.

'No fur too long,' said Big Al. 'Remember Nick always slept on the bottom bunk.'

34

'NICK WAS FIVE MONTHS older than me,' said Danny, 'and half an inch shorter.'

'How dae ye know that?' asked Big Al nervously.

'It's all in his diaries,' replied Danny. 'I've just reached the point where I turn up in this cell and you two have to decide what story you're going to tell me.' Big Al frowned. 'I've been blind for the past two years, when all the time it was staring me in the face.' Big Al still didn't speak. 'You were the staff sergeant who shot those two Kosovan Albanians when Nick's platoon was ordered to guard a group of Serbian prisoners.'

'Wurse,' said Big Al. 'It wis efter Captain Moncrieff hud given a clear order no tae fire till he'd issued a warnin' in both English and Serbo-Croat.'

'And you chose to ignore that order.'

'There's nae point issuing warnings tae someone who's already firing at ye.'

'But two UN observers told the court martial that the Albanians were only firing their weapons into the air.'

'An observation made fae the safety of their hotel suite on the other side of the square.'

'And Nick ended up carrying the can.'

'Aye,' said Big Al. 'Despite the fact that I told the provost marshal exactly whit happened, they chose tae take Nick's word over mine.'

'Which resulted in you being charged with manslaughter.'

'An only being sentenced tae ten years rather than twenty-two for murder with nae hope of remission.'

'Nick writes a lot about your courage, and how you saved half the platoon, including himself, while you were serving in Iraq.'

'He exaggerated.'

'Not his style,' said Danny, 'although it does explain why he was willing to shoulder the blame, even though you had disobeyed his orders.'

'I told the court martial the truth,' repeated Big Al, 'but they still stripped Nick of his commission and sentenced him tae eight years fur being reckless and negligent in the course of his duty. Do ye imagine a day goes by when I don't think aboot the sacrifice he made fur me? But I'm certain of wan thing – he wouldae wanted ye tae take his place.'

'How can you be so sure?'

'Read on, Danny boy, read on.'

◄○►

'Something doesn't ring quite true about this whole episode,' said Ray Pascoe.

'What are you getting at?' asked the governor. 'You know as well as I do that it's not uncommon for a lifer to commit suicide within days of his appeal being turned down.'

'But not Cartwright. He had too much to live for.'

'We can't begin to know what was going on in his mind,' said the governor. 'Don't forget that he tore his cell apart and ended up in segregation. He also refused to see his fiancée or his child whenever they turned up for a visit – wouldn't even open her letters.'

'True. But is it just a coincidence that this happens within days of Leach threatening to get even with him?'

'You wrote in your latest report that there's been no contact between the two of them since the library-book incident.'

'That's what worries me,' said Pascoe. 'If you intended to kill someone, the last thing you'd do is be seen anywhere near them.'

'The doctor has confirmed that Cartwright died of a broken neck.'

'Leach is quite capable of breaking someone's neck.'

'Because he didn't return a library book?'

'And ended up in segregation for a month,' said Pascoe.

'What about that tape you've been banging on about?'

Pascoe shook his head. 'I'm none the wiser on that subject,' he admitted. 'It's still just a gut feeling . . .'

'You'd better have a little more to go on than a gut feeling, Ray, if you expect me to open a full inquiry.'

'A few minutes before the body was found, Leach bumped into me quite purposely.'

'So what?' said the governor.

'He was wearing a brand new pair of trainers.'

'Is this leading somewhere?'

'I noticed that he was wearing his blue prison gym shoes when the match started, so how come he was wearing brand-new Adidas trainers when it ended? It doesn't add up.'

'Much as I admire your powers of observation, Ray, that's hardly enough proof to convince me that we need to open an inquiry.'

'His hair was wet.'

'Ray,' said the governor, 'we've got two choices. Either we accept the doctor's report and confirm to our masters at the Home Office that it was suicide, or we call in the police and ask them to mount a full investigation. If it's the latter, I'll need a little more to go on than wet hair and a new pair of trainers.'

'But if Leach—'

'The first question we'd be asked is why, if we knew about Leach's threat to Cartwright, we didn't recommend that he was transferred to another prison the same day.'

There was a gentle tap on the door.

'Come in,' said the governor.

'Sorry to disturb you,' said his secretary, 'but I thought you'd want to see this immediately.' She handed him a sheet of lined prison paper.

He read the short note twice before passing it across to Ray Pascoe.

'Now that's what I call proof,' said the governor.

—◦—

Payne was showing a client round a penthouse apartment in Mayfair when his mobile phone began to ring. He would normally have switched it off whenever he was with a potential buyer, but when the name Spencer appeared on the screen he excused himself for a moment and went into the next room to take the call.

'Good news,' said Craig. 'Cartwright's dead.'

'Dead?'

'He committed suicide – he was found hanging in the showers.'

'How do you know?'

'It's on page seventeen of the *Evening Standard*. He even left a suicide note, so that's the end of our problems.'

'Not while that tape still exists,' Payne reminded him.

'No one is going to be interested in a tape of one dead man talking about another.'

—◦—

The cell door swung open and Pascoe walked in. He stared at Danny for some time, but didn't speak. Danny looked up from the diary; he'd reached the date of Nick's interview with Hurst from the Parole Board. The same day his appeal had been turned down. The day he trashed the cell and ended up in segregation.

'OK, lads, grab a meal and then get back to work. And, Moncrieff,' said Pascoe, 'I'm sorry about your friend Cartwright. I for one never thought he was guilty.' Danny tried to think of a suitable reply, but Pascoe was already unlocking the next door cell.

'He knows,' said Big Al quietly.

'Then we're done for,' said Danny.

'I don't think so,' said Big Al. 'Fur some reason he's gon' along wi' the suicide, an ma bet is that he's no the only wan who's got his doubts. By the way, Nick, whit made ye change yer mind?'

Danny picked up the diary, flicked back a few pages and read out the words: *If I could change places with Danny, I would. He has far more right to his freedom than I do.*

35

DANNY STOOD as inconspicuously as possible at the back of the churchyard as Father Michael raised his right hand and gave the sign of the cross.

The governor had granted Nick's request to attend Danny Cartwright's funeral at St Mary's in Bow. He turned down a similar application from Big Al on the grounds that he still had at least fourteen months to serve, and had not yet been granted parole.

As the unmarked car had swung into Mile End Road, Danny looked out of the window, checking for familiar sights. They passed his favourite chippie, his local, the Crown and Garter, and the Odeon where he and Beth used to sit in the back row every Friday night. When they stopped at the lights outside Clement Attlee comprehensive, he clenched his fist as he thought of the wasted years he had spent there.

He tried not to look when they passed Wilson's garage, but he couldn't stop himself. There were few signs of life in the little yard. It would take more than a fresh coat of paint to make anyone think about buying a second-hand car from Wilson's. He turned his attention to Monty Hughes's place on the other side of the road: row upon row of gleaming new Mercedes with smartly dressed salesmen displaying cheerful smiles.

The governor had reminded Moncrieff that although he had only five weeks left to serve, he would still have to be accompanied by two officers, who would never leave his side. And if he were to disobey any of the strictures placed upon him, the governor would not hesitate to recommend to the Parole Board that they rescind their decision for an early release, which would result in him having to serve another four years.

'But you already know all this,' Michael Barton had gone on to say, 'because the same strictures were placed on you when you attended your father's funeral just a couple of months ago.' Danny didn't comment.

The governor's strictures, as he called them, rather suited Danny, as he was not allowed to mix with the Cartwright family, their friends or any members of the public. In fact, he was not permitted to speak to anyone other than the accompanying officers until he was back inside the prison walls. The possibility of another four years in Belmarsh was quite enough to concentrate the mind.

Pascoe and Jenkins stood on either side of him, some way back from the mourners who surrounded the grave. Danny was relieved to find that Nick's clothes might have been tailor-made for him – well, perhaps the trousers could have been an inch longer, and although he had never worn a hat before, it had the advantage of shielding his face from any curious onlookers.

Father Michael opened the service with a prayer while Danny watched a gathering that was far larger than he had anticipated. His mother looked pale and drawn, as if she had been weeping for days, and Beth was so thin that a dress he well remembered now hung loosely on her, no longer emphasizing her graceful figure. Only his two-year-old daughter, Christy, was oblivious to the occasion as she played quietly by her mother's side; but then, she had only ever come into contact with her dad briefly, followed by month-long intervals, so she'd probably long forgotten him. Danny hoped that the only memory of her father wouldn't be of visiting him in prison.

Danny was touched to see Beth's father standing by her side, head bowed, and just behind the family, a tall elegant young man in a black suit, lips pursed, a look of smouldering anger in his eyes. Danny suddenly felt guilty that he hadn't replied to any of Alex Redmayne's letters since the appeal.

When Father Michael had finished intoning the prayers, he bowed his head before delivering his eulogy. 'The death of Danny Cartwright is a modern tragedy,' he told his parishioners as he looked down at the coffin. 'A young man who had lost his way, and so troubled was he in this world that he took his own life. Those of us who knew Danny well still find it hard to believe that such a gentle, considerate man could have committed any crime, let alone the slaying of his closest friend. Indeed, many of us in this parish,' he glanced at an innocent constable standing by the entrance to the church, 'have still to be convinced that the police arrested the right person.' A smattering of applause broke out among some of the mourners encircling the grave. Danny was pleased to see that Beth's father was among them.

Father Michael raised his head. 'But for now, let us remember the son, the young father, the gifted leader and sportsman, for many of us believe that had Danny Cartwright lived, his name would have echoed far beyond the streets of Bow.' Applause broke out a second time. 'But that was not the Lord's will, and in His divine mystery He chose to take our son away, to spend the rest of his days with our saviour.' The priest sprinkled holy water around the grave and, as the coffin was lowered into the ground, he began to intone, 'May eternal rest be granted unto Danny, O Lord.'

As the young choir softly chanted the 'Nunc Dimittis', Father Michael, Beth and the rest of the Cartwright family knelt by the graveside. Alex Redmayne along with several other mourners waited behind to pay their last respects. Alex bowed his head as if in prayer, and spoke a few words that neither Danny nor anyone else present could hear: 'I will clear your name so that you may finally rest in peace.'

Danny wasn't allowed to move until the last mourners had departed, including Beth and Christy, who never once looked in his direction. When Pascoe finally turned to tell Moncrieff that they should leave, he found him in tears. Danny wanted to explain that his tears were shed not only for his dear friend Nick, but for the privilege of being one of those rare individuals who discover how much they are loved by those closest to them.

36

DANNY SPENT every spare moment reading and rereading Nick's diaries, until he felt there was nothing left to know about the man.

Big Al, who had served with Nick for five years before they were both court-martialled and sent to Belmarsh, was able to fill in several gaps, including how Danny should react if he ever bumped into an officer of the Cameron Highlanders, and he also taught him how to spot the regimental tie at thirty paces. They endlessly discussed the first thing Nick would have done the moment he was released.

'He'd go straight up tae Scotland,' said Big Al.

'But all I'll have is forty-five pounds and a rail voucher.'

'Mr Munro will be able tae sort all that oot fur ye. Don't forget that Nick said ye'd huv handled him far better than he did.'

'If I'd been him.'

'Ye ur him,' said Big Al, 'thanks to Louis and Nick, who between them huv done a brilliant job, so Munro shouldnae be too difficult. Just be sure that when he sees ye fur the first time—'

'The second time.'

' – but he only saw Nick fur an hour, and he'll be expecting tae see Sir Nicholas Moncrieff, not someone he's never met before. The bigger problem will be whit tae dae efter that.'

'I'll come straight back to London,' said Danny.

'Then make sure ye keep away fae the East End.'

'There are millions of Londoners who have never been to the East End,' said Danny with some feeling. 'And although I don't know where The Boltons is, I'm pretty sure it's west of Bow.'

'So whit will ye dae wance yur back in London?'

'After attending my own funeral and having to watch Beth suffer, I'm more determined than ever to ensure that she isn't the only person who knows I didn't kill her brother.'

'Bit like that Frenchman ye told me aboot – whit's his name?'

'Edmond Dantès,' said Danny. 'And like him, I will not be satisfied until I have had revenge on the men whose deceit has ruined my life.'

'Yur gonnae kill them aw?'

'No, that would be too easy. They must suffer, to quote Dumas, *a fate worse than death.* I've had more than enough time to think how I'd go about it.'

'Perhaps ye should add Leach tae that list,' said Big Al.

'Leach? Why should I bother with him?'

'Because I think it wis Leach who killed Nick. I keep asking maself, why would he top hisself six weeks before he wis gonnae be released?'

'But why would Leach kill Nick? If he had a quarrel with anyone, it was me.'

'It was nae Nick he wis efter,' said Big Al. 'Don't forget ye were wearing Nick's silver chain, watch and ring while he wis in the shower.'

'But that means—'

'Leach killed the wrong man.'

'But he can't have wanted to kill me just because I asked him to return a library book.'

'An ended up back in segregation.'

'You think that would be enough to make him murder someone?'

'Perhaps not,' said Big Al. 'But you cin be sure that Craig wouldnae've paid up fur the wrong tape. And I doubt if ye're on Mr Hagen's Christmas card list.'

Danny tried not to think about the fact that he might have been unwittingly responsible for Nick's death.

'But don't worry yersel, Nick. Once you're oot ay here, a fate worse than death isnae whit I huv planned for Leach.'

—◦—

Spencer Craig didn't need to look at the menu, because it was his favourite restaurant. The maitre d' was used to seeing him accompanied by different women – sometimes two or three times in the same week.

'Sorry I'm late,' said Sarah as she sat down opposite him. 'I was held up by a client.'

'You work too hard,' said Craig. 'But then you always did.'

'This particular client always makes an appointment for an hour and then expects me to clear my diary for the rest of the afternoon. I didn't even have time to go home and change.'

'I would never have guessed,' said Craig. 'In any case, I find white blouses, black skirts and black stockings quite irresistible.'

'I see you've lost none of your charm,' said Sarah, as she began to study the menu.

'The food here is excellent,' said Craig. 'I can recommend—'

'I only ever have one course in the evenings,' said Sarah. 'One of my golden rules.'

'I remember your golden rules from Cambridge,' said Craig. 'They're the reason you ended up with a first while I only got a two-one.'

'But you also managed a boxing blue, if I recall?' said Sarah.

'What a good memory you have.'

'Said Little Red Riding Hood. By the way, how's Larry? I haven't seen him since opening night.'

'Nor me,' said Craig. 'But then, he's no longer able to come out and play in the evenings.'

'I hope he wasn't too hurt by those vicious reviews.'

'Can't imagine why he should have been,' said Craig. 'Actors are like barristers – it's only the jury's opinion that matters. I never give a damn what the judge thinks.'

A waiter reappeared by their side. 'I'll have the John Dory,' said Sarah, 'but please no sauce, even on the side.'

'Steak for me, so rare that the blood is almost running,' said Craig. He handed the menu to the waiter and turned his attention back to Sarah.

'It's good to see you after all this time,' he said, 'especially as we didn't part on the best of terms. *Mea culpa.*'

'We're both a little older now,' Sarah replied. 'In fact, aren't you being tipped to be among the youngest QCs of our generation?'

—◄o►—

The cell door swung open, which surprised Danny and Big Al because lock-up had been called over an hour before.

'You put in a written request to see the governor, Moncrieff.'

'Yes, Mr Pascoe,' said Danny, 'if that's possible.'

'He'll give you five minutes at eight o'clock tomorrow morning.' The door slammed without further explanation.

'Ye sound mer like Nick every day,' said Big Al. 'Carry on like this and I'll soon be saluting and calling ye sir.'

'Carry on, sergeant,' said Danny.

Big Al laughed, but then asked, 'How come ye want tae see the governor? Ye're no changing yer mind?'

'No,' said Danny, thinking on his feet. 'There are two young lads in education who would benefit from sharing a cell, as they're both studying the same subject.'

'But cell allocation is Mr Jenkins's responsibility. Why not huv a word wi' him?'

'I would, but there's an added problem,' said Danny, trying to think of one.

'And whit's that?' asked Big Al.

'They've both applied to be the librarian. I was going to suggest to the governor that he appoints two librarians in future, otherwise one of them could end up back on the wing as a cleaner.'

'Good try, Nick, but ye dinnae expect me tae believe that load of bullshit, dae ye?'

'Yes,' said Danny.

'Well, if yur gonnae try and bluff an auld soldier like me, make sure you're no taken by surprise – always have yer story well prepared.'

'So if you'd been asked why you wanted to see the governor,' said Danny, 'how would you have replied?'

'Mind yer own business.'

—◄o►—

'Can I give you a lift home?' asked Craig, as the waiter handed him back his credit card.

'Only if it's not out of your way,' said Sarah.

'I was hoping it would be on my way,' he replied, delivering a well-honed line.

Sarah rose from the table but didn't respond. Craig accompanied her to the door and helped her on with her coat. He then took her by the arm and led her across the road to where his Porsche was parked. He opened the passenger door and admired her legs as she climbed in.

'Cheyne Walk?' he asked.

'How did you know that?' asked Sarah as she fastened her seatbelt.

'Larry told me.'

'But you said—'

Craig turned on the ignition, revved up for several seconds then suddenly shot off. He swung sharply round the first bend, causing Sarah to lurch towards him. His left hand ended up on her thigh. She gently removed it.

'Sorry about that,' said Craig.

'Not a problem,' said Sarah, but she was surprised when he tried the same move as he rounded the next corner, and this time she removed the hand more firmly. Craig didn't try again during the rest of the journey, satisfying himself with small talk until he drew up outside her flat in Cheyne Walk.

Sarah unclipped her seatbelt, expecting Craig to get out and open the door for her, but he leant across and attempted to kiss her. She turned her head away so that his lips only brushed against her cheek. Craig then wrapped an arm firmly round her waist and pulled her towards him. Her breasts were pressed against his chest, and he placed his other hand on her thigh. She tried to push him away, but she had forgotten how strong he was. He smiled at her and attempted to kiss her again. She pretended to give in, leant forward and bit his tongue. He fell back and shouted, 'You bitch!'

This allowed Sarah enough time to open the door, although she quickly discovered just how difficult it was to get out of a Porsche.

She turned back to confront him. 'And to think I was living under the illusion that you might have changed,' she said angrily. She slammed the door, and didn't hear him say, 'I don't know why I bothered. You weren't that good a lay the first time.'

◄◊►

Pascoe marched him into the governor's office.

'Why did you want to see me, Moncrieff?' asked Barton.

'It's a delicate matter,' Danny replied.

'I'm listening,' said the governor.

'It concerns Big Al.'

'Who, if I remember correctly, was a staff sergeant in your platoon?'

'That's right, sir, which is why I feel somewhat responsible for him.'

'Naturally,' said Pascoe. 'After your four years in this place, Moncrieff, we know you're not a nark and will have Crann's best interests at heart. So out with it.'

'I overheard a heated row between Big Al and Leach,' said Danny. 'Of course, it's possible that I'm overreacting, and I'm confident I can keep the lid on it while I'm still around, but if anything were to happen to Big Al after I left, I would feel responsible.'

'Thank you for the warning,' said the governor. 'Mr Pascoe and I have already discussed what we should do about Crann once you've been released. While you're here, Moncrieff,' continued the governor, 'do you have a view on who should be the next librarian?'

'There are two lads, Sedgwick and Potter, who are both well capable of doing the job. I'd split the role between them.'

'You'd have made a good governor, Moncrieff.'

'I think you'll find that I lack the necessary qualifications.'

It was the first time Danny had heard either man laugh. The governor nodded, and Pascoe opened the door so that he could accompany Moncrieff to work.

'Mr Pascoe, perhaps you could remain behind for a moment. I'm sure Moncrieff can find his way to the library without your help.'

'Right, governor.'

'How much longer has Moncrieff got to serve?' asked Barton after Danny had closed the door behind him.

'Ten more days, sir,' said Pascoe.

'Then we'll have to move quickly if we're going to ship Leach out.'

'There is an alternative, sir,' said Pascoe.

―◆―

Hugo Moncrieff tapped his boiled egg with a spoon while he considered the problem. His wife Margaret was sitting at the other end of the table reading the *Scotsman*. They rarely spoke at breakfast; a routine that had been established over many years.

Hugo had already sifted through the morning post. There was a letter from the local golf club and another from the Caledonian Society, along with several circulars which he put on one side, until he finally came across the one he was looking for. He picked up the butter knife, slit the envelope open, extracted the letter and then did what he always did, checked the signature at the bottom of the last page: Desmond Galbraith. He left his egg untouched as he began to consider his lawyer's advice.

At first he smiled, but by the time he had reached the last paragraph he was frowning. Desmond Galbraith was able to confirm that following Hugo's brother's funeral, his nephew, Sir Nicholas, had attended a meeting with his solicitor. Fraser Munro had called Galbraith the following morning, and did not raise the subject of the two mortgages. This led Galbraith to believe that Sir Nicholas would not be disputing Hugo's right to the two million pounds that had been raised using his grandfather's two homes as security. Hugo smiled, removed the top from his egg and took a spoonful. It had taken a lot of persuading to get his brother Angus to agree to take out mortgages on both the estate and his London home without consulting Nick, especially after Fraser Munro had advised so firmly against it. And Hugo had had to move quickly once Angus's doctor confirmed that his brother had only a few weeks to live.

Since Angus had left the regiment, single malt had become his constant companion. Hugo regularly visited Dunbroathy Hall to partake of a wee dram with his brother, and he rarely left before they'd finished the bottle. Towards the end, Angus was willing to sign almost any document placed in front of him: first a mortgage on the London property he rarely visited, followed by another on the estate, which Hugo was able to convince him was in dire need of repair. Finally Hugo persuaded him to end his professional association with Fraser Munro, who in Hugo's opinion had far too great a sway over his brother.

To take over the family's affairs Hugo appointed Desmond Galbraith, a lawyer who believed in abiding by the letter of the law, but took no more than a passing interest in its spirit.

Hugo's final triumph had been Angus's last Will and Testament, which was signed only a few nights before his brother passed away. Hugo had it witnessed by a magistrate who just happened to be the secretary of the local golf club, and the local parish priest.

When Hugo came across an earlier will in which Angus had bequeathed the bulk of the estate to his only son Nicholas, he shredded it, and tried not to show the relief he felt when his brother died just a few months before Nick was due to be released. A reunion and reconciliation between father and son hadn't formed any part of his plans. However, Galbraith had failed to prise out of Mr Munro the original copy of Sir Alexander's earlier will, as the old solicitor had correctly pointed out that he now represented the main beneficiary, Sir Nicholas Moncrieff.

Once he had finished off his first egg, Hugo reread the paragraph of Galbraith's letter that had made him frown. He cursed, which caused his wife to look up from her paper, surprised by this break in their well-ordered routine.

'Nick is claiming that he knows nothing about the key his grandfather left him. How can that be when we've all seen him wearing the damn thing round his neck?'

'He didn't wear it at the funeral,' said Margaret. 'I looked most carefully when he knelt down to pray.'

'Do you think he knows what that key unlocks?' said Hugo.

'He may well do,' Margaret replied, 'but that doesn't mean he knows where to look for it.'

'Father should have told us where he had hidden his collection in the first place.'

'You and your father were hardly on speaking terms towards the end,' Margaret reminded him. 'And he considered Angus to be weak, and far too fond of the bottle.'

'True, but that doesn't solve the problem of the key.'

'Perhaps the time has come for us to resort to more robust tactics.'

'What do you have in mind, old gal?'

'I think the vulgar expression is "putting a tail on him". Once Nick is released, we can have him followed. If he does know where the collection is, he'll lead us straight to it.'

'But I wouldn't know how to . . .' said Hugo.

'Don't even think about it,' said Margaret. 'Leave it all to me.'

'Whatever you say, old gal,' said Hugo as he attacked his second egg.

37

DANNY LAY AWAKE on the lower bunk and thought about everything that had taken place since Nick's death. He couldn't sleep, despite the fact that Big Al wasn't snoring. He knew his last night at Belmarsh would be as long as the first – another night he would never forget.

During the past twenty-four hours, several officers and inmates had dropped in to say goodbye and to wish him luck, confirming just how popular and respected Nick had been.

The reason Big Al wasn't snoring was that he'd been shipped out of Belmarsh the previous morning and transferred to Wayland prison in Norfolk, while Danny had been revising for his A levels in Nick's name. Danny still had the maths papers to look forward to, but was disappointed to have to forgo the English exams as Nick was not taking them. By the time Danny returned to his cell that afternoon, there was no sign of Big Al. It was almost as if he had never existed. Danny hadn't even been given the chance to say goodbye.

By now Big Al would have worked out why Danny had been to see the governor, and he'd be fuming. But Danny knew that he'd calm down once he settled into his C cat, with a television in every cell, food that was almost edible, an opportunity to visit a gym that wasn't overcrowded and, most important of all, being allowed out of his cell fourteen hours a day. Leach had also disappeared, but no one knew where, and few cared enough to ask a second time.

During the past few weeks Danny had begun to form a plan in his mind, but in his mind it had remained, because he couldn't risk committing anything to paper. If he was discovered, it would condemn him to another twenty years in hell. He slept.

He woke. His first thought was of Bernie, who had been robbed of his life by Craig and the misnamed Musketeers. His second was of Nick, who had made it possible for him to be given another chance. His final thoughts were of Beth, when he was reminded once again that the decision had made it impossible for him ever to see her again.

He began to think about tomorrow. Once he'd had his meeting with Fraser Munro and tried to sort out Nick's immediate problems in Scotland, he would return to London and put into motion the plans he'd been working on for the past six weeks. He'd become realistic about the chances of clearing his name, but that wouldn't stop him seeking justice of a different kind – what the Bible called retribution, and what Edmond Dantès described less subtly as revenge. Whatever. He slept.

He woke. He would stalk his prey like an animal, observing them at a distance while they relaxed in their natural habitat: Spencer Craig in the courtroom, Gerald Payne in his Mayfair offices, and Lawrence Davenport on stage. Toby Mortimer, the last of the four Musketeers, had suffered a death even more dreadful than any he could have devised. But first Danny must travel to Scotland, meet up with Fraser Munro and find out if he could pass his initiation test. If he fell at the first hurdle, he would be back in Belmarsh by the end of the week. He slept.

He woke. The early morning sun was producing a feeble square of light on his cell floor, but it could not disguise the fact that he was in prison, for the bars were clearly reflected on the cold grey stones. A lark attempted a cheerful tune to greet the dawn, but quickly flew away.

Danny pulled aside the green nylon sheet and placed his bare feet on the ground. He walked across to the tiny steel washbasin, filled it with luke-warm water and shaved carefully. Then, with the assistance of a sliver of soap, he washed, wondering how long the smell of prison would remain in the pores of his skin.

He studied himself in the small steel mirror above the basin. The bits he could see appeared to be clean. He put on his prison clothes for the last time: a pair of boxer shorts, a blue and white striped shirt, jeans, grey socks and Nick's trainers. He sat on the end of the bed and waited for Pascoe to appear, jangling keys and with his usual morning greeting, 'Let's be having you, lad. It's time to go to work.' Not today. He waited.

When the key eventually turned in the lock and the door opened, Pascoe had a broad grin on his face. 'Morning, Moncrieff,' he said. 'Look lively, and follow me. It's time for you to pick up your personal belongings from the stores, be on your way and leave us all in peace.'

As they walked down the corridor at a prison pace, Pascoe ventured, 'The weather's on the turn. You should have a nice day for it,' as if Danny was off on a day trip to the seaside.

'How do I get from here to King's Cross?' Danny asked. Something Nick wouldn't have known.

'Take the train from Plumstead station to Cannon Street, then the tube to King's Cross,' said Pascoe as they reached the store room. He banged on the double doors, and a moment later they were pulled open by the stores manager.

'Morning, Moncrieff,' said Webster. 'You must have been looking forward to today for the past four years.' Danny didn't comment. 'I've got everything ready for you,' continued Webster, taking two full plastic bags from the shelf behind him and placing them on the counter. He then disappeared into the back, returning a moment later with a large leather suitcase that was covered in dust and bore the initials N.A.M. in black. 'Nice piece of kit, that,' he said. 'What does the A stand for?'

Danny couldn't remember if it was Angus, after Nick's father, or Alexander, after his grandfather.

'Get on with it, Moncrieff,' said Pascoe. 'I don't have all day to stand around chatting.'

Danny tried manfully to pick up both the plastic bags in one hand and the large leather suitcase with the other, but found that he had to stop and change hands every few paces.

'I'd like to help you, Moncrieff,' whispered Pascoe, 'but if I did, I'd never hear the end of it.'

Eventually they ended up back outside Danny's cell. Pascoe

unlocked the door. 'I'll return in about an hour to fetch you. I have to get some of the lads off to the Old Bailey before we can think about releasing you.' The cell door slammed in Danny's face for the last time.

Danny took his time. He opened the suitcase and placed it on Big Al's bed. He wondered who would sleep in his bunk tonight; someone who would be appearing at the Old Bailey later that morning, hoping the jury would find him not guilty. He emptied the contents of the plastic bags on to the bed, feeling like a robber surveying his swag: two suits, three shirts, what the diary described as a pair of cavalry twills, along with a couple of pairs of brogues, one black, one brown. Danny selected the dark suit he'd worn at his own funeral, a cream shirt, a striped tie and a pair of smart black shoes that even after four years didn't require a polish.

Danny Cartwright stood in front of the mirror and stared at Sir Nicholas Moncrieff, officer and gentleman. He felt like a fraud.

He folded up his prison gear and placed it on the end of Nick's bed. He still thought of it as Nick's bed. Then he packed the rest of the clothes neatly in the suitcase before retrieving Nick's diary from under the bed, along with a file of correspondence marked *Fraser Munro* – twenty-eight letters that Danny knew almost off by heart. Once he'd finished packing, all that remained were a few of Nick's personal belongings, which Danny had put on the table, and the photo of Beth taped to the wall. He carefully peeled off the sellotape before putting the photo in a side pocket of the suitcase, which he then snapped closed and placed by the cell door.

Danny sat back down at the table and looked at his friend's personal belongings. He strapped on Nick's slim Longines watch with 11.7.91 stamped on the back – a gift from his grandfather on his twenty-first birthday – then he slipped on a gold ring which bore the Moncrieff family crest. He stared at a black leather wallet and felt even more like a thief. Inside it he found seventy pounds in cash and a Coutts chequebook with an address in The Strand printed on the cover. He put the wallet in an inside pocket, turned the plastic chair round to face the cell door, sat down and waited for Pascoe to reappear. He was ready to escape. As he sat there, he recalled one of Nick's favourite misquotes: *In prison, time and tide wait for every man.*

He reached inside his shirt and touched the small key that was hanging from the chain around his neck. He was no nearer to discovering what it unlocked – it unlocked the prison gate. He had searched through the diaries for the slightest clue, over a thousand pages, but had come up with nothing. If Nick had known, he had taken the secret to his grave.

Now a very different key was turning in the lock of his cell door. It opened to reveal Pascoe standing alone. Danny quite expected him to say, 'Good try, Cartwright, but you didn't really expect to get away with it, did you?' But all he said was, 'It's time to go, Moncrieff, look sharp about it.'

Danny rose, picked up Nick's suitcase and walked out on to the landing. He didn't look back at the room that had been his home for the past two years. He followed Pascoe along the landing and down the spiral staircase. As he left the block he was greeted with cheers and jeers from those who were soon to be released and those who would never see the light of day again.

They continued down the blue corridor. He'd forgotten how many sets of double-barred gates there were between B block and reception, where Jenkins was seated behind his desk waiting for him.

'Good morning, Moncrieff,' he announced cheerfully; he had one voice for those coming in, quite another for those who were leaving. He checked the open ledger in front of him. 'I see that over the past four years you have saved two hundred and eleven pounds, and as you are also entitled to forty-five pounds discharge allowance, that makes in all two hundred and fifty-six pounds.' He counted out the money slowly and carefully, before passing it over to Danny. 'Sign here,' he said. Danny wrote Nick's signature for the second time that morning before putting the money in his wallet. 'You are also entitled to a rail warrant to any part of the country you decide on. It's one way, of course, as we don't want to see you back here again.' Prison humour.

Jenkins handed him a rail warrant to Dunbroath in Scotland, but not before Danny had falsely signed another document. It wasn't surprising that his handwriting resembled Nick's – after all, it was Nick who had taught him to write.

'Mr Pascoe will accompany you to the gate,' said Jenkins once he'd checked the signature. 'I'll say goodbye, as I have a feeling we'll never meet again, which sadly I'm not able to say all that often.'

Danny shook his hand, picked up the suitcase and followed Pascoe out of reception, down the steps and into the yard.

Together they walked slowly across a bleak concrete square which acted as a car park for the prison vans and private vehicles that made their legal entrance and exit every day. In the gatehouse sat an officer Danny had never seen before.

'Name?' he demanded without looking up from the list of discharges on his clipboard.

'Moncrieff,' Danny replied.

'Number?'

'CK4802,' said Danny without thinking.

The officer ran a finger slowly down his list. A puzzled look appeared on his face.

'CK1079,' whispered Pascoe.

'CK1079,' repeated Danny, shaking.

'Ah, yes,' said the officer, his finger coming to rest on Moncrieff. 'Sign here.'

Danny's hand was shaking as he scribbled Nick's signature in the little rectangular box. The officer checked the name against the prison number and the photograph, before looking up at Danny. He hesitated for a moment.

'Don't hang around, Moncrieff,' said Pascoe firmly. 'Some of us have got a day's work to do, haven't we, Mr Tomkins?'

'Yes, Mr Pascoe,' replied the gate officer, and quickly pressed the red button beneath his desk. The first of the massive electric gates slowly began to open.

Danny stepped out of the gatehouse, still not sure in which direction he would be heading. Pascoe said nothing.

Once the first gate had slipped into the gap in the wall, Pascoe finally offered, 'Good luck, lad, you'll need it.'

Danny shook him warmly by the hand. 'Thank you, Mr Pascoe,'

he said. 'For everything.' Danny picked up Nick's suitcase and stepped into the void between the two different worlds. The first gate slid back into place behind him, and a moment later the second one began to open.

Danny Cartwright walked out of prison a free man. The first inmate ever to escape from Belmarsh.

BOOK THREE

FREEDOM

38

As Nick Moncrieff crossed the road, one or two passers-by glanced at him in mild surprise. It wasn't that they were unaccustomed to seeing prisoners coming out of that gate, but not someone carrying a leather suitcase and dressed like a country gentleman.

Danny never once looked back as he walked to the nearest station. After he'd bought a ticket – his first handling of cash for over two years – he boarded the train. He stared out of the window, feeling strangely insecure. No walls, no razor wire, no barred gates and no screws – prison officers. Look like Nick, talk like Nick, think like Danny.

At Cannon Street, Danny switched to the tube. The commuters were moving at a different pace from the one he had become accustomed to in prison. Several of them were dressed in smart suits, speaking in smart accents and dealing in smart money, but Nick had shown him that they were no smarter than he was; they had just started life in a different cot.

At King's Cross, Nick disembarked, lugging his heavy suitcase. He passed a policeman who didn't even glance at him. He checked the departures board. The next train to Edinburgh was scheduled to leave at eleven, arriving at Waverley station at 3.20 that afternoon. He still had time for breakfast. He grabbed a copy of *The Times* from a stand outside W.H. Smith. He'd walked a few paces before he realized he hadn't paid for the paper. Sweating profusely, Danny ran back and quickly joined the queue at the till. He remembered being told about a prisoner who had just been released and while he was on his way home to Bristol had taken a

Mars Bar from a display cabinet on Reading station. He was arrested for shoplifting and was back in Belmarsh seven hours later; he'd ended up serving another three years.

Danny paid for the paper and walked into the nearest café, where he joined another queue. When he reached the hotplate he passed his tray across to the girl behind the counter.

'What would you like?' she asked, ignoring the proffered tray.

Danny wasn't sure how to respond. For over two years he had just taken whatever ended up on his plate. 'Eggs, bacon, mushrooms and . . .'

'You may as well have the full English breakfast while you're at it,' she suggested.

'Fine, the full English breakfast,' said Danny. 'And, and . . .'

'Tea or coffee?'

'Yes, coffee would be great,' he said, aware that it was going to take him a little time to become used to being given whatever he asked for. He found a seat at a table in the corner. He picked up the bottle of HP sauce and shook an amount on to the side of the plate that Nick would have approved of. He then opened his paper and turned to the business pages. Look like Nick, talk like Nick, think like Danny.

Internet companies were still falling by the wayside as their owners discovered that the meek rarely inherit the earth. By the time Danny had reached the front pages, he'd finished his meal and was enjoying a second cup of coffee. Someone had not only walked over to his table and refilled his cup, but also smiled when he said thank you. Danny began to read the lead article on the front page. The leader of the Conservative Party, Iain Duncan Smith, was under attack again. If the Prime Minister called an election, Danny would have voted for Tony Blair. He suspected that Nick would have supported Iain Duncan Smith; after all, he was another old soldier. Perhaps he would abstain. No, he must stay in character if he hoped to fool the voters, let alone remain in office.

Danny finished his coffee, but didn't move for some time. He needed Mr Pascoe to tell him he could return to his cell. He smiled to himself, rose from his seat and strolled out of the café. He knew the time had come to face his first test. When he spotted a row of phone booths, he took a deep breath. He took out his wallet – Nick's wallet – extracted a card, and dialled the number embossed in the bottom right-hand corner.

'Munro, Munro and Carmichael,' announced a voice.

'Mr Munro, please,' said Nick.

'Which Mr Munro?'

Danny checked the card. 'Mr Fraser Munro.'

'Who shall I say is calling?'

'Nicholas Moncrieff.'

'I'll put you straight through, sir.'

'Thank you.'

'Good morning, Sir Nicholas,' said the next lilting voice Danny heard. 'How nice to hear from you.'

'Good morning, Mr Munro.' Danny spoke slowly. 'I'm thinking of travelling up to Scotland later today and I wondered if you might be free to see me some time tomorrow.'

'Of course, Sir Nicholas. Would ten o'clock suit you?'

'Admirably,' said Danny, recalling one of Nick's favourite words.

'Then I'll look forward to seeing you here in my office at ten o'clock tomorrow morning.'

'Goodbye, Mr Munro,' said Danny, just stopping himself from asking where his office was. Danny put the phone down. He was covered in sweat. Big Al had been right. Munro was expecting a call from Nick. Why would he have thought for a moment that he might be speaking to someone else?

Danny was among the first to board the train. While he waited for it to depart he turned his attention to the sports pages. The football season was still a month away, but he had high hopes for West Ham, who had finished seventh in the Premier League the previous season. He felt a tinge of sadness at the thought that he would never be able to risk visiting Upton Park again for fear of being recognized. No more 'I'm forever blowing bubbles'. Try to remember, Danny Cartwright is dead – and buried.

The train pulled slowly out of the station, and Danny watched London pass by giving way to the countryside. He was surprised how quickly they reached full speed. He had never been to

Scotland before – the farthest north he had ever been was Vicarage Road, Watford.

Danny felt exhausted, and he'd only been out of prison for a few hours. The pace of everything was so much quicker and, hardest of all, you had to make decisions. He checked Nick's watch – his watch – a quarter past eleven. He tried to go on reading the paper, but his head fell back.

'Tickets please.'

Danny woke with a start, rubbed his eyes and handed his rail warrant to the ticket collector. 'I'm sorry, sir, but this ticket isn't valid for the express train. You'll have to pay a supplement.'

'But I was—' began Danny. 'I do apologize, how much will that be?' asked Nick.

'Eighty-four pounds.'

Danny couldn't believe he'd made such a stupid mistake. He took out his wallet and handed over the cash. The ticket collector printed out a receipt.

'Thank you, sir,' he said after he'd issued Danny with his ticket. Danny noticed that he called him sir without thinking about it, not mate, as an East End bus driver would have addressed him.

'Will you be having lunch today, sir?'

Once again, simply because of his dress and accent. 'Yes,' said Danny.

'The dining car is a couple of carriages forward. They'll begin serving in about half an hour.'

'I'm grateful.' Another of Nick's expressions.

Danny looked out of the window and watched the countryside flying by. After they passed through Grantham he returned to the financial pages, but was interrupted by a voice over the tannoy announcing that the dining car was now open. He made his way forward and took a seat at a small table hoping that no one would join him. He studied the menu carefully, wondering which dishes Nick would have chosen. A waiter appeared by his side.

'The pâté,' Danny said. He knew how to pronounce it, although he had no idea what it would taste like. In the past his golden rule had been never to order anything that had a foreign name. 'Followed by the steak and kidney pie.'

'And for pudding?'

Nick had taught him that you should never order all three courses at once. 'I'll think about it,' said Danny.

'Of course, sir.'

By the time Danny had finished his meal, he had read everything *The Times* had to offer, including the theatre reviews, which only made him think about Lawrence Davenport. But for now, Davenport would have to wait. Danny had other things on his mind. He had enjoyed the meal, until the waiter gave him a bill for twenty-seven pounds. He handed over three ten-pound notes, aware that his wallet was becoming lighter by the minute.

According to Nick's diary, Mr Munro believed that if the estate in Scotland and the London house were placed on the market, they would fetch handsome sums, although he had cautioned that it could be several months before a sale was completed. Danny knew that he couldn't survive for several months on less than two hundred pounds.

He returned to his seat, and began to give some thought to his meeting with Munro the following morning. When the train stopped at Newcastle upon Tyne, Danny unbuckled the leather straps around the suitcase, opened it and found Mr Munro's file. He extracted the letters. Although they contained all of Munro's replies to Nick's questions, Danny had no way of knowing what Nick had written in his original letters. He had to try to second-guess what questions Nick must have asked after reading Munro's answers, with only the dates and the diary entries as reference points. After reading the correspondence again, he wasn't in any doubt that Uncle Hugo had taken advantage of the fact that Nick had been locked up for the past four years.

Danny had come across customers like Hugo when he worked at the garage – loan sharks, property dealers and barrow boys who thought they could get the better of him, but they never did, and none of them ever discovered that he couldn't read a contract. He found his mind drifting to the A levels he'd taken only days before being released. He wondered if Nick had passed with flying colours – another Nick expression. He had promised his cellmate that if he won his appeal, the first thing he would do was study for a degree.

He intended to keep that promise and take the degree in Nick's name. Think like Nick, forget Danny, he reminded himself. You are Nick, *you are Nick*. He went over the letters once again as if he was revising for an exam; an exam he couldn't afford to fail.

The train arrived at Waverley station at three thirty, ten minutes late. Danny joined the crowd as they walked along the platform. He checked the departure board for the time of the next train to Dunbroath. Another twenty minutes. He bought a copy of the *Edinburgh Evening News* and satisfied himself with a bacon baguette from Upper Crust. Would Mr Munro realize that he wasn't upper crust? He went in search of his platform, then sat down on a bench. The paper was full of names and places he had never heard of: problems with the planning committee in Duddlingston, the cost of the unfinished Scottish Parliament building and a supplement giving details of something called the Edinburgh Festival, which was taking place the following month. Hearts' and Hibs' prospects in the forthcoming season dominated the back pages, rudely replacing Arsenal and West Ham.

Ten minutes later Danny climbed on board the cross-country train to Dunbroath, a journey that took forty minutes, stopping at several stations whose names he couldn't even pronounce. At four forty, the little train trundled into Dunbroath station. Danny lugged his case along the platform and out on to the pavement, relieved to see a single taxi waiting on the stand. Nick climbed into the front seat while the driver put his case in the boot.

'Where to?' asked the driver once he was back behind the wheel.

'Perhaps you can recommend a hotel?'

'There is only one,' said the taxi driver.

'Well, that solves the problem,' said Danny, as the car moved off.

Three pounds fifty later, plus a tip, and Danny was dropped outside the Moncrieff Arms. He walked up the steps, through the swing doors and dumped his suitcase by the reception desk.

'I need a room for the night,' he told the woman behind the counter.

'Just a single?'

'Yes, thank you.'

'Would you please sign the booking form, sir?' Danny could now sign Nick's name almost without thinking. 'And can I take an imprint of your credit card?'

'But I don't . . .' began Danny. 'I'll be paying cash,' said Nick.

'Of course, sir.' She swivelled the form round, checked the name and tried to hide her surprise. She then disappeared into a back room without another word. A few moments later a middle-aged man wearing a plaid sweater and brown corduroys emerged from the office.

'Welcome home, Sir Nicholas. I'm Robert Kilbride, the hotel manager, and I do apologize, but we weren't expecting you. I'll transfer you to the Walter Scott suite.'

Transfer is a word every prisoner dreads. 'But—' began Danny, recalling how little cash was left in his wallet.

'At no extra cost,' added the manager.

'Thank you,' said Nick.

'Will you be joining us for dinner?'

Yes, said Nick. 'No,' said Danny, remembering his diminishing reserves. 'I've already eaten.'

'Of course, Sir Nicholas. I'll have a porter take your case up to the room.'

A young man accompanied Danny to the Walter Scott suite.

'My name's Andrew,' he said as he unlocked the door. 'If you need anything, just pick up the phone and let me know.'

'I need a suit pressed and a shirt washed in time for a ten o'clock meeting tomorrow morning,' said Danny.

'Of course, sir. You'll have them back well in time for your meeting.'

'Thank you,' said Danny. Another tip.

Danny sat on the end of the bed and turned on the television. He watched the local news, delivered in an accent that reminded him of Big Al. It wasn't until he switched channels to BBC2 that he was able to follow every word, but within a few minutes he had fallen asleep.

39

DANNY WOKE to find he was fully dressed and the credits were running at the end of a black and white film starring someone called Jack Hawkins. He switched it off, undressed and decided to take a shower before going to bed.

He stepped into a shower which sent down a steady stream of warm water that didn't turn itself off every few seconds. He washed himself with a bar of soap the size of a bread roll, and dried himself with a large fluffy towel. He felt clean for the first time in years.

He climbed into a bed with a thick comfortable mattress, clean sheets and more than one blanket before resting his head on a feather pillow. He fell into a deep sleep. He woke. The bed was too comfortable. It even changed shape when he moved. He peeled off one of the blankets and dumped it on the floor. He turned over and fell asleep again. He woke. The pillow was too soft, so it joined the blanket on the floor. He fell asleep again, and when the sun rose accompanied by a cacophony of unrecognizable bird tunes, he woke again. He looked around, expecting to see Mr Pascoe standing in the doorway, but this door was different: it was wooden, not steel, and it had a handle on the inside that he could open whenever he pleased.

Danny climbed out of bed and walked across the soft carpet to the bathroom – a separate room – to take another shower. This time he washed his hair, and shaved with the aid of a circular glass mirror that magnified his image.

There was a polite tap on the door, which remained closed, instead of being heaved open. Danny put on a hotel dressing gown and opened the door to find the porter standing there holding a neat package.

'Your clothes, sir.'

'Thank you,' said Danny.

'Breakfast will be served until ten o'clock in the dining room.'

Danny put on a clean shirt and a striped tie before trying on his freshly pressed suit. He looked at himself in the mirror. Surely no one would doubt that he was Sir Nicholas Moncrieff. Never again would he have to wear the same shirt for six days in a row, the same jeans for a month, the same shoes for a year – that was assuming Mr Munro was about to solve all his financial problems. That was also assuming Mr Munro . . .

Danny checked the wallet that had felt so thick only yesterday. He cursed; he wouldn't have much left once he had settled the hotel bill. He opened the door, and once he'd closed it he immediately realized that he'd left the key inside. He would have to ask Pascoe to open the door for him. Would he end up on report? He cursed again. Damn. A Nick curse. He went off in search of the dining room.

A large table in the centre of the room was brimming over with a choice of cereals and juices, and the hotplate offered porridge, eggs, bacon, black pudding and even kippers to order. Danny was shown to a table by the window and offered a morning paper, the *Scotsman*. He turned to the financial pages to find that the Royal Bank of Scotland was expanding its property portfolio. While he was in prison, Danny had watched with admiration the RBS's takeover of the NatWest Bank; a minnow swallowing a whale, and not even burping.

He looked around, suddenly fearful that the staff might be commenting on the fact that he didn't have a Scottish accent. But Big Al had once told him that officers never do. Nick certainly didn't. A pair of kippers was placed in front of him. His father would have considered them a right treat. First thoughts of his father since he had been released.

'Would you care for anything else, sir?'

'No, thank you,' said Danny. 'But would you be kind enough to have my bill ready?'

'Of course, sir,' came back the immediate reply.

He was just about to leave the dining room when he remembered he had no idea where Mr Munro's office was. According to his business card it was 12 Argyll Street, but he couldn't ask the receptionist for directions, because everyone thought he'd been brought up in Dunbroath. Danny picked up another key from reception and returned to his room. It was nine thirty. He still had thirty minutes to find out where Argyll Street was.

There was a knock on the door. It was still going to be a little time before he didn't leap up and stand at the end of the bed and wait for the door to be opened.

'Can I take your luggage, sir?' asked the porter. 'And will you need a taxi?'

'No, I'm only going to Argyll Street,' Danny risked.

'Then I'll put your case in reception and you can pick it up later.'

'Is there still a chemist shop on the way to Argyll Street?' Danny asked.

'No, it closed a couple of years ago. What do you need?'

'Just some razor blades and shaving cream.'

'You'll be able to get those at Leith's, a few doors down from where Johnson's used to be.'

'Many thanks,' said Danny, parting with another pound, although he had no idea where Johnson's used to be.

Danny checked Nick's watch: 9.36 a.m. He walked quickly downstairs and headed for reception, where he tried a different ploy.

'Do you have a copy of *The Times*?'

'No, Sir Nicholas, but we could pick one up for you.'

'Don't trouble yourself. I could do with the exercise.'

'They'll have one at Menzies,' said the receptionist. 'Turn left as you go out of the hotel, about a hundred yards . . .' She paused. 'But of course you know where Menzies is.'

Danny slipped out of the hotel and turned left, and soon spotted the Menzies sign. He strolled inside. No one recognized him. He bought a copy of *The Times*, and the girl behind the counter, much to his relief, addressed him as neither 'sir' nor 'Sir Nicholas'.

'Am I far from Argyll Street?' he asked her.

'A couple of hundred yards. Turn right out of the shop, go past the Moncrieff Arms . . .'

Danny walked quickly back past the hotel, checking every intersection until he finally saw the name Argyll Street carved in large letters on a stone slab above him. He checked his watch as he turned into the street: 9.54. He still had a few minutes to spare, but he couldn't afford to be late. Nick was always on time. He recalled one of Big Al's favourite lines: 'Battles are lost by armies who turn up late. Ask Napoleon.'

As he passed numbers 2, 4, 6, 8, his pace became slower and slower; number 10, and then he came to a halt outside 12. A brass plate on the wall that looked as if it had been polished that morning, and on ten thousand mornings before, displayed the faded imprint of Munro, Munro and Carmichael.

Danny took a deep breath, opened the door and marched in. The girl behind the reception desk looked up. He hoped she couldn't hear his heart pounding. He was about to give his name when she said, 'Good morning, Sir Nicholas. Mr Munro is expecting you.' She rose from her seat and said, 'Please follow me.'

Danny had passed the first test, but he hadn't opened his mouth yet.

◄○►

'Following the death of your partner,' said a woman officer standing behind the counter, 'I'm authorized to pass over all of Mr Cartwright's personal belongings to you. But first I need to see some form of identification.'

Beth opened her bag and pulled out her driving licence.

'Thank you,' said the officer, who checked the details carefully before passing it back. 'If I read out the description of each item, Miss Wilson, perhaps you'd be kind enough to identify them.' The officer opened a large cardboard box and removed a pair of designer jeans. 'One pair of jeans, light blue,' she said. When Beth saw the jagged tear where the knife had entered Danny's leg, she burst into tears. The officer waited until she had composed herself, before she continued. 'One West Ham shirt; one belt, brown leather; one ring, gold; one pair of socks, grey; one pair of boxer shorts, red; one pair of shoes, black; one wallet containing thirty-five pounds and a membership card for the Bow Street Boxing Club. If you'd be kind enough to sign here, Miss Wilson,' she said finally, placing a finger on a dotted line.

Once Beth had signed her name she put all Danny's possessions neatly back in the box. 'Thank you,' she said. As she turned to leave she came face to face with another prison officer.

'Good afternoon, Miss Wilson,' he said. 'My name is Ray Pascoe.'

Beth smiled. 'Danny liked you,' she said.

'And I admired him,' said Pascoe, 'but that's not why I'm here. Allow me to carry that for you,' he said, taking the box from her as they started to walk down the corridor. 'I wanted to find out if you still intend to try to have the appeal verdict overturned.'

'What's the point,' said Beth, 'now that Danny's dead.'

'Would that be your attitude if he was still alive?' asked Pascoe.

'No, of course it wouldn't,' said Beth sharply. 'I'd go on fighting to prove his innocence for the rest of my life.'

When they reached the front gates Pascoe handed the box back to her and said, 'I have a feeling Danny would like to see his name cleared.'

40

'GOOD MORNING, Mr Munro,' said Danny, thrusting out his hand. 'How nice to see you again.'

'And you, Sir Nicholas,' Munro replied. 'I trust you had a pleasant journey.'

Nick had described Fraser Munro so well that Danny almost felt he knew him. 'Yes, thank you. The train journey allowed me to go over our correspondence once again, and reconsider your recommendations,' said Danny as Munro ushered him into a comfortable chair by the side of his desk.

'I fear my latest letter may not have reached you in time,' said Munro. 'I would have telephoned, but of course . . .'

'That wasn't possible,' said Danny, only interested in what the latest letter contained.

'I fear it's not good news,' said Munro, tapping his fingers on the desk – a habit Nick hadn't mentioned. 'A writ has been issued against you' – Danny gripped the arms of his chair. Were the police waiting for him outside? – 'by your uncle Hugo.' Danny breathed an audible sigh of relief. 'I should have seen it coming,' said Munro, 'and therefore I blame myself.'

Get on with it, Danny wanted to say. Nick said nothing.

'The writ claims that your father left the estate in Scotland and the house in London to your uncle and that you have no legal claim over either of them.'

'But that's nonsense,' said Danny.

'I entirely agree with you, and with your permission I will reply that we intend to defend the action vigorously.' Danny accepted

Munro's judgement, although he realized that Nick would have been more cautious. 'To add insult to injury,' Munro continued, 'your uncle's lawyers have come up with what they describe as a compromise.' Danny nodded, still unwilling to offer an opinion. 'If you were to accept your uncle's original offer, namely that he retains possession of both properties along with responsibility for the mortgage payments, he will give instructions to withdraw the writ.'

'He's bluffing,' said Danny. 'If I recall correctly, Mr Munro, your original advice was to take my uncle to court and make a claim for the money my father borrowed against both houses, a matter of two million, one hundred thousand pounds.'

'That was indeed my advice,' continued Munro. 'But if I recall your response at the time, Sir Nicholas – ' he placed his half-moon spectacles back on the end of his nose and opened a file – 'yes, here it is. Your exact words were, "If those were my father's wishes, I will not go against them".'

'That was how I felt at the time, Mr Munro,' said Danny, 'but circumstances have changed since then. I do not believe my father would have approved of Uncle Hugo issuing a writ against his nephew.'

'I agree with you,' said Munro, unable to hide his surprise at his client's change of heart. 'So can I suggest, Sir Nicholas, that we call his bluff?'

'And how would we go about that?'

'We could issue a counter-writ,' replied Munro, 'asking the court to make a judgement on whether your father had the right to borrow money against the two properties without consulting you in the first place. Although I am by nature a cautious man, Sir Nicholas, I would go as far as to suggest that the law is on our side. However, I'm sure that you read *Bleak House* in your youth.'

'Quite recently,' admitted Danny.

'Then you will be acquainted with the risks of becoming embroiled in such an action.'

'But unlike Jarndyce and Jarndyce,' said Danny, 'I suspect Uncle Hugo will agree to settle out of court.'

'What makes you think that?'

'He won't want to see his picture on the front page of the *Scotsman* and the *Edinburgh Evening News*, both of which would be only too happy to remind their readers where his nephew had been residing for the past four years.'

'A point I had not taken into consideration,' said Munro. 'But on reflection, I have to agree with you.' He coughed. 'When we last met, you did not seem to be of the opinion that . . .'

'When we last met, Mr Munro, I was preoccupied with other matters, and was therefore unable to fully grasp the significance of what you were telling me. Since then I have had time to consider your advice, and . . .' Danny had rehearsed these sentences again and again in his cell, with Big Al playing the role of Mr Munro.

'Quite so,' said Munro, removing his spectacles and looking more carefully at his client. 'Then with your permission, I will take up the cudgels on your behalf. However, I must warn you that the matter may not be resolved quickly.'

'How long?' asked Danny.

'It could be a year, even a little longer, before the case comes to court.'

'That might be a problem,' said Danny. 'I'm not sure there's enough money in my account at Coutts to cover . . .'

'No doubt you will advise me once you have been in touch with your bankers.'

'Certainly,' said Danny.

Munro coughed again. 'There are one or two other matters I feel we ought to discuss, Sir Nicholas.' Danny simply nodded, as Munro put his half-moon spectacles back on and rummaged among the papers on his desk once again. 'You recently executed a will while you were in prison,' said Munro, extracting a document from the bottom of the pile.

'Remind me of the details,' said Danny, recognizing Nick's familiar hand on the lined prison paper.

'You have left the bulk of your estate to one Daniel Cartwright.'

'Oh my God,' said Danny.

'From that, am I to assume that you wish to reconsider your position, Sir Nicholas?'

JEFFREY ARCHER

'No,' said Danny, recovering quickly. 'It's just that Danny Cartwright died recently.'

'Then you will need to make a new will at some time in the future. But frankly, there are far more pressing matters for us to consider at this moment in time.'

'Like what?' asked Danny.

'There is a key that your uncle seems most anxious to get his hands on.'

'A key?'

'Yes,' said Munro. 'It seems that he is willing to offer you one thousand pounds for a silver chain and key that he believes are in your possession. He realizes that they have little intrinsic value, but he would like them to remain in the family.'

'And so they will,' responded Danny. 'I wonder if I might ask you in confidence, Mr Munro, if you have any idea what the key opens?'

'No, I do not,' admitted Munro. 'On that particular subject your grandfather did not confide in me. Though I might make so bold as to suggest that if your uncle is so keen to lay his hands on it, I think we can assume that the contents of whatever the key opens will be worth far more than a thousand pounds.'

'Quite so,' said Danny, mimicking Munro.

'How do wish me to respond to this offer?' Munro asked.

'Tell him that you are not aware of the existence of such a key.'

'As you wish, Sir Nicholas. But I have no doubt that he'll not be that easily dissuaded, and will come back with a higher offer.'

'My reply will be the same whatever he offers,' said Danny firmly.

'So be it,' said Munro. 'May I enquire if it is your intention to settle in Scotland?'

'No, Mr Munro. I shall be returning to London shortly to sort out my financial affairs, but be assured I will stay in touch.'

'Then you will require the keys to your London residence,' said Munro, 'which have been in my safekeeping since your father's death.' He rose from his chair and walked across to a large safe in the corner of the room. He entered a code and pulled open the heavy door to reveal several shelves stacked with documents. He took two envelopes from the top shelf. 'I am in possession of the keys to both the house in The Boltons and your estate here in Scotland, Sir Nicholas. Would you care to take charge of them?'

'No, thank you,' said Danny. 'For the time being I only require the keys for my home in London. I would be obliged if you retained the keys to the estate. After all, I can't be in two places at once.'

'Quite so,' said Munro, handing over one of the bulky envelopes.

'Thank you,' said Danny. 'You have served our family loyally over many years.' Munro smiled. 'My grandfather—'

'Ah,' said Munro with a sigh. Danny wondered if he'd gone too far. 'I apologize for interrupting you, but the mention of your grandfather reminds me that there is a further matter that I should bring to your attention.' He returned to the safe, and after rummaging around for a few moments, extracted a small envelope. 'Ah, here it is,' he declared, a look of triumph on his face. 'Your grandfather instructed me to hand this to you in person, but not until after your father had died. I should have carried out his wishes at our previous meeting, but with all the, er, constraints you were under at that time, I confess it quite slipped my mind.' He passed the envelope to Danny who looked inside, but found nothing.

'Does this mean anything to you?' Danny asked.

'No, it doesn't,' confessed Munro. 'But recalling your grandfather's lifelong hobby, perhaps the stamp might be of some significance.'

Danny placed the envelope in an inside pocket without further comment.

Munro rose from his chair. 'I hope, Sir Nicholas, that it will not be too long before we see you in Scotland again. In the meantime, should you require my assistance, do not hesitate to call.'

'I don't know how to repay your kindness,' said Danny.

'I'm sure that after we have dealt with the problem of your uncle Hugo, I shall be more than adequately compensated.' He smiled drily, then accompanied Sir Nicholas to the door, shook him warmly by the hand and bade him farewell.

As Munro watched his client stride back in the direction of the hotel, he couldn't help thinking how like his grandfather Sir Nicholas had turned out to be, although he wondered if it had been wise of him to wear the regimental tie – given the circumstances.

◄o►

'He's done what?' said Hugo, shouting down the phone.

'He's issued a counter-writ against you, making a claim for the two million one hundred thousand you raised on the two properties.'

'Fraser Munro must be behind this,' said Hugo. 'Nick wouldn't have the nerve to oppose his father's wishes. What do we do now?'

'Accept service of the writ and tell them we'll see them in court.'

'But we can't afford to do that,' said Hugo. 'You've always said that if this case were to end up in court, we'd lose – and the press would have a field day.'

'True, but it will never come to court.'

'How can you be so sure?'

'Because I'll make certain that the case drags on for at least a couple of years, and your nephew will have run out of money long before then. Don't forget, we know how much is in his bank account. You'll just need to be patient while I bleed him dry.'

'What about the key?'

'Munro is claiming that he doesn't know anything about a key.'

'Offer him more money,' said Hugo. 'If Nick ever discovers what that key opens, he'll be able to watch me bleed to death.'

41

ON THE TRAIN back to London, Danny took a closer look at the envelope Nick's grandfather must have wanted him to have without his father knowing. But why?

Danny turned his attention to the stamp. It was French, value five francs, and showed the five circles of the Olympic emblem. The envelope was postmarked Paris and dated 1896. Danny knew from Nick's diaries that his grandfather, Sir Alexander Moncrieff, had been a keen collector, so the stamp might possibly be rare and valuable, but he had no idea who to turn to for advice. He found it hard to believe that the name and address could be of any significance: *Baron de Coubertin, 25 rue de la Croix-Rouge, Genève, La Suisse.* The baron must have been dead for years.

From King's Cross, Danny took the tube to South Kensington – not a part of London in which he felt at home. With the aid of an A–Z bought from a station kiosk, he walked down Old Brompton Road in the direction of The Boltons. Although Nick's suitcase was becoming heavier by the minute, he didn't feel he could waste any more of his rapidly dwindling reserves on a taxi.

When he finally reached The Boltons, Danny came to a halt outside number 12. He couldn't believe that only one family had lived there; the double garage alone was larger than his home in Bow. He opened a squeaky iron gate and walked up a long path covered in weeds to the front door. He pressed the bell. He couldn't think why, except that he didn't want to put the key in the lock until he was certain the house was unoccupied. No one answered.

Danny made several attempts at turning the key in the lock before the door reluctantly opened. He switched on the hall light. Inside, the house was exactly as Nick had described it in his diary. A thick green carpet, faded; red-patterned wallpaper, faded; and long antique lace curtains that hung from ceiling to floor, and had been allowed to attract moths over the years. There were no pictures on the walls, just less faded squares and rectangles to show where they had once hung. Danny wasn't in much doubt who had removed them, and in whose home they were now hanging.

He walked slowly around the rooms trying to get his bearings. It felt like a museum rather than someone's home. Once he'd explored the ground floor, he climbed the stairs to the landing and walked down another corridor before entering a large double bedroom. In a wardrobe hung a row of dark suits that could have been hired out for a period drama, along with shirts with wing collars, and on a rail at the bottom were several pairs of heavy black brogues. Danny assumed that this must have been Nick's grandfather's room, and clearly his father had preferred to stay in Scotland. Once Sir Alexander had died, Uncle Hugo must have removed the pictures and anything else of value that wasn't nailed down, before committing Nick's father to a million-pound mortgage on the house while Nick was safely locked up in prison. Danny was beginning to think that he might have to settle with Hugo before he could turn his attention to the Musketeers.

Having checked all the bedrooms – seven in all – Danny selected one of the smaller rooms in which to spend his first night. After he'd looked through the wardrobe and the chest of drawers, he concluded that it had to be Nick's old room, because there was a rack of suits, a drawer full of shirts and a row of shoes that fitted him perfectly, but looked as if they had been worn by a soldier who spent most of his time in uniform and had little interest in fashion.

Once Danny had unpacked, he decided to venture higher and find out what was on the top floor. He came across a children's room that looked as if it had never been slept in, next door to a nursery full of toys that no child had ever played with. His thoughts turned to Beth and Christy. He looked out of the nursery window on to a large garden. Even in the fading light of dusk he could see that the lawn was overgrown from years of neglect.

Danny returned to Nick's room, undressed and ran himself a bath. He sat in it, deep in thought, and didn't move until the water had turned cold. Once he'd dried himself, he decided against wearing Nick's silk pyjamas and climbed straight into bed. Within minutes he was fast asleep. The mattress was more like the one he had become accustomed to in prison.

‑‹o›‑

Danny leapt out of bed the following morning, pulled on a pair of pants, grabbed a silk dressing gown that was hanging on the back of the door, and went in search of the kitchen.

He descended a small uncarpeted staircase to a dark basement, where he discovered a large kitchen with an Aga and shelves full of glass bottles containing he knew not what. He was amused by a line of little bells attached to the wall, marked 'Drawing Room', 'Master Bedroom', 'Study', 'Nursery' and 'Front Door'. He began to search for some food, but couldn't find anything that hadn't passed its sell-by date years before. He now realized what the smell was that pervaded the whole house. If there was any money in Nick's bank account, the first thing he needed to do was employ a cleaner. He pulled open one of the large windows to allow a gust of fresh air to enter the room, into which it hadn't been invited for some time.

Having failed to find anything to eat, Danny returned to the bedroom to get dressed. He chose the least conservative garments he could find from Nick's wardrobe, but still ended up looking like a Guards captain on furlough.

As eight o'clock struck on the church clock in the square, Danny picked up the wallet from the bedside table and put it in his jacket pocket. He looked at the envelope Nick's grandfather had left him, and decided the stamp had to be the secret. He sat down at the desk by the window and wrote out a cheque to Nicholas Moncrieff for five hundred pounds. Was there five hundred pounds in Nick's account? There was only one way he was going to find out.

When he left the house a few minutes later he pulled the door

251

closed, but this time he remembered to take the keys with him. He strolled to the top of the road, turned right and walked in the direction of South Kensington tube station, only stopping to drop into a newsagent and pick up a copy of *The Times*. As he was leaving the shop, he spotted a noticeboard offering various services. 'Massage, Sylvia will come to your home, £100.' 'Lawnmower for sale, only used twice, £250 o.n.o.' He would have bought it if he had been confident there was £250 in Nick's bank account. 'Cleaner, five pounds an hour, references supplied. Call Mrs Murphy on . . .' Danny wondered if Mrs Murphy had a thousand hours to spare. He made a note of her mobile number, which reminded him of something else he needed to put on his shopping list, but that would also have to wait until he had discovered how much money there was in Nick's account.

By the time he got off the tube at Charing Cross, Danny had settled on two plans of action, depending on whether the manager of Coutts knew Sir Nicholas well, or had never come across him before.

He walked along the Strand looking for the bank. On its grey cover Nick's chequebook simply stated *Coutts & Co, The Strand, London*; clearly it was too grand an establishment to admit it had a number. He had not gone far before he spotted a large glass-fronted bronze building on the other side of the road, discreetly displaying two crowns above the name Coutts. He crossed the road, nipping in and out of the traffic. He was about to find out the extent of his wealth.

He entered the bank through the revolving doors, and quickly tried to get his bearings. Ahead of him, an escalator led up to the banking hall. He made his way up to a large, glass-roofed room with a long counter running the length of one wall. Several tellers, dressed in black frock coats, were serving customers. Danny selected a young man who looked as if he had only just started shaving. He walked up to his window. 'I would like to make a withdrawal.'

'How much do you require, sir?' the teller asked.

'Five hundred pounds,' said Danny, handing over the cheque he had written out earlier that morning.

The teller checked the name and number on his computer, and hesitated. 'Would you be kind enough to wait for one moment, Sir Nicholas?' he asked. Danny's mind started racing. Was Nick's account overdrawn? Had the account been closed? Were they unwilling to deal with an ex-con? A few moments later an older man appeared, and gave him a warm smile. Had Nick known him?

'Sir Nicholas?' he ventured.

'Yes,' said Danny, one of his questions answered.

'My name is Mr Watson. I'm the manager. It's a pleasure to meet you after all this time.' Danny shook him warmly by the hand before the manager added, 'Perhaps we could have a word in my office?'

'Certainly, Mr Watson,' said Danny, trying to appear confident. He followed the manager across the banking floor and through a door that led into a small wood-panelled office. There was a single oil painting of a gentleman in a long black frock coat hanging on the wall behind his desk. Under the portrait was the legend *John Campbell, Founder, 1692.*

Mr Watson began speaking even before Danny had sat down. 'I see that you haven't made a withdrawal for the past four years, Sir Nicholas,' he said, looking at his computer screen.

'That's correct,' said Danny.

'Perhaps you have been abroad?'

'No, but in future I will be a more regular customer. That is, if you have been handling my account with care while I've been away.'

'I hope you will think so, Sir Nicholas,' responded the manager. 'We have been paying interest at three per cent per annum into your current account year on year.'

Danny wasn't impressed, but only asked, 'And how much is in my current account?'

The manager glanced at the screen. 'Seven thousand, two hundred and twelve pounds.'

Danny breathed a sigh of relief, then asked, 'Are there any other accounts, documents or valuables in my name which you are holding at the present time?' The manager looked a little surprised. 'It's just that my father died recently.'

The manager nodded. 'I'll just check, sir,' he said, before pressing some keys on his computer. He shook his head. 'It seems that your father's account was closed two months ago, and all his assets were transferred to the Clydesdale Bank in Edinburgh.'

'Ah yes,' said Danny. 'My uncle Hugo.'

'Hugo Moncrieff was indeed the recipient,' confirmed the manager.

'Just as I thought,' said Danny.

'Is there anything else I can do for you, Sir Nicholas?'

'Yes, I'll need a credit card.'

'Of course,' said Watson. 'If you fill in this form,' he added, pushing a questionnaire across the table, 'we'll send one to your home address in the next few days.'

Danny tried to remember Nick's date and place of birth and his middle name; he wasn't sure what to put under 'occupation' or 'annual earnings'.

'There's one other thing,' said Danny once he'd completed the form. 'Would you have any idea where I can get this valued?' He took out the little envelope from an inside pocket and slid it across the desk.

The manager looked at the envelope carefully. 'Stanley Gibbons,' he replied without hesitation. 'They are leaders in the field, and they have an international reputation.'

'Where would I find them?'

'They have a branch just up the road. I would recommend that you have a word with Mr Prendergast.'

'I'm lucky that you're so well informed,' said Danny suspiciously.

'Well, they have banked with us for almost a hundred and fifty years.'

—◇—

Danny walked out of the bank with an extra £500 in his wallet, and set off in search of Stanley Gibbons. On the way he passed a mobile phone shop, which allowed him to tick another item off his shopping list. After he'd selected the latest model, he asked the young assistant if he knew where Stanley Gibbons was.

'Another fifty yards on your left,' he replied.

Danny continued down the road until he saw the sign over the door. Inside, a tall thin man was leaning on the counter turning the pages of a catalogue. He stood up straight the moment Danny came in.

'Mr Prendergast?' asked Danny.

'Yes,' he said. 'How may I help you?'

Danny took out the envelope and put it on the counter. 'Mr Watson at Coutts suggested that you might be able to value this for me.'

'I'll do my best,' said Mr Prendergast, picking up a magnifying glass from under the counter. He studied the envelope for some time before he ventured an opinion. 'The stamp is a first-edition five franc imperial, issued to mark the founding of the modern Olympic Games. The stamp itself is of little value, no more than a few hundred pounds. But there are two other factors that could possibly add to its importance.'

'And what are they?' asked Danny.

'The postmark is dated April sixth, 1896.'

'And why is that of any significance?' asked Danny, trying not to sound impatient.

'That was the date of the opening ceremony of the first modern Olympic Games.'

'And the second factor?' asked Danny, not waiting this time.

'The person the envelope is addressed to,' said Prendergast, sounding rather pleased with himself.

'Baron de Coubertin,' said Danny, not needing to be reminded.

'Correct,' said the dealer. 'It was the baron who founded the modern Olympics, and that is what makes your envelope a collector's item.'

'Are you able to place a value on it?' asked Danny.

'That's not easy, sir, as the item is unique. But I would be willing to offer you two thousand pounds for it.'

'Thank you, but I'd like a little time to think about it,' replied Danny, and turned to leave.

'Two thousand two hundred?' said the dealer as Danny closed the door quietly behind him.

42

DANNY SPENT the next few days settling into The Boltons, not that he thought he'd ever really feel at home in Kensington. That was until he met Molly.

Molly Murphy hailed from County Cork and it was some time before Danny could understand a word she was saying. She must have been about a foot shorter than Danny, and was so thin that he wondered if she had the strength to manage more than a couple of hours' work a day. He had no idea of her age, although she looked younger than his mother and older than Beth. Her first words to him were, 'I charge five pounds an hour, cash. I won't be paying any tax to those English bastards,' she had added firmly after learning that Sir Nicholas hailed from north of the border, 'and if you don't think I'm up to it, I'll leave at the end of the week.'

Danny kept an eye on Molly for the first couple of days, but it soon became clear that she had been forged in the same furnace as his mother. By the end of the week he was able to sit down anywhere in the house without a cloud of dust rising, climb into a bath that didn't have a water mark, and open the fridge to grab something without fearing he'd be poisoned.

By the end of the second week, Molly had started making his supper as well as washing and ironing his clothes. By the third week he wondered how he had ever survived without her.

Molly's enterprise allowed Danny to concentrate on other things. Mr Munro had written to let him know that he had served a writ on his uncle. Hugo's solicitor had allowed the full twenty-one days to pass before acknowledging service.

Mr Munro warned Sir Nicholas that Galbraith had a reputation for taking his time, but assured him that he would keep snapping at his ankles whenever the opportunity arose. Danny wondered how much this snapping would cost. He found out when he turned the page. Attached to Munro's letter was a bill for four thousand pounds, which covered all the work he had done since the funeral, including the serving of the writ.

Danny checked his bank statement, which had arrived, along with a credit card, in the morning post. Four thousand pounds would make a very large dent on the bottom line and Danny wondered how long he could survive before he would have to throw in the towel; it might have been a cliché but the expression did remind him of happier times in Bow.

During the past week, Danny had bought a laptop and a printer, a silver photo frame, several files, assorted pens, pencils and erasers, as well as reams of paper. He had already begun to build a database on the three men who had been responsible for Bernie's death, and he spent most of the first month entering everything he knew about Spencer Craig, Gerald Payne and Lawrence Davenport. That didn't amount to a great deal, but Nick had taught him that it's easier to pass exams if you've put in the research. He had just been about to begin that research when he received Munro's invoice, which reminded him how quickly his funds were drying up. Then he remembered the envelope. The time had come to seek a second opinion.

He picked up *The Times* – brought in by Molly every morning – and turned to an article he'd spotted on the Arts pages. An American collector had bought a Klimt for fifty-one million pounds in an auction at somewhere called Sotheby's.

Danny opened his laptop and Googled *Klimt* to discover that he was an Austrian Symbolist painter, 1862–1918. He next turned his attention to Sotheby's, which turned out to be an auction house that specialized in fine art, antiques, books, jewellery and other collectable items. After a few clicks of the mouse, he discovered that collectable items included stamps. Those wishing to seek advice could do so by calling Sotheby's or by visiting their offices in New Bond Street.

Danny thought he'd take them by surprise, but not today,

because he was going to the theatre, and not to see the play. The play was not the thing.

—◦—

Danny had never been to a West End theatre before, unless he counted a trip on Beth's twenty-first to see *Les Misérables* at the Palace Theatre. He hadn't enjoyed it that much, and didn't think he'd bother with another musical.

He had phoned the Garrick the previous day and booked a seat for a matinee performance of *The Importance of Being Earnest*. They had told him to pick up his ticket from the box office fifteen minutes before the curtain rose. Danny arrived a little early, to find that the theatre was almost deserted. He collected his ticket, bought a programme and with the assistance of an usher made his way to the stalls, where he found his seat at the end of row H. Just a handful of people were dotted around.

He opened his programme and read for the first time about how Oscar Wilde's play had been an instant hit in 1895 when it was first performed at the St James's Theatre in London. He had to keep standing up to allow other people to take their seats in row H as a steady stream of ticket holders made their way into the theatre.

By the time the lights went down, the Garrick was almost full and the majority of seats seemed to be occupied by young girls. When the curtain rose, Lawrence Davenport was nowhere to be seen, but Danny didn't have to wait long, because he made his entrance a few moments later. A face he would never forget. One or two of the audience immediately began clapping. Davenport paused before delivering his first line, as though he expected nothing less.

Danny was tempted to charge up on to the stage and tell the assembled gathering what sort of a man Davenport really was, and what had taken place at the Dunlop Arms the night their hero had stood and watched Spencer Craig stab his best friend to death. How differently he had acted in the alley from the swaggering, confident man he now portrayed. On that occasion he had given a far more convincing performance as a coward.

Like the young girls in the audience, Danny's eyes never left

Davenport. As the performance continued, it became clear that if there was a mirror to gaze in, Davenport would find it. By the time the curtain fell for the interval, Danny felt he had seen quite enough of Lawrence Davenport to know just how much he'd appreciate a few matinees in jail. Danny would have returned to The Boltons and brought his file up to date if he hadn't found to his surprise how much he was enjoying the play.

He followed the jostling crowd into a packed bar and waited in a long queue while one barman tried manfully to serve all his would-be customers. Finally Danny gave up, and decided to use the time to read his programme and learn more about Oscar Wilde, who he wished had featured on the A-level syllabus. He became distracted by a high-pitched conversation that was taking place between two girls standing at the corner of the bar.

'What did you think of Larry?' asked the first.

'He's wonderful,' came back the reply. 'Pity he's gay.'

'But are you enjoying the play?'

'Oh, yes. I'm coming again on closing night.'

'How did you manage to get tickets?'

'One of the stage hands lives in our street.'

'Does that mean you'll be going to the party afterwards?'

'Only if I agree to be his date for the night.'

'Do you think you'll get to meet Larry?'

'It's the only reason I said I'd go out with him.'

A bell sounded three times and several customers quickly downed their drinks before drifting back into the auditorium to take their seats. Danny followed in their wake.

When the curtain rose again, Danny became so engrossed in the play that he almost forgot his real purpose for being there. While the girls' attention remained firmly focused on Dr Beresford, Danny sat back waiting to find out which one of two men would turn out to be Earnest.

When the curtain fell and the cast took their bows, the audience rose to their feet, shouting and screaming, just as Beth had done that night, but a different kind of scream. It only made Danny more determined that they should find out the truth about their flawed idol.

After the final curtain call, the chattering crowd spilled out of the theatre on to the pavement. Some headed straight for the stage door, but Danny made his way back to the box office.

The box office manager smiled. 'Enjoy the show?'

'Yes, thank you. Do you by any chance have a ticket for the closing night?'

'Afraid not, sir. Sold out.'

'Just a single?' said Danny hopefully. 'I don't mind where I sit.'

The box office manager checked his screen and studied the seating plan for the last performance. 'I do have a single seat in row W.'

'I'll take it,' said Danny, passing over his credit card. 'Does that allow me to attend the party afterwards?'

'No, I'm afraid not,' said the manager with a smile. 'That's by invitation only.' He swiped Danny's card, 'Sir Nicholas Moncrieff,' he said, looking at him more closely.

'Yes, that's right,' said Danny.

The manager printed out a single ticket, took an envelope from below the counter and slipped the ticket inside.

Danny continued to read the programme on the tube journey back to South Kensington, and after he'd devoured every word on Oscar Wilde and read about the other plays he'd written, he opened the envelope to check his ticket. C9. They must have made a mistake. He looked inside the envelope and pulled out a card which read:

THE GARRICK THEATRE

invites you to the closing-night party of

The Importance of Being Earnest

at the Dorchester

Saturday 14th September 2002

Admittance by ticket only
11.00 p.m. till heaven knows when

Danny suddenly realized the importance of being Sir Nicholas.

43

'HOW INTERESTING. How very interesting,' said Mr Blundell as he placed his magnifying glass back on the table and smiled at his potential customer.

'How much is it worth?' asked Danny.

'I have no idea,' Blundell admitted.

'But I was told you were one of the leading experts in the field.'

'And I like to think I am,' replied Blundell, 'but in thirty years in the business I've never come across anything quite like this.' He picked up his magnifying glass again, bent down and studied the envelope more closely. 'The stamp itself is not all that uncommon, but one franked on the day of the opening ceremony is far more rare. And for the envelope to be addressed to Baron de Coubertin . . .'

'The founder of the modern Olympics,' said Danny. 'Must be even rarer.'

'If not unique,' suggested Blundell. He ran the magnifying glass over the envelope once again. 'It's extremely difficult to put a value on it.'

'Could you give me a rough estimate, perhaps?' asked Danny hopefully.

'If the envelope was purchased by a dealer, two thousand two hundred to two thousand five hundred would be my guess; by a keen collector, perhaps as much as three thousand. But should two collectors want it badly enough, who can say? Allow me to give you an example, Sir Nicholas. Last year an oil painting entitled *A Vision of Fiammetta* by Dante Gabriel Rossetti came under the hammer here at Sotheby's. We put an estimate on it of two and a half to three million pounds, which was certainly at the high end of the market, and, indeed, all the well-known dealers had fallen out some time before it reached the high estimate. However, because Andrew Lloyd Webber and Elizabeth Rothschild both wanted to add the picture to their collections, the hammer came down for the final time at nine million pounds, more than double the previous record for a Rossetti.'

'Are you suggesting that my envelope might sell for more than double its valuation?'

'No, Sir Nicholas, I am simply saying that I have no idea how much it might sell for.'

'But can you make sure that Andrew Lloyd Webber and Elizabeth Rothschild turn up for the sale?' asked Danny.

Blundell lowered his head, fearing Sir Nicholas might see that he was amused by such a suggestion. 'No,' he said, 'I have no reason to believe that either Lord Lloyd Webber or Elizabeth Rothschild has any interest in stamps. However, if you decide to put your envelope into our next sale, it would be featured in the catalogue, and sent to all the leading collectors in the world.'

'And when will your next stamp sale be?' asked Danny.

'September the sixteenth,' replied Blundell. 'Just over six weeks' time.'

'That long?' said Danny, who had assumed that they would be able to sell his envelope within a few days.

'We are still preparing the catalogue, and will be mailing it to all our clients at least two weeks prior to the sale.'

Danny thought back to his meeting with Mr Prendergast at Stanley Gibbons, who had offered him £2,200 for the envelope, and probably would have gone as high as £2,500. If he accepted his offer he wouldn't have to wait for another six weeks. Nick's latest bank statement showed that he only had £1,918, so he might well be overdrawn by September 16th with still no prospect of any further income.

Blundell did not hurry Sir Nicholas, who was clearly giving the matter his serious consideration, and if he was the grandson of . . . this could be the beginning of a long and fruitful relationship.

Danny knew which of the two options Nick would have settled for. He would have accepted the original offer of £2,000 from Mr Prendergast, walked back to Coutts and banked the money immediately. That helped Danny come to a decision. He picked up the envelope, handed it to Mr Blundell and said, 'I'll leave you to find the two people who want my envelope.'

'I'll do my best,' said Blundell. 'Nearer the time, Sir Nicholas, I'll see that you are sent a catalogue, along with an invitation to the sale. And may I add how much I always enjoyed assisting your grandfather in the building of his magnificent collection.'

'His magnificent collection?' repeated Danny.

'Should you wish to add to that collection, or indeed to sell any part of it, I would be only too happy to offer my services.'

'Thank you,' said Danny. 'I may well be in touch.' He left Sotheby's without another word – he couldn't risk asking Mr Blundell questions to which he himself would be expected to know the answers. But how else was he going to find out about Sir Alexander's magnificent collection?

No sooner was Danny back out on Bond Street than he wished he had accepted Prendergast's original offer, because even if the envelope raised as much as six thousand, it still wouldn't be nearly enough to cover the costs of a prolonged legal battle with Hugo Moncrieff, and if he were to settle the writ before the expenses ran out of control, he'd still have enough money to survive on for a few more weeks while he looked for a job. But unfortunately, Sir Nicholas Moncrieff was not qualified to work as an East End garage mechanic; in fact, Danny was beginning to wonder what he was qualified to do.

Danny strolled on up Bond Street and into Piccadilly. He thought about the significance, if any, of Blundell's words 'your grandfather's magnificent collection'. He didn't notice that some-one was following him. But then, he was a professional.

◄○►

Hugo picked up the phone.

'He's just left Sotheby's and he's standing at a bus stop in Piccadilly.'

'So he must be running out of funds,' said Hugo. 'Why did he go to Sotheby's?'

'He left an envelope with a Mr Blundell, the head of the philatelic department. It will come up for auction in six weeks' time.'

'What was on the envelope?' asked Hugo.

'A stamp issued to mark the first modern Olympics, which Blundell estimated to be worth between two and two and a half thousand.'

'When's the sale?'

'September sixteenth.'

'Then I'll have to be there,' said Hugo, putting down the phone.

'How unlike your father to allow one of his stamps to be put up for sale. Unless . . .' said Margaret as she folded her napkin.

'I'm not following you, old gal. Unless what?' said Hugo.

'Your father devotes his life to putting together one of the world's finest stamp collections, which not only disappears on the day he dies, but isn't even mentioned in his will. But what *is* mentioned are a key and an envelope, which he leaves to Nick.'

'I'm still not sure what you're getting at, old gal?'

'The key and the envelope are clearly connected in some way,' said Margaret.

'What makes you think that?'

'Because I don't believe the stamp is of any importance.'

'But two thousand pounds would be a great deal of money to Nick at the present time.'

'But not to your father. I suspect that the name and address on the envelope are far more important, because they will lead us to the collection.'

'But we still won't have the key,' said Hugo.

'The key will be of little importance if you can prove that you are the rightful heir to the Moncrieff fortune.'

―◦―

Danny jumped on a bus for Notting Hill Gate, hoping he'd be in time for the monthly meeting with his probation officer. Another ten minutes and he would have had to take a cab. Ms Bennett had written to say that something of importance had come up. Those words made him nervous, though Danny knew that if they had found out who he really was, he wouldn't have been informed by a letter from his probation officer, but would have woken in the middle of the night to find the house surrounded by police.

Although he was becoming more and more confident with his new persona, not a day passed when he wasn't reminded that he was an escaped prisoner. Anything could give him away: a second glance, a misunderstood remark, a casual question to which he didn't know the answer. Who was your housemaster at Loretto? Which college were you in at Sandhurst? Which rugby team do you support?

Two men stepped off the bus when it came to a halt in Notting Hill Gate. One of them began to jog towards the local probation office; the other followed close behind, but didn't enter the building. Although Danny checked in at reception with a couple of minutes to spare, he still had to wait for another twenty minutes before Ms Bennett was free to see him.

Danny entered a small, sparse office that contained only one table and two chairs, no curtains, and a threadbare carpet that would have been left orphaned at a car-boot sale. It wasn't much of an improvement on his cell at Belmarsh.

'How are you, Moncrieff?' asked Ms Bennett as he sat down in the plastic chair opposite her. No 'Sir Nicholas', no 'sir', just 'Moncrieff'.

Behave like Nick, think like Danny. 'I'm well, thank you, Ms Bennett. And you?'

She didn't reply, simply opened a file in front of her that revealed a list of questions that had to be answered by all former prisoners once a month while they are on probation. 'I just want to bring myself up to date,' she began. 'Have you had any success in finding a job as a teacher?'

Danny had forgotten that Nick intended to return to Scotland and teach once he'd been released from prison.

'No,' Danny replied. 'Sorting out my family problems is taking a little longer than I had originally anticipated.'

'Family problems?' repeated Ms Bennett. That wasn't the reply she had expected. Family problems spelt trouble. 'Do you wish to discuss these problems?'

'No, thank you, Ms Bennett,' said Danny. 'I'm just trying to sort out my grandfather's will. There's nothing for you to worry about.'

'I will be the judge of that,' responded Ms Bennett sharply. 'Does this mean you are facing financial difficulties?'

'No, Ms Bennett.'

'Have you found any employment yet?' she asked, returning to her list of questions.

'No, but I expect to be looking for a job in the near future.'

'Presumably as a teacher.'

'Let's hope so,' said Danny.

'Well, if that proves difficult, perhaps you should consider other employment.'

'Like what?'

'Well, I see that you were a librarian in prison.'

'I'd certainly be willing to consider that,' said Danny, confident that would achieve another tick in another box.

'Do you have somewhere to live at the present time, or are you staying in a prison hostel?'

'I have somewhere to live.'

'With your family?'

'No, I have no family.'

One tick, one cross and one question mark. She continued. 'Are you in rented accommodation, or staying with a friend?'

'I live in my own house.'

Ms Bennett looked perplexed. No one had ever given that reply to the question before. She decided on a tick. 'I have just one more question for you. Have you, during the past month, been tempted to commit the same crime as the one you were sent to prison for?'

Yes, I've been tempted to kill Lawrence Davenport, Danny wanted to tell her, but Nick replied, 'No, Ms Bennett, I have not.'

'That will be all for now, Moncrieff. I'll see you again in a month's time. Don't hesitate to get in touch if you feel I can be of any assistance in the meantime.'

'Thank you,' said Danny, 'but you mentioned in your letter that there was something of importance . . .'

'Did I?' said Ms Bennett as she closed the file on her desk to reveal an envelope. 'Ah yes, you're quite right.' She handed him a letter addressed to *N. A. Moncrieff, Education Department, HMP Belmarsh.* Danny began to read a letter to Nick from the UK Matriculation Board to discover what Ms Bennett considered important.

> The results of your A level exams are listed below:
>
> Business Studies A*
>
> Maths A

Danny leapt up and punched his fist in the air as if he was at Upton Park and West Ham had scored the winning goal against Arsenal. Ms Bennett wasn't sure if she should congratulate Moncrieff or press the button under her desk to summon security. When his feet touched the ground, she asked, 'If it's still your intention to take a degree, Moncrieff, I'll be happy to assist you with your application for a grant.'

—o—

Hugo Moncrieff studied the Sotheby's catalogue for some considerable time. He had to agree with Margaret, it could only be Lot 37: *A rare envelope displaying a first-edition stamp celebrating the opening of the modern Olympics addressed to the founder of the Games, Baron Pierre de Coubertin, estimate £2,200–£2,500.*

'Perhaps I should attend one of the viewing days and take a closer look?' he suggested.

'You will do nothing of the sort,' said Margaret firmly. 'That would only alert Nick, and he might even work out that it's not the stamp we're interested in.'

'But if I went down to London the day before the sale and found out the address on the envelope, we'd know where the collection is, without having to waste any money buying it.'

'But then we wouldn't have a calling card.'

'I'm not sure I'm following you, old gal.'

'We may not be in possession of the key, but if your father's only surviving son turns up with the envelope as well as the new will, we must have a chance of convincing whoever is holding the collection on his behalf that you are the rightful heir.'

'But Nick might be at the sale.'

'If he hasn't worked out by then that it's the address that matters, not the stamp, it will be too late for him to do anything about it. Just be thankful of one thing, Hugo.'

'And what's that, old gal?'

'Nick doesn't think like his grandfather.'

◄о►

Danny opened the catalogue once again. He turned to Lot 37 and studied the entry more carefully. He was pleased to find such a full description of his envelope, if not a little disappointed that, unlike several of the other items, there was no photograph accompanying it.

He started to read the conditions of sale and was horrified to discover that Sotheby's deduct 10 per cent of the hammer price from the seller as well as loading a further 20 per cent premium on the buyer. If he ended up with only £1,800, he would have been better off selling the envelope to Stanley Gibbons – which was exactly what Nick would have done.

Danny closed the catalogue and turned his attention to the only other letter he had received that morning: a booklet and an application form from London University to apply for one of its degree courses. He spent some time considering the various options. He finally turned to the section marked grant applications, aware that if he did honour his promise to Nick and Beth, it was going to mean a considerable change in lifestyle.

Nick's current account was down to £716, with not a single addition to the entry column since he had been released from prison. He feared his first sacrifice would have to be Molly, in which case the house would soon return to the state he'd found it in when he had first opened the front door.

Danny had avoided calling Mr Munro for a progress report on his battle with Uncle Hugo for fear it would only prompt another bill. He sat back and thought about the reason he had been willing to take Nick's place. Big Al had convinced him that if he were able to escape, anything was possible. He was, in fact, quickly discovering that a penniless man working on his own was in no position to take on three highly successful professionals, even if they did think he was dead and long forgotten. He thought of the plans he had begun to put in place, starting with tonight's visit to the final performance of *The Importance of Being Earnest*. Its real purpose would come after the curtain had fallen, when he attended the closing-night party and came face to face with Lawrence Davenport for the first time.

44

DANNY ROSE FROM his place and joined the standing ovation, not least because if he hadn't, he would have been one of the few people in the theatre who was still sitting. He had enjoyed the play even more a second time, but that was possibly because he'd now had a chance to read the script.

Sitting in the third row among the family and friends of the cast had only added to his enjoyment. The set designer sat on one side of him, and the wife of the producer on the other. They invited him to join them for a drink in the extended interval. He listened to theatre talk, rarely feeling confident enough to offer an opinion. It didn't seem to matter, as they all had unshakeable views on everything from Davenport's performance to why the West End was full of musicals. Danny appeared to have only one thing in common with theatre folk: none of them seemed to know what their next job would be.

After Davenport had taken countless curtain calls, the audience slowly made their way out of the theatre. As it was a clear night, Danny decided he would walk to the Dorchester. The exercise would do him good, and in any case, he couldn't afford the expense of a cab.

He began to stroll towards Piccadilly Circus, when a voice behind him said, 'Sir Nicholas?' He looked round to see the box office manager hailing him with one hand, while holding a taxi door open with the other. 'If you're going to the party, why don't you join us?'

'Thank you,' said Danny, and climbed in to find two young women sitting on the back seat.

'This is Sir Nicholas Moncrieff,' said the box office manager as he unfolded one of the seats and sat down to face them.

'Nick,' insisted Danny as he sat on the other folding seat.

'Nick, this is my girlfriend Charlotte. She works in props. And this is Katie, who's an understudy. I'm Paul.'

'Which part do you understudy?' Nick asked Katie.

'I stand in for Eve Best, who's been playing Gwendolen.'

'But not tonight,' said Danny.

'No,' admitted Katie, as she crossed her legs. 'In fact, I've only done one performance during the entire run. A matinee when Eve had to fulfil a commitment for the BBC.'

'Isn't that a little frustrating?' asked Danny.

'It sure is, but it beats being out of work.'

'Every understudy lives in hope that they'll be discovered while the lead is indisposed,' said Paul. 'Albert Finney took over from Larry Olivier when he was playing Coriolanus at Stratford, and became a star overnight.'

'Well, it didn't happen the one afternoon I was on stage,' said Katie with feeling. 'What about you, Nick, what do you do?'

Danny didn't reply immediately, partly because no one except his probation officer had ever asked him that question. 'I used to be a soldier,' he said.

'My brother's a soldier,' said Charlotte. 'I'm worried that he might be sent to Iraq. Have you ever served there?'

Danny tried to recall the relevant entries in Nick's diary. 'Twice,' he replied. 'But not recently,' he added.

Katie smiled at Danny as the cab drew up outside the Dorchester. He remembered so well the last young woman who had looked at him that way.

Danny was the last to climb out of the taxi. He heard himself saying, 'Let me get this one,' quite expecting Paul's reply to be, *Certainly not.*

'Thanks, Nick,' said Paul, as he and Charlotte strolled into the hotel. Danny took out his wallet and parted with another ten pounds he could ill afford – one thing was certain, he would be walking home tonight.

Katie hung back and waited for Nick to join her. 'Paul tells me this is the second time you've seen the show,' she said as they made their way into the hotel.

'I came on the off-chance you'd be playing Gwendolen,' said Danny with a grin.

She smiled and kissed his cheek. Something else Danny hadn't experienced for a long time. 'You're sweet, Nick,' she said as she took his hand and led him into the ballroom.

'So what are you hoping to do next?' asked Danny, almost having to shout above the noise of the crowd.

'Three months of rep with the English Touring Company.'

'Understudying again?'

'No, they can't afford understudies on tour. If anyone falls out, the programme seller takes your place. So this is going to be my chance to be on stage, and your chance to come and see me.'

'Where will you be performing?' asked Danny.

'Take your choice – Newcastle, Sheffield, Birmingham, Cambridge or Bromley.'

'I think it will have to be Bromley,' said Danny as a waiter offered them champagne.

He looked around the overcrowded room. Everyone seemed to be talking at once. Those that weren't were drinking champagne, while others continually moved from person to person, hoping to impress directors, producers and casting agents in an endless quest to land their next job.

Danny let go of Katie's hand, recalling that, not unlike the out-of-work actors, he had a purpose for being there. He slowly scanned the room in search of Lawrence Davenport, but there was no sign of him. Danny assumed that he would make an entrance later.

'Bored with me already?' asked Katie, grabbing another glass of champagne from a passing waiter.

'No,' said Danny unconvincingly, as a young man joined them.

'Hi, Katie,' he said, kissing her on the cheek. 'Have you got another job lined up or are you resting?'

Danny took a sausage from a passing tray, remembering that he wouldn't be having anything else to eat that night. Once again he looked around the room in search of Davenport. His eyes rested on another man he should have realized might be there that evening. He was standing in the centre of the room chatting to a couple of girls who were hanging on his every word. He wasn't as tall as Danny remembered from their last encounter, but then, it had been in an unlit alley, and his only interest had been in saving Bernie's life.

Danny decided to take a closer look. He took a pace towards him, and then another, until he was just a few feet away. Spencer Craig looked straight at him. Danny froze, then realized Craig was looking over his shoulder, probably at another girl.

Danny stared at the man who had killed his best friend and thought he'd got away with it. 'Not while I'm still alive,' said Danny, almost loud enough for Craig to hear. He took another pace forward, emboldened by Craig's lack of interest. Another pace, and a man in Craig's group, who had his back to Danny, instinctively turned round to see who was invading his territory. Danny came face to face with Gerald Payne. He'd put on so much weight since the trial that it was a few seconds before Danny recognized him. Payne turned back, uninterested. Even when he had appeared in the witness box, he hadn't given Danny a second look – no doubt part of the tactics Craig had advised him to adopt.

Danny helped himself to a smoked salmon blini while listening to Craig's conversation with the two girls. He was delivering an obviously well-rehearsed line about the courtroom being rather like the theatre, except that you never know when the curtain will fall. Both girls dutifully laughed.

'Very true,' said Danny in a loud voice. Craig and Payne both looked at him, but without a flicker of recognition, despite the fact that they had seen him in the dock only two years before, but at that time his hair had been a lot shorter, he had been unshaven and wearing prison clothes. In any case, why should they give Danny Cartwright a thought? After all, he was dead and buried.

'How are you getting on, Nick?' Danny turned to find Paul standing by his side.

'Very well, thank you,' said Danny. 'Better than I expected,' he added without explanation. Danny took a pace closer to Craig and

Payne so that they could hear his voice, but nothing seemed to distract them from their conversation with the two girls.

A burst of applause erupted around the room, and all heads turned to watch Lawrence Davenport as he made his entrance. He smiled and waved as if he were visiting royalty. He made his way slowly across the floor, receiving plaudits and praise with every step he took. Danny remembered Scott Fitzgerald's haunting line: *While the actor danced, he could find no mirrors, so he leant back to admire his image in the chandeliers.*

'Would you like to meet him?' asked Paul, who had noticed that Danny couldn't take his eyes off Davenport.

'Yes, I would,' said Danny, curious to discover if the actor would treat him with the same indifference as his fellow Musketeers.

'Then follow me.' They began to make slow progress across the crowded ballroom, but before they reached Davenport, Danny came to a sudden halt. He stared at the woman the actor was addressing, with whom it was clear he was on intimate terms.

'So good-looking,' said Danny.

'Yes he is, isn't he,' agreed Paul, but before Danny could correct him, he said, 'Larry, I want you to meet a friend of mine, Nick Moncrieff.'

Davenport didn't bother to shake hands with Danny; he was just another face in the crowd hoping for an audience. Danny smiled at Davenport's girlfriend.

'Hello,' she said. 'I'm Sarah.'

'Nick. Nick Moncrieff,' he replied. 'You must be an actress.'

'No, far less glamorous. I'm a solicitor.'

'You don't look like a solicitor,' said Danny. Sarah didn't respond. She had clearly heard that dull response before.

'And are you an actor?' she asked.

'I'll be whatever you want me to be,' Danny replied, and this time she did smile.

'Hi, Sarah,' said another young man, putting an arm round her waist. 'You are without question the most gorgeous woman in the room,' he said before kissing her on both cheeks.

Sarah laughed. 'I'd be flattered, Charlie, if I didn't know that it's my brother you really fancy, not me.'

'Are you Lawrence Davenport's sister?' said Danny in disbelief.

'Someone has to be,' said Sarah. 'But I've learnt to live with it.'

'What about your friend?' said Charlie, smiling at Danny.

'I don't think so,' said Sarah. 'Nick, this is Charlie Duncan, who produced the play.'

'Pity,' said Charlie, and turned his attention to the young men surrounding Davenport.

'I think he fancies you,' said Sarah.

'But I'm not . . .'

'I'd just about worked that out,' said Sarah with a grin.

Danny continued to flirt with Sarah, aware that he no longer needed to bother with Davenport when his sister could undoubtedly tell him everything he needed to know.

'Perhaps we might—' began Danny, when another voice said, 'Hi, Sarah, I was wondering if . . .'

'Hello, Spencer,' she said coldly. 'Do you know Nick Moncrieff?'

'No,' he replied, and after a cursory handshake, he continued his conversation with Sarah. 'I was just coming across to tell Larry how brilliant he was when I spotted you.'

'Well, now's your chance,' said Sarah.

'But I was also hoping to have a word with you.'

'I was just about to leave,' said Sarah, checking her watch.

'But the party's only just begun, can't you hang around a little longer?'

'I'm afraid not, Spencer. I need to go over some papers before briefing counsel.'

'It's just that I was hoping . . .'

'Just as you were on the last occasion we met.'

'I think we got off on the wrong foot.'

'I seem to remember it being the wrong hand,' said Sarah, turning her back on him.

'Sorry about that, Nick,' said Sarah. 'Some men don't know when to take no for an answer, while others . . .' She gave him a gentle smile. 'I hope we'll meet again.'

'How do I—' began Danny, but Sarah was already halfway across the ballroom; the kind of woman who assumes that if you want to find her, you will. Danny turned back to see Craig looking more closely at him.

'Spencer, good of you to come,' said Davenport. 'Was I all right tonight?'

'Never better,' said Craig.

Danny thought it was time to leave. He no longer needed to talk to Davenport, and like Sarah, he also had a meeting he had to prepare for. He intended to be wide awake when the auctioneer called for an opening bid for Lot 37.

'Hi, stranger. Where did you disappear to?'

'Ran into an old enemy,' said Danny. 'And you?'

'The usual bunch. So boring,' said Katie. 'I've had enough of this party. How about you?'

'I was just leaving.'

'Good idea,' said Katie, taking him by the hand. 'Why don't we jump ship together?'

They walked across the ballroom and headed towards the swing doors. Once Katie had stepped out on to the pavement, she hailed a taxi.

'Where to, miss?' asked the driver.

'Where are we going?' Katie asked Nick.

'Twelve The Boltons.'

'Right you are, guv,' said the cabbie, which brought back unhappy memories for Danny.

Danny hadn't even sat down before he felt a hand on his thigh. Katie's other arm draped around his neck, and she pulled him towards her.

'I'm sick of being the understudy,' she said. 'I'm going to take the lead for a change.' She leant across and kissed him.

By the time the taxi drew up outside Nick's home, there were very few buttons left to undo. Katie jumped out of the cab and ran up the drive as Danny paid for a second taxi that night.

'I wish I was your age,' remarked the cabbie.

Danny laughed and joined Katie at the front door. It took him some time to get the key in the lock, and as they stumbled into the hall she pulled off his jacket. They left a trail of clothes all the way from the front door to the bedroom. She dragged him on to the bed and pulled him on top of her. Something else Danny hadn't experienced for a long time.

45

DANNY JUMPED OFF the bus and began walking up Bond Street. He could see a blue flag fluttering in the breeze, boldly displaying in gold the legend *Sotheby's*.

Danny had never attended an auction before, and was beginning to wish he'd sat in on one or two other sales before he lost his virginity. The uniformed officer on the door saluted him as he walked in, as if he were a regular who thought nothing of spending a few million on a minor Impressionist.

'Where is the stamp sale being held?' Danny asked the woman behind the reception desk.

'Up the stairs,' she said, pointing to her right, 'on the first floor. You can't miss it. Do you want a paddle?' she asked. Danny wasn't sure what she meant. 'Will you be bidding?'

'No,' said Danny. 'Collecting, I hope.'

Danny climbed the stairs and walked into a large, brightly lit room, to find half a dozen people milling around. He wasn't certain if he was in the right place until he spotted Mr Blundell talking to a man in smart green overalls. The room was filled with rows and rows of chairs, although only a few were occupied. At the front, where Blundell was standing, was a highly polished circular podium, from which Danny assumed the auction would be conducted. On the wall behind it was a large screen giving the conversion rates of several different currencies, so that any bidders from abroad would know how much they were expected to pay, while on the right-hand side of the room a row of white telephones were evenly spaced on a long table.

Danny hung around at the back of the room as more people began to stroll in and take their places. He decided to sit at the far end of the back row so that he could keep his eye on all those who were bidding, as well as the auctioneer. He felt like an observer rather than a participant. Danny leafed through the pages of the catalogue, although he had already read it several times. His only real interest was Lot 37, but he noticed that Lot 36, an 1861 Cape of Good Hope four penny red, had a low estimate of £40,000 and a high of £60,000, making it the most expensive item in the sale.

He looked up to see Mr Prendergast from Stanley Gibbons enter the room and join a small group of dealers who were whispering among themselves at the back of the room.

Danny began to relax as more and more people carrying paddles strolled in and took their seats. He checked his watch – the one Nick's grandfather had given him for his twenty-first birthday – it was ten to ten. He couldn't help noticing when a man who must have weighed over twenty-five stone waddled into the room, carrying a large unlit cigar in his right hand. He made his way slowly down the aisle before taking a seat on the end of the fifth row that appeared to have been reserved for him.

When Blundell spotted the man – not that he could have missed him – he left the group he was with and walked across to greet him. To Danny's surprise they both turned and looked in his direction. Blundell raised his catalogue in acknowledgement, and Danny nodded. The man with the cigar smiled as if he recognized Danny, and then continued his conversation with the auctioneer.

The seats were quickly beginning to fill as seasoned customers appeared only moments before Blundell returned to the front of the sale room. He mounted the half-dozen steps of the podium, smiled down at his potential customers, and then filled a glass with water before checking the clock on the wall. He tapped his microphone and said, 'Good morning, ladies and gentlemen, and welcome to our biannual auction of rare stamps. Lot number one.' An enlarged image of the stamp displayed in the catalogue appeared on the screen by his side.

'We begin today with a penny black, dated eighteen forty-one, in near mint condition. Do I see an opening bid of one thousand pounds?' A dealer standing in Prendergast's small group at the back raised his paddle. 'One thousand two hundred?' This was met by an immediate response from a bidder in the third row who, six bids later, ended up purchasing the stamp for £1,800.

Danny was delighted that the penny black had sold for a far higher price than its estimate, but as each new lot came under the hammer, the prices achieved were inconsistent. There seemed no reason to Danny why some of them exceeded the high estimate, while others failed to reach the low, after which the auctioneer said quietly, 'No sale.' Danny didn't want to think about the consequences of 'no sale' when it came to Lot 37.

Danny occasionally glanced at the man with the cigar, but there was no sign that he was bidding for any of the early lots. He hoped his interest was in the de Coubertin envelope, otherwise why would Blundell have pointed him out?

By the time the auctioneer had reached Lot 35, an assortment of Commonwealth stamps which was disposed of in less than thirty seconds for £1,000, Danny was becoming increasingly nervous. Lot No. 36 caused an outbreak of chatter, which made Danny check his catalogue once again: the 1861 Cape of Good Hope four penny red, one of only six known in the world.

Blundell opened the bidding at £30,000, and after some dealers and a few minor collectors had dropped out, the only two bidders left appeared to be the man with the cigar and an anonymous telephone bidder. Danny watched the man with the cigar very closely. He didn't seem to give any sign that he was bidding, but when Blundell finally received a shake of the head from the woman on the phone, he turned back to him and said, 'Sold to Mr Hunsacker for seventy-five thousand pounds.' The man smiled and removed the cigar from his mouth.

Danny had become so engrossed in the bidding war that had just taken place that he was taken by surprise when Blundell announced, 'Lot number thirty-seven, a unique envelope showing an 1896 first edition of a stamp issued by the French government to celebrate the opening ceremony of the modern Olympic Games. The envelope is addressed to the founder of the Games, Baron

Pierre de Coubertin. Do I have an opening bid of a thousand pounds?' Danny was disappointed that Blundell had started the bidding at such a low figure, until he saw several paddles being raised around the room.

'Fifteen hundred?' Almost as many.

'Two thousand?' Not quite as many.

'Two thousand five hundred?' Mr Hunsacker kept the unlit cigar in his mouth.

'Three thousand?' Danny craned his neck and peered around the room, but couldn't see where the bidding was coming from.

'Three thousand five hundred?' The cigar remained in the mouth.

'Four thousand. Four thousand five hundred. Five thousand. Five thousand five hundred. Six thousand.' Hunsacker removed his cigar and frowned.

'Sold, to the gentleman in the front row, for six thousand pounds,' said the auctioneer as he brought the hammer down. 'Lot thirty-eight, a rare example of . . .'

Danny tried to see who was seated in the front row, but he couldn't work out which one of them had bought his envelope. He wanted to thank them for bidding three times the high estimate. He felt a tap on his shoulder, and looked round to see the man with the cigar towering over him.

'My name is Gene Hunsacker,' he said in a voice almost as loud as the auctioneer's. 'If you'd care to join me for a coffee, Sir Nicholas, it's possible that we may have something of mutual interest to discuss. I'm a Texan,' he said, shaking Danny by the hand, 'which may not come as a big surprise as we met in Washington. I had the honour of knowing your grand-daddy,' he added as they left the room and walked down the stairs together. Danny didn't say a word. Never offer hostages, he had learnt since he had begun playing the role of Nick. When they reached the ground floor, Hunsacker led him into the restaurant and headed for another seat that appeared to be his by right.

'Two black coffees,' he said to a passing waiter, without giving Danny any choice. 'Now, Sir Nicholas. I'm puzzled.'

'Puzzled?' said Danny, speaking for the first time.

'I can't work out why you let the de Coubertin come up for auction, and then allowed your uncle to outbid me for it. Unless you and he were working together, and hoped you could force me to go even higher.'

'My uncle and I are not on speaking terms,' said Danny, selecting his words carefully.

'That's something you have in common with your late grand-daddy,' said Hunsacker.

'You were a friend of my grandfather's?' asked Danny.

'*Friend* would be presumptuous,' said the Texan. 'Pupil and follower would be nearer the mark. He once outfoxed me for a rare two penny blue way back in 1977 when I was still a rookie collector, but I learnt quickly from him and, to be fair, he was a generous teacher. I keep reading in the press that I have the finest stamp collection on earth, but it just ain't true. That honour goes to your late grand-daddy.' Hunsacker sipped his coffee before adding, 'Many years ago he tipped me off that he'd be leaving the collection to his grandson, and not to either of his sons.'

'My father is dead,' Danny said.

Hunsacker looked surprised. 'I know – I was at his funeral. I thought you saw me.'

'I did,' said Danny, recalling Nick's description of the *vast American* in his diary. 'But they would only allow me to speak to my solicitor,' he added quickly.

'Yes, I know,' said Hunsacker. 'But I managed to have a word with your uncle and let him know that I was in the market should you ever want to dispose of the collection. He promised to keep in touch. That's when I realized that he hadn't inherited it, and that your grand-daddy must have kept his word and left the collection to you. So when Mr Blundell phoned to tell me that you'd put the de Coubertin up for sale, I flew back across the pond in the hope that we might meet.'

'I don't even know where the collection is,' admitted Danny.

'Maybe that explains why Hugo was willing to pay so much for your envelope,' said the Texan, 'because he has absolutely no interest in stamps. There he is now.' Hunsacker pointed his cigar at a man standing at the reception desk. So that's Uncle Hugo, Danny thought, taking a closer look at him. He could only wonder why he wanted the envelope so badly that he'd been willing to pay three times its estimated value. Danny watched as Hugo passed a cheque to Mr Blundell, who in return handed over the envelope.

'You're an idiot,' muttered Danny, rising from his place.

'What did you say?' asked Hunsacker, the cigar falling out of his mouth.

'Me, not you,' said Danny quickly. 'It's been staring me in the face for the past two months. It's the address he's after, not the envelope, because that's where Sir Alexander's collection has to be.'

Gene looked even more puzzled. Why would Nick describe his grandfather as Sir Alexander?

'I have to go, Mr Hunsacker, I apologize. I should never have sold the envelope in the first place.'

'I wish I knew what in hell's name you were talking about,' said Hunsacker, taking a wallet from an inside pocket. He passed a card across to Danny. 'If you ever decide to sell the collection, at least give me first option. I'd offer you a fair price with no ten per cent deduction.'

'And no twenty per cent premium either,' said Danny with a grin.

'A chip off the older block,' said Gene. 'Your grand-daddy was a brilliant and resourceful gentleman, unlike your uncle Hugo, as I'm sure you realize.'

'Goodbye, Mr Hunsacker,' said Danny as he tucked the card into Nick's wallet. His eyes never left Hugo Moncrieff, who had just put the envelope into a briefcase. He walked across the lobby to join a woman Danny hadn't noticed until that moment. She linked her arm in his and the two of them left the building quickly.

Danny waited for a few seconds before following them. Once he was back on Bond Street, he looked left and then right, and when he spotted them he was surprised by how much ground they'd already covered. It was clear they were in a hurry. They turned right as they passed the statue of Churchill and Roosevelt sitting on a bench, and then left when they reached Albemarle Street, where they crossed the road and walked for a few more yards before disappearing into Brown's Hotel.

Danny hung around outside the hotel for a few moments while he considered his options. He knew that if they spotted him they would think it was Nick. He entered the building cautiously, but there was no sign of either of them in the lobby. Danny took a seat that was half concealed by a pillar, but still allowed him a clear view of the lifts as well as reception. He didn't pay any attention to a man who had just sat down on the other side of the lobby.

Danny waited for another thirty minutes, and began to wonder if he'd missed them. He was about to get up and check with reception when the lift doors opened, and out stepped Hugo and the woman pulling two suitcases. They walked across to the reception desk, where the woman settled the bill before they quickly left the hotel by a different door. Danny rushed out on to the pavement to see them climbing into the back of a black cab. He hailed the next one on the rank, and even before he had closed the door shouted, 'Follow that cab.'

'I've waited all my life to hear someone say that,' the cabbie responded as he pulled away from the kerb.

The taxi in front turned right at the end of the road and made its way towards Hyde Park Corner, through the underpass, along Brompton Road and on to the Westway.

'Looks like they're heading for the airport,' said the cabbie. Twenty minutes later he was proved right.

When the two cabs emerged from the Heathrow underpass, Danny's driver said, 'Terminal two. So they must be flying to somewhere in Europe.' They both came to a halt outside the entrance. The meter read £34.50, and Danny handed over forty pounds but remained in the cab until Hugo and the woman had disappeared inside the terminal.

He followed them in, and watched as they joined a queue of business-class passengers. The screen above the check-in desk read *BA0732, Geneva, 13.55.*

'Idiot,' Danny muttered again, recalling the address on the envelope. But where exactly in Geneva had it been? He looked at his watch. He still had enough time to buy a ticket and catch the plane. He ran across to the British Airways sales counter, and had to wait some time before he reached the front of the queue.

'Can you get me on the 13.55 to Geneva?' he asked, trying not to sound desperate.

'Do you have any luggage, sir?' asked the assistant behind the sales counter.

'None,' said Danny.

She checked her computer. 'They haven't closed the gate yet, so you should still be able to make it. Business or economy?'

'Economy,' said Danny, wanting to avoid the section where Hugo and the woman would be seated.

'Window or aisle?'

'Window.'

'That will be £217, sir.'

'Thank you,' said Danny as he passed over his credit card.

'May I see your passport, please?'

Danny had never had a passport in his life. 'My passport?'

'Yes, sir, your passport.'

'Oh no, I must have left it at home.'

'Then I'm afraid you won't be in time to catch the plane, sir.'

'Idiot, idiot,' said Danny.

'I beg your pardon?'

'I'm so sorry,' said Danny. 'Me, not you,' he repeated. She smiled.

Danny turned round and walked slowly back across the concourse, feeling helpless. He didn't notice Hugo and the woman leave through the gate marked *Departures, Passengers only*, but someone else did, who had been watching both them and Danny closely.

◄○►

Hugo pressed the green button on his mobile just as the tannoy announced, 'Final call for all passengers travelling to Geneva on flight BA0732. Please make your way to gate nineteen.'

'He followed you from Sotheby's to the hotel, and then from the hotel to Heathrow.'

'Is he on the same flight as us?' asked Hugo.

'No, he didn't have his passport with him.'

'Typical Nick. Where is he now?'

'On his way back to London, so you should have at least a twenty-four-hour start on him.'

'Let's hope that's enough, but don't let him out of your sight for a moment.' Hugo turned off his phone, as he and Margaret left their seats to board the aircraft.

◄○►

'Have you come across another heirloom, Sir Nicholas?' asked Mr Blundell hopefully.

'No, but I do need to know if you have a copy of the envelope from this morning's sale,' said Danny.

'Yes, of course,' replied Blundell. 'We retain a photograph of every item sold at auction, in case a dispute should arise at some later date.'

'Would it be possible to see it?' asked Danny.

'Is there a problem?' asked Blundell.

'No,' Danny replied. 'I just need to check the address on the envelope.'

'Of course,' repeated Blundell. He tapped some keys on his computer, and a moment later an image of the envelope appeared on the screen. He swivelled the screen round so that Danny could see it.

Baron de Coubertin
25 rue de la Croix-Rouge
Genève
La Suisse

Danny copied down the name and address. 'Do you by any chance know if Baron de Coubertin was a serious stamp collector?' asked Danny.

'Not to my knowledge,' said Blundell. 'But of course his son was the founder of one of the most successful banks in Europe.'

'Idiot,' said Danny. 'Idiot,' he repeated as he turned to leave.

'I do hope, Sir Nicholas, that you are not dissatisfied with the result of this morning's sale?'

Danny turned back. 'No, of course not, Mr Blundell, I do apologize. Yes, thank you.' Another of those moments when he should have behaved like Nick, and only thought like Danny.

—◄○►—

The first thing Danny did when he arrived back at The Boltons was to search for Nick's passport. Molly knew exactly where it was. 'And by the way,' she added, 'a Mr Fraser Munro called, and asked you to phone him.'

Danny retreated to the study, called Munro and told him everything that had happened that morning. The old solicitor listened to all his client had to say, but didn't comment.

'I'm glad you phoned back,' he eventually said, 'because I have some news for you, although it might be unwise to discuss it over the phone. I was wondering when you next expected to be in Scotland.'

'I could catch the sleeper train tonight,' said Danny.

'Good, and perhaps it might be wise for you to bring your passport with you this time.'

'For Scotland?' said Danny.

'No, Sir Nicholas. For Geneva.'

46

MR AND MRS MONCRIEFF were ushered into the boardroom by the chairman's secretary.

'The chairman will be with you in a moment,' she said. 'Would you care for coffee or tea while you're waiting?'

'No, thank you,' said Margaret, as her husband began pacing around the room. She took a seat in one of the sixteen Charles Rennie Mackintosh chairs placed around the long oak table, and that should have made her feel at home. The walls were painted in a pale Wedgwood blue with full-length oil portraits of past chairmen hanging on every available space, giving an impression of stability and wealth. Margaret said nothing until the secretary had left the room and closed the door behind her.

'Calm down, Hugo. The last thing we need is for the chairman to think we're unsure about your claim. Now come and sit down.'

'It's all very well, old gal,' said Hugo, continuing his perambulations, 'but don't forget that our whole future rests on the outcome of this meeting.'

'All the more reason for you to behave in a calm and rational manner. You must appear as if you've come to claim what is rightfully yours,' she said as the door at the far end of the room opened.

An elderly gentleman entered the room. Although he stooped and carried a silver cane, such was his air of authority that no one would have doubted he was the bank's chairman.

'Good morning, Mr and Mrs Moncrieff,' he said, and shook hands with both of them. 'My name is Pierre de Coubertin, and it's a pleasure to meet you,' he added. His English revealed no trace of an accent. He took a seat at the head of the table, below a portrait of an elderly gentleman who, but for a large grey moustache, was a reflection of himself. 'How may I assist you?'

'Rather simple, really,' responded Hugo. 'I have come to claim the inheritance left to me by my father.'

Not a flicker of recognition passed across the chairman's face. 'May I ask what your father's name was?' he said.

'Sir Alexander Moncrieff.'

'And what makes you think that your father conducted any business with this bank?'

'It was no secret within the family,' said Hugo. 'He told both my brother Angus and myself on several occasions about his long-standing relationship with this bank, which, among other things, was the guardian of his unique stamp collection.'

'Do you have any evidence to support such a claim?'

'No, I do not,' said Hugo. 'My father considered it unwise to commit such matters to paper, given our country's tax laws, but he assured me that you were well aware of his wishes.'

'I see,' said de Coubertin. 'Perhaps he furnished you with an account number?'

'No, he did not,' said Hugo, beginning to show a little impatience. 'But I have been briefed on my legal position by the family's solicitor, and he assures me that as I am my father's sole heir following my brother's death, you have no choice but to release what is rightfully mine.'

'That may well be the case,' confirmed de Coubertin, 'but I must enquire if you are in possession of any documents that would substantiate your claim.'

'Yes,' said Hugo, placing his briefcase on the table. He flicked it open and produced the envelope he had bought from Sotheby's the previous day. He pushed it across to the other side of the table. 'This was left to me by my father.'

De Coubertin spent some time studying the envelope addressed to his grandfather. 'Fascinating,' he said, 'but it does not prove that your father held an account with this bank. It may be wise at this juncture for me to ascertain if that was indeed the case.

Perhaps you'd be kind enough to excuse me for a moment?' The old man rose slowly from his place, bowed low and left the room without another word.

'He knows perfectly well that your father did business with this bank,' said Margaret, 'but for some reason he's playing for time.'

—◦—

'Good morning, Sir Nicholas,' said Fraser Munro as he rose from behind his desk. 'I trust you had a comfortable journey?'

'It might have been more comfortable if I hadn't been painfully aware that my uncle is at this moment in Geneva trying to relieve me of my inheritance.'

'Rest assured,' responded Munro, 'that in my experience Swiss bankers do not make hasty decisions. No, we will come to Geneva in good time. But for the moment, we must deal with more pressing matters that have arisen on our own doorstep.'

'Is this the problem you felt unable to discuss over the phone?' asked Danny.

'Precisely,' said Munro, 'and I fear that I am not the bearer of glad tidings. Your uncle is now claiming that your grandfather made a second will, only weeks before his death, in which he disinherited you and left his entire estate to your father.'

'Do you have a copy of this will?' asked Danny.

'I do,' replied Munro, 'but as I was not satisfied with a facsimile I travelled to Edinburgh to attend Mr Desmond Galbraith in his chambers in order that I could inspect the original.'

'And what conclusion did you come to?' asked Danny.

'The first thing I did was to compare your grandfather's signature with the one on the original will.'

'And?' said Danny, trying not to sound anxious.

'I was not convinced, but if it is a fake, it's a damned good one,' replied Munro. 'On a brief inspection, I could also find no fault with the paper or the ribbon, which appeared to be of the same vintage as those of the original will he executed on your behalf.'

'Can it get any worse?'

'I'm afraid so,' said Munro. 'Mr Galbraith also mentioned a

letter purportedly sent to your father by your grandfather a short time before he died.'

'Did they allow you to see it?'

'Yes. It was typewritten, which surprised me, because your grandfather always wrote his letters by hand; he distrusted machinery. He described the typewriter as a new-fangled invention that would be the death of fine writing.'

'What did the letter say?' asked Danny.

'That your grandfather had decided to disinherit you, and that he had accordingly written a new will, leaving everything to your father. Particularly clever.'

'Clever?'

'Yes. If the estate had been divided between both of his sons, it would have looked suspicious, because too many people were aware that he and your uncle hadn't been on speaking terms for years.'

'But this way,' said Danny, 'Uncle Hugo still ends up with everything, because my father left his entire estate to him. But you used the word "clever". Does that mean that you have your doubts about whether my grandfather actually wrote the letter?'

'I most certainly do,' said Munro, 'and not simply because it was typed. It was on two sheets of your grandfather's personal stationery, which I recognized immediately, but for some inexplicable reason the first page was typed, while the second was handwritten and bore only the words, *These are my personal wishes and I rely on you both to see they are carried out to the letter, your loving father, Alexander Moncrieff.* The first page, the typewritten one, detailed those personal wishes, while the second was not only handwritten, but was identical in every word to the one that was attached to the original will. Quite a coincidence.'

'But surely that alone must be enough proof . . . ?'

'I fear not,' said Munro. 'Although we may have every reason to believe that the letter is a fake, the facts are that it was written on your grandfather's personal stationery, the typewriter used is of the correct vintage, and the writing on the second page is unquestionably in your grandfather's hand. I doubt if there's a court in the land that would uphold our claim. And if that weren't enough,' continued Munro, 'your uncle served a trespass order on us yesterday.'

'A trespass order?' said Danny.

'Not satisfied that the new will claims he is now the rightful heir to both the estate in Scotland and the house in The Boltons, he is also demanding that you vacate the latter within thirty days, or he will serve you with a court order demanding rent that is commensurate with that of similar properties in the area, back-dated to the day you took over occupation.'

'So I've lost everything,' said Danny.

'Not quite,' said Munro. 'Although I admit that matters do look a little bleak on the home front, but when it comes to Geneva, you still have the key. I suspect that the bank will be loath to hand over anything that belonged to your grandfather to someone who is unable to produce that key.' He paused for a moment before he delivered the next sentence. 'And of one thing I am certain. If your grandfather had been placed in this position, he would not have taken it lying down.'

'And neither would I,' said Danny, 'if I had the finances to take Hugo on. But despite yesterday's sale of the envelope, it will only be a matter of weeks before my uncle can add a writ for bankruptcy to the long list of actions we are already defending.'

Mr Munro smiled for the first time that morning. 'I had anticipated this problem, Sir Nicholas, and yesterday afternoon my partners and I discussed what we should do about your current dilemma.' He coughed. 'They were of the unanimous opinion that we should break with one of our long-held customs, and not present any further bills until this action has reached a satisfactory conclusion.'

'But should the case fail when it comes to court – and let me assure you, Mr Munro, that I have some experience in these matters – I would end up being perpetually in your debt.'

'Should *we* fail,' replied Munro, 'no bills will be presented, because this firm remains perpetually in your grandfather's debt.'

◄○►

The chairman returned after a few minutes, and resumed the place opposite his would-be customers. He smiled. 'Mr Moncrieff,' he began. 'I have been able to confirm that Sir Alexander did indeed conduct some business with this bank. We must now attempt to establish your claim to be the sole heir to his estate.'

'I can supply you with any documentation you require,' said Hugo with confidence.

'First, I must ask you if you are in possession of a passport, Mr Moncrieff?'

'Yes I am,' replied Hugo, who opened his briefcase, extracted his passport and handed it across the table.

De Coubertin turned to the back page and studied the photograph for a moment before returning the passport to Hugo. 'Do you have your father's death certificate?' he asked.

'Yes,' replied Hugo, taking a second document from his briefcase and pushing it across the table.

This time the chairman studied the document a little more carefully before nodding and handing it back. 'And do you also have your brother's death certificate?' he asked. Hugo passed over a third document. Once again de Coubertin took his time before handing it back. 'I will also need to see your brother's will, to confirm that he left the bulk of the estate to you.' Hugo handed over the will and put another tick against the long list Galbraith had prepared for him.

De Coubertin did not speak for some time while he studied Angus Moncrieff's will. 'That all seems to be in order,' he said eventually. 'But most important of all, are you in possession of your father's will?'

'Not only am I able to supply you with his last Will and Testament,' said Hugo, 'signed and dated six weeks before his death, but I am also in possession of a letter he wrote to my brother Angus and myself that was attached to that will.' Hugo slid both documents across the table, but de Coubertin made no attempt to study either of them.

'And finally, Mr Moncrieff, I must ask if there was a key among your father's bequests?'

Hugo hesitated.

'There most certainly was,' said Margaret, speaking for the first time, 'but unfortunately it has been mislaid, although I have seen it many times over the years. It's quite small, silver, and, if I remember correctly, it has a number stamped on it.'

'And do you recall that number by any chance, Mrs Moncrieff?' asked the chairman.

'Unfortunately I do not,' Margaret finally admitted.

'In that case, I'm sure you will appreciate the bank's dilemma,' said de Coubertin. 'As you can imagine, without the key, we are placed in an invidious position. However,' he added before Margaret could interrupt, 'I will ask one of our experts to study the will, which as I'm sure you are aware is common practice in such circumstances. Should they consider it to be authentic, we will hand over any possessions we are holding in Sir Alexander's name.'

'But how long will that take?' asked Hugo, aware that it would not take Nick long to work out where they were, and what they were up to.

'A day, a day and a half at the most,' said the chairman.

'When should we return?' asked Margaret.

'To be on the safe side, let us say three o'clock tomorrow afternoon.'

'Thank you,' said Margaret. 'We look forward to seeing you then.'

De Coubertin accompanied Mr and Mrs Moncrieff to the bank's front door without discussing anything more significant than the weather.

—◦—

'I've booked you on a BA business-class flight to Barcelona,' said Beth. 'You fly from Heathrow on Sunday evening, and you'll be staying at the Arts Hotel.' She handed her boss a folder which contained all the documents he would need for the trip, including the names of several recommended restaurants and a guide to the city. 'The conference opens at nine o'clock with a speech from the International President, Dick Sherwood. You'll be sitting on the platform along with the other seven VPs. The organizers have asked you to be in your place by eight forty-five.'

'How far away from the conference centre is the hotel?' asked Mr Thomas.

'It's just across the road,' said Beth. 'Is there anything else you need to know?'

'Just one thing,' Thomas replied. 'How would you like to join me for the trip?'

Beth was taken by surprise, something Thomas didn't manage that often, and admitted, 'I've always wanted to visit Barcelona.'

'Well, now's your chance,' said Thomas, giving her a warm smile.

'But would there be enough for me to do while I was there?' asked Beth.

'For a start, you could make sure I'm sitting in my place on time next Monday morning.' Beth didn't respond. 'I was rather hoping you might relax for a change,' Thomas added. 'We could go to the opera, take in the Thyssen Collection, study Picasso's early work, see Miró's birthplace, and they tell me that the food . . .'

You do realize that Mr Thomas fancies you. Danny's words came flooding back, and caused Beth to smile. 'It's very kind of you, Mr Thomas, but I think it might be wiser if I were to stay behind and make sure that everything runs smoothly while you're away.'

'Beth,' said Thomas, sitting back and folding his arms, 'you're a bright, beautiful young woman. Don't you think Danny would have wanted you to enjoy yourself occasionally? God knows you've earned it.'

'It's very thoughtful of you, Mr Thomas, but I'm not quite ready to consider . . .'

'I understand,' said Thomas, 'of course I do. In any case, I'm quite content to wait until you're ready. Whatever it was that Danny possessed, I haven't yet calculated the premium that's required to insure against it.'

Beth laughed. 'He's like the opera, the art galleries and the finest wine all wrapped up in one,' she replied, 'and even then you won't have captured Danny Cartwright.'

'Well, I don't intend to give up,' said Thomas. 'Maybe I'll be able to tempt you next year, when the annual conference is in Rome and it will be my turn to be president.'

'Caravaggio,' sighed Beth.

'Caravaggio?' repeated Thomas, looking puzzled.

'Danny and I had planned to spend our honeymoon in St Tropez – that was until he was introduced to Caravaggio by his cellmate Nick Moncrieff. In fact, one of the last things Danny promised me before he died' – Beth could never get herself to utter the words *committed suicide* – 'was that he would take me to Rome, so I could also meet Signor Caravaggio.'

'I don't have a chance, do I?' said Thomas.

Beth didn't reply.

◄○►

Danny and Mr Munro touched down at Geneva airport later that evening. Once they had cleared customs, Danny went in search of a taxi. The short journey into the city ended when the driver pulled up outside the Hôtel Les Armeurs, situated in the old town near the cathedral – his personal recommendation.

Munro had called de Coubertin before leaving his office. The chairman of the bank had agreed to see them at ten o'clock the following morning. Danny was beginning to think that the old man was rather enjoying himself.

Over dinner, Mr Munro – Danny didn't consider, even for a moment, calling him Fraser – took Sir Nicholas through the list of documents he anticipated would be required for their meeting in the morning.

'Are we missing anything?' asked Danny.

'Certainly not,' said Munro. 'That is, assuming you've remembered to bring the key.'

◄○►

Hugo picked up the phone on his bedside table. 'Yes?'

'He took the overnight train to Edinburgh, and then travelled on to Dunbroath,' said a voice.

'In order to see Munro, no doubt.'

'In his office at ten o'clock this morning.'

'Did he then return to London?'

'No, he and Munro left the office together, drove to the airport and caught a BA flight. They should have landed an hour ago.'

'Were you on the same flight?'

'No,' said the voice.

'Why not?' asked Hugo sharply.

'I didn't have my passport with me.'

Hugo put the phone down and looked across at his wife, who was fast asleep. He decided not to wake her.

47

DANNY LAY AWAKE, considering the precarious position he was in. Far from vanquishing his foes, he seemed only to have created new ones who were bent on bringing him to his knees.

He rose early, showered and dressed, and went down to the breakfast room to find Munro seated at a corner table, a pile of documents by his side. They spent the next forty minutes going over any questions Munro thought de Coubertin might ask. Danny stopped listening to his lawyer when a fellow guest entered the room and went straight to a table by the window that overlooked the cathedral. Another seat that he evidently assumed would be reserved for him.

'Should de Coubertin ask you that question, Sir Nicholas, how will you respond?' asked Munro.

'I think the world's leading stamp collector has decided to join us for breakfast,' whispered Danny.

'From that I assume your friend Mr Gene Hunsacker is among us?'

'No less. I can't believe it's a coincidence that he's in Geneva at the same time as we are.'

'Certainly not,' said Munro. 'And he'll also be aware that your uncle is in Geneva.'

'What can I do about it?' asked Danny.

'Not a lot for the moment,' said Munro. 'Hunsacker will circle like a vulture until he discovers which of you has been anointed as the legitimate heir to the collection, and only then will he swoop.'

'He's a little overweight for a vulture,' suggested Danny, 'but

I take your point. What do I tell him if he starts asking me questions?'

'You say nothing until after we've had our meeting with de Coubertin.'

'But Hunsacker was so helpful and friendly the last time we met, and it was obvious that he doesn't care for Hugo, and would prefer to deal with me.'

'Don't deceive yourself. Hunsacker will be happy to do business with whoever de Coubertin decides is the rightful heir to your grandfather's collection. He's probably already made your uncle an offer.' Munro rose from the table and left the dining room without even glancing in Hunsacker's direction. Danny followed him into the lobby.

'How long will it take for us to get to the Banque de Coubertin by taxi?' Munro asked the concierge.

'Three, possibly four minutes, depending on the traffic,' came back the reply.

'And if we walk?'

'Three minutes.'

◄○►

A waiter tapped softly on the door. 'Room service,' he announced before entering. He set up a breakfast table in the centre of the room and placed a copy of the *Telegraph* on a side plate; the only newspaper Margaret Moncrieff would consider reading if the *Scotsman* wasn't available. Hugo signed for the breakfast as Margaret took her place and poured them both coffee.

'Do you think we'll get away with it, old gal, without the key?' asked Hugo.

'If they're convinced the will is genuine,' said Margaret, 'they'll have no choice, unless they're prepared to involve themselves in a lengthy court battle. And as anonymity is a Swiss banker's mantra, they'll avoid that at all costs.'

'They're not going to find anything wrong with the will,' said Hugo.

'Then my bet is that we'll be in possession of your father's collection by this evening, in which case all you'll have to do is agree a price with Hunsacker. As he offered you forty million dollars when he came up to Scotland for your father's funeral, I feel sure he'd be willing to go to fifty,' said Margaret. 'In fact, I have already instructed Galbraith to draw up a contract to that effect.'

'With whichever one of us secures the collection,' said Hugo, 'because by now Nick will have worked out why we're here.'

'But he can't do anything about it,' said Margaret. 'Not while he's stranded in England.'

'There's nothing to stop him jumping on the next plane. I wouldn't be surprised if he's here already,' added Hugo, not wanting to admit that he knew Nick was in Geneva.

'You've obviously forgotten, Hugo, that he's not allowed to travel abroad while he's on probation.'

'If it was me, I'd be willing to take that risk,' said Hugo, 'for fifty million dollars.'

'You might,' said Margaret, 'but Nick would never disobey an order. And even if he did, it would only take one phone call to help de Coubertin decide which branch of the Moncrieff family he wants to do business with – the one threatening to take him to court, or the one who will be spending another four years in jail.'

◄○►

Although Danny and Fraser Munro arrived at the bank a few minutes early, the chairman's secretary was waiting in reception to accompany them to the boardroom. Once they were seated, she offered them both a cup of English tea.

'I won't be having any of your English tea, thank you,' said Munro, giving her a warm smile. Danny could only wonder if she had understood a word the Scotsman had said, let alone comprehended his particular brand of humour.

'Two coffees, please,' said Danny. She smiled and left the room.

Danny was admiring a portrait of the founder of the modern Olympic Games when the door opened and the present holder of the title entered the room.

'Good morning, Sir Nicholas,' he said, walking up to Munro, offering his hand.

'No, no, my name is Fraser Munro, I am Sir Nicholas's legal representative.'

'I apologize,' said the old man, trying to hide his embarrassment. He smiled shyly as he shook hands with Danny. 'I apologize,' he repeated.

'Not at all, baron,' said Danny. 'An understandable mistake.'

De Coubertin gave him a slight bow. 'Like me, you are the grandson of a great man.' He invited Sir Nicholas and Mr Munro to join him at the boardroom table. 'What can I do for you?' he asked.

'I had the great honour of representing the late Sir Alexander Moncrieff,' began Munro, 'and I now have the privilege of advising Sir Nicholas.' De Coubertin nodded. 'We have come to claim my client's rightful inheritance,' said Munro, opening his briefcase and placing on the table one passport, one death certificate and Sir Alexander's will.

'Thank you,' said de Coubertin, not giving any of the documents even a cursory glance. 'Sir Nicholas, may I ask if you are in possession of the key that your grandfather left you?'

'Yes, I am,' Danny replied. He undid the chain that hung round his neck and handed the key across to de Coubertin, who studied it for a moment before returning it to Danny. He then rose from his place and said, 'Please follow me, gentlemen.'

'Don't say a word,' whispered Munro as they followed the chairman out of the room. 'It's clear that he's carrying out your grandfather's instructions.' They walked down a long corridor, passing even more oil paintings of partners of the bank, until they came to a small elevator. When the doors slid open, de Coubertin stood to one side to allow his guests to step in, then joined them and pressed a button marked –2. He didn't speak until the doors opened again, when he stepped out and repeated, 'Please follow me, gentlemen.'

The soft Wedgwood blue of the boardroom walls had been replaced by a dull ochre as they walked on down a brick corridor that displayed no pictures of the bank's past office-holders. At the end of the corridor was a large steel barred gate which brought back unhappy memories for Danny. A guard unlocked the gate the moment he spotted the chairman. He then accompanied the three of them until they came to a halt outside a massive steel door with two locks. De Coubertin took a key from his pocket, placed it in the top lock and turned it slowly. He nodded to Danny, who put his key in the lock below and also turned it. The guard pulled open the heavy steel door.

A two-inch-wide yellow strip had been painted on the ground just inside the doorway. Danny crossed it and walked into a small square room whose walls were covered from floor to ceiling with shelves, crammed with thick leather-bound books. On each shelf were printed cards, indicating the years 1840 to 1992.

'Please join me,' said Danny, as he removed one of the thick leather books from the top shelf and began to leaf through the pages. Munro walked in, but de Coubertin did not follow.

'I apologize,' he said, 'but I am not allowed to cross the yellow line – one of the bank's many regulations. Perhaps you would be kind enough to inform the guard when you wish to leave, and then do come and join me back in the boardroom.'

Danny and Munro spent the next half hour turning the pages of album after album, and began to understand why Gene Hunsacker had flown all the way from Texas to Geneva.

'I'm none the wiser,' said Munro as he looked at an unperforated sheet of forty-eight penny blacks.

'You will be after you've had a look at this one,' said Danny, passing him the only leather-bound book in the entire collection that was not dated.

Munro turned the pages slowly, to be reacquainted with the neat, calligraphic hand he remembered so well: column after column listing when, where and from whom Sir Alexander had purchased each new acquisition and the price he'd paid. He handed the meticulous record of the collector's life back to Danny and suggested, 'You're going to have to study each entry most carefully before you next bump into Mr Hunsacker.'

Mr and Mrs Moncrieff were shown into the boardroom at 3.00 p.m. Baron de Coubertin was seated at the far end of the table, with three colleagues on each side of him. All seven men rose from their chairs as the Moncrieffs entered the room, and didn't resume their places until Mrs Moncrieff had sat down.

'Thank you for allowing us to inspect your late father's will,' said de Coubertin, 'as well as the attached letter.' Hugo smiled. 'However, I must inform you that in the considered opinion of one of our experts, the will is invalid.'

'Are you suggesting that it's a fake?' said Hugo, angrily rising from his place.

'We are not suggesting for a moment, Mr Moncrieff, that you were aware of this. However, we have decided that these documents do not stand up to the scrutiny required by this bank.' He passed the will and the letter across the table.

'But . . .' began Hugo.

'Are you able to tell us what in particular prompted you to reject my husband's claim?' asked Margaret quietly.

'No, madam, we are not.'

'Then you can expect to hear from our lawyers later today,' said Margaret as she gathered up the documents, placed them back in her husband's briefcase and rose to leave.

All seven members of the board stood as Mr and Mrs Moncrieff were escorted from the room by the chairman's secretary.

48

WHEN FRASER MUNRO joined Danny in his room the following morning, he found his client sitting cross-legged on the floor in his dressing gown, surrounded by sheets of paper, a laptop and a calculator.

'I apologize for disturbing you, Sir Nicholas. Shall I come back later?'

'No, no,' said Danny as he leapt up, 'come in.'

'I trust you slept well?' said Munro as he looked down at the mass of paperwork littering the floor.

'I haven't been to bed,' admitted Danny. 'I was up all night checking over the figures again and again.'

'And are you any the wiser?' asked Munro.

'I hope so,' said Danny, 'because I have a feeling that Gene Hunsacker didn't lose any sleep wondering what this lot is worth.'

'Do you have any idea . . . ?'

'Well,' said Danny, 'the collection consists of twenty-three thousand, one hundred and eleven stamps, purchased over a period of more than seventy years. My grandfather bought his first stamp in 1920 at the age of thirteen, and he continued collecting until 1998, only a few months before he died. In total, he spent £13,729,412.'

'No wonder Hunsacker thinks it's the finest collection on earth,' said Munro.

Danny nodded. 'Some of the stamps are incredibly rare. There is, for example, a 1901 US one cent "inverted centre", a Hawaiian two cent blue from 1851, and a Newfoundland 1857 two penny scarlet, which he paid $150,000 for in 1978. But the pride of the collection has to be an 1856 British Guiana one cent black on magenta, which he bought at auction in April 1980 for $800,000. That's the good news,' said Danny. 'The not so good news is that it would take a year, possibly even longer, to have every stamp valued. Hunsacker knows that, of course, but in our favour is that he won't want to hang around waiting for a year, because among other things I've picked up from the odd article my grandfather kept is that Hunsacker has a rival, a Mr Tomoji Watanabe, a commodities dealer from Tokyo. It appears,' Danny said as he bent down to pick up an old cutting from *Time Magazine*, 'to be a matter of opinion which one of their collections was second only to my grandfather's. That argument would be settled the moment one of them gets his hands on this,' said Danny, holding up the inventory.

'That piece of knowledge, may I suggest,' said Munro, 'places you in a very strong position.'

'Possibly,' said Danny, 'but when you get into amounts of this size – and on a quick calculation the collection must be worth around fifty million dollars – there are very few people on earth, and I suspect in this case only two, who could even consider joining in the bidding, so I can't afford to overplay my hand.'

'I'm lost,' said Munro.

'Let's hope I'm not once the game of poker begins, because I suspect that if the next person to knock on that door isn't the waiter wanting to set up breakfast, it will be Mr Gene Hunsacker hoping to buy a stamp collection he's been after for the past fifteen years. So I'd better take a shower and get dressed. I wouldn't want him to think I've been up all night trying to work out how much I ought to be asking for.'

◄○►

'Mr Galbraith, please.

'Who shall I say is calling?'

'Hugo Moncrieff.'

'I'll put you straight through, sir.'

'How did you get on in Geneva?' were Galbraith's first words.

'We left empty-handed.'

'What? How can that be possible? You had every document you needed to validate your claim, including your father's will.'

'De Coubertin said the will was a fake, and virtually threw us out of his office.'

'But I don't understand,' said Galbraith, sounding genuinely surprised. 'I had it examined by the leading authority in the field, and it passed every known test.'

'Well, de Coubertin clearly doesn't agree with your leading authority, so I'm phoning to ask what our next move should be.'

'I'll call de Coubertin immediately, and advise him to expect service of a writ both in London and Geneva. That will make him think twice about doing business with anyone else until the authenticity of the will has been resolved in the courts.'

'Perhaps the time has come for us to set in motion the other matter we discussed before I flew to Geneva.'

'All I'll need if I'm to do that,' said Galbraith, 'is your nephew's flight number.'

◄○►

'You were right,' said Munro when Danny emerged from the bathroom twenty minutes later.

'About what?' asked Danny.

'The next person to knock on that door was the waiter,' Munro added as Danny took his place at the breakfast table. 'A bright young man who was happy to give me a great deal of information.'

'Then he can't have been Swiss,' said Danny as he unfolded his napkin.

'It appears,' continued Munro, 'that Mr Hunsacker booked into the hotel two days ago. The management sent a limousine to the airport to pick him up from his private jet. The young man was also able to tell me, in return for ten Swiss francs, that his hotel booking is open-ended.'

'A sound investment,' said Danny.

'Even more interesting is the fact that the same limousine drove Hunsacker to the Banque de Coubertin yesterday morning, where he had a forty-minute meeting with the chairman.'

'To view the collection, no doubt,' suggested Danny.

'No,' said Munro. 'De Coubertin would never allow anyone near that room without your authority. That would break every tenet of the bank's policy. In any case, it wouldn't have been necessary.'

'Why not?' asked Danny.

'Surely you remember that when your grandfather put his entire collection on display at the Smithsonian Institution in Washington to celebrate his eightieth birthday, one of the first people to walk through the doors on the opening morning was Mr Gene Hunsacker.'

'What else did the waiter tell you?' asked Danny without missing a beat.

'Mr Hunsacker is at this moment having breakfast in his room on the floor above us, presumably waiting for you to knock on his door.'

'Then he's going to have a long wait,' said Danny, 'because I don't intend to be the first to blink.'

'Pity,' said Munro, 'I'd been looking forward to the encounter. I once had the privilege of attending a negotiation in which your grandfather was involved. By the end of the meeting, I left feeling battered and bruised – and I was on *his* side.' Danny laughed.

There was a knock on the door.

'Sooner than I thought,' said Danny.

'It might be your uncle Hugo brandishing another writ,' suggested Munro.

'Or just the waiter coming to take away the breakfast things. Either way, I'll need a moment to clear up these papers. Can't have Hunsacker thinking I don't know what the collection is worth.' Danny knelt down on the floor and Munro joined him as they began gathering up reams of scattered papers.

There was another knock on the door, this time a little louder. Danny disappeared into the bathroom with all the papers, while Munro went across to open the door.

'Good morning, Mr Hunsacker, how nice to see you again. We met in Washington,' he added, offering his hand, but the Texan barged past him, clearly looking for Danny. The bathroom door opened a moment later, and Danny reappeared wearing a hotel dressing gown. He yawned and stretched his arms.

'What a surprise, Mr Hunsacker,' he said. 'To what do we owe this unexpected pleasure?'

'Surprise be damned,' said Hunsacker. 'You saw me at breakfast yesterday. I'm pretty hard to miss. And you can cut out the yawning act, I know you've already had breakfast,' he said, glancing at a half-eaten piece of toast.

'At a cost of ten Swiss francs, no doubt,' said Danny with a grin. 'But do tell me what brings you to Geneva,' he added as he sank back in the only comfortable chair in the room.

'You know damn well why I'm in Geneva,' said Hunsacker, lighting his cigar.

'This is a non-smoking floor,' Danny reminded him.

'Crap,' said Hunsacker, flicking ash on to the carpet. 'So how much do you want?'

'For what, Mr Hunsacker?'

'Don't play games with me, Nick. How much do you want?'

'I confess I was discussing that very subject with my legal adviser only moments before you knocked on the door, and he wisely recommended that I should wait a little longer before I commit myself.'

'Why wait? You don't have any interest in stamps.'

'True,' said Danny, 'but perhaps there are others who do.'

'Like who?'

'Mr Watanabe, for example,' suggested Danny.

'You're bluffing.'

'That's what he said about you.'

'You've already been in touch with Watanabe?'

'Not yet,' admitted Danny, 'but I'm expecting him to call any minute.'

'Name your price.'

'Sixty-five million dollars,' said Danny.

'You're crazy. That's double what it's worth. And you do realize that I'm the only person on earth who can afford to buy the collection. It would only take you one phone call to discover that Watanabe's not in my league.'

'Then I shall have to split the collection up,' said Danny. 'After all, Mr Blundell assured me that Sotheby's could guarantee me a large income for the rest of my life, without ever having to flood the market. That would give both you and Mr Watanabe the chance to cherry-pick any particular items you are keen to add to your collection.'

'While at the same time you paid a ten per cent seller's premium on everything in the collection,' Hunsacker said, jabbing his cigar at Danny.

'And don't let's forget your twenty per cent buyer's premium,' Danny countered. 'And let's face it, Gene, I'm thirty years younger than you, so I'm not the one who's in a hurry.'

'I'd be willing to pay fifty million,' said Hunsacker.

Danny was taken by surprise as he had expected Hunsacker to open the bidding at around forty million, but he didn't blink. 'I'd be willing to drop to sixty.'

'You'd be willing to drop to fifty-five,' said Hunsacker.

'Not for a man who flew halfway round the world in his private jet simply to find out who would end up owning the Moncrieff collection.'

'Fifty-five,' Hunsacker repeated.

'Sixty,' insisted Danny.

'No, fifty-five is my limit. And I'll wire the full amount to any bank in the world, which means it would be in your account within the next couple of hours.'

'Why don't we toss for the last five million?'

'Because that way you can't lose. Fifty-five is what I said. You can take it or leave it.'

'I think I'll leave it,' said Danny, rising from his chair. 'Have a good flight back to Texas, Gene, and do give me a call if there is a particular stamp you'd like to make an offer for before I phone Mr Watanabe.'

'OK, OK. I'll toss you for the last five million.'

Danny turned back to his lawyer. 'Would you be kind enough to act as referee, Mr Munro?'

'Umpire,' said Hunsacker.

'Yes, of course,' Munro replied. Danny handed him a pound

coin, and was surprised to see that Munro's hand was shaking as he balanced it on the end of his thumb. He tossed it high in the air.

'Heads,' called Hunsacker. The coin landed in the thick rug by the fireplace. It was standing upright on its edge.

'Let's settle on $57,500,000,' said Danny.

'It's a deal,' said Hunsacker, who bent down, picked up the coin and put it in his pocket.

'I think you'll find that's mine,' said Danny, holding out his hand.

Hunsacker handed over the coin and grinned. 'Now give me the key, Nick, so I can inspect the goods.'

'There's no need for that,' said Danny. 'After all, you saw the whole collection when it was on display in Washington. However, I will allow you to have my grandfather's ledger,' he said, picking up the thick leather book from a side table and handing it to him. 'As for the key,' he added with a smile, 'Mr Munro will deliver it to you the moment the money is lodged in my account. I think you said it would take a couple of hours.'

'Hunsacker started walking towards the door.

'And, Gene.' Hunsacker turned back. 'Try to make it before the sun sets in Tokyo.'

◄o►

Desmond Galbraith picked up the private line on his desk.

'I'm reliably informed by one of the hotel staff,' said Hugo Moncrieff, 'that they are both booked on BA flight 737 which leaves here at 8.55 p.m. and touches down at Heathrow at 9.45 p.m.'

'That's all I need to know,' said Galbraith.

'We'll be flying back to Edinburgh first thing in the morning.'

'Which should give de Coubertin more than enough time to reflect on which branch of the Moncrieff family he'd prefer to do business with.'

◄o►

'Would you care for a glass of champagne?' asked the stewardess.

'No thank you,' said Munro, 'just a scotch and soda.'

'And for you, sir?'

'I'll have a glass of champagne, thank you,' said Danny. After the stewardess had gone he turned to ask Munro, 'Why do you think the bank didn't take my uncle's claim seriously? After all, he must have shown de Coubertin the new will.'

'They must have spotted something I missed,' said Munro.

'Why don't you call de Coubertin and ask him what it was?'

'That man wouldn't admit he'd ever met your uncle, let alone seen your grandfather's will. Still, now that you have almost sixty million dollars in the bank, I presume you'll want me to defend all the writs?'

'I wonder what Nick would have done,' mumbled Danny as he fell into a deep sleep.

Munro raised an eyebrow, but didn't press his client further when he remembered that Sir Nicholas hadn't been to bed the previous night.

Danny woke with a start when the wheels touched down at Heathrow. He and Munro were among the first to disembark from the aircraft. As they walked down the steps they were surprised to see three policemen standing on the tarmac. Munro noticed that they were not carrying machine guns, so they couldn't be security. As Danny's foot touched the bottom step two of the policemen grabbed him, while the third pinned his arms behind his back and handcuffed him.

'You're under arrest, Moncrieff,' said one of them as they marched him off.

'On what charge?' demanded Munro, but he didn't get a response because the police car, siren blaring, was already speeding away.

Danny had spent most days since his release wondering when they'd finally catch up with him. The only surprise was that they'd called him Moncrieff.

━◦━

Beth could no longer bear to look at her father, whom she hadn't spoken to for days. Despite being forewarned by the doctor, she couldn't believe how emaciated he'd become in such a short time.

Father Michael had visited his parishioner every day since he had been bedridden, and that morning he had asked Beth's mother to gather the family and close friends around the bedside that evening, as he could no longer delay conducting the last rites.

'Beth.'

Beth was taken by surprise when her father spoke. 'Yes, Dad,' she said, taking his hand.

'Who's running the garage?' he asked in a piping voice that was almost inaudible.

'Trevor Sutton,' she replied softly.

'He's not up to it. You'll have to appoint someone else, and soon.'

'I will, Dad,' Beth replied dutifully. She didn't tell him that no one else wanted the job.

'Are we alone?' he asked after a long pause.

'Yes, Dad. Mum's in the front room talking to Mrs . . .'

'Mrs Cartwright?'

'Yes,' admitted Beth.

'Thank God for her common sense.' Her father paused to take another breath before adding, 'Which you've inherited.'

Beth smiled. Even the effort of talking was now almost beyond him. 'Tell Harry,' he suddenly said, his voice even weaker, 'I'd like to see them both before I die.'

Beth had stopped saying 'You're not going to die' some time ago, and simply whispered in his ear, 'Of course I will, Dad.'

Another long pause, another struggle for breath, before he whispered, 'Promise me one thing.'

'Anything.'

He gripped his daughter's hand. 'You'll fight on to clear his name.' The grip suddenly weakened, and his hand went limp.

'I will,' said Beth, although she knew he couldn't hear her.

49

MR MUNRO'S OFFICE had left several messages on his mobile asking him to call urgently. He had other things on his mind.

Sir Nicholas had been whisked off in a police car to spend the night in a cell at Paddington Green police station. When Mr Munro left him, he made his way by taxi to the Caledonian Club in Belgravia. He blamed himself for not remembering that Sir Nicholas was still on probation and was not allowed to leave the country. Perhaps it was simply that he could never think of him as a criminal.

When Munro arrived at his club just after eleven thirty, he found Miss Davenport waiting for him in the guest lounge. The first thing he needed to ascertain, and very quickly, was whether she was up to the job. That took him about five minutes. He had rarely come across anyone who grasped the salient points of a case so quickly. She asked all the right questions and he could only hope that Sir Nicholas had all the right answers. By the time they parted, just after midnight, Munro was in no doubt that his client was in good hands.

Sarah Davenport hadn't needed to remind Munro of the court's attitude to prisoners who broke their parole conditions, and how rarely exceptions were made, especially when it came to travelling abroad without seeking approval from their probation officer. Both she and Munro were fully aware that a judge would probably send Nick back to prison to complete the remaining four years of his sentence. Miss Davenport would of course plead 'mitigating circumstances', but she wasn't at all optimistic about the outcome.

Munro had never cared for lawyers who were optimistic. She promised to call him in Dunbroath the moment the judge had delivered his verdict.

As Munro was about to make his way upstairs to his room, the porter told him there was another message, to call his son as soon as possible.

'So what's so urgent?' was Munro's first question as he sat on the end of the bed.

'Galbraith has withdrawn all his pending writs,' whispered Hamish Munro, not wanting to wake his wife, 'as well as the trespass order demanding that Sir Nicholas vacate his home in The Boltons within thirty days. Is this total capitulation, Dad, or am I missing something?' he asked after he'd quietly closed the bathroom door.

'The latter, I fear, my boy. Galbraith's done no more than sacrifice the irrelevant in order to capture the only prize that's really worth having.'

'Getting the court to legitimize Sir Alexander's second will?'

'You've got it in one,' said Munro. 'If he is able to prove that Sir Alexander's new will leaving everything to his brother Angus supersedes any previous wills, then it will be Hugo Moncrieff, and not Sir Nicholas, who inherits the estate, including a bank account in Switzerland that is now showing a balance of at least $57,500,000.'

'Galbraith must be confident that the second will is genuine?'

'He may well be, but I know someone else who isn't quite so confident.'

'By the way, Dad, Galbraith called again just as I was leaving the office. He wanted to know when you'd be returning to Scotland.'

'Did he indeed?' said Munro. 'Which begs the question, how did he know I wasn't in Scotland?'

◄○►

'When I told you that I hoped we'd meet again,' said Sarah, 'an interview room at Paddington Green police station wasn't exactly what I had in mind.' Danny smiled ruefully as he looked across the small wooden table at his new solicitor. Munro had explained that he could not represent him in an English court of law; however, he could recommend— 'No,' Danny had responded, 'I know exactly who I want to represent me.'

'I'm flattered,' Sarah continued, 'that when you found yourself in need of legal advice, I was your first choice.'

'You were my only choice,' admitted Danny. 'I don't know any other solicitors.' He regretted his words the moment he'd said them.

'And to think I've been up half the night—'

'I'm sorry,' said Danny. 'That's not what I meant. It's just that Mr Munro told me—'

'I know what Mr Munro told you,' said Sarah with a smile. 'Now, we don't have any time to waste. You'll be up in front of the judge at ten o'clock, and although Mr Munro has fully briefed me on what you've been up to for the past couple of days, I still have a few questions of my own that need answering, as I don't want to be taken by surprise once we're in the court. So please be frank – and by that I mean honest. Have you at any time in the past twelve months travelled abroad, other than on this one occasion when you visited Geneva?'

'No,' Danny replied.

'Have you failed to attend any meetings with your probation officer since you left prison?'

'No, never.'

'Did you at any time make an attempt to contact . . .'

◄○►

'Good morning, Mr Galbraith,' said Munro. 'I apologize for not contacting you earlier, but I have a feeling that you are only too aware of what caused me to be detained.'

'Indeed I am,' responded Galbraith, 'which is precisely the reason I needed to speak to you so urgently. You will know that my client has withdrawn all pending actions against Sir Nicholas, so I'd rather hoped, given these circumstances, that your client will wish to respond in the same magnanimous manner, and withdraw his writ disputing the validity of his grandfather's most recent will?'

'You can assume nothing of the sort,' retorted Munro sharply. 'That would only result in your client ending up with everything, including the kitchen sink.'

'Your response comes as no surprise to me, Munro. Indeed, I have already forewarned my client that would be your attitude, and we would be left with no choice but to contest your vexatious writ. However,' Galbraith added before Munro could respond, 'may I suggest that as there is now only one dispute outstanding between the two parties, namely whether Sir Alexander's most recent will is valid or invalid, it might be in the best interest of both parties to expedite matters by making sure this action comes before the court at the first possible opportunity?'

'May I respectfully remind you, Mr Galbraith, that it has not been this firm that has been responsible for holding up proceedings. Nevertheless, I welcome your change of heart, even at this late juncture.'

'I am delighted that that is your attitude, Mr Munro, and I'm sure you will be pleased to learn that Mr Justice Sanderson's clerk rang this morning to say that his lordship has a clear day in his diary on the first Thursday of next month, and would be happy to sit in judgement on this case if that were convenient to both sides.'

'But that gives me less than ten days to prepare my case,' said Munro, realizing he had been ambushed.

'Frankly, Mr Munro, you either have proof that the will is invalid, or you do not,' said Galbraith. 'If you do, Mr Justice Sanderson will rule in your favour, which, to quote you, would result in your client ending up with everything, including the kitchen sink.'

—◦—

Danny looked down at Sarah from the dock. He had answered all her questions truthfully, and was relieved to find that she only seemed interested in his reasons for travelling abroad. But then, how could she possibly know anything about the late Danny Cartwright? She had warned him that he would probably be back at Belmarsh in time for lunch, and should anticipate having to spend the next four years in prison. She had advised him to plead guilty, as they had no defence to the charge of breaking his probation order and therefore she could do no more than plead mitigating circumstances. He'd agreed.

'My lord,' began Sarah as she rose to face Mr Justice Callaghan. 'My client does not deny his breach of licence, but he did so only in order to establish his rights in a major financial case which he anticipates will shortly be coming before the High Court in Scotland. I should also point out, my lord, that my client was accompanied at all times by the distinguished Scottish solicitor Mr Fraser Munro, who is representing him in that case.' The judge made a note of the name on the pad in front of him. 'You may also consider it to be relevant, my lord, that my client was out of the country for less than forty-eight hours, and returned to London of his own volition. The charge that he failed to inform his probation officer is not entirely accurate, because he rang Ms Bennett, and when he received no reply, left a message on her answerphone. That message was recorded and can be supplied to the court if your lordship pleases.

'My lord, this uncharacteristic lapse has been the only occasion on which my client has failed to abide strictly by his licence conditions, and he has never missed or ever been late for a meeting with his probation officer. I would add,' continued Sarah, 'that since being released from prison, my client's behaviour, with the exception of this one blemish, has been exemplary. Not only has he at all times abided by his licence, but he has continued his efforts to further his educational qualifications. He has recently been granted a place at London University, which he hopes will lead to an honours degree in business studies.

'My client unreservedly apologizes for any inconvenience he has caused the court or the probation service, and he has assured me that this will never happen again.

'In conclusion, my lord, I would hope that after you have taken all these matters into consideration, you will agree that no purpose will be served by sending this man back to prison.' Sarah closed her file, bowed and resumed her place.

The judge went on writing for some time before he put down

his pen. 'Thank you, Miss Davenport,' he eventually said. 'I would like a little time to consider your submission before I pass judgement. Perhaps we could take a short break, and convene again at noon.'

The court rose. Sarah was puzzled. Why would a judge of Mr Justice Callaghan's experience need time to come to a decision on such a mundane matter? And then she worked it out.

◄o►

'Could I speak to the chairman, please?'

'Who shall I say is calling?'

'Fraser Munro.'

'I'll see if he's free to take your call, Mr Munro.' Munro tapped his fingers on the desk while he waited.

'Mr Munro, how nice to hear from you again,' said de Coubertin. 'How can I assist you on this occasion?'

'I thought I would let you know that the matter which concerns us both will be resolved on Thursday of next week.'

'Yes, I am fully aware of the latest developments,' replied de Coubertin, 'as I have also had a call from Mr Desmond Galbraith. He assured me that his client has agreed to accept whatever judgement the court reaches. I must therefore ask if your client is willing to do the same.'

'Yes, he is,' replied Munro. 'I shall be writing to you later today confirming that is our position.'

'I am most grateful,' said de Coubertin, 'and will inform our legal department accordingly. As soon as we learn which of the two parties has won the action, I will give instructions to deposit the $57,500,000 into the relevant account.'

'Thank you for that assurance,' said Munro. He coughed. 'I wondered if I might have a word with you off the record?'

'Not an expression we Swiss have come to terms with,' replied de Coubertin.

'Then perhaps in my capacity as a trustee of the late Sir Alexander Moncrieff's estate, I could seek your guidance.'

'I will do my best,' replied de Coubertin, 'but I will not under any circumstances breach client confidentiality. And that applies whether the client is dead or alive.'

'I fully understand your position,' said Munro. 'I have reason to believe that you had a visit from Mr Hugo Moncrieff before you saw Sir Nicholas, and that therefore you must have considered the documents that constitute the evidence in this case.' De Coubertin did not offer an opinion. 'Can I assume from your silence,' said Munro, 'that is not in dispute.' De Coubertin still did not respond. 'Among those documents would have been copies of both of Sir Alexander's wills, the legitimacy of which will decide the outcome of this case.' Again, de Coubertin didn't offer an opinion, making Munro wonder if the line had gone dead. 'Are you still there, chairman?' he asked.

'Yes, I am,' de Coubertin replied.

'As you were willing to see Sir Nicholas after your meeting with Mr Hugo Moncrieff, I can only assume that the reason you rejected his uncle's claim was because the bank, like myself, is not convinced that the second will is valid. So that there is no misunderstanding between us,' added Munro, 'your bank concluded that it is a fake.' Mr Munro could now hear the chairman breathing. 'Then in the name of justice, man, I must ask you what it was that convinced you that the second will was invalid, but which I have failed to identify.'

'I'm afraid I am unable to assist you, Mr Munro, as it would be a breach of client confidentiality.'

'Is there anyone else that I can turn to for advice on this matter?' pressed Munro.

There was a long silence before de Coubertin eventually said, 'In keeping with the bank's policy, we sought a second opinion from an outside source.'

'And can you divulge the name of your source?'

'No, I cannot,' replied de Coubertin. 'Much as I might like to, that would also be contrary to the bank's policy on such matters.'

'But—' began Munro.

'However,' continued de Coubertin, ignoring the interruption, 'the gentleman who advised us is unquestionably the leading authority in his field, and hasn't yet left Geneva to return to his own country.'

—◦—

'All rise,' said the usher as twelve o'clock struck and Mr Justice Callaghan walked back into the courtroom.

Sarah turned to smile encouragingly at Danny, who was standing in the dock, with a look of resignation on his face. Once the judge had settled in his chair, he peered down at defence counsel. 'I have given a great deal of thought to your submission, Miss Davenport. However, you must understand that it is my responsibility to ensure that prisoners are fully aware that while they are on licence, they are still serving part of their sentence, and that if they fail to keep to the conditions set down in their parole order, they are breaking the law.

'I have of course,' he continued, 'taken into consideration your client's overall record since his release, including his efforts to obtain further academic qualifications. This is all very commendable, but does not alter the fact that he abused his position of trust. He must therefore be punished accordingly.' Danny bowed his head. 'Moncrieff,' said the judge, 'I intend to sign an order today which will ensure that you will be locked up for a further four years should you break any of your licence conditions in the future. For the period of your licence you may not under any circumstances travel abroad, and you will continue to report to your probation officer once a month.'

He removed his spectacles. 'Moncrieff, you have been most fortunate on this occasion, and what tipped the balance in your favour was the fact that you were accompanied on your injudicious foreign excursion by a senior member of the Scottish legal profession, whose reputation on both sides of the border is beyond reproach.' Sarah smiled. Mr Justice Callaghan had needed to make one or two phone calls so that he could confirm something Sarah already knew. 'You are free to leave the court,' were Mr Justice Callaghan's final words.

The judge rose from his place, bowed low and shuffled out of the courtroom. Danny remained in the dock, despite the fact that the two policemen who'd been guarding him had already disappeared downstairs. Sarah walked across as the usher opened the little gate to allow him to step out of the dock and into the well of the court.

'Can you join me for lunch?' he asked.

'No,' said Sarah, switching off her mobile. 'Mr Munro has just texted to say he wants you on the next flight to Edinburgh – and please call him on the way to the airport.'

50

'IN CHAMBERS' was a term Danny had not come across before. Mr Munro explained in great detail why he and Mr Desmond Galbraith had agreed on this approach for settling the dispute between the two parties.

Both sides had agreed that it would not be wise to air any family grievances in public. Galbraith went as far as to admit that his client had a loathing of the press, and Munro had already warned Sir Nicholas that if their grievances were to be picked over in open court, his period in prison would end up covering far more column inches than any disagreement over his grandfather's will.

Both sides also accepted that the case should be tried in front of a high court judge, and that his decision would be final: once judgement had been made, neither side would be given leave to appeal. Sir Nicholas and Mr Hugo Moncrieff both signed a binding legal agreement to this effect before the judge would agree to consider proceeding.

Danny sat at a table next to Mr Munro on one side of the room, while Hugo and Margaret Moncrieff sat alongside Mr Desmond Galbraith on the other. Mr Justice Sanderson was seated at his desk facing them. None of the participants was dressed in court garb, which allowed a far more relaxed atmosphere to prevail. The judge opened proceedings by reminding both parties that despite the case being heard privately in chambers, the outcome still carried the full weight of the law. He seemed pleased to see both counsel nodding.

Mr Justice Sanderson had not only proved acceptable to both sides, but was, in the words of Munro, 'a wise old bird'.

'Gentlemen,' he began. 'Having acquainted myself with the background to this case, I am aware just how much is at stake for both parties. Before I begin, I am bound to ask if every attempt to reach a compromise has been made?'

Mr Desmond Galbraith rose from his place and stated that Sir Alexander had written an uncompromising letter, making it clear that he wished to disinherit his grandson after he had been court-martialled, and his client, Mr Hugo Moncrieff, simply wished to carry out his late father's wishes.

Mr Munro rose to state that his client had not issued the original writ, and had never sought this quarrel in the first place, but that like Mr Hugo Moncrieff he felt that it was imperative that his grandfather's wishes were carried out. He paused. 'To the letter.'

The judge shrugged his shoulders and resigned himself to not being able to achieve any form of compromise between the two parties. 'Then let's get on with it,' he said. 'I have read all the papers put before me and I have also considered any further submissions entered by both parties as evidence. With that in mind, I intend to state from the outset what I consider to be relevant in this case, and what I consider to be irrelevant. Neither side disputes that Sir Alexander Moncrieff executed a will on January seventeenth, 1997, in which he left the bulk of his estate to his grandson Nicholas, then a serving officer in Kosovo.' He looked up to seek confirmation, and both Galbraith and Munro nodded.

'However, what is being claimed by Mr Galbraith, on behalf of his client Mr Hugo Moncrieff, is that this document was not Sir Alexander's last Will and Testament, and that at a later date – ' the judge looked down at his notes – 'November first, 1998, Sir Alexander executed a second will, leaving the entire estate to his son Angus. Sir Angus died on the twentieth of May 2002, and in his last Will and Testament he in turn left everything to his younger brother, Hugo.

'Also offered in evidence by Mr Galbraith on behalf of his client is a letter signed by Sir Alexander stating his reasons for this change of heart. Mr Munro does not dispute the authenticity of the signature on the second page of this letter, but suggests that the first page was in fact drawn up at a later date. He states that although he will not be putting forward any evidence to support this claim, its truth will become self-evident when the second will is proved to be invalid.

'Mr Munro has also made it known to the court that he will not be suggesting that Sir Alexander was, to use the legal term, not of sound mind at the relevant time. On the contrary, they spent an evening together only a week before Sir Alexander died, and after dinner his host soundly beat him at a game of chess.

'So I am bound to say to both parties that in my opinion the only question to be settled in this dispute is the validity of the second will, which Mr Galbraith claims on behalf of his client was Sir Alexander Moncrieff's last Will and Testament, while Mr Munro states, without putting too fine a point on it, that it's a fake. I hope that both sides consider this to be a fair assessment of the present position. If so, I will ask Mr Galbraith to present his case on behalf of Mr Hugo Moncrieff.'

Desmond Galbraith rose from his place. 'My lord, my client and I for our part accept that the only disagreement between the two parties concerns the second will, which as you have stated we are in no doubt was Sir Alexander's last Will and Testament. We offer the will and the attached letter as proof of our claim, and we would also like to present a witness who we believe will put this matter to rest once and for all.'

'By all means,' said Mr Justice Sanderson. 'Please call your witness.'

'I call Professor Nigel Fleming,' said Galbraith, looking towards the door.

Danny leant across and asked Munro if he knew the professor. 'Only by reputation,' Munro replied as a tall, elegant man with a full head of grey hair walked into the room. As he took the oath, Danny thought that the professor reminded him of the sort of visiting dignitary who used to come to Clement Attlee comprehensive once a year to present the prizes – though never to him.

'Please have a seat, Professor Fleming,' said Mr Justice Sanderson.

Galbraith remained standing. 'Professor, I feel it is important for the court to be made aware of the expertise and authority you bring to this case, so I hope you will forgive me if I ask you a few questions concerning your background.'

The professor gave a slight bow.

'What is your present position?'

'I am the Professor of Inorganic Chemistry at Edinburgh University.'

'And have you written a book on the relevance of that field to crime, which has become the standard work on the subject and is taught as part of the legal syllabus in most universities?'

'I cannot speak for *most* universities, Mr Galbraith, but that is certainly the case at Edinburgh.'

'Have you in the past, professor, represented several governments to advise them on disputes of this nature?'

'I would not wish to overstate my authority, Mr Galbraith. I have on three occasions been called in by governments to advise them on the validity of documents when a disagreement has arisen between two or more nations.'

'Quite so. Then let me ask you, professor, if you have ever given evidence in court when the validity of a will has been called into question?'

'Yes, sir, on seventeen separate occasions.'

'And will you tell the court, professor, how many of those cases ended with a judgement that supported your findings.'

'I would not for a moment suggest the verdicts given in those cases were solely determined by my evidence.'

'Nicely put,' said the judge with a wry smile. 'However, professor, the question is, how many of the seventeen verdicts backed up your opinion?'

'Sixteen, sir,' replied the professor.

'Please continue, Mr Galbraith,' said the judge.

'Professor, have you had the opportunity to study the late Sir Alexander Moncrieff's will, which is at the centre of this case?'

325

'I have studied both wills.'

'Can I ask you some questions about the second will?' The professor nodded. 'Is the paper on which the will is written of a type that would have been available at that time?'

'What time is that precisely, Mr Galbraith?' asked the judge.

'November 1998, my lord.'

'Yes it is,' replied the professor. 'It is my belief, based on scientific evidence, that the paper is the same vintage as that used for the first will, which was executed in 1997.'

The judge raised an eyebrow, but didn't interrupt. 'Was the red ribbon attached to that second will also of the same vintage?' asked Galbraith.

'Yes. I carried out tests on both ribbons, and it turned out that they were produced at the same time.'

'And were you, professor, able to come to any conclusion about Sir Alexander's signature as it appears on both wills?'

'Before I answer that question, Mr Galbraith, you must understand that I am not a calligraphic expert, but I can tell you that the black ink used by the signatory was manufactured some time before 1990.'

'Are you telling the court,' asked the judge, 'that you are able to date a bottle of ink to within a year of its production?'

'Sometimes within a month,' said the professor. 'In fact, I would submit that the ink used for the signature on both wills came from a bottle manufactured by Waterman's in 1985.'

'And now I should like to turn to the typewriter used for the second will,' said Mr Galbraith. 'What make was it, and when did it first come on to the market?'

'It is a Remington Envoy II, which came on to the market in 1965.'

'So just to confirm,' added Galbraith, 'the paper, the ink, the ribbon and the typewriter were all in existence before November 1998.'

'Without question, in my judgement,' said the professor.

'Thank you, professor. If you would be kind enough to wait there, I have a feeling that Mr Munro will have some questions for you.'

Munro rose slowly from his place. 'I have no questions for this witness, my lord.'

The judge did not react. However, the same could not be said of Galbraith, who stared at his opposite number in disbelief. Hugo Moncrieff asked his wife to explain the significance of Munro's words, while Danny looked straight ahead, showing no emotion, just as Munro had instructed him to do.

'Will you be presenting any other witnesses, Mr Galbraith?' asked the judge.

'No, my lord. I can only assume that my learned friend's refusal to cross-examine Professor Fleming means that he accepts his findings.' He paused. 'Without question.'

Munro didn't rise, in any sense of the expression.

'Mr Munro,' said the judge, 'do you wish to make an opening statement?'

'Briefly, if it so pleases your lordship,' said Munro. 'Professor Fleming has confirmed that Sir Alexander's first Will and Testament, made in favour of my client, is indisputably authentic. We accept his judgement in this matter. As you stated at the beginning of this hearing, my lord, the only question which concerns this court is the validity or otherwise of the second will, which—'

'My lord,' said Galbraith, jumping up from his place. 'Is Mr Munro suggesting to the court that the expertise the professor applied to the first will can conveniently be discounted when it comes to his opinion of the second?'

'No, my lord,' said Munro. 'Had my learned friend shown a little more patience, he would have discovered that that is not what I am suggesting. The professor told the court that he was not an expert on the authenticity of signatures—'

'But he also testified, my lord,' said Galbraith, leaping up again, 'that the ink used to sign both of the wills came from the same bottle.'

'But not from the same hand, I would suggest,' said Munro.

'Will you be calling a calligraphy expert?' asked the judge.

'No, my lord, I will not.'

'Do you have any evidence to suggest that the signature is a forgery?'

'No, my lord, I do not,' repeated Munro.

This time the judge did raise an eyebrow. 'Will you be calling any witnesses, Mr Munro, in support of your case?'

'Yes, my lord. Like my esteemed colleague, I will be calling only one witness.' Munro paused for a moment, aware that, with the exception of Danny, who didn't even blink, everyone in the room was curious to know who this witness could possibly be. 'I call Mr Gene Hunsacker.'

The door opened, and the vast frame of the Texan ambled slowly into the room. Danny felt that something wasn't right, then realized that it was the first time he'd seen Hunsacker without his trademark cigar.

Hunsacker took the oath, his voice booming around the small room.

'Please have a seat, Mr Hunsacker,' said the judge. 'As we are such a small gathering, perhaps we might address each other in more conversational tones.'

'I'm sorry, your honour,' said Hunsacker.

'No need to apologize,' said the judge. 'Please proceed, Mr Munro.'

Munro rose from his place and smiled at Hunsacker. 'For the record, would you be kind enough to state your name and occupation?'

'My name is Gene Hunsacker the third, and I'm retired.'

'And what did you do before you retired, Mr Hunsacker?' asked the judge.

'Not a lot, sir. My pa, like my grand-daddy before him, was a cattle rancher, but I myself never took to it, especially after oil was discovered on my land.'

'So you're an oilman,' said the judge.

'Not exactly, sir, because at the age of twenty-seven I sold out to a British company, BP, and since then I've spent the rest of my life pursuing my hobby.'

'How interesting. What, may I ask—' began the judge.

'We'll come to your hobby in a moment, Mr Hunsacker,' said Munro firmly. The judge sank back in his chair, an apologetic look on his face. 'Mr Hunsacker, you have stated that having made a considerable fortune following the sale of your land to BP, you are not in the oil business.'

'That's correct, sir.'

'I would also like to establish for the court's benefit what else you are *not* an expert on. For example, are you an expert on wills?'

'No, sir, I am not.'

'Are you an expert on paper and ink technology?'

'No, sir.'

'Are you an expert on ribbons?'

'I tried to remove a few from girls' hair when I was a younger man, but I wasn't even very good at that,' said Gene.

Munro waited for the laughter to die down before he continued. 'Then perhaps you are an expert on typewriters?'

'No, sir.'

'Or even signatures?'

'No, sir.'

'However,' said Munro, 'would I be right in suggesting that you are considered the world's leading authority on postage stamps?'

'I think I can safely say it's either me or Tomoji Watanabe,' Hunsacker replied, 'depending on who you talk to.'

The judge couldn't control himself any longer. 'Can you explain what you mean by that, Mr Hunsacker?'

'Both of us have been collectors for over forty years, your honour. I have the larger collection, but to be fair to Tomoji, that's possibly because I'm a darn sight richer than he is, and keep outbidding the poor bastard.' Even Margaret Moncrieff couldn't stifle a laugh. 'I sit on the board of Sotheby's, and Tomoji advises Philips. My collection has been put on display at the Smithsonian Institution in Washington DC, his at the Imperial Museum in Tokyo. So I can't tell you who's the world's leading authority, but whichever one of us is number one, the other guy is certainly number two.'

'Thank you, Mr Hunsacker,' said the judge. 'I am satisfied that your witness is an expert in his chosen field, Mr Munro.'

'Thank you, my lord,' said Munro. 'Mr Hunsacker, have you studied both of the wills involved in this case?'

'I have, sir.'

'And what is your opinion, your professional opinion, of the second will, the one that leaves Sir Alexander's fortune to his son Angus?'

'It's a fake.'

Desmond Galbraith was immediately on his feet. 'Yes, yes, Mr Galbraith,' said the judge, waving him back in his place. 'I do hope, Mr Hunsacker, that you are going to supply the court with some concrete evidence for this assertion. By "concrete evidence", I do not mean another dose of your homespun philosophy.'

Hunsacker's jovial smile disappeared. He waited for some time before saying, 'I shall prove, your honour, in what I believe you describe in this country as beyond reasonable doubt, that Sir Alexander's second will is a fake. In order to do so, I will require you to be in possession of the original document.' Mr Justice Sanderson turned to Galbraith, who shrugged his shoulders, rose from his place and handed the second will across to the judge. 'Now, sir,' said Hunsacker, 'if you would be kind enough to turn to the second page of the document, you will see Sir Alexander's signature written across a stamp.'

'Are you suggesting that the stamp is a fake?' said the judge.

'No, sir, I am not.'

'But as you have already stated, Mr Hunsacker, you are not an expert on signatures. What exactly are you suggesting?'

'That is clear for all to see, sir,' said Hunsacker, 'as long as you know what you're looking for.'

'Please enlighten me,' said the judge, sounding a little exasperated.

'Her Majesty the Queen ascended the British throne on February second, 1952,' said Hunsacker, 'and was crowned at Westminster Abbey on June second, 1953. The Royal Mail produced a stamp to mark that occasion – indeed I am the proud owner of a mint sheet of first editions. That stamp shows the Queen as a young woman, but because of the remarkable length of Her Majesty's reign, the Royal Mail has had to issue a new edition every few years to reflect the fact that the monarch has grown a little older. The edition which is affixed to this will was issued in March 1999.' Hunsacker swung round in his chair to look at

Hugo Moncrieff, wondering if the significance of his words had sunk in. He couldn't be sure, although the same could not be said of Margaret Moncrieff, whose lips were pursed, while the blood was quickly draining from her face.

'Your honour,' said Hunsacker, 'Sir Alexander Moncrieff died on December seventeen 1998 – three months *before* the stamp was issued. So one thing is for certain: that sure can't be his signature scrawled across Her Majesty.'

BOOK FOUR

REVENGE

51

Revenge is a dish best served cold.

Danny placed *Les Liaisons Dangereuses* in his briefcase as the plane began its descent through a bank of murky clouds that hung over London. He had every intention of exacting cold revenge on all three men who had been responsible for the death of his closest friend, for preventing him from marrying Beth, for depriving him of being able to bring up his daughter Christy, and for causing him to be imprisoned for a crime he did not commit.

He now had the financial resources to pick them off slowly, one by one, and it was his intention that by the time he'd completed the task, all three of them would consider death a preferable option.

'Would you please fasten your seatbelt, sir, we'll be landing at Heathrow in a few minutes.'

Danny smiled up at the stewardess who had interrupted his thoughts. Mr Justice Sanderson hadn't been given the opportunity to pass judgement in the case of Moncrieff v. Moncrieff, as one of the parties had withdrawn its claim soon after Mr Gene Hunsacker had left the judge's chambers.

Mr Munro had explained to Nick over dinner at the New Club in Edinburgh that if the judge had reason to believe a crime had been committed, he would have no choice but to send all the relevant papers to the Procurator Fiscal. Elsewhere in the city, Mr Desmond Galbraith was informing his client that if that were to happen, Hugo's nephew might not be the only Moncrieff to experience the slamming of the iron door.

Munro had advised Sir Nicholas not to press charges, despite the fact that Danny was in no doubt who had been responsible for the three policemen waiting for him on the last occasion he had landed at Heathrow. Munro had added, in one of those rare moments when his guard came down, 'But if your uncle Hugo causes any trouble in the future, then all bets are off.'

Danny had tried inadequately to thank Munro for all he had done *over the years* – think like Nick – and was surprised by his response, 'I'm not sure whom I enjoyed defeating more, your uncle Hugo or that prig Desmond Galbraith.' The guard remained down. Danny had always thought how lucky he was to have Mr Munro in his corner, but he had only recently become aware what it would be like to have him as an opponent.

When coffee was served, Danny had asked Fraser Munro to become a trustee of the family estate as well as its legal adviser. He had bowed low and said, 'If that is your wish, Sir Nicholas.' Danny had also made it clear that he wanted Dunbroathy Hall and the surrounding land to be handed over to the National Trust for Scotland, and that he intended to allocate whatever funds were necessary for its upkeep.

'Precisely as your grandfather envisaged,' said Munro. 'Although I have no doubt your uncle Hugo, with the help of Mr Galbraith, would have found some ingenious way of wriggling out of that commitment.'

Danny was beginning to wonder if Munro had had a wee dram too many. He couldn't imagine how the old solicitor would react were he to find out what Danny had in mind for another member of his profession.

The plane touched down at Heathrow just after eleven. Danny was meant to have caught the 8.40 flight, but had overslept for the first time in weeks.

He put Spencer Craig out of his mind when the aircraft came to a halt at its docking gate. He unbuckled his seatbelt and joined the other passengers standing in the aisle waiting for the door to swing open. This time there would be no policemen waiting outside for him. After the case had come to its premature end, Hunsacker had slapped the judge on the back and offered him a cigar. Mr

Justice Sanderson was briefly lost for words, but he did manage a smile before politely refusing.

Danny pointed out to Hunsacker that if he had stayed in Geneva, he would still have ended up with Sir Alexander's collection, because Hugo would have been happy to sell it to him and probably for a lower price.

'But I wouldn't have kept my pact with your grand-daddy,' Hunsacker replied. 'Now I've done something to repay his kindness and shrewd advice over so many years.'

An hour later Gene took off for Texas in his private jet, accompanied by 173 leather-bound albums, which Danny knew would keep him engrossed for the entire journey, and probably the rest of his life.

As Danny climbed aboard the Heathrow Express, his thoughts turned to Beth. He desperately wanted to see her again. Maupassant summed up his feelings so well: 'What's the point of triumph if you've no one to share it with?' But he could hear Beth asking, 'What's the point of revenge now you have so much to live for?' He would have reminded her first of Bernie and then of Nick, who had also had so much to live for. She would realize that the money meant nothing to him. He would have happily exchanged every penny for . . .

If only he could turn the clock back . . .

If only they had gone up to the West End the following night . . .

If only they hadn't gone to that particular pub . . .

If only they had left by the front door . . .

If only . . .

The Heathrow Express pulled into Paddington station seventeen minutes later. Danny checked his watch; he still had a couple of hours before his meeting with Ms Bennett. This time he'd go by taxi, and would be waiting in reception long before his appointment. The judge's words were still ringing in his ears: 'I intend to sign an order today which will ensure that you will be returned to prison for a further four years should you break any of your licence conditions in the future.'

Although settling scores with the three Musketeers remained Danny's first priority, he would have to put aside enough time to work on his degree, and honour his promise to Nick. He was even beginning to wonder if Spencer Craig might have played some role in Nick's death. Had Leach, as Big Al suggested, murdered the wrong man?

The taxi drew up outside his house in The Boltons. For the first time Danny really felt as if it was his home. He paid the fare, and opened the gate to find a tramp lounging on his doorstep.

'This is going to be your lucky day,' Danny said as he took out his wallet. The dozing figure was dressed in an open-neck blue and white striped shirt, a pair of well-worn jeans and a pair of black shoes that must have been polished that morning. He stirred and raised his head.

'Hi, Nick.'

Danny threw his arms around him, just as Molly opened the door. She put her hands on her hips. 'He said he was a friend of yours,' she said, 'but I still told him to wait outside.'

'He is my friend,' said Danny. 'Molly, meet Big Al.'

Molly had already prepared an Irish stew for Nick, and as her portions were always too large, there was more than enough for both of them.

'So tell me everything,' Danny said once they were seated at the kitchen table.

'No a lot tae tell, Nick,' said Big Al between mouthfuls. 'Like you, they released me after I'd served half my sentence. Thank God they shipped me oot, otherwise I might've been there fur the rest of ma life.' He reluctantly put down his spoon and added with a smile, 'An we know who wis responsible fur that.'

'So what have you got planned?' asked Danny.

'Nothing at the moment, but ye did say tae come and see you wance I got oot.' He paused. 'I hoped ye'd let me stay fur a night.'

'Stay as long as you like,' said Danny. 'My housekeeper will prepare the guest bedroom,' he added with a grin.

'I'm not your housekeeper,' said Molly sharply. 'I'm your cleaner what occasionally cooks.'

'Not any longer, Molly, you're now the housekeeper, as well as cook, on ten pounds an hour.' Molly was speechless. Danny took advantage of this unusual state of affairs to add, 'And what's more, you'll need to hire a cleaner to help you now that Big Al's joining us.'

'No, no,' said Big Al. 'I'll be out of here just as soon as I find a job.'

'You were a driver in the army, weren't you?' asked Danny.

'I wis *your* driver fur five years,' whispered Big Al, nodding his head in the direction of Molly.

'Then you've got your old job back,' said Danny.

'But you haven't got a car,' Molly reminded him.

'Then I shall have to get one,' said Danny. 'And who better to advise me?' he added, winking at Big Al. 'I've always wanted a BMW,' he said. 'Having worked in a garage, I know the exact model . . .'

Big Al put a finger up to his lips.

Danny knew Big Al was right. Yesterday's triumph must have gone to his head, and he'd slipped back to behaving like Danny – a mistake he couldn't afford to make too often. Think like Danny, act like Nick. He snapped back into his unreal world.

'But first you'd better go and buy some clothes,' he said to Big Al, 'before you even think about a car.'

'And some soap,' said Molly, filling Big Al's plate for a third time.

'Then Molly can scrub your back.'

'I will do no such thing,' said Molly. 'But I'd better go and make up one of the guest bedrooms if Mr Big Al is going to be with us – for a few days.' Danny and Big Al laughed as she took off her apron and left the kitchen.

Once the door was closed, Big Al leant across the table. 'Are ye still planning tae get they bastards that—'

'Yes, I am,' said Danny quietly, 'and you couldn't have turned up at a better time.'

'So when dae we start?'

'You start by having a bath, and then go and buy yourself some clothes,' said Danny, taking out his wallet for a second time. 'Meanwhile, I've got an appointment with my probation officer.'

◄○►

'And how have you spent the past month, Nicholas?' was Ms Bennett's first question.

Danny tried to keep a straight face. 'I've been busy sorting out those family problems I mentioned at our last meeting,' he replied.

'And has everything worked out as planned?'

'Yes, thank you, Ms Bennett.'

'Have you found a job yet?'

'No, Ms Bennett. I'm currently concentrating on my business studies degree at London University.'

'Ah yes, I remember. But surely the grant isn't sufficient to live on?'

'I can just about get by,' said Danny.

Ms Bennett returned to her list of questions. 'Are you still living in the same house?'

'Yes.'

'I see. I think perhaps I should come and inspect the property at some time, just to make sure it meets with the minimum Home Office standards.'

'You would be most welcome to visit any time that suits you,' said Danny.

She read out the next question. 'Have you been associating with any former prisoners you were in jail with?'

'Yes,' said Danny, aware that concealing anything from his probation officer would be regarded as a breach of his probation conditions. 'My former driver has just been released, and is currently staying with me.'

'Is there enough room in the house for both of you?'

'More than enough, thank you, Ms Bennett.'

'And does he have a job?'

'Yes, he's going to be my driver.'

'I think you're in enough trouble as it is, Nicholas, without being facetious.'

'It's no more than the truth, Ms Bennett. My grandfather has left me with sufficient funds to allow me to employ a driver.'

Ms Bennett looked down at the questions that the Home Office expected her to ask at monthly meetings. There didn't appear to be anything there about employing your own driver. She tried again.

'Have you been tempted to commit a crime since our last meeting?'

'No, Ms Bennett.'

'Have you been taking any drugs?'

'No, Ms Bennett.'

'Are you at present drawing unemployment benefit?'

'No, Ms Bennett.'

'Do you require any other assistance from the probation service?'

'No, thank you, Ms Bennett.'

Ms Bennett had come to the end of her list of questions, but had only spent half the time she was allocated for each client. 'Why don't you tell me what you've been up to for the past month?' she asked desperately.

—◄◦►—

'I'm going to have to let you go,' said Beth, resorting to the euphemism Mr Thomas always fell back on whenever he sacked a member of staff.

'But why?' asked Trevor Sutton. 'If I go, you won't have a manager. Unless you've already got someone else lined up to replace me.'

'I have no plans to replace you,' said Beth. 'But since my father's death, the garage has been steadily losing money. I can't afford this state of affairs to continue any longer,' she added, reading from the script Mr Thomas had prepared for her.

'But you haven't given me enough time to prove myself,' protested Sutton.

Beth wished that it was Danny who was sitting in her place – but if Danny had been around, the problem would never have arisen in the first place.

'If we have another three months like the last three,' Beth said, 'we'll be out of business.'

'What am I expected to do?' demanded Sutton, leaning forward and putting his elbows on the table. 'Because I know one thing, the boss would never have treated me this way.'

Beth felt angry that he had mentioned her father. But Mr

Thomas had advised her to try to put herself in Trevor's shoes, and to imagine how he must be feeling, especially since he'd never worked anywhere else since the day he left Clement Attlee comprehensive.

'I've had a word with Monty Hughes,' said Beth, trying to remain calm, 'and he assured me that he'd be able to find you a place on his staff.' What she didn't add was that Mr Hughes only had a junior mechanic's job available, which would mean a considerable drop in pay for Trevor.

'That's all very well,' he said angrily, 'but what about compensation? I know my rights.'

'I'm willing to pay you three months' wages,' said Beth, 'and also to give you a reference saying that you've been among the hardest workers.' *And among your most stupid*, Monty Hughes had added when Beth had consulted him. While she waited for Trevor's response, she recalled Danny's words, *but only because he can't add up*. Beth pulled open the drawer of her father's desk and extracted a bulky package and a single sheet of paper. She ripped open the package and emptied its contents on to the desk. Sutton stared down at the pile of fifty-pound notes and licked his lips as he tried to calculate just how much money was on the table. Beth slid a contract across the desk that Mr Thomas had prepared for her the previous afternoon. 'If you sign here,' she said, placing her finger on a dotted line, 'the seven thousand pounds will be yours.' Trevor hesitated, while Beth tried not to show just how desperate she was for him to sign the contract. She waited for Trevor to spend the money, although it seemed an age before he eventually picked up the proffered pen and wrote the only two words he could spell with confidence. He suddenly gathered up the cash and, without uttering another word, turned his back on Beth and marched out of the room.

Once Trevor had kicked the door closed behind him, Beth breathed a sigh of relief that wouldn't have left him in any doubt that he could have demanded far more than seven thousand, though, in truth, withdrawing that amount of cash from the bank had just about emptied the garage's account. All that was left for Beth to do now was to sell off the property as quickly as possible.

The young estate agent who had looked over the property had assured her that the garage was worth at least two hundred thousand. After all, it was a freehold site, situated in an excellent location with easy access to the City. Two hundred thousand pounds would solve all of Beth's financial problems, and mean there was enough left over to ensure that Christy could have the education she and Danny had always planned for her.

52

DANNY WAS READING Milton Friedman's *Tax Limitation, Inflation and the Role of Government*, and taking notes on the chapter about the property cycle and the effects of negative equity when the phone rang. After two hours of studying, he was beginning to feel that anything would be an improvement on Professor Friedman. He picked up the phone to hear a woman's voice.

'Hi, Nick. It's a voice from your past.'

'Hi, voice from my past,' said Danny, desperately trying to put a name to it.

'You said you were going to come and see me while I was on tour. Well, I keep looking out into the audience, but you're never there.'

'So where are you performing at the moment?' asked Danny, still racking his brains, but no name came to his rescue.

'Cambridge, the Arts Theatre.'

'Great, which play?'

'*A Woman of No Importance.*'

'Oscar Wilde again,' said Danny, aware that he didn't have much longer.

'Nick, you don't even remember my name, do you?'

'Don't be silly, Katie,' he said, just in time. 'How could I ever forget my favourite understudy?'

'Well, I've got the lead now, and I was hoping you'd come and see me.'

'Sounds good,' said Danny, flicking through the pages of his diary, although he knew that almost every evening was free. 'How about Friday?'

'Couldn't be better. We can spend the weekend together.'

'I have to be back in London for a meeting on Saturday morning,' said Danny, looking at a blank page in his diary.

'So it will have to be another one-night stand,' said Katie. 'I can live with that.' Danny didn't respond. 'Curtain's up at seven thirty. I'll leave a ticket for you at the box office. Come alone, because I don't intend to share you with anybody.'

Danny put the phone down and stared at the photograph of Beth that was in a silver frame on the corner of his desk.

◄○►

'There are three men coming up the path,' said Molly as she looked out of the kitchen window. 'They look foreign.'

'They're quite harmless,' Danny assured her. 'Just show them into the living room and tell them I'll join them in a moment.'

Danny ran up the stairs to his study and grabbed the three files that he had been working on in preparation for the meeting, then quickly made his way back downstairs.

The three men who were waiting for him looked identical in every way except for their age. They wore well-tailored dark blue suits, white shirts and anonymous ties, and each carried a black leather briefcase. You would have passed them in the street without giving them a second look – which would have pleased them.

'How nice to see you again, baron,' said Danny.

De Coubertin bowed low. 'We are touched that you invited us to your beautiful home, Sir Nicholas. May I introduce Monsieur Bresson, the bank's chief executive, and Monsieur Segat, who handles our major accounts.' Danny shook hands with all three men as Molly reappeared carrying a tray laden with tea and biscuits.

'Gentlemen,' said Danny as he sat down. 'Perhaps I could begin by asking you to bring me up to date on the current state of my account.'

'Certainly,' said Monsieur Bresson, opening an unmarked brown file. 'Your number-one account is showing a balance of just over fifty-seven million dollars, which is currently accumulating interest at the rate of 2.75 per cent per annum. Your number-two account,' he continued, 'has a balance of just over one million dollars. This was known at the bank as your grandfather's stamp account, which he used whenever he wanted to add to his collection at short notice.'

'You can combine the two accounts,' said Danny, 'as I won't be buying any stamps.' Bresson nodded. 'And I have to say, Monsieur Bresson, that I find a 2.75 per cent return on my capital unacceptable, and that I shall in future be putting my money to better use.'

'Can you tell us what you have in mind?' asked Segat.

'Yes,' said Danny. 'I shall be investing in three areas – property, stocks and shares, and possibly bonds, which incidentally are showing a current return of 7.12 per cent across the board. I will also set aside a small amount, never more than ten per cent of my total worth, for speculative ventures.'

'Then may I suggest in the circumstances,' said Segat, 'that we move your money into three separate accounts that cannot be traced back to you, while appointing nominee directors as your representatives.'

'In the circumstances?' repeated Danny.

'Since 9/11, the Americans and the British are taking far more interest in anyone who moves large sums of money around. It would not be wise for your name to keep popping up on their radar.'

'Good thinking,' said Danny.

'Assuming that you agree to our setting up these accounts,' added Bresson, 'may I ask whether you will wish to make additional use of the bank's expertise in managing your investments? I mention this, because our property department, for example, employs over forty specialists in the field – seven of them in London – who currently manage a portfolio of just under one hundred billion dollars, and our investment department is considerably larger.'

'I shall take advantage of everything you have to offer,' said Danny, 'and do not hesitate to let me know if you think I am making a wrong decision. However, over the past couple of years I have spent a considerable amount of time following the fortunes of twenty-eight particular companies and I have decided to invest some of my capital in eleven of them.'

'What will be your policy when it comes to purchasing shares in those companies?' asked Segat.

'I would want you to buy in small tranches whenever they come on the market – never aggressively, as I do not wish to be responsible for influencing the market either way. Also, I never want to hold more than two per cent of any one company.' Danny handed Bresson a list of the companies whose progress he had been monitoring long before he had escaped from prison.

Bresson ran his finger down the names, and smiled. 'We have been keeping an eye on several of these companies ourselves, but I am fascinated to see that you have identified one or two that we have not yet considered.'

'Then please double-check them, and if you have any doubts, tell me.' Danny picked up one of his files. 'When it comes to property, I intend to act aggressively,' he said. 'And I will expect you to move quickly if immediate payment will secure a more realistic price.'

Bresson handed over a card. It had no name on it, no address, just a phone number embossed in black. 'That is my private line. We can wire any amount of money you require to any country on earth at the touch of a button. And when you call, you need never give your name, as the line is voice-activated.'

'Thank you,' said Danny, placing the card in an inside pocket. 'I also require your advice on a more pressing matter, namely my day-to-day living expenses. I have no desire for the taxman to be prying into my affairs, and as I live in this house and employ a housekeeper and driver, while apparently subsisting on nothing more than a student grant, it may be the Inland Revenue's radar that I keep popping up on.'

'If I might make a suggestion?' said de Coubertin. 'We used to transfer one hundred thousand pounds a month to an account in London for your grandfather. It came from a trust we set up on his behalf. He paid tax on this income in full, and even carried out some of his smaller transactions through a company registered in London.'

'I should like you to continue that arrangement,' said Danny. 'How do I go about it?'

De Coubertin extracted a slim file from his briefcase, removed a single sheet of paper and said, pointing to a dotted line, 'If you sign here, Sir Nicholas, I can assure you that everything will be set up and administered to your satisfaction. All I will need to know is to which bank we should make the monthly transfer.'

'Coutts and Co in the Strand,' said Danny.

'Just like your grandfather,' said the chairman.

◄o►

'How long will it take to get to Cambridge?' Danny asked Big Al moments after the three Swiss bankers had disappeared into thin air.

'Aboot an hour and a half. So we ought tae be leaving fairly soon, boss.'

'Fine,' said Danny. 'I'll go and change and pack an overnight bag.'

'Molly's already done that,' said Big Al. 'I put it in the boot of the car.'

The Friday evening traffic was heavy, and it wasn't until they joined the M11 that Big Al managed to push the speedometer above thirty miles an hour. He drove into King's Parade only minutes before the curtain was due to rise.

Danny had been so preoccupied during the past few weeks that this was going to be his first visit to the theatre since seeing Lawrence Davenport in *The Importance of Being Earnest*.

Lawrence Davenport. Although Danny had begun to form plans for all three of his antagonists, every time he thought about Davenport, Sarah came into his mind. He was aware that he might well have been back in Belmarsh had it not been for her, and also that he would need to see her again, as she could open doors to which he didn't have a key.

Big Al brought the car to a halt outside the theatre. 'What time will ye be gon' back tae London, boss?'

'I haven't decided yet,' said Danny, 'but not before midnight.'

He picked up his ticket from the box office, handed over three pounds in exchange for a programme, and followed a group of fellow latecomers into the stalls. Once he'd found his seat, he began to turn the pages of the programme. He'd meant to read the play before this evening, but it had remained on his desk unopened while he tried to keep up with Milton Friedman.

Danny stopped at a page that displayed a large, glamorous headshot of Katie Benson. Unlike so many actresses, it was not a photograph that had been taken some years before. He read the brief résumé of her credits. *A Woman of No Importance* was clearly the most significant role she had played in her short career.

When the curtain rose, Danny became lost in another world, and resolved that in future he would go to the theatre on a regular basis. How he wished that Beth was sitting next to him and sharing in his enjoyment. Katie was standing on stage arranging some flowers in a vase, but all he could think about was Beth. But as the play unfolded, he had to admit that Katie was giving a polished performance, and he soon became engrossed in the story of a woman who suspected her husband of being unfaithful.

During the interval, Danny made a decision, and by the time the curtain came down, Mr Wilde had even shown him how to go about it. He waited for the theatre to empty before he made his way to the stage door. The doorman gave him a suspicious look when he asked if he could see Miss Benson.

'What's your name?' he demanded, checking his clipboard.

'Nicholas Moncrieff.'

'Ah, yes. She's expecting you. Dressing room seven, first floor.'

Danny walked slowly up the stairs and when he reached the door marked 7, he waited for a moment before knocking.

'Come in,' said a voice he remembered.

He opened the door to find Katie sitting in front of a mirror wearing only a black bra and panties. She was removing her stage make-up.

'Shall I wait outside?' he asked.

'Don't be silly, darling, I've got nothing new to show you, and in any case, I was hoping to arouse a few memories,' she added, turning to face him.

She stood up and stepped into a black dress, which strangely made her look even more desirable. 'You were wonderful,' he said lamely.

'Are you sure, darling?' she asked, looking at him more closely. 'You don't sound altogether convinced.'

'Oh, yes,' Danny said. 'I really enjoyed the play.'

Katie stared at him. 'Something's wrong.'

'I have to get back to London. I have some urgent business.'

'On a Friday night? Oh, come on, Nick, you can do better than that.'

'It's just that—'

'It's another woman, isn't it?'

'Yes,' admitted Danny.

'Then why did you bother to come in the first place?' she said angrily, turning her back on him.

'I'm sorry. I'm very sorry.'

'Don't bother to apologize, Nick. You couldn't have made it more obvious that I'm a woman of no importance.'

53

'SORRY, BOSS, but I thought ye said no before midnight,' said Big Al, quickly finishing his hamburger.

'I changed my mind.'

'I thought that was a lady's prerogative?'

'So did she,' said Danny.

By the time they reached the M11 fifteen minutes later, Danny was already fast asleep. He didn't wake until the car came to a halt at a traffic light on Mile End Road. If Danny had woken a few moments earlier he would have asked Big Al to take a different route.

The light changed, and they sped through green light after green light, as if someone else knew that Danny shouldn't be there. He leant back and closed his eyes, though he knew there were some familiar landmarks he wouldn't be able to pass without at least a fleeting glance: Clement Attlee comprehensive, St Mary's church, and of course Wilson's garage.

He opened his eyes, and wished he'd kept them closed. 'It can't be possible,' he said. 'Pull over, Al.'

Big Al brought the car to a halt, and looked around to make sure the boss was all right. Danny was staring across the road in disbelief. Big Al tried to work out what he was looking at, but couldn't see anything unusual.

'Wait here,' said Danny, opening the back door. 'I'll only be a couple of minutes.'

Danny walked across the road, stood on the pavement and stared up at a sign that was attached to the wall. He took a pen and a piece of paper out of an inside pocket and wrote down the number below the words FOR SALE. When he saw some locals spilling out of a nearby pub, he ran quickly back across the road and joined Big Al in the front of the car.

'Let's get out of here,' he said without explanation.

—◄○►—

Danny thought of asking Big Al to drive him back to the East End on Saturday morning so he could have a second look, but he knew he couldn't take the risk of someone even thinking they recognized him.

A plan began to form in his mind, and by Sunday evening it was nearly in place. Every detail would have to be followed to the letter. One mistake and all three of them would work out exactly what he was up to. But the bit-part players, the understudies, had to be in their positions long before the three lead actors could be allowed to walk on to the stage.

When Danny woke on Monday morning and went down to breakfast, he left *The Times* unopened on the kitchen table. He played over in his mind what needed to be done, because he couldn't afford to commit anything to paper. If Arnold Pearson QC had asked him as he left the kitchen what Molly had given him for breakfast that morning, he wouldn't have been able to tell him. He retreated to his study, locked the door and sat at his desk. He picked up the phone and dialled the number on the card.

'I will need to move a small amount of money some time today, and very quickly,' he said.

'Understood.'

'I will also require someone to advise me on a property transaction.'

'They will be in touch with you later today.'

Danny replaced the phone and checked his watch. No one would be at their desks before nine. He paced around the room, using the time to rehearse his questions, questions that mustn't sound prepared. At one minute past nine, he took the piece of paper out of his pocket and dialled the number.

'Douglas Allen Spiro,' said a morning voice.

'You have a for-sale sign outside a property on Mile End Road,' said Danny.

'I'll put you through to Mr Parker, he deals with properties in that area.'

Danny heard a click. 'Roger Parker.'

'You have a property for sale on Mile End Road,' repeated Danny.

'We have several properties in that area, sir. Can you be more specific?'

'Wilson's garage.'

'Oh yes, first-class property, freehold. It's been in the same family for over a hundred years.'

'How long has it been on the market?'

'Not long, and we've already had a lot of interest.'

'How long?' repeated Danny.

'Five, perhaps six months,' admitted Parker.

Danny cursed to himself as he thought about the anxiety Beth's family must have been going through, and he'd done nothing to help. He wanted to ask so many questions that he knew Mr Parker couldn't answer. 'What's the asking price?'

'Two hundred thousand,' said Parker, 'or near offer, which of course includes the fixtures and fittings. Can I take your name, sir?'

Danny replaced the receiver. He stood up and walked across to a shelf that had three files on it marked *Craig, Davenport* and *Payne*. He took down Gerald Payne's file and checked the phone number of the youngest partner in Baker, Tremlett and Smythe's history, as Mr Arnold Pearson QC had been so keen to inform the jury. But Danny had no plans to speak to Payne today. Payne had to come to him, desperate to be part of the deal. Today was saved for the messenger. He dialled the number.

'Baker, Tremlett and Smythe.'

'I'm thinking of buying a property on Mile End Road.'

'I'll put you through to the department that handles East London.'

There was a click on the end of the line. Would whoever picked up the phone ever discover they had been randomly selected to be the messenger and shouldn't later be blamed when the earthquake erupted? 'Gary Hall. How can I help you?'

'Mr Hall, my name is Sir Nicholas Moncrieff and I wonder – ' slowly, very slowly, ' – if I've got the right man.'

'Tell me what it is you need, sir, and I'll see if I can help.'

'There's a property for sale in Mile End Road that I'd like to buy, but I don't want to deal directly with the vendor's estate agent.'

'I understand, sir. You can be assured of my discretion.' I hope not, thought Danny. 'What number in Mile End Road is it?'

'One four three,' Danny replied. 'It's a garage – Wilson's garage.'

'Who are the vendor's agents?'

'Douglas Allen Spiro.'

'I'll have a word with my opposite number there and find out all the details,' said Hall, 'then give you a bell back.'

'I'll be in your area later today,' said Danny. 'Perhaps you could join me for a coffee?'

'Of course, Sir Nicholas. Where would you like to meet?'

Danny could only think of one place he'd ever been to that was anywhere near Baker, Tremlett and Smythe's offices. 'The Dorchester,' he said. 'Shall we say twelve o'clock?'

'I'll see you there at twelve, Sir Nicholas.'

Danny remained seated at his desk. He put three ticks on a long list in front of him, but he still needed several other players to be in place before midday if he was going to be ready for Mr Hall. The phone on his desk began to ring. Danny picked it up.

'Good morning, Sir Nicholas,' said a voice. 'I manage the bank's property desk in London.'

―◦―

Big Al drove Danny to Park Lane, and drew up outside the terrace entrance of the Dorchester just after eleven thirty. A doorman walked down the steps and opened the back door of the car. Danny stepped out.

'My name is Sir Nicholas Moncrieff,' he said as he walked up the steps. 'I'm expecting a guest to join me around twelve – a Mr

Hall. Could you tell him I'll be in the lounge?' He took out his wallet and handed the doorman a ten-pound note.

'I certainly will, sir,' said the doorman, raising his top hat.

'And your name is?' asked Danny.

'George.'

'Thank you, George,' said Danny, and walked through the revolving doors and into the hotel.

He paused in the lobby, and introduced himself to the head concierge. After a short conversation with Walter, he parted with another ten-pound note.

On Walter's advice, Danny made his way to the lounge and waited for the maitre d' to return to his post. This time Danny took a ten-pound note out of his wallet before he'd made his request.

'Why don't I put you in one of our more private alcoves, Sir Nicholas? I'll see that Mr Hall is brought across to you the moment he arrives. Would you care for anything while you're waiting?'

'A copy of *The Times* and a hot chocolate,' said Danny.

'Of course, Sir Nicholas.'

'And your name is?' asked Danny.

'Mario, sir.'

George, Walter and Mario had unwittingly become members of his team, at a cost of thirty pounds. Danny turned to the business section of *The Times* to check on his investments while he waited for the innocent Mr Hall to appear. At two minutes to twelve, Mario was standing by his side. 'Sir Nicholas, your guest has arrived.'

'Thank you, Mario,' Danny said as if he were a regular customer.

'It's a pleasure to meet you, Sir Nicholas,' said Hall as he took the seat opposite Danny.

'What would you like to drink, Mr Hall?' said Danny.

'Just a coffee, thank you.'

'A coffee and my usual, please, Mario.'

'Of course, Sir Nicholas.'

The young man who had joined Danny was dressed in a beige suit, green shirt and a yellow tie. Gary Hall would never have been offered a position at the Banque de Coubertin. He opened his briefcase and took out a file. 'I think I have all the information you require, Sir Nicholas,' said Hall, flicking open the cover. 'Number 143 Mile End Road – used to be a garage, owned by a Mr George Wilson, who died recently.' The blood drained from Danny's face as he realized just how far the ramifications of Bernie's death had extended: a single incident that had changed so many lives.

'Are you feeling all right, Sir Nicholas?' asked Hall, looking genuinely concerned.

'Yes, I'm fine, just fine,' said Danny, quickly recovering. 'You were saying?' he added as a waiter placed a hot chocolate in front of him.

'After Mr Wilson retired, the business was carried on for a couple of years under a man called . . .' Hall referred to his file, though Danny could have told him. 'Trevor Sutton. But during that time the company ran up considerable debts, so the owner decided to cut her losses and put it up for sale.'

'*Her* losses?'

'Yes, the site is now owned – ' he once again checked his file – 'by a Miss Elizabeth Wilson, the daughter of the previous owner.'

'What's the asking price?' said Danny.

'The site is approximately five thousand square feet, but if you are considering making an offer, I could do a survey and confirm the exact measurements.' 4,789 square feet, Danny could have told him. 'There's a pawn shop on one side, and a Turkish carpet warehouse on the other.'

'What's the asking price?' repeated Danny.

'Oh yes, sorry. Two hundred thousand, including fixtures and fittings, but I'm fairly confident you could pick it up for a hundred and fifty. There hasn't been much interest shown in the property, and there's a far more successful garage trading on the other side of the road.'

'I can't afford to waste any time haggling,' said Danny, 'so listen carefully. I'm prepared to pay the asking price, and I also want you to approach the owners of the pawn shop and the carpet warehouse, as I intend to make an offer for their properties.'

'Yes, of course, Sir Nicholas,' said Hall, writing down his every word. He hesitated for a moment. 'I'll need a deposit of twenty thousand pounds before we can proceed.'

'By the time you get back to your office, Mr Hall, two hundred thousand pounds will have been deposited in your client account.' Hall didn't look convinced, but managed a thin smile. 'As soon as you know about the other two properties, call me.'

'Yes, Sir Nicholas.'

'And I must make one thing clear,' said Danny. 'The owner must never find out who she is dealing with.'

'You can rely on my discretion, Sir Nicholas.'

'I hope so,' said Danny, 'because I found I couldn't rely on the discretion of the last company I dealt with, and that's how they lost my business.'

'I understand,' said Hall. 'How do I get in touch with you?' Danny took out his wallet and handed him a freshly minted embossed card. 'And finally, may I ask, Sir Nicholas, which solicitors will be representing you in this transaction?'

This was the first question Danny hadn't anticipated. He smiled. 'Munro, Munro and Carmichael. You should only deal with Mr Fraser Munro, the senior partner, who handles all my personal affairs.'

'Of course, Sir Nicholas,' said Hall, rising from his place once he had written the name down. 'I'd better get straight back to the office and talk to the vendor's agents.'

Danny watched Hall as he scuttled away, his coffee untouched. He was confident that within the hour the whole office would have heard about the eccentric Sir Nicholas Moncrieff, who clearly had more money than sense. They would undoubtedly tease young Hall about his wasted morning, until they discovered the £200,000 in the client account.

Danny flicked open his mobile phone and dialled the number. 'Yes,' said a voice.

'I want two hundred thousand pounds to be transferred to the client account of Baker, Tremlett and Smythe in London.'

'Understood.'

Danny closed the phone and thought about Gary Hall. How quickly would he discover that Mrs Isaacs had wanted her husband to sell the pawn shop for years, and that the carpet warehouse only just about broke even, and Mr and Mrs Kamal hoped to retire to Ankara so that they could spend more time with their daughter and grandchildren?

Mario placed the bill discreetly on the table by his side. Danny left a large tip. He needed to be remembered. As he passed through reception, he paused to thank the head concierge.

'My pleasure, Sir Nicholas. Do let me know if I can be of any service in the future.'

'Thank you, Walter. I may well be in touch.'

Danny pushed his way through the swing doors and walked out on to the terrace. George rushed across to the waiting car and opened the back door. Danny extracted another ten-pound note.

'Thank you, George.'

George, Walter and Mario were now all paid-up members of his cast, although the curtain had only fallen on the first act.

54

DANNY TOOK the file marked *Davenport* off the shelf and placed it on his desk. He turned to the first page.

Davenport, Lawrence, actor – pages 2–11

Davenport, Sarah, sister, solicitor – pages 12–16

Duncan, Charlie, producer – pages 17–20

He turned to page 17. Another bit-part player was about to become involved in Lawrence Davenport's next production. Danny dialled his number.

'Charles Duncan Productions.'

'Mr Duncan, please.'

'Who shall I say is calling?'

'Nick Moncrieff.'

'I'll put you through, Mr Moncrieff.'

'I'm trying to remember where we met,' said the next voice on the line.

'At the Dorchester, for *The Importance of Being Earnest* closing-night party.'

'Oh, yes, now I remember. So what can I do for you?' asked a suspicious-sounding voice.

'I'm thinking of investing in your next production,' said Danny. 'A friend of mine put a few thousand in *Earnest* and he tells me he made a handsome profit, so I thought this might be the right time for me to—'

'You couldn't have called at a better time,' said Duncan. 'I've got the very thing for you, old boy. Why don't you join me at the Ivy for a spot of lunch some time so we can discuss it?'

Could anyone really fall for that line, thought Danny. If they could, this was going to be easier than he had imagined. 'No, let me take you to lunch, old boy,' said Danny. 'You must be extremely busy, so perhaps you'd be kind enough to give me a call when you're next available.'

'Well, funnily enough,' said Duncan, 'I've just had a cancellation for tomorrow, so if you happened to be free.'

'Yes, I am,' said Danny, before baiting the trap. 'Why don't you join me at my local pub?'

'Your local pub?' said Duncan, not sounding quite so enthusiastic.

'Yes, the Palm Court Room at the Dorchester. Shall we say one o'clock?'

'Ah, yes, of course. I'll see you there, one o'clock,' said Duncan. 'It's *Sir* Nicholas, isn't it?'

'Nick's just fine,' said Danny, before putting the phone down and making an entry in his diary.

◄○►

Professor Amirkhan Mori smiled benevolently as he peered into the packed auditorium. His lectures were always well attended, and not just because he imparted so much wisdom and knowledge, but he also managed to do it with humour. It had taken Danny some time to realize that the professor enjoyed provoking discussion and argument by offering up outrageous statements to see what reaction he would arouse from his students.

'It would have been better for the economic stability of our nation if John Maynard Keynes had never been born. I cannot think of one worthwhile thing that he achieved in his lifetime.' Twenty hands shot into the air.

'Moncrieff,' he said. 'What example do you have to offer of a legacy that Keynes could be proud of?'

'He founded the Cambridge Arts Theatre,' said Danny, hoping to play the professor at his own game.

'He also played Orsino in *Twelfth Night* when he was a student at King's College,' said Mori. 'But that was before he went on to prove to the world that it made economic sense for wealthy countries to invest in and encourage developing nations.' The clock on the wall behind him struck one. 'I've had enough of you lot,' said the professor, and marched off the platform and disappeared out of the swing doors to laughter and applause.

Danny knew he wouldn't have time even to grab a quick lunch in the canteen if he wasn't going to be late for the meeting with his probation officer, but as he dashed out of the lecture theatre he found Professor Mori waiting in the corridor.

'I wonder if we might have a word, Moncrieff,' said Mori, and without waiting for a reply, charged off down the corridor. Danny followed him into his office, prepared to defend his views of Milton Friedman, as he knew his latest essay was not in line with the professor's oft-expressed opinions on the subject.

'Have a seat, dear boy,' Mori said. 'I'd offer you a drink, but frankly I don't have anything worth drinking. But to more important matters. I wanted to know if you had considered entering your name for the Jennie Lee Memorial Prize essay competition.'

'I hadn't given it a thought,' admitted Danny.

'Then you should,' said Professor Mori. 'You're by far the brightest student of your intake, which isn't saying a lot, but I still think you could win the prize. If you have the time, you ought to give it your serious consideration.'

'What sort of commitment would it require?' asked Danny, whose studies were still only the second priority in his life.

The professor picked up a booklet that was lying on his desk, turned to the first page and began reading out loud. 'The essay should be no less than ten thousand words and no more than twenty, on a subject of the entrant's choice, and it must be handed in by the end of Michaelmas Term.'

'I'm flattered that you think I'm up to it,' said Danny.

'I'm only surprised that your masters at Loretto didn't advise you to go to Edinburgh or Oxford, rather than join the army.'

Danny would like to have told the professor that no one from Clement Attlee comprehensive had ever been to Oxford, including the head teacher.

'Perhaps you'd like to think it over,' said the professor. 'Let me know when you've come to a decision.'

'I certainly will,' said Danny as he rose to leave. 'Thank you, professor.'

Once he was back in the corridor, Danny began running towards the entrance. As he charged through the front doors, he was relieved to see Big Al waiting by the car.

Danny mulled over Professor Mori's words as Big Al drove along the Strand and through The Mall on his way to Notting Hill Gate. He continually broke the speed limit as he didn't want the boss to be late for his appointment. Danny made it clear that he'd rather pay a speeding fine than spend another four years in Belmarsh. It was unfortunate that Big Al drew up outside the probation office just as Ms Bennett stepped off her bus. She stared through the car window as Danny tried to conceal himself behind Big Al's hulking frame.

'She probably thinks ye huv robbed a bank,' said Big Al, 'an I'm the getaway driver.'

'I did rob a bank,' Danny reminded him.

Danny was made to wait in reception for longer than usual before Ms Bennett reappeared and beckoned him into her office. Once he was seated on his plastic chair on the opposite side of the formica table, she said, 'Before I begin, Nicholas, perhaps you can explain whose car you arrived in this afternoon?'

'It's mine,' replied Danny.

'And who was the driver?' asked Ms Bennett.

'He's my chauffeur.'

'How can you afford to own a BMW and have a chauffeur when your only declared source of income is a student grant?' she asked.

'My grandfather set up a trust fund for me which pays out a monthly income of a hundred thousand pounds and—'

'Nicholas,' said Ms Bennett sharply, 'these meetings are meant to be an opportunity for you to be open and frank about any problems you are facing so that I can offer you advice and assistance. I am going to allow you one more chance to answer my questions honestly. If you continue to act in this frivolous manner, I will have no choice but to mention it in my next report to the

Home Office, and we both know what the consequences of that will be. Do I make myself clear?'

'Yes, Ms Bennett,' said Danny, recalling what Big Al had told him when he had faced the same problem with his probation officer. 'Tell them what they want tae hear, boss. It makes life so much easier.'

'Let me ask you once again. Who owns the car you arrived in this afternoon?'

'The man who was driving it,' said Danny.

'And is he a friend? Or do you work for him?'

'I knew him when I was in the army, and because I was running late, he offered me a lift.'

'And can you tell me if you have any source of income other than your student grant?'

'No, Ms Bennett.'

'That's more like it,' said Ms Bennett. 'You see how much more smoothly everything goes when you cooperate? Now, is there anything else you want to discuss with me?'

Danny was tempted to tell her about his meeting with the three Swiss bankers, take her through the property deal he was trying to put together, or let her know what he had in mind for Charlie Duncan. He settled on, 'My professor wants me to enter for the Jennie Lee Memorial Prize essay competition, and I wondered what your advice would be.'

Ms Bennett smiled. 'Do you think it will enhance your chances of becoming a teacher?'

'Yes, I suppose it might,' said Danny.

'Then I would advise you to enter the competition.'

'I am most grateful, Ms Bennett.'

'Not at all,' she replied. 'After all, that's what I'm here for.'

Danny's unplanned late-night visit to Mile End Road had rekindled those glowing embers that lifers call their demons. Returning to the Old Bailey in broad daylight would mean that he had to face an even greater challenge.

As Big Al swung the car into St Paul's Yard, Danny looked up at the statue perched on top of the Central Criminal Court: a woman was attempting to balance a pair of scales. When Danny had flicked through his diary to see if he was free to have lunch with Charlie Duncan, he had been reminded how he had planned to spend that morning. Big Al drove past the public entrance, swung right at the end of the road and made his way round to the back of the building, where he parked outside a door marked *Visitors' Entrance.*

Once Danny had been cleared through security he began the long climb up the steep stone steps that led to the galleries that overlook the different courts. When he reached the top floor, a court official wearing a long black schoolmaster's gown asked him if he knew which court he wished to attend.

'Number four,' he told the officer, who pointed down the corridor to the second door on the right. Danny followed his instructions and made his way into the public gallery. A handful of onlookers – family and friends of the accused, and a few of the simply curious – were seated on a bench in the front row peering down into the court. He didn't join them.

Danny had no interest in the accused man. He had come to watch his adversary performing on his home ground. He slipped into a place in the corner of the back row. Like a skilled assassin, he had a perfect sighting of his quarry as he went about his business, while Spencer Craig would have had to turn round and stare up into the gallery if he were to have any chance of seeing him, and even then Danny would appear as an irrelevant speck on his landscape.

Danny watched every move Craig made, much as a boxer does when sparring with an opponent, looking for flaws, searching for weaknesses. Craig displayed very few to the untrained eye. As the morning progressed, it became clear that he was skilful, cunning and ruthless, all necessary weapons in the armoury of his chosen profession; but he also appeared willing to stretch the elastic of the law to breaking point if it would advance his cause, as Danny had already learnt to his cost. He knew that when the time came to face Craig head on, he would have to be at his sharpest, because this opponent wasn't going to lie down until the last breath had been knocked out of him.

Danny felt that he now knew almost everything there was to know about Spencer Craig, which only made him more cautious. While Danny had the advantage of preparation and the element of surprise, he also had the disadvantage of having dared to enter an arena that Craig considered to be nothing less than his birthright, whereas Danny had only inhabited the same terrain for a few months. With every day that he played his role it became more of a reality, so that now, no one he came across ever doubted that he was Sir Nicholas Moncrieff. But Danny remembered that Nick had written in his diary that whenever you face a skilful enemy, you must lure him off his own ground, so that he does not feel at ease, because that is when you have the best chance of taking him by surprise.

Danny had been testing his new skills every day, but getting himself invited to a closing-night party, giving the impression that he was a regular customer at the Dorchester, fooling a young estate agent who was desperate to close a deal, and convincing a theatrical producer that he might invest in his latest production, were simply the opening rounds of a long competition in which Craig was undoubtedly the number-one seed. If Danny were to lower his guard even for a moment, the man strutting his hour upon the courtroom floor below would not hesitate to strike again, and this time he would make sure that Danny was sent back to Belmarsh for the rest of his life.

He had to lure this man into a swamp from which he could not hope to escape. Charlie Duncan might be able to help him strip Lawrence Davenport of his adoring fans; Gary Hall could even cause Gerald Payne to be humiliated in the eyes of his colleagues and friends; but it would take far more to ensure that Spencer Craig would end his legal career, not sitting in judgement on the bench wearing a wig and red gown while being addressed as m'lord, but standing in the dock being convicted by a jury of his fellow citizens on a charge of murder.

55

'GOOD MORNING, George,' said Danny as the doorman opened the back door of the car for him.

'Good morning, Sir Nicholas.'

Danny strolled into the hotel and waved at Walter as he passed through the reception area. Mario's face lit up the moment he spotted his favourite customer.

'A hot chocolate and *The Times*, Sir Nicholas?' he asked once Danny had settled into his alcove seat.

'Thank you, Mario. I'd also like a table for lunch tomorrow at one o'clock, somewhere I can't be overheard?'

'That won't be a problem, Sir Nicholas.'

Danny leant back and thought about the meeting that was about to take place. His advisers from de Coubertin's property department had called three times during the past week: no names, no small talk, just facts and considered advice. Not only had they come up with a realistic price for the pawn shop and the carpet warehouse, but they had also drawn his attention to a barren plot of land that ran behind the three properties and was owned by the local council. Danny didn't tell them he knew every inch of that land, because when he was a kid he'd played striker while Bernie was in goal in their private cup final.

They had also been able to inform him that for some years the council's planning committee had wanted to build 'affordable housing' on that particular site, but that with a garage so close to the site, the health and safety committee had vetoed the idea. The minutes of the relevant committee meetings had arrived in a brown envelope the following morning. Danny had plans to solve their problems.

'Good morning, Sir Nicholas.'

Danny looked up from his newspaper. 'Good morning, Mr Hall,' he said as the young man took the seat opposite him. Hall opened his briefcase and took out a thick file marked *Moncrieff*, then removed a document and handed it to Danny.

'These are the deeds for Wilson's garage,' he explained. 'Contracts were exchanged when I met up with Miss Wilson this morning.' Danny thought his heart would stop beating. 'A charming young woman who seemed relieved to have the problem off her hands.'

Danny smiled. Beth would deposit the £200,000 with her local branch of the HSBC, content to see it earning 4.5 per cent per annum, although he knew exactly who would benefit most from the windfall.

'And the two buildings on either side?' asked Danny. 'Have you made any progress with them?'

'To my surprise,' said Hall, 'I think we can close a deal on both sites.' This came as no surprise to Danny. 'Mr Isaacs says he'd let the pawn shop go for two hundred and fifty thousand, while Mr Kamal is asking three hundred and sixty thousand for the carpet warehouse. Together they would just about double the size of your holding, and our investment people estimate that the marriage value alone could double your original outlay.'

'Pay Mr Isaacs his asking price. Offer Mr Kamal three hundred thousand and settle for three hundred and twenty.'

'But I still think I can get you a better deal,' said Hall.

'Don't even think about it,' said Danny. 'I want you to close both deals on the same day, because if Mr Kamal were to find out what we're up to, he'd know he's got a ransom strip.'

'Understood,' said Hall, as he continued to write down Danny's instructions.

'Once you've closed both deals, let me know immediately so I can open negotiations with the council about the strip of land behind the three sites.'

'We could even draw you up some outline plans before we

approach them,' said Hall. 'It might be an ideal site for a small office block, even a supermarket.'

'No it would not, Mr Hall,' said Danny firmly. 'If you did that, you'd be wasting your time and my money.' Hall looked embarrassed. 'There's a branch of Sainsbury's only a hundred yards away, and if you study the council's ten-year development plan for the area, you'll see that the only projects they're giving planning permission for are affordable dwellings. My experience tells me that if you make a council think something is their idea in the first place, you have a far better chance of closing a deal. Don't get greedy, Mr Hall. Remember, that was another mistake my last agent made.'

'I'll remember,' said Hall.

Danny's advisers had done their homework so well that he had no difficulty in running circles around Hall.

'Meanwhile, I'll deposit five hundred and seventy thousand pounds in your client account today, so that you can close both deals as soon as possible – but don't forget, on the same day, and without either side finding out about the other sale and certainly without them becoming aware of my involvement.'

'I won't let you down,' said Hall.

'I hope not,' said Danny. 'Because if you succeed in this little enterprise, I've been working on something far more interesting. But as there is an element of risk involved, it will need the backing of one of your partners, preferably someone young, who's got balls and imagination.'

'I know exactly the right man,' said Hall.

Danny didn't bother to say and so do I.

◄○►

'How are you, Beth?' asked Alex Redmayne as he rose from behind his desk and ushered her towards a comfortable chair by the fire.

'I'm well, thank you, Mr Redmayne.'

Alex smiled as he took a seat by her side. 'I never could get Danny to call me Alex,' he said, 'even though I like to think that towards the end we became friends. Perhaps I'll be more successful with you.'

'The truth, Mr Redmayne, is that Danny was even shyer than I am; shy and stubborn. You mustn't think that because he didn't call you by your first name he didn't consider you a friend.'

'I wish he was sitting there now telling me that,' said Alex, 'although I was delighted when you wrote asking to see me.'

'I wanted to seek your advice,' said Beth, 'but until recently, I haven't been in a position to do so.'

Alex leant across and took her hand. He smiled when he saw the engagement ring, which she hadn't worn on the previous occasion. 'How can I help?'

'It's just that I thought I should let you know that something strange took place when I went to Belmarsh to pick up Danny's personal belongings.'

'That must have been a dreadful experience,' said Alex.

'In some ways it was worse than the funeral,' replied Beth. 'But as I left, I bumped into Mr Pascoe.'

'Bumped into,' said Alex, 'or had he been hanging around hoping to see you?'

'Possibly he had, but I couldn't be sure. Does it make any difference?'

'A world of difference,' said Alex. 'Ray Pascoe is a decent, fair-minded man, who never doubted Danny was innocent. He once told me that he had met a thousand murderers in his time, and Danny wasn't one of them. So what did he have to say?'

'That's the strange thing,' said Beth. 'He told me he had a feeling Danny would like his name cleared, not *would have liked*. Don't you find that odd?'

'A slip of the tongue, perhaps,' said Alex. 'Did you press him on the point?'

'No,' said Beth. 'By the time I'd thought about it he was gone.'

Alex didn't speak for some time while he considered the implications of Pascoe's words. 'There's only one course of action open to you if you still hope to clear Danny's name, and that's to make an application to the Queen for a royal pardon.'

'A royal pardon?'

'Yes. If the Law Lords can be convinced that an injustice has been done, the Lord Chancellor can recommend to the Queen that the appeal court's decision be overturned. It was quite common in the days of capital punishment, although it's far rarer now.'

'And what would be the chances of Danny's case even being considered?' asked Beth.

'It's rare for an application for pardon to be granted, although there are many people, some in high places, who consider Danny suffered an injustice – myself included.'

'You seem to forget, Mr Redmayne, that I was in the pub when Craig provoked the row, I was in the alley when he attacked Danny, and I held Bernie in my arms when he told me that it was Craig who had stabbed him. My story has never wavered – not because, as Mr Pearson suggested, I'd prepared every word before the trial, but because I was telling the truth. There are three other people who know that I was telling the truth, and a fourth – Toby Mortimer – who confirmed my story only days before he took his own life, but despite your efforts at the appeal hearing, the judge wouldn't even listen to the tape. Why should it be any different this time?'

Alex didn't reply immediately, as it took him a moment to recover from Beth's rebuke. 'If you were able to rekindle a campaign among Danny's friends,' he eventually managed, 'like the one you mounted when he was alive, there would be an outcry if the Law Lords didn't reopen the case. But,' he continued, 'if you do decide to go down that particular road, Beth, it will be a long and arduous journey, and although I would be happy to offer my services pro bono, it still wouldn't come cheap.'

'Money is no longer a problem,' said Beth confidently. 'I recently managed to sell the garage for far more than I would have thought possible. I've put half the money aside for Christy's education, because Danny wanted her to have a better start in life than he did, and I'd be happy to spend the other half trying to have the case reopened if you believe there's the slightest chance of clearing his name.'

Alex once again leant across and took her hand. 'Beth, can I ask you a personal question?'

'Anything. Whenever Danny spoke about you, he always used to say, "He's a diamond, you can tell him anything."'

'I consider that a great compliment, Beth. It gives me the confidence to ask you something that's been preying on my mind for some time.' Beth looked up, the fire bringing a warm glow to her cheeks. 'You are a young and beautiful woman, Beth, with rare qualities that Danny recognized. But don't you think the time has come to move on? It's six months since Danny's death.'

'Seven months, two weeks and five days,' said Beth, lowering her head.

'Surely he wouldn't want you to mourn him for the rest of your life.'

'No, he wouldn't,' said Beth. 'He even tried to break off our relationship after his appeal had failed, but he didn't mean it, Mr Redmayne.'

'How can you be sure?' asked Alex.

She opened her handbag, took out the last letter Danny had ever sent her and handed it over to Alex.

'It's almost impossible to read,' he said.

'And why's that?'

'You know the answer only too well, Beth. Your tears . . .'

'No, Mr Redmayne, not my tears. Although I've read that letter every day for the past eight months, those tears were not shed by me, but by the man who wrote them. He knew how much I loved him. We would have made a life together even if we could only spend one day a month with each other. I'd have been happy to wait twenty years, more, in the hope that I would eventually be allowed to spend the rest of my life with the only man I'll ever love. I adored Danny from the day I met him, and no one will ever take his place. I know I can't bring him back, but if I could prove his innocence to the rest of the world, that would be enough, quite enough.'

Alex stood up, walked over to his desk and picked up a file. He didn't want Beth to see the tears streaming down his cheeks. He looked out of the window at a statue of a blindfolded woman perched on top of a building, holding up a pair of scales for the world to see. He said quietly, 'I'll write to the Lord Chancellor today.'

'Thank you, Alex.'

56

DANNY WAS SEATED at a corner table fifteen minutes before Charlie Duncan was due to appear. Mario had chosen the ideal spot to ensure that they could not be overheard. There were so many questions that Danny needed to ask, all filed away in his memory.

Danny studied the menu so that he would be familiar with it before his guest arrived. He expected that Duncan would be on time; after all, he was desperate for Danny to invest in his latest show. Perhaps at some time in the future he might even work out the real reason he'd been invited to lunch . . .

At two minutes to one, Charlie Duncan entered the Palm Court restaurant wearing an open-necked shirt and smoking a cigarette – a walking Bateman cartoon. The head waiter had a discreet word with him before offering him an ashtray. Duncan stubbed out his cigarette while the maître d' rummaged around in a drawer in his desk and produced three striped ties, all of which clashed with Duncan's salmon-pink shirt. Danny suppressed a smile. If it had been a tennis match, he would have started the first set five-love up. The head waiter accompanied Duncan across the room to Danny's table. Danny made a mental note to double his tip.

Danny rose from his place to shake hands with Duncan, whose cheeks were now the same colour as his shirt.

'You're obviously a regular here,' said Duncan, taking his seat. 'Everyone seems to know you.'

'My father and grandfather always used to stay here whenever they came down from Scotland,' said Danny. 'It's a bit of a family tradition.'

'So, what do you do, Nick?' asked Duncan while he glanced at the menu. 'I don't recall seeing you at the theatre before.'

'I used to be in the army,' Danny replied, 'so I've been abroad a lot of the time. But since my father's death, I've taken over responsibility for the family trust.'

'And you've never invested in the theatre before?' asked Duncan as the sommelier showed Danny a bottle of wine. Danny studied the label for a moment, then nodded.

'And what will you have today, Sir Nicholas?' asked Mario.

'I'll have my usual,' said Danny. 'And keep it on the rare side,' he added, remembering Nick once delivering those words to the servers behind the hotplate at Belmarsh. It had caused so much laughter that Nick had nearly ended up on report. The sommelier poured a little wine into Danny's glass. He sniffed the bouquet before sipping it, then nodded again – something else Nick had taught him, using Ribena, water and a plastic mug to swill the liquid in.

'I'll have the same,' said Duncan, closing his menu and handing it back to the maître d'. 'But make mine medium.'

'The answer to your question,' said Danny, 'is no, I've never invested in a play before. So I'd be fascinated to learn how your world operates.'

'The first thing a producer has to do is identify a play,' said Duncan. 'Either a new one, preferably by an established play-wright, or a revival of a classic. Your next problem is to find a star.'

'Like Lawrence Davenport?' said Danny, topping up Duncan's glass.

'No, that was a one-off. Larry Davenport's not a stage actor. He can just about get away with light comedy as long as he's backed up by a strong cast.'

'But he can still fill a theatre?'

'We were running a little thin towards the end of the run,' admitted Duncan, 'once his Dr Beresford fans had dried up. Frankly, if he doesn't get back on television fairly soon, he won't be able to fill a phone box.'

'So how does the finance work?' asked Danny, having already had three of his questions answered.

'To put a play on in the West End nowadays costs four to five hundred thousand pounds. So once a producer has settled on a piece, signed up the star and booked the theatre – and it's not always possible to get all three at the same time – he relies on his angels to raise the capital.'

'How many angels do you have?' asked Danny.

'Every producer has his own list, which he guards like the crown jewels. I have about seventy angels who regularly invest in my productions,' said Duncan as a steak was placed in front of him.

'And how much do they invest, on average?' asked Danny, pouring Duncan another glass of wine.

'On a normal production, units would start around ten thousand pounds.'

'So you need fifty angels per play.'

'You're sharp when it comes to figures, aren't you?' said Duncan, cutting into his steak.

Danny cursed to himself. He hadn't meant to drop his guard, and quickly moved on. 'So how does an angel, a punter, make a profit?'

'If the theatre is sixty per cent full for the entire run, he'll break even and get his money back. Above that figure, he can make a handsome profit. Below it, he can lose his shirt.'

'And how much are the stars paid?' asked Danny.

'Badly, by their usual standards, is the answer. Sometimes as little as five hundred a week. Which is the reason so many of them prefer to do television, the odd advertisement, or even voiceovers rather than get themselves involved in real work. We only paid Larry Davenport one thousand.'

'A thousand a week?' said Danny. 'I'm amazed he got out of bed for that.'

'So were we,' admitted Duncan as the wine waiter drained the bottle. Danny nodded when he held it up enquiringly.

'Fine wine, that,' said Duncan. Danny smiled. 'Larry's problem is that he hasn't been offered much lately, and at least *Earnest* kept his name on the billboards for a few weeks. Soap stars, like footballers, soon get used to earning thousands of pounds a week, not to mention the lifestyle that goes with it. But once that tap is turned off, even if they've accumulated a few assets along the way, they can quickly run out of cash. It's been a problem for so many actors, especially the ones who believe their own publicity and don't put anything aside for a rainy day, and then find themselves facing a large tax bill.'

Another question answered. 'So what are you planning to do next?' asked Danny, not wanting to show too much interest in Lawrence Davenport in case Duncan became suspicious.

'I'm putting on a piece by a new playwright called Anton Kaszubowski. He won several awards at the Edinburgh Festival last year. It's called *Bling Bling*, and I have a feeling it's just what the West End is looking for. Several big names are already showing interest, and I'm expecting to make an announcement in the next few days. Once I know who's taking the lead, I'll drop you a line.' He toyed with his glass. 'What sort of figure would you be thinking of investing?' he asked.

'I'd begin with something small,' said Danny, 'say ten thousand. If that works out, I could well become a regular.'

'I survive on my regulars,' said Duncan and drained his glass. 'I'll be in touch as soon as I've signed up a lead actor. By the way, I always throw a small drinks party for the investors when I launch a new show, which inevitably attracts a few stars. You'll be able to see Larry again. Or his sister, depending on your preference.'

'Anything else, Sir Nicholas?' asked the head waiter.

Danny would have called for a third bottle, but Charlie Duncan had already answered all his questions. 'Just the bill, thank you, Mario.'

◄○►

After Big Al had returned him to The Boltons, Danny went straight up to his study and took the Davenport file off the shelf. He spent the next hour making notes. Once he had written down everything of relevance that Duncan had told him, he replaced the file between Craig's and Payne's and returned to his desk.

He began to read through his attempt at a prize essay, and after only a few paragraphs his suspicions that it wouldn't be good enough to impress Professor Mori, let alone the panel of judges, were confirmed. The only good thing about the time he had spent on it was that it had occupied the endless hours of waiting before he could make his next move. He had to avoid the temptation to speed things up, which might well result in him making a fatal error.

It was several weeks before Gary Hall managed to close the two property deals in Mile End Road, without either seller becoming aware what he was up to. Like a good fisherman, Danny cast his fly with a single purpose: not to catch the minnows like Hall that hang around the surface, but to tempt the bigger fish, like Gerald Payne, to leap out of the water.

He also had to wait for Charlie Duncan to find a star for his new show before he could legitimately meet up with Davenport again. He also had to wait for— The phone rang. Danny picked it up. 'That problem you mentioned,' said a voice. 'I believe we may have come up with a solution. We should meet.' The line went dead. Danny was beginning to discover why Swiss bankers continue to hold on to the accounts of the rich who value discretion.

He picked up his pen, returned to his essay and tried to think of a more arresting opening line. *John Maynard Keynes would surely have known the popular song, 'Ain't We Got Fun', with its damning line, 'There's nothing surer, the rich get rich and the poor get children'. He may well have speculated on its application to nations as well as individuals . . .*

57

'JAPANESE KNOTWEED?'

'Yes, we believe that Japanese knotweed is the answer,' said Bresson. 'Although I'm bound to say that we were both puzzled by the question.'

Danny made no attempt to enlighten them, as he was just beginning to learn how to play the Swiss at their own game. 'And why is it the answer?' he asked.

'If Japanese knotweed is discovered on a building site, it can hold up planning permission for at least a year. Once it's been identified, experts have to be brought in to destroy the weed, and building cannot commence until the local health and safety committee have deemed the site to have passed all the necessary tests.'

'So how do you get rid of Japanese knotweed?' asked Danny.

'A specialist company moves in and sets fire to the entire site. Then you have to wait another three months to make sure that every last rhizome has been removed before you can reapply for planning permission.'

'That wouldn't come cheap?'

'No, it certainly doesn't come cheap for the owner of the land. We came across a classic example in Liverpool,' added Segat. 'The city council discovered Japanese knotweed on a thirty-acre site that had already been granted planning permission for a hundred council houses. It took more than a year to remove it at a cost of just over three hundred thousand pounds. By the time the houses had been built, the developer was lucky to break even.'

'Why is it so dangerous?' asked Danny.

'If you don't destroy it,' said Bresson, 'it will eat its way into the foundations of any building, even reinforced concrete, and ten years later, without warning, the whole edifice comes tumbling down, leaving you with an insurance bill that would bankrupt most companies. In Osaka, Japanese knotweed destroyed an entire apartment block, which is how it acquired its name.'

'So how do I get hold of some?' asked Danny.

'Well, you certainly won't find a packet on the shelves of your local garden centre,' said Bresson. 'However, I suspect that any company which specializes in destroying it could point you in the right direction.' Bresson paused for a moment. 'It would of course be illegal to plant it on someone else's land,' he said, looking directly at Danny.

'But not on your own land,' Danny replied, which silenced both bankers. 'Have you come up with a solution for the other half of my problem?'

It was Segat who answered him. 'Once again, your request was to say the least unusual, and it certainly falls into the high-risk category. However, my team feel they may have identified a piece of land in East London that fulfils all your criterion.' Danny recalled Nick correcting him on the proper use of the word *criteria*, but decided not to enlighten Segat. 'London, as you will be well aware,' continued Segat, 'is bidding to host the 2012 Olympics, with most of the major events provisionally planned to take place at Stratford in East London. Although the success or failure of the bid has not yet been decided, this has already created a large speculative market for sites in the area. Among the sites the Olympic Committee are currently considering is the venue for a velodrome which would accommodate all the indoor cycling events. My contacts inform me that six potential sites have been identified, of which only two are likely to be on the shortlist. You are in the happy position of being able to purchase both sites, and although you would initially have to pay a heavy premium, there is still potential for a handsome profit.'

'How heavy a premium?' asked Danny.

'We have valued the two sites,' said Bresson, 'at around a million pounds each, but both of the current owners are asking for a million and a half. But if they were both to make the short-list, they could end up being worth as much as six million. And if one of them turned out to be the winner, that figure could be doubled.'

'But if it doesn't,' said Danny, 'I stand to lose three million.' He paused. 'I'll have to consider your report very carefully before I'm willing to risk that amount.'

'You've only got a month to make up your mind,' said Bresson, 'because that's when the shortlist will be announced. If both of the sites are on it, you certainly wouldn't be able to pick them up at that price.'

'You'll find all the material you need to help make your decision in here,' added Segat, handing Danny two files.

'Thank you,' said Danny. 'I'll let you know what I've decided by the end of the week.' Segat nodded. 'Now, I'd like an update on how your negotiations with Tower Hamlets over the Wilson garage site on Mile End Road are progressing.'

'Our London lawyer had a meeting with the council's chief planning officer last week,' said Segat, 'to try to discover what his committee would regard as acceptable were you to apply for outline planning permission. The council has always envisaged a block of affordable flats on that piece of land, but they accept that the developer has to make a profit. They've come up with a proposal that if seventy flats were to be built on the site, one third of them would have to be classified as affordable dwellings.'

'That's not mathematically possible,' said Danny.

Segat smiled for the first time. 'We didn't consider it wise to point out that there would have to be either sixty-nine or seventy-two flats, allowing us some room for negotiation. However, if we were to agree in principle to their suggestion, they would sell us the plot for four hundred thousand pounds, and grant outline planning permission at the same time. On that basis, we would recommend that you accept their offer price, but try to get the council to allow you to build ninety flats. The chief planning officer felt that this would cause heated debate in the council chamber, but if we were to raise our offer to, say, five hundred thousand, he could see his way to recommending our proposal.'

'If this were to be approved by the council,' said Bresson, 'you'd end up owning the whole site for just over a million pounds.'

'If we managed to achieve that, what do you suggest should be my next move?'

'You have two choices,' said Bresson. 'You can either sell on to a developer, or you can build and manage the project yourself.'

'I have no interest in spending the next three years on a building site,' said Danny. 'In that case once we've agreed terms and provisional planning permission has been granted, just sell the site on to the highest bidder.'

'I agree that might be the wisest solution,' said Segat. 'And I'm confident that you will still double your investment in the short term.'

'You've done well,' said Danny.

'We could not have moved so swiftly,' said Segat, 'had it not been for your knowledge of the site and its past history.'

Danny didn't react to what was clearly a fishing expedition. 'Finally, perhaps you could bring me up to date on my current financial position.'

'Certainly,' said Bresson, extracting another file from his brief-case. 'We have merged your two accounts as requested and formed three trading companies, none of them in your name. Your personal account currently stands at $55,373,871, slightly down on where it was three months ago. However, you have made several investments during that time, which should eventually show a handsome return. We have also purchased on your behalf some of the shares you identified when we last met, making a further investment of just over two million pounds – you'll find the details on page nine of your green file. Again, following your instructions, we have placed any surplus cash with triple-A institutions on the overnight currency markets, which is presently showing a year-on-year return of approximately eleven per cent.'

Danny decided not to comment on the difference between the 2.75 per cent interest the bank had originally been paying and the 11 per cent he was now accruing. 'Thank you,' he said. 'Perhaps we could meet again in a month's time.' Segat and Bresson nodded and began to gather up their files. Danny rose from his place and, aware that neither banker had any interest in small talk, accompanied them to the front door.

'I'll be back in touch,' he said, 'the moment I've come to a decision on those two Olympic sites.'

After they had been driven away, Danny went upstairs to his study, removed Gerald Payne's file from the shelf, placed it on his desk and spent the rest of the morning transferring all the details that would assist in his plan to destroy him. If he were to purchase the two sites, he would then need to meet Payne face to face. Had he ever heard of Japanese knotweed?

◄○►

Are parents always more ambitious for their children than they are for themselves, Beth wondered as she entered the headmistress's study.

Miss Sutherland stepped forward from behind her desk and shook hands with Beth. The headmistress didn't smile as she ushered her into a chair and then reread the application form. Beth tried not to show just how nervous she was.

'Am I to understand, Miss Wilson,' said the headmistress, emphasizing the word *miss*, 'you are hoping that your daughter will be able to join our pre-school group at St Veronica's next term?'

'Yes, I am,' replied Beth. 'I think Christy would greatly benefit from the stimulus your school has to offer.'

'There is no doubt that your daughter is advanced for her years,' said Miss Sutherland, glancing at her entrance papers. 'However, as I'm sure you will appreciate, before she can be offered a place at St Veronica's, there are other concerns I will have to take into consideration.'

'Naturally,' said Beth, fearing the worst.

'For instance, I can find no mention of the child's father on the application form.'

'No,' said Beth. 'He died last year.'

'I'm sorry to hear that,' said Miss Sutherland, not sounding at all sorry. 'May I enquire, what was the cause of death?'

Beth hesitated, as she always found it difficult to utter the words. 'He committed suicide.'

'I see,' said the headmistress. 'Were you married to him at the time?'

'No,' admitted Beth. 'We were engaged.'

'I'm sorry to have to ask this question, Miss Wilson, but what were the circumstances of your fiancé's death?'

'He was in prison at the time,' said Beth softly.

'I see,' said Miss Sutherland. 'May I ask what offence he was convicted of?'

'Murder,' said Beth, now certain that Miss Sutherland already knew the answer to every question she was asking.

'In the eyes of the Catholic Church both suicide and murder are, as I'm sure you are aware, Miss Wilson, mortal sins.' Beth said nothing. 'I also feel it is my duty to point out,' the headmistress continued, 'that there are no illegitimate children currently registered at St Veronica's. However, I will give your daughter's application my most serious consideration, and will let you know my decision in the next few days.'

At that moment, Beth felt that Slobodan Milosevic had a better chance of winning the Nobel Peace Prize than Christy did of entering St Veronica's.

The headmistress rose from behind her desk, walked across the room and opened the study door.

'Goodbye, Miss Wilson.'

Once the door had been closed behind her, Beth burst into tears. Why should the sins of the father . . .

58

DANNY WONDERED how he would react to meeting Gerald Payne. He couldn't afford to show any emotion, and certainly if he were to lose his temper all the hours that he'd spent planning Payne's downfall would have been wasted.

Big Al drew up outside Baker, Tremlett and Smythe a few minutes early, but when Danny pushed through the swing doors and walked into the foyer, he found Gary Hall standing by the reception desk waiting to greet him.

'He's a quite exceptional man,' Hall enthused as they walked across to a bank of lifts. 'The youngest partner in the history of the company,' he added as he pressed a button that would whisk them up to the top floor. 'And quite recently he's landed a safe parliamentary seat, so I don't suppose he'll be with us for much longer.'

Danny smiled. His plan had only involved Payne being sacked. Having to give up a parliamentary seat as well would be an added bonus.

When they stepped out of the lift, Hall led his most important client along the partners' corridor until they reached a door with the name *Gerald Payne* printed in gold. Hall knocked softly, opened it and stood aside to allow Danny to enter. Payne leapt up from behind his desk and tried to do up his jacket as he walked towards them, but it was clear that it had been some time since the middle button had reached the buttonhole. He thrust out his hand and gave Danny an exaggerated smile. Try as he might, Danny couldn't return it.

'Have we met before?' asked Payne, looking at Danny more closely.

'Yes,' said Danny. 'At Lawrence Davenport's closing-night party.'

'Oh, yes, of course,' said Payne, before inviting Danny to take a seat on the opposite side of the desk. Gary Hall remained standing.

'Let me begin, Sir Nicholas . . .'

'Nick,' said Danny.

'Gerald,' said Payne. Danny nodded.

'As I was saying, let me begin by expressing my admiration for your little coup with Tower Hamlets council over the site in Bow – a deal which, in my opinion, will see you double your outlay in under a year.'

'Mr Hall did most of the spadework,' said Danny. 'I'm afraid I've been distracted by something far more demanding.'

Payne leant forward. 'And will you be involving our firm in your latest venture?' he enquired.

'Certainly in the final stages,' said Danny, 'although I've already completed most of the research. But I'll still need someone to represent me when it comes to putting in an offer for the site.'

'We'll be happy to assist in any way we can,' said Payne, the smile returning to his face. 'Do you feel able to take us into your confidence at this stage?' he added.

Danny was pleased to find that Payne was clearly only interested in what might be in it for him. This time he returned the smile. 'Everyone knows that if London is awarded the 2012 Olympics, there will be a lot of money to be made during the run-up,' said Danny. 'With a budget of ten billion available, there should be enough washing around for all of us.'

'I would normally agree with you,' said Payne, looking a little disappointed, 'but don't you think that market is already rather overcrowded?'

'Yes I do,' said Danny, 'if your mind is only focused on the main stadium, the swimming pool, the gymnastics hall, the athletes' village or even the equestrian centre. But I've identified an opportunity that hasn't attracted press attention or any public interest.'

Payne leant forward and placed his elbows on the table as Danny sat back and relaxed for the first time. 'Almost no one has noticed,' Danny continued, 'that the Olympic Committee has been considering six sites for the building of a velodrome. How many people can even tell you what takes place in a velodrome?'

'Cycling,' said Gary Hall.

'Well done,' said Danny. 'And in a fortnight's time we'll learn which two sites the Olympic Committee has provisionally short-listed. My bet is that even after the announcement is made, it won't get much more than the odd paragraph in the local paper, and then only on the sports pages.' Neither Payne nor Hall interrupted him. 'But I have some inside information,' said Danny, 'which I acquired at a cost of four pounds ninety-nine.'

'Four ninety-nine?' repeated Payne, looking mystified.

'The price of *Cycling Monthly*,' said Danny, removing a copy from his briefcase. 'In this month's issue, they leave no doubt which two sites the Olympic Committee will be shortlisting, and their editor clearly has the ear of the minister.' Danny passed the magazine over to Payne, open at the relevant page.

'And you say the press haven't followed this up?' said Payne once he'd finished reading the magazine's leader.

'Why should they?' said Danny.

'But once the site has been announced,' said Payne, 'dozens of developers will apply for the contract.'

'I'm not interested in building the velodrome,' said Danny. 'I intend to have made my money long before the first excavator moves on to the site.'

'And how do you expect to do that?'

'That, I admit, has cost me a little more than four ninety-nine, but if you look on the back of *Cycling Monthly*,' said Danny, turning the magazine over, 'you'll see the name of the publishers printed in the bottom right-hand corner. The next edition won't be on the stands for another ten days, but for a little more than the cover price I managed to get my hands on an early proof. There's an article on page seventeen by the president of the British Cycling Federation, in which he says that the minister has assured him that only two sites are being taken seriously. The minister will be making an announcement to that effect in the House of Commons the day before the magazine goes on sale. But he goes on to point out which of the two sites his committee will be backing.'

'Brilliant,' said Payne. 'But surely the owners of that site must be aware that they may be sitting on a fortune?'

'Only if they can get their hands on next month's *Cycling Monthly*, because at the moment they still think they're on a shortlist of six.'

'So what are you planning to do about it?' asked Payne.

'The site that is favoured by the Cycling Federation changed hands quite recently for three million pounds, although I haven't been able to identify the buyer. However, once the minister has made her announcement, the site could be worth fifteen, perhaps even twenty million. While there are still six possible sites on the shortlist, if someone were to offer the present owner say four or five million, I suspect they might be tempted to take a quick turn rather than risk ending up with nothing. Our problem is that we have less than a fortnight before the shortlist of two is announced, and once the views of the Cycling Federation's president become public, there will be nothing left in it for us.'

'Can I make a suggestion?' said Payne.

'Go ahead,' said Danny.

'If you're so certain there are only two sites in contention, why not purchase both of them? Your profit may not be as large, but it would be impossible for you to lose.'

Danny now realized why Payne had become the youngest partner in the firm's history.

'Good idea,' said Danny, 'but there's not much point in doing that until we've found out if the site we're really interested in can be purchased. That's where you come in. You'll find all the details you need in this file, apart from who owns the site; after all, you have to do something to earn your money.'

Payne laughed. 'I'll get straight on to it, Nick, and be back in touch with you as soon as I've tracked down the owner.'

'Don't hang about,' said Danny, standing up. 'The rewards will only be high if we can move quickly.'

Payne produced the same smile as he stood to shake hands with his new client. As Danny turned to leave, he spotted a familiar invitation on the mantelpiece. 'Will you be at Charlie Duncan's drinks party this evening?' he asked, sounding surprised.

'Yes, I will. I occasionally invest in his shows.'

'Then I may see you there,' said Danny. 'In which case you'll be able to bring me up to date.'

'Will do,' said Payne. 'Can I just check on one thing before I get started?'

'Yes, of course,' said Danny, trying not to sound anxious.

'When it comes to the investment, will you be putting up the full amount yourself?'

'Every penny,' said Danny.

'And you wouldn't consider allowing anyone else to have a piece of the action?'

'No,' said Danny firmly.

'Forgive me, Father, for I have sinned,' said Beth. 'It's been two weeks since my last confession.'

Father Michael smiled the moment he recognized Beth's gentle voice. He was always moved by her confessions, because what she considered to be a sin, most of his parishioners would not have thought worthy of mention.

'I am ready to hear your confession, my child,' he said, as if he had no idea who it was on the other side of the lattice window.

'I have thought unworthily of another, and wished them ill.'

Father Michael stirred. 'Are you able to tell me what caused you to have such evil thoughts, my child?'

'I wanted my daughter to have a better start in life than I did, and I felt that the headmistress of the school I had chosen did not give me a fair hearing.'

'Is it possible that you were unable to see things from her point of view?' said Father Michael. 'After all, you may have misjudged her motives.' When Beth didn't respond, he added, 'You must always remember, my child, that it is not for us to judge the Lord's will, as He might have other plans for your little girl.'

'Then I must ask for the Lord's forgiveness,' said Beth, 'and wait to discover what is His will.'

'I think that would be the wise course to take, my child. Meanwhile, you should pray and seek the Lord's guidance.'

'And what penance should I perform, Father, for my sins?'

'You must learn to be contrite, and to forgive those who cannot hope to understand your problems,' said Father Michael. 'You will say one Our Father and two Hail Marys.'

'Thank you, Father.'

Father Michael waited until he heard the little door close and was sure that Beth had departed. He sat alone for some time while he gave Beth's problem considerable thought, only relieved that he was not interrupted by another parishioner. He stepped out of the confessional box and headed for the vestry. He walked quickly past Beth who was on her knees, head bowed, a rosary in her hand.

Once he'd reached the vestry, Father Michael locked the door, went over to his desk and dialled a number. This was one of those rare occasions when he felt the Lord's will needed a little assistance.

◄○►

Big Al dropped the boss outside the front door a few minutes after eight. Once Danny had entered the building, he didn't need to be told where Charlie Duncan's office was. The sound of laughter and exuberant chatter was coming from the first floor, and one or two of the guests had spilled out on to the landing.

Danny climbed the shabby, badly lit staircase, passing framed posters of previous shows Duncan had produced, not one of which Danny remembered being a hit. He made his way past an intertwined young couple who didn't give him as much as a glance. He walked into what was clearly Duncan's office and quickly discovered why people were spilling out on to the landing. It was so crowded, the guests could hardly move. A young girl standing by the door offered him a drink and Danny asked for a glass of water

– after all, he needed to concentrate if his investment was to show a dividend.

Danny glanced around the room looking for someone he knew, and spotted Katie. She turned away the moment she saw him. It only made him smile and think of Beth. She'd always teased him about how shy he was, especially when he entered a room full of strangers. If Beth had been there, by now she would have been chatting to a group of people she'd never met before. How he missed her. Someone touched his arm, interrupting his thoughts, and he turned to find Gerald Payne standing by his side.

'Nick,' he said as if they were old friends. 'Good news. I've tracked down the bank which represents the owner of one of the sites.'

'And do you have any contacts there?'

'Unfortunately not,' admitted Payne, 'but as they are based in Geneva, the owner may well be a foreigner who has no idea of the site's potential value.'

'Or he may be an Englishman who knows only too well.' Danny had already discovered that Payne's bottles were always three-quarters full.

'Either way,' said Payne, 'we'll find out tomorrow because the banker, a Monsieur Segat, has promised to call back in the morning and let me know if his client is willing to sell.'

'And the other site?' asked Danny.

'Not much point in chasing after that if the owner of the first site is unwilling to sell.'

'You're probably right,' said Danny, not bothering to point out that was what he had recommended in the first place.

'Gerald,' said Lawrence Davenport, leaning down to kiss Payne on both cheeks.

Danny was surprised to see that Davenport was unshaven, and wearing a shirt that had clearly already been worn more than once that week. As the two men exchanged greetings, he felt such loathing for both of them that he found himself unable to join in the conversation.

'Do you know Nick Moncrieff?' asked Payne.

Davenport showed neither recognition nor interest.

'We met at your closing-night party,' said Danny.

'Oh, right,' said Davenport, showing a little more interest.

'I saw the play twice.'

'How flattering,' said Davenport, giving him the smile reserved for his fans.

'Will you be starring in Charlie's next production?' asked Danny.

'No,' replied Davenport. 'Much as I adored being in *Earnest*, I can't afford to devote my talents to the stage alone.'

'Why's that?' asked Danny innocently.

'You have to turn down so many opportunities if you commit yourself to a long run. You never know when someone's going to ask you to star in a film, or take the lead in a new mini-series.'

'That's a pity,' said Danny. 'I would have invested considerably more if you'd been a member of the cast.'

'How nice of you to say so,' said Davenport. 'Perhaps you'll have another opportunity at some time in the future.'

'I do hope so,' said Danny, 'because you're a real star.' He was becoming aware that there was no such thing as over-the-top with Lawrence Davenport, as long as you were talking to Lawrence Davenport about Lawrence Davenport.

'Well,' said Davenport, 'if you really did want to make a shrewd investment, I have—'

'Larry!' said a voice. Davenport turned away and kissed another man, far younger than himself. The moment had gone, but Davenport had left the door wide open and Danny intended to barge in unannounced at some later date.

'Sad,' said Payne as Davenport drifted off.

'Sad?' prompted Danny.

'He was the star of our generation at Cambridge,' said Payne. 'We all assumed he would have a glittering career, but it wasn't to be.'

'I notice that you call him Larry,' said Danny. 'Like Laurence Olivier.'

'That's about the only thing he has in common with Olivier.'

Danny almost felt sorry for Davenport when he recalled Dumas's words, *With friends like these* . . . 'Well, time is still on his side,' he added.

'Not with his problems, it isn't,' said Payne.

'His problems?' said Danny as he felt a slap on the back.

'Hi, Nick,' said Charlie Duncan, another instant friend that money attracts.

'Hi, Charlie,' replied Danny.

'Hope you're enjoying the party,' said Duncan, as he filled Danny's empty glass with champagne.

'Yes, thank you.'

'Are you still thinking of investing in *Bling Bling*, old boy?' whispered Duncan.

'Oh, yes,' said Danny. 'You can put me down for ten thousand.' He didn't add, despite its being an unfathomable script.

'Shrewd fellow,' said Duncan, and slapped him on the back again. 'I'll drop a contract in the post tomorrow.'

'Is Lawrence Davenport doing a film at the moment?' Danny asked.

'What makes you ask that?'

'The unshaven look and the shabby clothes. I thought they might involve some part he's playing.'

'No, no,' said Duncan laughing. 'He's not playing a part, he's only just got out of bed.' Once again he lowered his voice. 'I'd steer clear of him at the moment, old boy.'

'And why's that?' asked Danny.

'He's on the scrounge. Don't lend him anything, because you'll never get it back. God knows how much he owes just to the people in this room.'

'Thanks for the warning,' said Danny, putting the full glass of champagne on a passing tray. I must be off. But thanks, it's been a great party.'

'So soon? But you haven't even met the stars you'll be investing in.'

'Yes I have,' said Danny.

◄❍►

She picked up the phone on her desk, and recognized the voice immediately.

'Good evening, Father,' she said. 'How may I assist you?'

'No, Miss Sutherland, it is I who wish to assist you.'

'And what do you have in mind?'

'I was hoping to help you come to a decision concerning Christy Cartwright, a young member of my congregation.'

'Christy Cartwright?' said the headmistress. 'The name rings a bell.'

'As indeed it should, Miss Sutherland. Any conscientious head-mistress couldn't fail to notice that Christy is potentially scholarship material in this dreadful age of league tables.'

'And any conscientious headmistress could also not have failed to notice that the child's parents were unmarried, a state of affairs that the governors of St Veronica's still frown upon, as I'm sure you will recall from the days when you served on the board.'

'And rightly so, Miss Sutherland,' responded Father Michael. 'But let me put your mind at rest by assuring you that I read the marriage banns three times at St Mary's, and posted the date of their wedding on the church noticeboard as well as the parish magazine.'

'But unfortunately the marriage never took place,' the head-mistress reminded him.

'Due to unforeseen circumstances,' murmured Father Michael.

'I am sure that I don't have to remind you, Father, of Pope John Paul's encyclical *Evangelium Vitae* making it clear that suicide, and indeed murder, are still, in the eyes of the Church, mortal sins. This, I fear, leaves me with no choice but to wash my hands of the matter.'

'You wouldn't be the first person in history to do that, Miss Sutherland.'

'That was unworthy of you, Father,' snapped the headmis-tress.

'You are right to rebuke me, Miss Sutherland, and I apologize. I fear that I am only human, and am therefore prone to making mistakes. Perhaps one of them was when an exceptionally talented young woman made an application to be headmistress of St

Veronica's, and I failed to inform the governors that she had recently had an abortion. I'm sure I don't need to remind you, Miss Sutherland, that the Holy Father also considers that to be a mortal sin.'

59

FOR SEVERAL WEEKS, Danny had been avoiding Professor Mori. He feared his effort for the essay competition would not have impressed the garrulous professor.

But after he left the morning lecture, Danny saw Mori standing by the door of his office. There was no escaping the beckoning finger. Like a schoolboy who knows he's about to be given a flogging, Danny meekly followed him into his study. He waited for the stinging remarks, the barbed witticisms, the poisoned arrows aimed at a static target.

'I'm disappointed,' began Professor Mori as Danny lowered his head. How was it possible that he could handle Swiss bankers, West End impresarios, senior partners and seasoned solicitors, but was a quivering wreck in the presence of this man? 'So now you know,' continued the professor, 'how it must feel to be an Olympic finalist who fails to step on to the podium.'

Danny looked up, puzzled.

'Congratulations,' said a beaming Professor Mori. 'You came fourth in the prize essay competition. As it counts towards your degree, I'm expecting great things from you when you sit your final exams.' He rose, still smiling. 'Congratulations,' he repeated, shaking Danny warmly by the hand.

'Thank you, professor,' said Danny, trying to take in the news. He could hear Nick saying, *Damn good show, old chap*, and he only wished he could share the news with Beth. She would be so proud. How much longer could he survive without seeing her?

He left the professor and ran along the corridor, out of the door and down the steps, to see Big Al standing by the back door of the car looking anxiously at his watch. Danny inhabited three different worlds, and in the next one he couldn't afford to be late for his probation officer.

◄o►

Danny had decided not to tell Ms Bennett how he would be spending the rest of his afternoon, as he had no doubt that she would dismiss the very idea as frivolous. However, she did appear pleased to learn how he'd fared in the essay competition.

Molly had already served Monsieur Segat with a second cup of tea by the time Danny arrived back from his meeting with Ms Bennett. The Swiss banker rose from his place as Danny entered the room. He apologized for being a few minutes late, without offering an explanation.

Segat gave a slight nod before sitting back down. 'You are now the owner of both sites which are in serious contention for the Olympic velodrome,' he said. 'Although you can no longer expect to make quite such a large profit, you should still show a more than satisfactory return on your original investment.'

'Has Payne called back?' was all Danny wanted to know.

'Yes. He phoned again this morning, and made a bid of four million pounds for the site most likely to be selected. I presume you want me to turn the offer down?'

'Yes. But tell him that you would accept six million, on the understanding that the contract is signed before the minister announces her decision.'

'But that site will be worth at least twelve million if everything goes to plan.'

'Be assured, everything is going to plan,' said Danny. 'Has Payne shown any interest in the other site?'

'No. Why should he,' said Segat, 'when everyone seems to know which site is going to be selected?'

Having gained all the information he needed, Danny switched subjects. 'Who came up with the highest offer for our site on Mile End Road?'

'The highest bidder turned out to be Fairfax Homes, a first-class company which the council has worked with in the past. I've studied their proposal,' said Segat, handing Danny a glossy brochure, 'and have no doubt that subject to a few modifications from the planning committee, the scheme should get the green light within the next few weeks.'

'How much?' asked Danny, trying not to sound impatient.

'Ah, yes,' said Segat, checking his figures, 'remembering that your outlay was a little over a million pounds, I think you can be well satisfied that Fairfax Homes came in at £1,801,156, giving you a profit of over half a million pounds. Not a bad return on your capital, remembering that the money's been in play for less than a year.'

'How do you explain the figure of £1,801,156?' asked Danny.

'I would guess that Mr Fairfax expected that there would be several bids around the one point eight million mark and just stuck his date of birth on the end.'

Danny laughed as he began to study Fairfax's plans for a magnificent new block of luxury flats called City Reach on the site where he had once worked as a garage mechanic.

'Do I have your authority to call Mr Fairfax and let him know his was the successful bid?'

'Yes, do,' said Danny. 'And once you've spoken to him, I'd like a word.'

While Segat made the call, Danny continued to study Fairfax Homes' impressive plans for the new apartment block. He only had one query.

'I'll just pass you over to Sir Nicholas, Mr Fairfax,' said Segat. 'He would like to have a word with you.'

'I've just been studying your plans, Mr Fairfax,' said Danny, 'and I see you have a penthouse on the top floor.'

'That's right,' said Fairfax. 'Four beds, four baths, all ensuite, just over three thousand square feet.'

'Overlooking a garage on the other side of Mile End Road.'

'Less than a mile from the City,' retorted Fairfax. Both of them laughed.

'And you're putting the penthouse on the market at six hundred and fifty thousand, Mr Fairfax?'

'Yes, that's the asking price,' Fairfax confirmed.

'I'll close the deal at a million three,' said Danny, 'if you'll throw in the penthouse.'

'A million two and you've got yourself a deal,' said Fairfax.

'On one condition.'

'And what's that?'

Danny told Mr Fairfax the one change he wanted, and the developer agreed without hesitation.

◄○►

Danny had chosen the hour carefully: 11 a.m. Big Al drove around Redcliffe Square twice before stopping outside number 25.

Danny walked up a path that hadn't seen a trowel recently. When he reached the front door he rang the bell and waited for some time, but there was no reply. He banged the brass knocker twice, and could hear the sound echoing inside, but still no one answered the door. He rang the bell one more time before finally giving up, and deciding to try again in the afternoon. He had almost reached the gate when the door suddenly swung open and a voice demanded, 'Who the hell are you?'

'Nick Moncrieff,' said Danny, turning round and walking back up the path. 'You asked me to give you a call, but you're ex-directory, and as I just happened to be passing . . .'

Davenport was wearing a silk dressing gown and slippers. He clearly hadn't shaved for several days and began blinking in the morning sunlight like an animal that had come out of hibernation on the first day of spring. 'You told me you had an investment you thought I might be interested in,' Danny reminded him.

'Oh, yes, I remember now,' said Lawrence Davenport, sounding a little more receptive. 'Yes, come in.'

Danny entered an unlit corridor that brought back memories of what the house in The Boltons had been like before Molly had taken charge.

'Do have a seat while I get changed,' said Davenport. 'I'll only be a moment.'

Danny didn't sit. He strolled around the room admiring the paintings and fine furniture, even if they were covered in a layer of dust. He peered through the back window to see a large but unkempt garden.

The anonymous voice had called from Geneva that morning to say that houses in the square were currently changing hands at around three million pounds. Mr Davenport had purchased number 25 in 1995, when eight million viewers were tuning in to *The Prescription* every Saturday evening to find out which nurse Dr Beresford would be sleeping with that week. 'He has a mortgage of one million pounds with Norwich Union,' said the voice, 'and for the last three months he's fallen behind with his payments.'

Danny turned away from the window when Davenport walked back into the room. He was wearing an open-neck shirt, jeans and sneakers. Danny had seen better-dressed men in prison.

'Can I fix you a drink?' asked Davenport.

'It's a little early for me,' said Danny.

'It's never too early,' said Davenport as he poured himself a large whisky. He took a gulp and smiled. 'I'll get straight to the point, because I know you're a busy chap. It's just that I'm a little strapped for cash at the moment – only temporary, you understand – just until someone signs me up for another series. In fact, my agent was on the phone this morning with one or two ideas.'

'You need a loan?' said Danny.

'Yes, that's the long and the short of it.'

'And what can you put up as collateral?'

'Well, my paintings for a start,' said Davenport. 'I paid over a million for them.'

'I'll give you three hundred thousand for the entire collection,' said Danny.

'But I paid over . . .' spluttered Davenport, pouring himself another whisky.

'That's assuming you can provide evidence that the total you paid does amount to over a million.' Davenport stared at him, as he tried to recall where they had last met. 'I'll instruct my lawyer to draw up a contract, and you'll receive the money the day you sign it.'

Davenport took another gulp of whisky. 'I'll think about it,' he said.

'You do that,' said Danny. 'And if you repay the full amount within twelve months, I'll return the paintings at no extra charge.'

'So what's the catch?' asked Davenport.

'No catch, but if you fail to pay the money back within twelve months, the paintings will be mine.'

'I can't lose,' said Davenport, a broad grin spread across his face.

'Let's hope not,' said Danny, who stood up to join him as Davenport began walking towards the door.

'I'll send a contract round along with a cheque for three hundred thousand pounds,' said Danny as he followed him into the hall.

'That's good of you,' said Davenport.

'Let's hope your agent comes up with something that suits your particular talents,' said Danny as Davenport opened the front door.

'You don't have to concern yourself about that,' said Davenport. 'My bet is that you'll have your money back within a few weeks.'

'That's good to hear,' said Danny. 'Oh, and should you ever decide to sell this house . . .'

'My home?' said Davenport. 'No, never. Out of the question, don't even think about it.'

He closed the front door as if he'd been dealing with a tradesman.

60

DANNY READ THE REPORT in *The Times* as Molly poured him a black coffee.

An exchange which had taken place on the floor of the House between the Minister of Sport and Billy Cormack, the Member for Stratford South, was tucked in at the end of the paper's parliamentary report.

> Cormack (Lab, Stratford South): 'Can the minister confirm that she has shortlisted two sites for the proposed Olympic velodrome?'
>
> Minister: 'Yes I can, and I'm sure my honourable friend will be delighted to learn that the site in his constituency is one of the two still under consideration.'
>
> Cormack: 'I thank the minister for her reply. Is she aware that the president of the British Cycling Federation has written to me pointing out that his committee voted unanimously in favour of the site in my constituency?'
>
> Minister: 'Yes I am, partly because my honourable friend kindly sent me a copy of that letter (laughter). Let me assure him that I shall take the views of the British Cycling Federation very seriously before I make my final decision.'
>
> Andrew Crawford (Con, Stratford West): 'Does the minister realize that this news will not be welcomed in my constituency, where the other shortlisted site is located, as we have plans to build a new leisure centre on that land, and never wanted the velodrome in the first place.'
>
> Minister: 'I will take the honourable member's views into consideration before I make my final decision.'

Molly placed two boiled eggs in front of Danny just as his mobile phone rang. He wasn't surprised to see Payne's name flash up on the little screen, although he hadn't expected him to call quite so early. He flicked open the mobile and said, 'Good morning.'

'Morning, Nick. Sorry to ring at this hour, but I wondered if you'd read the parliamentary report in the *Telegraph*?'

'I don't take the *Telegraph*,' said Danny, 'but I have read the ministerial exchange in *The Times*. What's your paper saying?'

'That the president of the British Cycling Federation has been invited to address the Olympic Sites Committee next week, four days before the minister makes her final decision. Apparently it's no more than a formality – an inside source has told the *Telegraph* that the minister is only waiting for the surveyor's report before she confirms her decision.'

'*The Times* has roughly the same story,' said Danny.

'But that isn't why I phoned,' said Payne. 'I wanted you to know that I've already had a call from the Swiss this morning and they've turned down your offer of four million.'

'Hardly surprising, given the circumstances,' said Danny.

'But,' said Payne, 'they made it clear that they would accept six mill, as long as the full amount is paid before the minister announces her final decision in ten days' time.'

'That's still a no-brainer,' said Danny. 'But I've got some news too, and I'm afraid mine is not so good. My bank's not willing to advance me the full amount right now.'

'But why not?' said Payne. 'Surely they can see what an opportunity this is?'

'Yes, they can, but they still consider it's a risk. Perhaps I should have warned you that I'm a little overstretched at the moment, with one or two other projects that aren't going quite as well as I'd hoped.'

'But I thought you made a killing on the Mile End Road site?'

'It didn't turn out quite as well as I anticipated,' said Danny. 'I ended up with a profit of just over three hundred thousand. And as I told Gary Hall some time ago, my last agent let me down rather badly, and I'm now having to pay the price for his lack of judgement.'

'So how much can you put up?' asked Payne.

'A million,' said Danny. 'Which means that we'll be five million short, so I fear the deal is off.'

A long silence followed, during which Danny sipped his coffee and removed the tops of his two eggs.

'Nick, I don't suppose you'd allow me to offer this deal to some of my other clients?'

'Why not,' said Danny, 'remembering all the work you've put in. I'm just livid that I can't put up all the capital for the best deal I've come across for years.'

'That's very magnanimous of you,' said Payne. 'I won't forget it. I owe you one.'

'You sure do,' said Danny as he snapped his mobile closed.

He was just about to attack his egg when the phone rang again. He checked the screen to see if he could ask whoever was calling to ring back later, but realized he couldn't when the word *voice* flashed up. He opened the phone and listened.

'We've already had several calls this morning with offers for your site, including one of eight million. What do you want me to do about Mr Payne?'

'You'll be getting a call from him making an offer of six million. You will accept his offer,' Danny said before the voice could comment, 'on two conditions.'

'Two conditions,' repeated the voice.

'He must deposit six hundred thousand with the bank before close of business today and he must also pay the full amount before the minister makes her announcement in ten days' time.'

'I'll call you back once he's been in touch,' said the voice.

Danny looked down at a prison yolk. 'Molly, could you boil me another couple of eggs?'

61

Spencer Craig left chambers at five o'clock, as it was his turn to host the quarterly Musketeers' dinner. They still got together four times a year despite the fact that Toby Mortimer was no longer with them. The fourth dinner had become known as the Memorial Dinner.

Craig always used outside caterers so that he didn't have to worry about preparing the meal or the clearing up afterwards, although he did like to select the wine himself, and to sample the food before the first guest arrived. Gerald had rung him earlier in the day to say that he had some exciting news to share with the team that could change their whole lives.

Craig would never forget the previous occasion when a meeting of the Musketeers had changed their whole lives, but since Danny Cartwright had hanged himself, no one had ever referred to the subject again. Craig thought about his fellow Musketeers as he drove home. Gerald Payne had gone from strength to strength in his firm, and now that he had been selected for a safe Conservative seat in Sussex, he looked certain to be a Member of Parliament whenever the Prime Minister called the next election. Larry Davenport appeared more relaxed recently, and had even paid back the ten thousand pounds Craig had lent him a couple of years ago, which he hadn't expected to see again; perhaps Larry also had something to tell the team. Craig had his own piece of news to share with the Musketeers this evening, and although it was no more than he had expected, it was nevertheless gratifying.

The briefs had picked up again as he continued to win cases, and his appearance at the Danny Cartwright trial was becoming a hazy memory that most of his colleagues could hardly recall – with one exception. His private life remained patchy, to say the least: the occasional one-night stand, but other than Larry's sister, there was no one he wanted to see a second time. However, Sarah Davenport had made it all too clear that she wasn't interested, but he hadn't given up hope.

When Craig arrived back at his home in Hambledon Terrace, he checked the wine racks to find he had nothing worthy of a Musketeers' dinner. He strolled to his local on the corner of the King's Road and selected three bottles of Merlot, three of a vintage Australian Sauvignon and a magnum of Laurent Perrier. After all, he had something to celebrate.

As he walked back to the house carrying two bags full of bottles, he heard a siren in the distance, which brought back memories of that night. They didn't seem to fade with time, like other memories. He had called Detective Sergeant Fuller, then run home, stripped off his clothes, had a quick shower without allowing his hair to get wet, dressed in an almost identical suit, shirt and tie, and been back sitting at the bar seventeen minutes later.

If Redmayne had checked the distance between the Dunlop Arms and Craig's home before the opening of the trial, he might have been able to plant even more doubt in the jurors' minds. Thank God it was only his second case as a leader, because if *he'd* been up against Arnold Pearson he would have checked every paving stone on the route back to his home with a stopwatch in his hand.

Craig had not been surprised by how long it had taken DS Fuller before he walked into the pub, as he knew he would have far more important problems to deal with in the alley: a dying man, and an obvious suspect covered in blood. He would also have no reason to suspect that a complete stranger could have been involved, especially when three other witnesses corroborated his story. The barman had kept his mouth shut, but then he'd been in trouble with the police before, and would have made an unreliable witness, whichever side he appeared for. Craig had continued to purchase all his wine from the Dunlop Arms and when the bills were sent at the end of each month and didn't always add up, he made no comment.

Once he'd returned home, Craig left the wine on the kitchen table and put the champagne in the fridge. He then went upstairs to shower and change into something more casual. He'd just returned to the kitchen and started uncorking a bottle when the doorbell rang.

He couldn't remember when he'd last seen Gerald looking so buoyant, and assumed it must be because of the news he'd called about that afternoon.

'How are you enjoying the constituency work?' Craig asked as he hung up Payne's coat and led him into the drawing room.

'Great fun, but I can't wait for the general election so I can take my place in the Commons.' Craig poured him a glass of champagne and asked if he'd heard from Larry lately. 'I popped round to see him one evening last week, but he wouldn't let me inside the house, which I thought was a little strange.'

'The last time I visited him at home the place was in a dreadful state,' said Craig. 'It might have been no more than that, or perhaps just another boyfriend he didn't want you to meet.'

'He must be working,' said Payne. 'He sent me a cheque last week for a loan I'd given up on long ago.'

'You too?' said Craig as the doorbell rang a second time.

When Davenport strolled in to join them, all the swagger and self-confidence seemed to have returned. He kissed Gerald on both cheeks as if he were a French general inspecting his troops. Craig offered him a glass of champagne, and couldn't help thinking that Larry looked ten years younger than when he'd last seen him. Perhaps he was about to reveal something that would upstage them all.

'Let's begin the evening with a toast,' said Craig. 'To absent friends.' The three men raised their glasses and cried, 'Toby Mortimer.'

'So who shall we drink to next?' asked Davenport.

'Sir Nicholas Moncrieff,' said Payne without hesitation.

'Who the hell is he?' asked Craig.

'The man who's about to change all our fortunes.'

'How?' asked Davenport, unwilling to reveal the fact that Moncrieff was the reason he'd been able to pay back the money he'd borrowed from them both, as well as several other debts.

'I'll tell you the details over dinner,' said Payne. 'But tonight I insist on going last, because this time I'm confident that you won't be able to trump me.'

'I wouldn't be so sure of that, Gerald,' said Davenport, looking even more pleased with himself than usual.

A young woman appeared in the doorway. 'We're ready when you are, Mr Craig.'

The three men strolled through to the dining room recounting their days at Cambridge, the stories becoming more exaggerated by the year.

Craig took his place at the head of the table as portions of smoked salmon were placed in front of his two guests. Once he had tasted the wine and nodded his approval, he turned to Davenport and said, 'I can't wait any longer, Larry. Let's hear your news first. You've clearly had a change of fortune.'

Davenport leant back in his chair and waited until he was certain he had their undivided attention. 'A couple of days ago I had a call from the BBC, asking me to drop into Broadcasting House for a chat. That usually means they want to offer you a small part in a radio play with a fee that wouldn't cover the taxi fare from Redcliffe Square to Portland Place. But this time, I was taken out to lunch by a senior producer, who told me that they were going to write a new character into *Holby City*, and I was their first choice. It seems that Dr Beresford has faded in people's memory . . .'

'Blessed memory,' said Payne, raising his glass.

'They've asked me to do a screen test next week.'

'Bravo,' said Craig, also raising his glass.

'My agent tells me they're not considering anyone else for the part, so he should be able to close a three-year contract with residuals and a tough renewal clause.'

'Not bad, I must admit,' said Payne, 'but I'm confident I can still beat both of you. So what's your news, Spencer?'

Craig filled his glass and took a sip before he spoke.

'The Lord Chancellor has asked to see me next week.' He took another sip as he allowed the news to sink in.

'Is he going to offer you his job?' asked Davenport.

'All in good time,' said Craig. 'But the only reason he asks to see someone of my humble status is when he's going to invite them to take silk and become a QC.'

'And well deserved,' said Davenport, as he and Payne rose from their places to salute their host.

'It hasn't been announced yet,' said Craig, waving them back down, 'so whatever you do, don't breathe a word.'

Craig and Davenport leant back in their chairs and turned to Payne. 'Your turn, old chum,' said Craig. 'So what is it that's going to change our whole lives?'

◄○►

There was a knock on the door.

'Come in,' said Danny.

Big Al stood in the doorway, clutching a large parcel. 'It's jist been delivered, boss. Where wull I put it?'

'Just leave it on the table,' said Danny, continuing to read his book as if the package was of little importance. As soon as he heard the door close, he put down Adam Smith on the theory of free-market economics and walked across to the table. He looked at the package marked *Hazardous, Handle with Care* for some time before removing the brown paper wrapping to reveal a cardboard box. He had to peel off several layers of sellotape before he was finally able to lift the lid.

He took out a pair of black rubber boots, size 9½, and tried them on – a perfect fit. Next he removed a pair of thin latex gloves and a large torch. When he switched it on, the beam lit up the whole room. The next articles to be removed from the box were a black nylon jumpsuit and a mask to cover his nose and mouth. He had been given a choice of black or white, and had chosen black. The only thing Danny left in the box was a small plastic container covered in bubble wrap and marked 'Hazardous'. He didn't unwrap the container because he already knew what was inside. He placed the gloves, torch, boots, jumpsuit and mask back in the box, took a reel of thick tape from the top drawer of his desk and resealed the lid. Danny smiled. A thousand pounds well invested.

——◇——

'And how much will *you* be contributing to this little enterprise?' asked Craig.

'About a million of my own money,' said Payne, 'of which I've already transferred six hundred thousand in order to secure the contract.'

'Won't that stretch you?' asked Craig.

'To breaking point,' Payne admitted, 'but I'm unlikely to come across an opportunity like this again in my lifetime, and the profit will allow me enough to live on after I become an MP and have to resign my partnership.'

'Let me try to understand what you're proposing,' said Davenport. 'Whatever sum we put up, you'll guarantee to double it in less than a month.'

'You can never guarantee anything,' said Payne, 'but this is a two-horse race, and ours is the clear favourite. In simple terms, I have the opportunity to pick up a piece of land for six million, which will be worth fifteen to twenty million once the minister announces which site she's selected for the velodrome.'

'That's assuming she chooses your site,' said Craig.

'I've shown you the entry in Hansard reporting her exchange with those two MPs.'

'Yes, you have,' said Craig. 'But I'm still puzzled. If it's such a good deal, why doesn't this chap Moncrieff buy the site himself?'

'I don't think he ever had enough to cover the six million in the first place,' said Payne. 'But he's still putting up a million of his own money.'

'Something just doesn't feel right to me,' said Craig.

'You're such an old cynic, Spencer,' said Payne. 'Let me remind you what happened last time I presented the Musketeers with such a golden opportunity – Larry, Toby and I all doubled our money on that farmland in Gloucestershire in just under two years. Now I'm offering you an even safer bet, except this time you'll double your money in ten days.'

'OK, I'm willing to risk two hundred thousand,' said Craig. 'But I'll kill you if anything goes wrong.'

The blood drained from Payne's face, and Davenport was struck dumb. 'Come on, chaps, it was only a joke,' said Craig. 'So I'm good for two hundred thousand. What about you, Larry?'

'If Gerald's willing to risk a million, so am I,' said Davenport, quickly recovering. 'I'm fairly confident I can raise that amount on my house without it changing my lifestyle.'

'Your lifestyle is going to change in ten days' time, old chum,' said Payne. 'Neither of us will ever need to work again.'

'All for one and one for all,' said Davenport, trying to stand up.

'All for one and one for all!' cried Craig and Payne in unison. They all raised their glasses.

'How are you going to raise the rest of the money?' Craig asked. 'After all, the three of us will be putting in less than half.'

'Don't forget Moncrieff's million, and my chairman is stumping up half a million. I've also approached a few chums who I've made money for over the years, and even Charlie Duncan is considering investing, so I should have covered the full amount by the end of the week. And as I'm the host for the next get-together of the Musketeers,' he continued, 'I thought I'd book a table at Harry's Bar.'

'Or McDonald's,' said Craig, 'should the minister select the other site.'

62

ALEX WAS LOOKING across the Thames at the London Eye when she arrived. He rose from the bench to greet her.

'Have you ever been on the Eye?' he asked as she sat down beside him.

'Yes, once,' said Beth. 'I took my father on it when it first opened. You used to be able to see our garage from the top.'

'It won't be that long before you'll be able to see Wilson House,' said Alex.

'Yes. It was kind of the developer to name the building after my dad. He'd have enjoyed that,' said Beth.

'I have to be back in court by two o'clock,' said Alex. 'But I needed to see you urgently, as I have some news.'

'It was good of you to give up your lunch break.'

'I had a letter this morning from the Lord Chancellor's office,' said Alex, 'and he's agreed to reopen the case.' Beth threw her arms around him. 'But only if we can supply some fresh evidence.'

'Wouldn't the tape be considered as fresh evidence?' asked Beth. 'There's been mention of it in both local papers since we launched the campaign to have Danny pardoned.'

'I'm sure they'll take it into consideration this time, but if they believe the conversation was recorded under duress, they'll have to discount it.'

'But how will anyone be able to prove that either way?' asked Beth.

'Do you remember that Danny and Big Al shared a cell with a man called Nick Moncrieff?'

'Of course,' said Beth. 'They were good friends. He taught Danny to read and write and even attended his funeral, although none of us were allowed to speak to him.'

'Well, some weeks before Moncrieff was released, he wrote to me offering to help in any way he could, as he was convinced Danny was innocent.'

'But there are countless people who believe Danny is innocent,' said Beth, 'and if you felt Big Al would have made a bad witness, why should Nick be any different?'

'Because Danny once told me that Moncrieff kept a diary while he was in prison, so it's possible that the tape incident has been recorded. Courts take diaries very seriously, because they're contemporaneous evidence.'

'Then all you have to do is get in touch with Moncrieff,' said Beth, unable to hide her excitement.

'It's not quite that simple,' said Alex.

'Why not? If he was so keen to help . . .'

'Not long after his release he was arrested for breaking his parole.'

'So is he back inside?' asked Beth.

'No, that's the strange thing. The judge gave him one last chance. He must have had a hell of a lawyer defending him.'

'Then what's to stop you trying to get hold of his diaries?' asked Beth.

'It's possible that after his latest brush with the law, he might not welcome a letter from a lawyer he's never met, asking him to become involved in yet another court case.'

'Danny said you could always rely on Nick, come hell or high water.'

'Then I'll write to him today,' said Alex.

—◁o▷—

Danny picked up the phone.

'Payne transferred six hundred thousand pounds by wire this morning,' said the voice, 'so if he pays the remaining five million four hundred thousand by the end of the week, the velodrome site will be his. I thought you'd want to know that we've had another bid in this morning for ten million, which of course we had to turn down. I hope you know what you're doing.' The line went dead. It was the first time the voice had offered an opinion on anything.

Danny dialled the number of his bank manager at Coutts. He was about to convince Payne that the deal couldn't fail.

'Good morning, Sir Nicholas. How can I help you?'

'Good morning, Mr Watson. I want to transfer a million pounds from my current account to Baker, Tremlett and Smythe's client account.'

'Certainly, sir.' There was a long pause before Mr Watson added, 'You do realize that will leave your account overdrawn?'

'Yes, I do,' said Danny, 'but it will be covered on October first when you receive the monthly cheque from my grandfather's trust.'

'I'll do the paperwork today and be back in touch,' said Mr Watson.

'I don't care when you do the paperwork, Mr Watson, as long as the full amount is transferred before close of business this evening.' Danny replaced the receiver. 'Damn,' he said. Not the way Nick would have behaved in the circumstances. He must quickly return to Nick mode. He swung round to see Molly standing in the doorway. She was shaking, and seemed unable to speak.

'What's the matter, Molly?' asked Danny, jumping up from his chair. 'Are you all right?'

'It's him,' she whispered.

'Him?' said Danny.

'That actor.'

'What actor?'

'That Dr Beresford. You know, Lawrence Davenport.'

'Is it, indeed?' said Danny. 'You'd better show him into the drawing room. Offer him some coffee and tell him I'll be with him in a moment.'

As Molly ran downstairs, Danny made two new entries in the Payne file before placing it back on the shelf. He then took down the Davenport file and quickly brought himself up to date.

He was just about to close it when his eye caught a note under the heading 'Early life' which caused him to smile. He replaced the file on the shelf and went downstairs to join his uninvited guest.

Davenport leapt up as Danny entered the room, and this time he did shake hands. Danny was momentarily taken aback by his appearance. He was now clean-shaven, and wearing a well-tailored suit and a smart open-necked shirt. Was he about to return the £300,000?

'Sorry to barge in on you like this,' said Davenport. 'I wouldn't have done so if it wasn't a bit of an emergency.'

'Please don't concern yourself,' said Danny as he sat in the chair opposite him. 'How can I help?'

Molly placed a tray on the side table and poured Davenport a cup of coffee.

'Cream or milk, Mr Davenport?' she asked.

'Neither, thank you.'

'Sugar, Mr Davenport?'

'No, thank you.'

'Would you like a chocolate biscuit?' asked Molly.

'No, thank you,' Davenport said, patting his stomach.

Danny sat back and smiled. He wondered if Molly would be quite so awestruck if she realized that she had just served the son of a car-park attendant with the Grimsby Borough Council.

'Well, just let me know if you want anything else, Mr Davenport,' said Molly before backing out of the room, having quite forgotten to offer Danny his usual hot chocolate. Danny waited for the door to close. 'Sorry about that,' he said. 'She's normally quite sane.'

'Don't worry, old chap,' said Davenport. 'One gets used to it.'

Not for much longer, thought Danny. 'Now, how can I help?' he asked.

'I want to invest a rather large sum of money in a business venture. Only temporary, you understand. Not only will I repay you within a few weeks at the outside, but,' he said, looking up at the McTaggart above the fireplace, 'I'll also be able to reclaim my paintings at the same time.'

Danny would have been sad to lose his recent acquisitions, as he'd been surprised how quickly he'd become attached to them. 'I'm sorry, how thoughtless of me,' he said, suddenly aware that the room was full of Davenport's old pictures. 'Be assured, they will be returned the moment the loan is repaid.'

'That could turn out to be a lot sooner than I had originally anticipated,' said Davenport. 'Especially if you were able to help me out with this little enterprise.'

'What sort of sum did you have in mind?' asked Danny.

'A million,' said Davenport tentatively. 'The problem is that I've only got a week to come up with the money.'

'And what would your collateral be this time?' asked Danny.

'My house in Redcliffe Square.'

Danny recalled Davenport's words the last time they had met: *My home? No, never. Out of the question, don't even think about it.* 'And you say that you will pay the full sum back within a month, using your home as collateral?'

'Within a month, it's guaranteed – a racing certainty.'

'And if you fail to pay back the million in that time?'

'Then, just like my pictures, the house is yours.'

'We have a deal,' said Danny. 'And as you've only got a few days to come up with the money, I'd better get straight on to my lawyers and instruct them to draw up a contract.'

When they left the drawing room and walked out into the hallway, they found Molly standing by the front door clutching Davenport's overcoat.

'Thank you,' said Davenport after she had helped him on with his coat and opened the door.

'I'll be in touch,' said Danny, not shaking hands with Davenport as he stepped out on to the path. Molly almost curtsied.

Danny turned round and headed back to his study. 'Molly, I have some calls to make, so I could be a few minutes late for lunch,' he said over his shoulder. When he received no reply, he turned back to see his housekeeper standing at the door chatting to a woman.

'Is he expecting you?' asked Molly.

'No, he isn't,' replied Ms Bennett. 'I came on the off-chance.'

63

THE ALARM WENT OFF at 2 a.m. but Danny wasn't asleep. He jumped out of bed and quickly put on the pants, T-shirt, socks, slacks and trainers that he'd laid out on the chair by the window. He didn't turn on the light.

He checked his watch: six minutes past two. He closed the bedroom door and walked slowly downstairs. He opened the front door to see his car parked by the kerb. Although he couldn't see him, he knew Big Al would be seated behind the wheel. Danny looked around – there were one or two lights still on in the square, but no one to be seen. He climbed into the car but didn't speak. Big Al switched on the ignition and drove for a hundred yards before he put on the side lights.

Neither of them spoke as Big Al turned right and headed for the Embankment. He had done the run five times during the past week; twice during the day, three times at night – what he called 'night ops'. But the dry runs were over, and tonight the full operation would be carried out. Big Al was treating the whole thing like a military exercise, and his nine years in the army were being put to good use. During the day, the journey averaged around forty-three minutes, but at night he could cover the same distance in twenty-nine, never once exceeding the speed limit.

As they progressed past the House of Commons and along the north side of the Thames, Danny concentrated on what needed to be done once they had reached the target area. They drove through the City and into the East End. Danny's concentration was broken only for a moment when they passed a large construction site with a vast advertising hoarding displaying a magnificent mock-up of what Wilson House would look like once it was completed: sixty luxury flats, thirty affordable dwellings, it promised, nine already sold, including the penthouse. Danny smiled.

Big Al continued on down Mile End Road before turning left at a signpost indicating Stratford, *The home of the 2012 Olympics.* Eleven minutes later, he turned off the road and on to a gravel track. He switched the lights off, as he knew each twist and turn, almost every stone between there and the target area.

At the end of the track he drove past a sign that read, *Private Land: Keep Off.* He kept on going; after all, the land was owned by Danny, and would still be his for another eight days. Big Al brought the car to a halt behind a small mound, switched off the engine and pressed a button. The side window purred down. They sat still and listened, but the only sounds were night noises. During an afternoon recce they'd come across the occasional dog walker and a group of kids kicking a football around, but now there was nothing, not even a night owl to keep them company.

After a couple of minutes Danny touched Big Al's elbow. They climbed out of the car and walked round to the back. Big Al opened the boot while Danny slipped off his trainers. Big Al lifted the box out of the back and placed it on the ground, just as they had done the night before, when Danny had walked the course to see if he could locate the seventy-one white pebbles they had put in cracks, holes and crevices during the day. He had managed to find fifty-three. He'd do better tonight. Another dry run that afternoon had given him a chance to check the ones he'd missed.

In daylight he could cover the three acres in just over two hours. Last night had taken three hours, seventeen minutes, while tonight would take even longer because of the number of times he would have to drop to his knees.

It was a clear, still night, as promised by the weather forecasters, who were predicting light showers in the morning. Like any good farmer planting his seeds, Danny had chosen the day, even the hour, carefully. Big Al removed the black jumpsuit from the box and handed it to Danny, who unzipped the front and climbed in. Even this simple exercise had been practised several times in the dark. Big Al then passed him the rubber boots, followed by the gloves, the mask, the torch and finally the small plastic container marked 'Hazardous'.

Big Al stationed himself by the back of the car as the boss set off. When Danny reached the corner of his land, he walked another seven paces before he came across the first white pebble. He picked it up and dropped it into a deep pocket. He fell on his knees, switched on the torch and placed a tiny fragment of stem into a crack in the ground. He turned off the torch and stood up. Yesterday he had practised the exercise without the rhizome. Nine more paces and he came to the second pebble, where he repeated the whole process, and then only one pace before he reached the third pebble and knelt by a little crevice before carefully inserting the rhizome deep inside. Five more paces . . .

Big Al desperately wanted a smoke, but he knew it was a risk he couldn't take. Once in Bosnia a squaddie had lit up during a night op, and three seconds later he got a bullet through his head. Big Al knew the boss would be out there for at least three hours, so he couldn't afford to let his concentration slip, even for a moment.

Pebble number twenty-three was at the far corner of Danny's land. He shone his torch down a large hole, before dropping in some more rhizome. He placed another pebble in his pocket.

Big Al stretched and began to walk slowly round the car. He knew they planned to leave long before first light, which was at 6.48 a.m. He checked his watch: 4.17. They both looked up when a plane flew overhead, the first to land at Heathrow that morning.

Danny put pebble number 36 in his right-hand pocket, taking care to distribute the weight evenly. He repeated the process again and again: a few paces, kneel down, turn on the torch, drop some rhizome in the crack, pick up the pebble and drop it in a pocket, turn off the torch, stand up, walk on – it felt much more tiring than it had the night before.

Big Al froze as a car drove on to the site and parked about fifty yards away. He couldn't be sure if whoever was in the car had seen him. He fell on to his stomach and began to crawl towards the enemy. A cloud moved to reveal the moon, just a sliver of light –

even the moon was on their side. The car's headlights had been turned off, but an inside light remained on.

Danny thought he saw a car's lights, and immediately fell flat on the ground. They had arranged that Big Al would flash his torch three times to warn him if there was any danger. Danny waited for over a minute, but there was no flashing beam, so he stood up and headed towards the next pebble.

Big Al was now only a few yards from the parked car, and although the windows were steamed up, he could see that the inside light was still on. He pushed himself up on to his knees and peered through the rear window. It took all his discipline not to burst out laughing when he saw a woman stretched out on the back seat, her legs wide apart, moaning. Big Al couldn't see the face of the man who was on top of her, but felt a throbbing in his pants. He fell back down on his stomach and began the long crawl back to base.

When Danny reached pebble number sixty-seven, he cursed. He'd covered the entire area, and somehow missed four. As he walked slowly back towards the car, each pace became more cumbersome than the last. One thing he hadn't anticipated was the sheer weight of the pebbles.

Once Big Al was back at base, he still kept a wary eye on the car. He wondered if the boss had even been aware of its presence. Suddenly he heard the sound of an engine revving up, and the headlights were turned full on before the car swung round, back on to the gravel path and disappeared into the night.

When Big Al saw Danny coming towards him, he removed the empty box from the boot and put it on the ground in front of him. Danny began to take the pebbles out of his pockets and place them in the box; a painstaking exercise when the slightest sound might attract attention. Once the task had been completed, he took off the mask, the gloves, the boots and the jumpsuit. He handed them to Big Al, who put them in the box on top of the pebbles. The last things to be deposited were the torch and an empty plastic container.

Big Al closed the boot and climbed into the front of the car as the boss fastened his seatbelt. He turned on the ignition, swung the car round and drove slowly back towards the gravel track. Neither of them spoke, even when they reached the main road. The job wasn't finished yet.

During the week, Big Al had identified various skips and building sites where they could dispose of any evidence of their nocturnal enterprise. Big Al stopped seven times during a journey that took just over an hour instead of the usual forty minutes. By the time they drove into The Boltons, it was half past seven. Danny smiled when he saw a few drops of rain land on the windscreen and the automatic wipers switch themselves on. Danny stepped out of the car, walked up the path and unlocked the front door. He picked up a letter that was lying on the mat and tore it open as he climbed the staircase. When he saw the signature on the bottom of the page he went straight to his study and locked the door.

Once he had read the letter, he wasn't quite sure how he should reply. Think like Danny. Behave like Nick.

64

'NICK, HOW LOVELY to see you,' said Sarah. She leant across and whispered, 'Now tell me you've been a good boy.'

'Depends what you mean by good,' said Danny as he took the seat next to her.

'You haven't missed a meeting with your favourite lady?'

Danny thought about Beth, even though he knew Sarah was referring to Ms Bennett. 'Not one,' he said. 'In fact, she recently visited me at home and passed my accommodation as suitable, putting ticks in all the relevant boxes.'

'And you haven't even thought about going abroad?'

'Not unless you count travelling up to Scotland to visit Mr Munro.'

'Good. So what else have you been up to that's safe to tell your other solicitor?'

'Not a lot,' said Danny. 'How's Lawrence?' he asked, wondering if he had told her about the loan.

'Never better. He's doing a screen test for *Holby City* next Thursday – a new part that's been written specially for him.'

'So what's it called? Witness to murder?' asked Danny, regretting his words the moment he'd said them.

'No, no,' said Sarah, laughing. 'You're thinking of the part he played in *Witness for the Prosecution*, but that was years ago.'

'It certainly was,' said Danny. 'And it was a performance I'm unlikely to forget.'

'I didn't realize you'd known Larry that long.'

'Only from a distance,' said Danny. He was relieved to be

rescued by a familiar voice saying, 'Hello, Sarah.' Charlie Duncan bent down and kissed her on the cheek.

'Good to see you, Nick,' said Duncan. 'You two know each other, of course.'

'Of course,' said Sarah.

Duncan whispered, 'Be careful what you say, you're sitting behind a critic. Enjoy the show,' he added in a loud voice.

Danny had read the script of *Bling Bling*, but hadn't been able to follow it, so he was curious to see how the piece would work on stage, and what he had spent ten thousand pounds on. He opened the programme to find that the play was billed as 'a hilarious look at Britain during the Blair era'. He turned the page and began reading about the playwright, a dissident Czech who had escaped from . . . The lights went down and the curtain rose.

No one laughed for the first fifteen minutes of the performance, which surprised Danny as the play had been billed as a light-hearted comedy. When the star finally made his entrance, a few laughs followed in his wake, but Danny wasn't altogether sure that they were intended by the playwright. By the time the curtain came down for the interval, Danny found himself stifling a yawn.

'What do you think?' he asked Sarah, wondering if he had missed something.

Sarah put a finger to her lips and pointed to the critic in front of them, who was writing furiously. 'Let's go and have a drink,' she said.

Sarah touched his arm as they walked slowly up the aisle. 'Nick, it's my turn to seek your advice.'

'On what?' said Danny. 'Because I must warn you, I know nothing about the theatre.'

She smiled. 'No, I'm talking about the real world. Gerald Payne has recommended that I put some money in a property deal he's involved in. He mentioned your name, so I wondered if you thought it was a safe investment.'

Danny wasn't sure how to reply, because however much he loathed her brother, he had no quarrel with this charming woman, who had prevented him being sent back to jail.

'I never advise friends to put money in anything,' said Danny. 'It's a no-win situation – if they make a profit they forget that it was you who recommended it, and if they make a loss they never stop reminding you. My only advice would be not to gamble what you can't afford, and never to risk an amount that might cause you to lose a night's sleep.'

'Good advice,' said Sarah. 'I'm grateful.'

Danny followed her into the stalls bar. As they entered the crowded room, Danny spotted Gerald Payne standing by a table, pouring a glass of champagne for Spencer Craig. He wondered if Craig had been tempted to invest any money in his Olympic site, and hoped to find out later at the opening-night party.

'Let's avoid them,' said Sarah. 'Spencer Craig has never been my favourite man.'

'Mine neither,' said Danny as they made their way towards the bar.

'Hey, Sarah, Nick! We're over here,' shouted Payne, waving furiously at them. 'Come and have a glass of bubbly.'

Danny and Sarah reluctantly walked across to join them. 'You remember Nick Moncrieff,' said Payne, turning to Craig.

'Of course,' said Craig. 'The man who's about to make us all a fortune.'

'Let's hope so,' said Danny – one of his questions answered.

'We'll need all the help we can get after tonight's performance,' said Payne.

'Oh, it could have been worse,' said Sarah as Danny passed her a glass of champagne.

'It's shit,' said Craig. 'So that's one of my investments down the drain.'

'You didn't put too much into it, I hope,' said Danny, embarking on a fishing expedition.

'Nothing compared to what I've invested in your little enterprise,' said Craig, who couldn't take his eyes off Sarah.

Payne whispered conspiratorially to Danny, 'I transferred the full amount this morning. We'll be exchanging contracts some time in the next few days.'

'I'm delighted to hear it,' said Danny genuinely, although the Swiss had already informed him of the transfer just before he'd left for the theatre.

'By the way,' added Payne, 'because of my political connections, I've managed to get a couple of tickets for Parliamentary Questions next Thursday. So if you'd like to join me for the minister's statement, you'd be most welcome.'

'That's kind of you, Gerald, but wouldn't you rather take Lawrence or Craig?' He still couldn't bring himself to call him Spencer.

'Larry's got a screen test that afternoon, and Spencer has an appointment with the Lord Chancellor at the other end of the building. We all know what that's about,' he said, winking.

'Do we?' asked Danny.

'Oh, yes. Spencer's about to be made a QC,' Payne whispered.

'Congratulations,' said Danny, turning to his adversary.

'It's not official yet,' said Craig, not even glancing in his direction.

'But it will be next Thursday,' said Payne. 'So, Nick, why don't you meet me outside the St Stephen's entrance of the House of Commons at twelve thirty and we can listen to the minister's statement together before going off to celebrate our good fortune.'

'I'll see you there,' said Danny as three bells sounded. He glanced across at Sarah, who had been trapped in the corner by Craig. He would like to have rescued her, but was swept along by the crowd as it began a reverse stampede back into the theatre.

Sarah returned to her seat just as the curtain rose. The second half turned out to be a slight improvement on the first, but Danny suspected not nearly enough to please the man seated in front of him.

When the curtain fell, the critic was the first out of the stalls, and Danny felt like joining him. Although the cast managed three curtain calls, Danny didn't have to stand on this occasion, as no one else bothered to. When the lights finally came up, Danny turned to Sarah and said, 'If you're going to the party, why don't I give you a lift?'

'I'm not going,' said Sarah. 'And I suspect not many of this lot will be either.'

'It's my turn to seek your advice,' said Danny. 'Why not?'

'The pros can always smell a flop, so they'll avoid being seen at a party where people might think they're involved in some way.' She paused. 'I hope you didn't invest too much.'

'Not enough to lose a night's sleep,' said Danny.

'I won't forget your advice,' she said, linking her arm in his. 'So how do you feel about taking a lonely girl out to dinner?'

Danny recalled the last time he'd taken up such an offer, and how that evening had ended. He didn't want to have to explain to another girl, and particularly not this one. 'I'm sorry,' he said, 'but . . .'

'You're married?' asked Sarah.

'I only wish,' said Danny.

'I only wish I'd met you before she did,' said Sarah, unlinking her arm.

'That wouldn't have been possible,' said Danny, without explanation.

'Bring her along next time,' said Sarah. 'I'd like to meet her. Goodnight, Nick, and thanks again for your advice.' She kissed him on the cheek and drifted off to join her brother.

Danny only just stopped himself from warning her not to invest a penny in Payne's Olympic venture, but he knew that with a girl that bright it might be one risk too many.

He joined the silent throng as they disgorged themselves from the theatre as quickly as they could, but he still couldn't avoid a downcast Charlie Duncan who had stationed himself by the exit. He gave Danny a weak smile.

'Well, at least I won't have to spend any money on a closing-night party.'

65

DANNY MET Gerald Payne outside the St Stephen's entrance of the Palace of Westminster. It was his first visit to the House of Commons, and he was planning that it would be Payne's last.

'I have two tickets for the public gallery,' Payne announced in a loud voice to the policeman stationed at the entrance. It still took them a long time to pass through security.

Once they had emptied their pockets and passed through the metal detector, Payne guided Danny down a long marble corridor to the Central Lobby.

'They don't have tickets,' Payne explained as he marched past a row of visitors sitting on the green benches waiting patiently to be admitted to the public gallery. 'They won't get in until late this evening, if at all.'

Danny took in the atmosphere of the Central Lobby while Payne reported to the policeman on the desk and presented his tickets. Members were chatting to visiting constituents, tourists were staring up at the ornate mosaic ceiling, while others for whom it had all become commonplace strode purposefully across the lobby as they went about their business.

Payne seemed interested in only one thing: making sure he secured a good seat before the minister rose to make her statement from the dispatch box. Danny also wanted him to have the best possible view of proceedings.

The policeman pointed to a corridor on his right. Payne marched off, and Danny had to hurry to catch him up. Payne strode down the green-carpeted corridor and up a flight of steps to the first floor as if he were already a Member. He and Danny were met at the top of the stairs by an usher, who checked their tickets before escorting them into the Strangers' Gallery. The first thing that struck Danny was how small the gallery was, and how few places there were for visitors, which explained the number of people having to wait on the ground floor. The usher found them two seats in the fourth row and handed them both an order paper. Danny leant forward and looked down into the Chamber, surprised to see how few Members were present despite its being the middle of the day. It was clear that not many MPs were that interested in where the Olympic velodrome would be sited, even though some people's whole future rested on the minister's decision. One of them was sitting next to Danny.

'Mostly London Members,' Payne whispered as he turned to the relevant page on the Order Paper. His hand was shaking as he drew Danny's attention to the top of the page: 12.30 p.m., Statement by the Minister of Sport.

Danny tried to follow what was happening in the chamber below. Payne explained that it was a day allocated for questions to the Minister of Health, but that these would end promptly at 12.30. Danny was delighted to see just how impatient Payne was to swap his place in the gallery for a seat on the green benches below.

As the clock above the Speaker's chair edged ever nearer to 12.30, Payne began fidgeting with his order paper, his right leg twitching. Danny remained calm, but then he already knew what the minister was going to tell the House.

When the Speaker rose at 12.30 and bellowed, 'Statement by the Minister of Sport,' Payne leant forward to get a better view as the minister rose from the front bench and placed a red file on the dispatch box.

'Mr Speaker, with your permission I will make a statement concerning which site I have selected for the building of a prospective Olympic velodrome. Members will recall that I informed the House earlier this month that I had shortlisted two locations for consideration but would not make my final decision until I had received detailed surveyors' reports on both sites.' Danny glanced round at Payne; a bead of sweat had appeared on his forehead. Danny tried to look concerned too. 'Those reports were handed into my office yesterday, and copies were also sent to the Olympic Sites Committee, to the two honourable Members in whose constituencies the sites are located, and to the president of the British Cycling Federation. Members can obtain copies from the Order Office immediately following this statement.

'Having read the two reports, all the parties concerned agreed that only one site could possibly be considered for this important project.' A flicker of a smile appeared on Payne's lips. 'The surveyor's report revealed that one of the sites is unfortunately infested with a noxious and invasive plant known as Japanese knotweed (laughter). I can sense that honourable Members, like myself, have not come across this problem before, so I will spend a moment explaining its consequences. Japanese knotweed is an extraordinarily aggressive and destructive plant, which, once it takes hold, quickly spreads and renders the land on which it is growing unsuitable for any building project. Before making my final decision, I sought advice as to whether there was a simple solution to this problem. I was assured by experts in the field that Japanese knotweed can in fact be eradicated by chemical treatment.' Payne looked up, a glimmer of hope in his eyes. 'However, past experience has shown that first attempts are not always successful. The average time before land owned by councils in Birmingham, Liverpool and Dundee was cleared of the weed and passed fit to build on was just over a year.

'Honourable Members will appreciate that it would be irresponsible for my department to risk waiting another twelve months, or possibly even longer, before work can commence on the infested site. I have been left with no choice but to select the excellent alternative site for this project.' Payne's skin turned chalk white when he heard the word 'alternative'. 'I am therefore able to announce that my department, with the backing of the British Olympic Committee and the British Cycling Federation, has selected the site in Stratford South for the building of the new velodrome.' The minister resumed her place and waited for questions from the floor.

Danny looked at Payne, whose head was resting in his hands.

An usher came running down the steps. 'Is your friend feeling all right?' he asked, looking concerned.

'I'm afraid not,' said Danny, looking unconcerned. 'Can we get him to a lavatory? I have a feeling he's going to be sick.'

Danny took Payne by the arm and helped him to his feet, while the usher guided them both up the steps and out of the gallery. He ran ahead and opened the door to allow Payne to stagger into the washroom. Payne began to be sick long before he'd reached a washbasin.

He pulled his tie loose and undid the top button of his shirt, then began to retch again. As he bowed his head and clung on to the side of the basin, breathing heavily, Danny helped him off with his jacket. He deftly removed Payne's mobile from an inside pocket of his jacket and pressed a button that revealed a long list of names. He scrolled through them until he reached 'Lawrence'. As Payne stuck his head in the washbasin for the third time, Danny checked his watch. Davenport would be preparing for his screen test, one last look at the script before going off to make-up. He began to tap out a text message as Payne fell on his knees, sobbing, just as Beth had done when she watched her brother die. *Minister didn't select our site. Sorry. Thought you'd want to know.* He smiled and touched the 'send' button, before returning to the list of contacts. He scrolled on down, stopping when the name 'Spencer' appeared.

◄○►

Spencer Craig looked at himself in the full-length mirror. He had purchased a new shirt and silk tie especially for the occasion. He'd also booked a car to pick him up from chambers at 11.30 a.m. He couldn't risk being late for the Lord Chancellor. Everyone seemed to know about his appointment, as he continually received smiles and murmurs of congratulation – from the head of chambers down to the tea lady.

Craig sat alone in his office pretending to read through a brief that had landed on his desk that morning. There had been a lot of briefs lately. He waited impatiently for the clock to reach eleven thirty so that he could leave for his appointment at twelve. 'First he'll offer you a glass of dry sherry,' a senior colleague had told him. 'Then he'll chat for a few minutes about the dire state of English cricket, which he blames on sledging, and then suddenly without warning he'll tell you in the strictest confidence that he will be making a recommendation to Her Majesty – he gets very pompous at this point – that your name should be included in the next list of barristers to take silk and be appointed a QC. He then rambles on for a few minutes about the onerous responsibility such an appointment places on any new appointee blah blah.'

Craig smiled. It had been a good year, and he intended to celebrate the appointment in style. He pulled open a drawer, took out his chequebook and wrote out a cheque for two hundred thousand pounds payable to Baker, Tremlett and Smythe. It was the largest cheque he had ever written in his life, and he'd already asked his bank for a short-term overdraft facility. But then, he had never known Gerald to be so confident about anything before. He leant back in his chair and savoured the moment as he thought about what he would spend the profits on: a new Porsche, a few days in Venice. Even Sarah might fancy a trip on the Orient Express.

The phone on his desk rang.

'Your car has arrived, Mr Craig.'

'Tell him I'll be right down.' He put the cheque in an envelope, addressed it to Gerald Payne at Baker, Tremlett and Smythe, left it on his blotting pad and strolled downstairs. He would be a few minutes early, but he had no intention of keeping the Lord Chancellor waiting. He didn't speak to the driver during the short journey down the Strand, along Whitehall and into Parliament Square. The car stopped outside the entrance to the House of Lords. An officer on the gate checked his name on a clipboard and waved the car through. The driver turned left under a gothic archway and came to a halt outside the Lord Chancellor's office.

Craig remained seated and waited for the driver to open the door for him, savouring every moment. He walked through the little archway to be greeted by a badge messenger carrying another clipboard. His name was checked once again before the messenger accompanied him slowly up a red-carpeted staircase to the Lord Chancellor's office.

The messenger tapped on the heavy oak door, and a voice said, 'Come in.' He opened the door and stood aside to allow Craig to enter. A young woman was seated at a desk on the far side of the room. She looked up and smiled. 'Mr Craig?'

'Yes,' he replied.

'You're a little early, but I'll just check and see if the Lord Chancellor is free.'

Craig was about to tell her that he was happy to wait, but she had already picked up the phone. 'Mr Craig is here, Lord Chancellor.'

'Please send him in,' came back a stentorian voice.

The secretary rose from behind her desk, crossed the room, opened another heavy oak door and ushered Mr Craig into the Lord Chancellor's office.

Craig could feel the sweat on the palms of his hands as he walked into the magnificent oak-panelled room that overlooked the River Thames. Portraits of former Lord Chancellors were liberally displayed on every wall, and the ornate red and gold Pugin wallpaper left him in no doubt that he was in the presence of the most senior law officer in the land.

'Please have a seat, Mr Craig,' said the Lord Chancellor, opening a thick red folder that lay on the centre of his desk. There was no suggestion of a glass of dry sherry as he browsed through some papers. Craig stared at the old man with his high forehead and bushy grey eyebrows which had proved many a cartoonist's joy. The Lord Chancellor slowly raised his head and stared across the large, ornate desk at his visitor.

'I thought, given the circumstances, Mr Craig, I should have a word in private rather than your becoming aware of the details in the press.'

No mention of the state of English cricket.

'We have received an application,' he continued in a dry, even tone, 'for a royal pardon in the case of Daniel Arthur Cartwright.' He paused to allow Craig to take in the full implication of what he was about to say. 'Three law lords, led by Lord Beloff, have advised me that having reviewed all the evidence, it is their unanimous recommendation that I should advise Her Majesty to allow a full judicial review of the case.' He paused again, clearly not wishing to hurry his words. 'As you were a prosecution witness in the original trial, I felt I should warn you that their lordships are minded to call you to appear before them, along with – ' he looked back down and checked his folder – 'a Mr Gerald Payne and Mr Lawrence Davenport, in order to question the three of you concerning your evidence at the original hearing.'

Before he could continue, Craig jumped in. 'But I thought that before their lordships would even consider overturning an appeal, it was necessary for new evidence to be presented for their consideration?'

'New evidence has been forthcoming.'

'The tape?'

'There is nothing in Lord Beloff's report that mentions a tape. There is, however, a claim from Cartwright's former cellmate – ' once again the Lord Chancellor peered down at the folder – 'a Mr Albert Crann, who states that he was present when Mr Toby Mortimer, whom I believe was known to you, stated that he had witnessed the murder of Mr Bernard Wilson.'

'But this is nothing more than hearsay, coming from the lips of a convicted criminal. It wouldn't stand up in any court in the land.'

'In normal circumstances I would have to agree with that judgement, Mr Craig, and would have dismissed the application had not another fresh piece of evidence been presented to their lordships.'

'Another fresh piece of evidence?' repeated Craig, suddenly feeling a knot in the pit of his stomach.

'Yes,' said the Lord Chancellor. 'It appears that Cartwright shared a cell not only with Albert Crann, but also with another prisoner who kept a daily diary in which he meticulously recorded everything that he witnessed in prison, including verbatim accounts of conversations in which he took part.'

'So the sole source of these accusations is a diary which a convicted criminal claims he wrote while he was in prison.'

'No one is accusing you of anything, Mr Craig,' said the Lord

Chancellor quietly. 'However, it is my intention to invite the witness to appear before their lordships. Of course, you will be given every opportunity to present your side of the case.'

'Who is this man?' demanded Craig.

The Lord Chancellor turned a page of his folder and double-checked the name, before he looked up and said, 'Sir Nicholas Moncrieff.'

66

DANNY SAT IN his usual alcove seat at the Dorchester reading
The Times. The cycling correspondent reported the Minister of
Sport's surprise choice for the velodrome site. It managed a few
column inches, tucked in between canoeing and basketball.

Danny had checked through the sports pages of most of the
national newspapers earlier that morning and those which bothered
to report the minister's statement agreed that she had been left
with little choice. None of them, not even the *Independent*, had
had enough space to inform its readers what Japanese knotweed
was.

Danny checked his watch. Gary Hall was running a few minutes
late and Danny could only imagine the recriminations which must
be going on in the offices of Baker, Tremlett and Smythe. He
turned to the front page, and was reading about the latest twist
in the North Korea nuclear threat, when an out-of-breath Hall
appeared by his side.

'Sorry to be late,' he gasped, 'but the senior partner called me
in just as I was about to leave the office. Quite a bit of flack flying
around following the minister's statement. Everyone is blaming
everyone else.' He took a seat opposite Danny and tried to compose himself.

'Just relax and let me order you a coffee,' said Danny as Mario
walked across.

'And another hot chocolate for you, Sir Nicholas?' Danny
nodded, put down his paper and smiled at Hall. 'Well, at least no
one can blame you, Gary,' he said.

'Oh, no one thinks I was even involved,' said Hall. 'Which is why I've been promoted.'

'Promoted?' said Danny. 'Congratulations.'

'Thank you, but it wouldn't have happened if Gerald Payne hadn't been sacked.' Danny somehow managed to stifle a smile. 'He was summoned to the senior partner's office first thing this morning and told to clear his desk and be off the premises within an hour. One or two of us found ourselves promoted in the fallout.'

'But didn't they realize that it was you and me who took the idea to Payne in the first place?'

'No. Once it turned out that you couldn't raise the full amount, it suddenly became Payne's idea. In fact, you're regarded as some-one who's lost his investment, and may even have a claim against the company.' Something Danny hadn't even considered – until then.

'I wonder what Payne will do now?' said Danny, probing.

'He'll never get another job in our business,' said Hall. 'Or at least not if the senior partner has anything to do with it.'

'So what will the poor fellow do?' asked Danny, still fishing.

'His secretary tells me he's gone down to Sussex to stay with his mother for a few days. She's chairman of the local constituency that he's still hoping to represent at the next election.'

'I can't see why that should be a problem,' said Danny, hoping to be contradicted. 'Unless of course he advised any of his constitu-ents to invest in Japanese knotweed.'

Hall laughed. 'That man's a survivor,' he said. 'My bet is that he'll be a Member of Parliament in a couple of years' time and by then no one will even remember what all the fuss was about.'

Danny frowned, suddenly aware that he might have only wounded Payne, although he didn't expect Davenport or Craig to recover quite so easily. 'I have another job for you,' he said, opening his briefcase and extracting a bundle of papers. 'I need you to dispose of a property in Redcliffe Square; number twenty-five. The previous owner—'

'Hi, Nick,' said a voice.

Danny looked up. A tall, heavily built man he'd never seen before was towering over him. He was wearing a kilt, had a shock of brown wavy hair and a ruddy complexion, and must have been around the same age as Danny. Think like Danny, behave like Nick. Be Nick. Danny had realized that this situation was bound to arise at some time, but lately he had become so relaxed in his new persona that he didn't think it was still possible for him to be taken by surprise. He was wrong. First, he needed to find out if the man had been at school or in the army with Nick, because it certainly wasn't prison. He stood up.

'Hello,' said Danny, giving the stranger a warm smile and shaking him by the hand. 'Can I introduce you to a business associate of mine, Gary Hall.'

The man bent down and shook hands with Hall, saying, 'Pleased to meet you, Gary. I'm Sandy, Sandy Dawson,' he added in a strong Scottish accent.

'Sandy and I go back a long way,' said Danny, hoping to find out just how long.

'Sure do,' said Dawson. 'But I haven't seen Nick since we left school.'

'We were at Loretto together,' Danny said, smiling at Hall. 'So what have you been up to, Sandy?' he asked, desperately searching for another clue.

'Like my father, still in the meat business,' said Dawson. 'And ever thankful that Highland beef remains the most popular meat in the kingdom. What about you, Nick?'

'I've been taking it pretty easy since . . .' said Danny, attempting to discover if Dawson knew that Nick had been to prison.

'Yes, of course,' said Sandy. 'Terrible business, most unfair. But I'm delighted to see you've come through the whole experience unscathed.' A puzzled look appeared on Hall's face. Danny couldn't think of a suitable reply. 'I hope you're still finding time to play the occasional game of cricket,' said Dawson. 'Best fast bowler of our generation at school,' he said, turning to Hall. 'I should know – I was the wicketkeeper.'

'And a damn good one,' said Danny, slapping him on the back.

'Sorry to interrupt you,' said Dawson, 'but I couldn't just walk by without saying hello.'

'Quite right,' said Danny. 'It was good to see you, Sandy, after all this time.'

'You too,' said Dawson as he turned to leave. Danny sat back down, and hoped that Hall didn't hear the sigh of relief that followed Dawson's departure. He began taking some more papers out of his briefcase, when Dawson turned back. 'I don't suppose anyone has told you, Nick, that Squiffy Humphries died?'

'No, I'm sorry to hear that,' said Danny.

'Had a heart attack on the golf course while playing a round with the headmaster. The fifteen has never been the same since Squiffy retired.'

'Yes, poor old Squiffy. Great coach.'

'I'll leave you in peace,' said Dawson. 'I thought you'd want to know. The whole of Musselburgh turned out for his funeral.'

'No more than he deserved,' said Danny. Dawson nodded and walked away.

This time Danny didn't take his eyes off the man until he saw him leave the room.

'Sorry about that,' he said.

'Always embarrassing to meet up with old school chums years later,' said Hall. 'Half the time I can't even remember their names. Mind you, it would be difficult to forget that one. Quite a character.'

'Yes,' said Danny, quickly passing over the deeds of the house in Redcliffe Square.

Hall studied the document for some time before he asked, 'What sort of price are you expecting the property to fetch?'

'Around three million,' said Danny. 'There's a mortgage of just over a million, and I've put up another million, so anything above two point two, two point three should show me a profit.'

'The first thing I'll have to do is arrange for a survey.'

'Pity Payne didn't carry out a survey on the Stratford site.'

'He claims he did,' said Hall. 'My bet is the surveyor had never heard of Japanese knotweed. To be fair, neither had anyone else in the office.'

'I certainly hadn't,' said Danny. 'Well, not until quite recently.'

'Any problems with the present owner?' asked Hall as he turned the last page of the deeds. Then he added before Danny could reply, 'Is that who I think it is?'

'Yes, Lawrence Davenport, the actor,' said Danny.

'Did you know he's a friend of Gerald's?'

—◄o►—

'Yur on the front page of the *Evening Standard*, boss,' said Big Al as he pulled out of the Dorchester forecourt and joined the traffic heading towards Hyde Park Corner.

'What do you mean?' said Danny, fearing the worst.

Big Al passed the paper back to Danny. He stared at the banner headline: *Royal pardon for Cartwright*?

He skimmed through the article before reading it more carefully a second time.

'I don't know whit yur gonnae dae, boss, if they ask Sir Nicholas Moncrieff tae appear in front of a tribunal an gie evidence in defence of Danny Cartwright.'

'If all goes to plan,' said Danny, looking at a photo of Beth surrounded by hundreds of campaigners from Bow, 'it won't be me who's the defendant.'

67

CRAIG HAD SENT OUT for four pizzas, and there would be no waitresses to serve chilled wine for this particular gathering of the Musketeers.

Since leaving the Lord Chancellor's office, he had spent every spare moment trying to find out everything he could about Sir Nicholas Moncrieff. He had been able to confirm that Moncrieff had shared a cell with Danny Cartwright and Albert Crann while they were inmates at Belmarsh. He also discovered that Moncrieff had been released from prison six weeks after Cartwright's death.

What Craig couldn't work out was why anyone would be willing to devote his entire existence, as Moncrieff had clearly done, to tracking down and then attempting to destroy three men he had never met. Unless . . . It was when he placed the two photographs of Moncrieff and Cartwright next to each other that he first began to consider the possibility. It didn't take him too long to come up with a plan to discover if the possibility could in fact be a reality.

There was a knock on the front door. Craig opened it, to be greeted by the forlorn figure of Gerald Payne, clutching on to a cheap bottle of wine. All the self-assurance of their previous meeting had evaporated.

'Is Larry coming?' he asked, not bothering to shake hands with Craig.

'I'm expecting him at any minute,' said Craig as he led his old friend through to the drawing room. 'So where have you been hiding yourself?'

'I'm staying in Sussex with my mother until this all blows over,' Payne replied, sinking into a comfortable chair.

'Any trouble in the constituency?' Craig asked as he poured him a glass of wine.

'Could be worse,' said Payne. 'The Liberals are spreading rumours, but fortunately they do it so often no one takes much notice. When the editor of the local rag rang, I told him I'd resigned as a partner of Baker, Tremlett and Smythe because I wanted to devote more time to my constituency work in the run-up to the general election. He even wrote a supportive leader the following day.'

'I have no doubt you'll survive,' said Craig. 'Frankly, I'm far more worried about Larry. He not only failed to land the part in *Holby City*, but he's telling everyone that you texted him about the minister's statement just as he was about to take the screen test.'

'But that just isn't true,' said Payne. 'I was in such a state of shock I didn't get in touch with anyone, not even you.'

'Someone did,' said Craig. 'And I now realize if it wasn't you who sent us both a text, it had to be someone who knew about Larry's screen test as well as my meeting with the Lord Chancellor.'

'The same person who had access to my phone at that time.'

'The ubiquitous Sir Nicholas Moncrieff.'

'The bastard. I'll kill him,' said Payne, without thinking what he was saying.

'That's what we should have done when we had the chance,' said Craig.

'What do you mean?'

'You'll find out all in good time,' said Craig as the doorbell rang. 'That must be Larry.'

While Craig answered the door, Payne sat thinking about the text messages that Moncrieff must have sent to Larry and Spencer while he was out of action in the Commons washroom, but he was still no nearer to understanding why when the two of them joined him. Payne couldn't believe the change in Larry in such a short time. He was wearing a pair of faded jeans and a crumpled shirt.

He clearly hadn't shaved since he'd heard about the announcement. He slumped down in the nearest chair.

'Why, why, why?' were his opening words.

'You'll find out soon enough,' said Craig, handing him a glass of wine.

'It was obviously a well-organized campaign,' said Payne once Craig had refilled his glass.

'And there's no reason to believe that he's finished with us yet,' said Craig.

'But why?' repeated Davenport. 'Why lend me a million pounds of his own money if he knew I was going to lose every penny of it?'

'Because he had the security of your home to cover the loan,' said Payne. 'He couldn't lose.'

'And what do you think he did the next day?' said Davenport. 'He appointed your old firm to dispose of my house. They've already put a for-sale sign in the front garden and started showing potential buyers around.'

'He did what?' said Payne.

'And this morning I received a solicitor's letter telling me that if I didn't vacate the premises by the end of the month, they would have no choice but to . . .'

'Where will you live?' asked Craig, hoping Davenport wouldn't ask to move in with him.

'Sarah's agreed to put me up until this mess gets sorted out.'

'You've not told her anything?' asked Craig anxiously.

'No, not a thing,' said Davenport. 'Although she obviously knows something's wrong. And she keeps asking me when I first met Moncrieff.'

'You can't afford to tell her that,' said Craig, 'or we'll all end up in even more trouble.'

'How can we possibly be in any more trouble?' asked Davenport.

'We will be if Moncrieff is allowed to continue waging his vendetta,' said Craig. Payne and Davenport made no attempt to contradict him. 'We know that Moncrieff has handed over his diaries to the Lord Chancellor, and no doubt he'll be called on to give evidence before the law lords when they consider Cartwright's pardon.'

'Oh God,' said Davenport, a look of sheer desperation on his face.

'No need to panic,' said Craig. 'I think I've come up with a way of finishing off Moncrieff once and for all.' Davenport didn't look convinced. 'And what's more, there's a possibility that we can still all get our money back, which would include your house, Larry, as well as your paintings.'

'But how can that be possible?' asked Davenport.

'Patience, Larry, patience, and all will be revealed.'

'I understand his tactics with Larry,' said Payne, 'because he had nothing to lose. But why put up a million of his own money when he knew it was a bum deal?'

'That was a stroke of sheer genius,' admitted Craig.

'No doubt you're going to enlighten us,' said Davenport.

'Because by investing that million,' said Craig, ignoring his sarcasm, 'you were both convinced, as I was, that we must be on to a winner.'

'But he was still bound to lose his million,' said Payne, 'if he knew that the first site was doomed.'

'Not if he already owned the site in the first place,' said Craig.

Neither of his two guests spoke for some time, as they tried to work out the significance of his words.

'Are you suggesting that we were paying him to buy his own property?' said Payne eventually.

'Worse than that,' said Craig, 'because I think a piece of advice you gave him, Gerald, meant that he couldn't lose either way. So he ended up not only killing us, but making a killing himself.'

The doorbell rang.

'Who's that?' asked Davenport, nearly jumping out of his chair.

'Only our supper,' said Craig. 'Why don't you two go through to the kitchen? I'll let you know over our pizzas exactly what I have planned for Sir Nicholas Moncrieff, because the time has come for us to fight back.'

'I'm not sure I want another confrontation with that man,'

Davenport admitted as he and Payne walked through to the kitchen.

'We may not have much choice,' said Payne.

'Any idea who's joining us?' asked Davenport, when he saw the table had been laid for four.

Payne shook his head. 'Haven't a clue. But I think it's unlikely to be Moncrieff.'

'You're right, although it could just be one of his old school chums,' said Craig as he joined them in the kitchen. He took the pizzas out of their boxes and placed them in the microwave.

'Are you going to explain what the hell you've been hinting at all evening?' asked Payne.

'Not yet,' said Craig, checking his watch. 'But you'll only have to wait a few more minutes to find out.'

'At least tell me what you meant when you said that Moncrieff may have made a killing because of some advice I gave him,' demanded Payne.

'Wasn't it you who told him to buy the second site so that it would be impossible for him to lose out either way?'

'Yes, I did. But if you remember, he didn't have enough money to buy the first site.'

'Or that's what he told you,' said Craig. 'According to the *Evening Standard*, the other site is now expected to fetch twelve million.'

'But why put up a million of his own money for the first site,' asked Davenport, 'if he already knew he was going to make a killing on the second?'

'Because he always intended to make a killing on both sites,' said Craig. 'Except on the first one we were to be the victims, while he didn't lose a penny. If you'd told us that it was Moncrieff who was lending you the money in the first place,' he said to Davenport, 'we could have worked it out.'

Davenport looked sheepish, but made no attempt to defend himself.

'But what I still don't understand,' said Payne, 'is why he put us through all this. It can't just be because he shared a cell with Cartwright.'

'I agree, there has to be more to it than that,' said Davenport.

'There is,' said Craig. 'And if it's what I think it is, Moncrieff won't be bothering us for much longer.'

Payne and Davenport didn't look convinced.

'At least tell us,' said Payne, 'how you happened to come across one of Moncrieff's old school friends.'

'Ever heard of Old School Chums dot com?'

'So who have you been trying to get in touch with?' asked Payne.

'Anyone who knew Nicholas Moncrieff when he was at school or in the army.'

'Did anybody get in touch with you?' asked Davenport as the doorbell rang again.

'Seven, but only one had all the necessary qualifications,' said Craig as he left the kitchen to answer the door.

Davenport and Payne looked at each other, but didn't speak.

When Craig reappeared moments later, he was accompanied by a tall, heavily built man who had to lower his head as he passed through the kitchen doorway.

'Gentlemen, allow me to introduce Sandy Dawson,' said Craig. 'Sandy was in the same house at Loretto school as Nicholas Moncrieff.'

'For five years,' said Dawson, shaking hands with Payne and Davenport. Craig poured him a glass of wine before ushering him towards the vacant seat at the table.

'But why do we need someone who knew Moncrieff at school?' asked Davenport.

'Why don't you tell them, Sandy?' said Craig.

'I contacted Spencer under the impression that he was my old friend Nick Moncrieff, who I haven't seen since leaving school.'

'When Sandy got in touch,' interrupted Craig, 'I told him my reservations about the man claiming to be Moncrieff, and he agreed to put him to the test. It was Gerald who let me know that Moncrieff had an appointment with one of his colleagues, Gary Hall, at the Dorchester that morning. So Sandy turned up there a few minutes later.'

'It wasn't difficult to find him,' said Dawson. 'Everyone from the hall porter to the hotel manager seemed to know Sir Nicholas Moncrieff. He was sitting in an alcove, exactly where the concierge said I would find him. When I first spotted him I felt certain it was Nick, but as it was almost fifteen years since I'd last seen him, I thought I'd better double-check. But when I walked over to have a word with him, he didn't show the slightest sign of recognition, and it's not as if I'm that easy to forget.'

'That's one of the reasons I selected you,' said Craig. 'But it still doesn't constitute proof, not after all this time.'

'Which is why I decided to interrupt his meeting,' said Dawson, 'to see whether it really was Nick.'

'And?' asked Payne.

'Very impressive. Same look, same voice, even the same mannerisms, but I still wasn't convinced, so decided to put out a couple of feelers. When Nick was at Loretto he was captain of cricket, and a damn good fast bowler. This man knew that, but when I reminded him that I'd been the first eleven wicketkeeper, he didn't bat an eyelid. That was his first mistake. I never played cricket at school, detested the game. I was in the rugby fifteen, a second row forward – which may not come as a surprise – so I walked away, but I still wondered if he might have forgotten, so I went back to tell him the sad news that Squiffy Humphries had died, and that the whole town had turned out for his funeral. "Great coach," the man said. That was his second mistake. Squiffy Humphries was our house matron. She ruled the boys with a rod of iron; even I was frightened of her. There was no way he could ever have forgotten Squiffy. I don't know who that man at the Dorchester was, but I can tell you one thing for certain, he isn't Nicholas Moncrieff.'

'Then who the hell is he?' asked Payne.

'I know exactly who he is,' said Craig. 'And what's more, I can prove it.'

◄o►

Danny had brought all three files up to date. There was no doubt that he had wounded Payne, and even crippled Davenport, but he'd hardly laid a glove on Spencer Craig, other than possibly to delay his appointment as a QC. And now he'd blown his cover, all three of them would be aware who was responsible for their downfall.

While Danny had remained anonymous, he'd been able to pick off his opponents one by one, and even select the ground on which he would fight. But he no longer had that advantage. Now they were only too aware of his presence, leaving him, for the first time, vulnerable and exposed. They would want to exact revenge, and he didn't need to be reminded what had happened the last time they worked as a team.

Danny had hoped to defeat all three of them before they found out who they were up against. Now his only hope was to expose them in court. But that would mean revealing that it was Nick who had been killed in the shower at Belmarsh, not him, and if he was to risk that, his timing had to be perfect.

Davenport had lost his home and his art collection, and had been written out of *Holby City* even before he'd completed a screen test. He had moved in with his sister in Cheyne Walk, which made Danny feel guilty for the first time; he wondered how Sarah would react if she ever found out the truth.

Payne was on the verge of bankruptcy, but Hall had said that his mother might have bailed him out, and at the next election he could still expect to become the Honourable Member for Sussex Central.

And Craig had lost nothing compared to his friends, and certainly showed no signs of remorse. Danny wasn't in any doubt which one of the Musketeers would lead the counter-attack.

Danny put the three files back on the shelf. He had already planned his next move, which he was confident would see all three of them end up in jail. He would appear before the three law lords as Mr Redmayne had requested, and would supply the fresh evidence needed to expose Craig as a murderer, Payne as his accomplice, and Davenport as having committed perjury which had caused an innocent man to be sent to prison for a crime he did not commit.

68

BETH EMERGED from the darkness of Knightsbridge tube station. It was a bright, clear afternoon, and the pavements were busy with window-shoppers and locals walking off their Sunday lunch.

Alex Redmayne could not have been kinder or more supportive over the past weeks, and when she left him less than an hour ago, she had felt full of confidence. That confidence was now beginning to ebb away. As she walked in the direction of The Boltons, she tried to recall everything Alex had told her.

Nick Moncrieff was a decent man who had become a loyal friend of Danny's when they were in prison together. Some weeks before he was released, Moncrieff had written to Alex offering to do anything he could to assist Danny, who he was convinced was innocent.

Alex had decided to put that offer to the test, and after Moncrieff's release, he had written to him requesting to have sight of the diaries he had written while in prison, along with any contemporaneous notes concerning the taped conversation that had taken place between Albert Crann and Toby Mortimer. Alex ended the letter by asking if he would agree to appear before the tribunal and give evidence.

The first surprise came when the diaries were delivered to Alex's chambers the following morning. The second was the courier. Albert Crann could not have been more cooperative, answering all the questions Alex put to him, only becoming guarded when he was asked why his boss wouldn't agree to appear before the law lords – in fact, wouldn't even consider an off-the-record meeting with Mr Redmayne in chambers. Alex assumed it must have something to do with Moncrieff wanting to avoid any confrontation with the police until he had completed his probation order. But Alex wasn't willing to give up that easily. Over lunch he had convinced Beth that if she could get Moncrieff to change his mind and agree to give evidence before the law lords, it might be the deciding factor in having Danny's name cleared.

'No pressure,' Beth had said with a smile, but now she was on her own and beginning to feel that pressure more with every step she took.

Alex had showed her a photograph of Moncrieff and warned her that when she first saw him she might think just for a moment that she was looking at Danny. But she must concentrate, and not allow herself to be distracted.

Alex had selected the day, even the hour, that the meeting should take place: a Sunday afternoon around four o'clock. He felt that Nick would be more relaxed at that time and possibly vulnerable to a distressed damsel appearing on his doorstep unannounced.

When Beth left the main road and walked into The Boltons, her pace became even slower. It was only the thought of clearing Danny's name that kept her going. She walked around the semi-circular garden with its church in the centre until she reached number 12. Before she opened the gate she rehearsed the words she and Alex had agreed on. My name is Beth Wilson, and I apologize for disturbing you on a Sunday afternoon, but I think you shared a cell with Danny Cartwright, who was . . .

—◦—

By the time Danny had read through the third essay recommended by Professor Mori, he was beginning to feel a little more confident about facing his mentor. He turned to a piece he'd written over a year ago on J. K. Galbraith's theories on a low-tax economy producing . . . when the doorbell rang. He cursed. Big Al had gone to watch West Ham play Sheffield Utd. Danny had wanted to join him, but they both agreed that he couldn't take the risk. Would it be possible for him to visit Upton Park next season? He turned his attention back to Galbraith, in the hope that whoever it was would go away, and then the bell rang a second time.

He reluctantly stood up and pushed back his chair. Who would it be this time? A Jehovah's Witness or a double-glazing salesman? Whichever it turned out to be, he already had his first sentence prepared for whoever had decided to interrupt his Sunday afternoon. He jogged downstairs and walked quickly along the corridor, hoping that he could get rid of them before his concentration broke. The bell rang a third time.

He pulled open the door.

'My name is Beth Wilson, and I apologize for disturbing you on a Sunday . . .'

Danny stared at the woman he loved. He had thought about this moment every day for the past two years, and what he would say to her. He stood there, speechless.

Beth turned white, and began to shake. 'It can't be,' she said.

'It is, my darling,' Danny replied as he took her in his arms.

A man sitting in a car on the opposite side of the road continued to take photographs.

◄○►

'Mr Moncrieff?'

'Who is this?'

'My name is Spencer Craig. I'm a barrister, and I have a proposition to put to you.'

'And what might that be, Mr Craig?'

'If I were able to restore your fortune, your rightful fortune, what would that be worth to you?'

'Name your price.'

'Twenty-five per cent.'

'That sounds a bit steep.'

'To give you back your estate in Scotland, to kick out the present occupant of your house in The Boltons, to restore the full amount paid for your grandfather's stamp collection, not to mention ownership of a luxury penthouse in London which I suspect you don't even know about, and to reclaim your bank accounts in Geneva and London? No, I don't think that's particularly steep,

Mr Moncrieff. In fact, it's quite reasonable when the alternative is a hundred per cent of nothing.'

'But how could this be possible?'

'Once you've signed a contract, Mr Moncrieff, your father's fortune will be restored to you.'

'And there will be no fees or hidden charges?' asked Hugo suspiciously.

'No fees or hidden charges,' promised Craig. 'In fact, I'll throw in a little bonus which I suspect will even please Mrs Moncrieff.'

'And what's that?'

'You sign my contract, and by this time next week she'll be Lady Moncrieff.'

69

'DID YOU GET a photo of his leg?' asked Craig.

'Not yet,' replied Payne.

'Let me know the moment you do.'

'Hold on,' said Payne. 'He's coming out of the house.'

'With his driver?' asked Craig.

'No, with the woman who went inside yesterday afternoon.'

'Describe her.'

'Late twenties, five foot eight, slim, brown hair, great legs. They're both getting into the back of the car.'

'Stay with them,' said Craig, 'and keep me briefed on where they go.' He put the phone down, turned on his computer and pulled up a photo of Beth Wilson, not surprised that she fitted the description. However, he was surprised that Cartwright was willing to take such a risk. Did he now believe that he was invincible?

Once Payne had taken a photograph of Cartwright's left leg, Craig would make an appointment to see Detective Sergeant Fuller. He would then stand aside and let the policeman take all the credit for capturing an escaped murderer and his accomplice.

◄◦►

Big Al dropped Danny outside the entrance to the university. After Beth had given him a kiss, he jumped out of the car and ran up the steps and into the building.

All his plans had been blown away with one kiss, followed by a night with no sleep. When the sun rose the following morning,

Danny knew that he could no longer live a life that didn't include Beth, even if it meant leaving the country and having to live abroad.

⋅◦⋅

Craig slipped out of the court while the jury were considering their verdict. He stood on the steps of the Old Bailey and phoned Payne on his mobile.

'Where did they end up?' he asked.

'Cartwright was dropped off at London University. He's doing a Business Studies degree there.'

'But Moncrieff already has a degree in English.'

'True, but don't forget that when Cartwright was at Belmarsh he took A levels in maths and business studies.'

'Another small mistake that he's assumed no one would pick up,' said Craig. 'So where did the driver take the girl after he'd dropped Cartwright off?'

'They headed for the East End and—'

'Twenty-seven Bacon Road, Bow,' said Craig.

'How did you know?'

'It's the home of Beth Wilson, Cartwright's girlfriend – she was with him that night in the alley, don't you remember?'

'How could I forget,' snapped Payne.

'Did you manage to get a photograph of her?' asked Craig, ignoring the little outburst.

'Several.'

'Good, but I still need a shot of Cartwright's left leg just above the knee before I can pay a visit to Detective Sergeant Fuller.' Craig checked his watch. 'I'd better get back to court. The jury shouldn't take too long to find my client guilty. Where are you at the moment?'

'Outside twenty-seven Bacon Road.'

'Stay well out of sight,' said Craig. 'That woman would recognize you at a hundred paces. I'll call you as soon as the court rises.'

⋅◦⋅

During his lunch break, Danny decided to take a walk and grab a sandwich before he attended Professor Mori's lecture. He tried to recall the six theories of Adam Smith in case the professor's hovering finger ended up pointing at him. He failed to notice the man sitting on a bench on the other side of the road, a camera by his side.

◄○►

Craig dialled Payne on his mobile moments after the court had risen.

'She didn't leave the house for over an hour,' said Payne, 'and when she came out, she was carrying a large suitcase.'

'Where did she go?' asked Craig.

'She was driven to her office at Mason Street in the City.'

'And did she take the suitcase with her?'

'No, she left it in the boot of the car.'

'So she intends to stay at The Boltons for at least another night.'

'Looks that way. Or do you think they're planning to skip the country?' asked Payne.

'They're unlikely to consider doing that until after his final meeting with his probation officer on Thursday morning, when he will have completed his licence.'

'Which means we've only got another three days to gather all the evidence we need,' said Payne.

'So what's he been up to this afternoon?'

'He left the university at four, and was driven back to The Boltons. He went into the house, but the driver left again straight away. I followed him in case he was picking up the girl.'

'And was he?'

'Yes. He collected her from work and drove her back to the house.'

'And the suitcase?'

'He carried it inside.'

'Perhaps she thinks it's safe for her to move in now. Did he go for a run?'

'If he did,' said Payne, 'it must have been while I was following the girl.'

'Don't bother with her tomorrow,' said Craig. 'From now on concentrate on Cartwright, because if we're going to flush him out, only one thing matters.'

'The photograph,' said Payne. 'But what if he doesn't go for a run in the morning?'

'All the more reason to ignore the girl and stick with him,' said Craig. 'Meanwhile, I'll bring Larry up to date.'

'Is he doing anything to earn his keep?'

'Not a lot,' said Craig. 'But we can't afford to antagonize him while he's still living with his sister.'

—◦—

Craig was shaving when the phone rang. He cursed.

'They left the house together again.'

'So he didn't go for a run this morning?'

'Not unless it was before five a.m. I'll call again if there's any change in his routine.'

Craig flicked the phone closed and continued to shave. He cut himself. He cursed again.

He needed to be in court by ten o'clock, when the judge would pass sentence on his aggravated burglary case. His client would probably end up with a two-year sentence, despite the fact that he had asked for twenty-three other offences to be taken into consideration.

Craig dabbed on some aftershave as he thought about the charges Cartwright would end up facing: escaping from Belmarsh while impersonating another prisoner, theft of a stamp collection worth over fifty million dollars, falsifying cheques on two bank accounts, with at least twenty-three other offences to be taken into consideration. Once the judge had considered that lot, Cartwright wouldn't be seeing the light of day until he was eligible for his old-age pension. Craig suspected that the girl would also end up facing a long spell behind bars for aiding and abetting a criminal. And once they found out exactly what Cartwright had been up to since escaping from prison, no one would be talking about offering him a pardon. Craig was even beginning to feel confident that the Lord Chancellor would be calling him back again and this time he would be offered a dry sherry, while the two of them discussed the decline of English cricket.

—◄o►—

'Wur bein' followed,' said Big Al.

'What makes you think that?' asked Danny.

'I spotted a car following us yisterday. Now it's there again.'

'Take a left at the next junction and see if he stays with us.'

Big Al nodded, and without indicating, suddenly swung left.

'Is he still following us?' asked Danny.

'Naw, he drove straight on,' said Big Al, checking his rear-view mirror.

'What type of car was it?'

'A dark blue Ford Mondeo.'

'How many of those do you imagine there are in London?' asked Danny.

Big Al grunted. 'He wis following us,' he repeated as he turned into The Boltons.

'I'm going for a run,' said Danny. 'I'll let you know if I see anyone following me.'

Big Al didn't laugh.

—◄o►—

'Cartwright's chauffeur spotted me,' said Payne, 'so I had no choice but to drive on and keep out of sight for the rest of the day. I'm on my way to the hire company to exchange the car for a different model. I'll be back on duty first thing tomorrow morning. But I'm going to have to be more careful in future because Cartwright's driver is good. My bet is that he's ex-police or army, which means I'll need to change my car every day.'

'What did you just say?' asked Craig.

'I'm going to have to change—'

'No, before that.'

'Cartwright's driver must be police or army trained.'

'Of course he is,' said Craig. 'Don't forget that Moncrieff's driver was locked up in the same cell as him and Cartwright.'

'You're right,' said Payne. 'Crann, Albert Crann.'

'Better known as Big Al. I've got a feeling that Detective Sergeant Fuller is going to end up with a royal flush – king, queen and now jerk.'

'Do you want me to go back this evening and double-check?' asked Payne.

'No. Crann may well turn out to be a bonus, but we can't risk him working out that we're on to them. Keep well out of their way until tomorrow afternoon, because you can be sure that Crann will now be on the lookout for you. Once he drops Cartwright off at the house and leaves to pick up the girlfriend, that's when I think you'll find Cartwright'll go for his run.'

◄○►

As Danny walked down the corridor he was greeted by Professor Mori who was talking to some students who were sitting their exams.

'A year today, Nick,' he said, 'and it will be your turn to take your finals.' Danny had quite forgotten about how little time he had left before his exams, and didn't bother to tell the professor that he had no idea where he would be a year today. 'When I'll be expecting great things of you,' added the professor.

'Let's hope I live up to your expectations.'

'Nothing wrong with my expectations,' said Mori, 'although you're typical of someone who gets himself educated outside of the mainstream and then imagines he has a lot of catching up to do. I think you'll find, Nick, that when the time comes to take your exams, you'll have not only caught up, but overtaken most of your contemporaries.'

'I'm flattered, professor,' said Danny.

'I don't do flattery,' said the professor as he turned his attention to another student.

Danny marched out on to the street to find Big Al holding open the back door of his car. 'Anyone been following us today?'

'Naw, boss,' said Big Al, climbing behind the wheel.

Danny didn't let Big Al know that he thought it was quite possible that someone was following them. He wondered how much time he had left before Craig stumbled across the truth, if he hadn't done so already. Danny only needed a couple more days before his probation would be completed, and then the whole world would know the truth.

When they drew up outside The Boltons, Danny jumped out and ran into the house.

'Do you want some tea?' Molly asked as he bounded up the stairs.

'No thanks, I'm going for a run.'

Danny threw off his clothes and put on his running kit. He had decided to go on an extended run as he needed time to think about his meeting with Alex Redmayne the following morning. As he ran out of the front door, he saw Big Al making his way down to the kitchen, no doubt to grab a cup of tea with Molly before he left to pick up Beth. Danny jogged off down the road in the direction of the Embankment, a flood of adrenalin being released after sitting on his backside and listening to lectures for most of the day.

As he ran past Cheyne Walk he avoided looking up at Sarah's apartment, where he knew her brother was now living. If he had done so, he might have spotted another man he would have recognized standing by an open window taking a photograph of him. Danny continued towards Parliament Square, and when he passed the St Stephen's entrance to the House of Commons he thought about Payne and wondered where he was now.

He was standing on the opposite side of the road focusing his camera, trying to look like a tourist taking a picture of Big Ben.

◄○►

'Did you get a half-decent photograph?' asked Craig.

'Enough to fill a gallery,' replied Payne.

'Well done. Bring them over to my place now, and we can have a look at them over dinner.'

'Pizza again?' said Payne.

'Not for much longer. Once Hugo Moncrieff pays up, we'll not only finish off Cartwright, but make a handsome profit at the same time, which I'm fairly confident wasn't part of his long-term plan.'

'I'm not quite sure what Davenport has done to deserve his million.'

'I agree, but he's still a bit flaky, and we don't need him opening his mouth at the wrong time, especially now he's living with Sarah. See you soon, Gerald.'

Craig put the phone down, poured himself a drink and thought about what he was going to say before he called the man he'd been looking forward to having a word with all week.

'Could I speak to Detective Sergeant Fuller?' he said when the phone was answered.

'Inspector Fuller,' said a voice. 'Who shall I say is calling?'

'Spencer Craig. I'm a barrister.'

'I'll put you through, sir.'

'Mr Craig, it's been a long time since I've heard from you. I'm unlikely to forget the last occasion you called.'

'Nor me,' said Craig, 'and that's the reason I'm phoning this time, *inspector* – many congratulations.'

'Thank you,' said Fuller, 'but I find it hard to believe that's the only reason you called.'

'You're right,' said Craig, laughing. 'But I do have a piece of information that might make your promotion to chief inspector even quicker.'

'You have my full attention,' said Fuller.

'But I have to make it clear, inspector, that you didn't get the information from me. I'm sure you'll understand why, once you discover who's involved. And I'd rather not talk about it over the phone.'

'Of course,' said Fuller, 'so where and when would you like to meet?'

'The Sherlock Holmes, twelve fifteen tomorrow?'

'How appropriate,' said Fuller. 'I'll see you there, Mr Craig.'

Craig put the phone down and thought he'd make one more call before Gerald turned up, but just as he picked up the phone, the doorbell rang. When he opened the door he found Payne standing under the porch, grinning. He hadn't seen him looking so pleased with himself for some time. Payne walked straight past Craig without uttering a word, marched into the kitchen and spread six photographs out on the table.

Craig looked down at the images and immediately understood why Payne was so smug. Just above the knee on Danny's left leg was a scar from a wound that Craig remembered inflicting, and although the scar had faded, it was still clear to the naked eye.

'That's all the evidence Fuller will need,' said Craig as he picked up the kitchen phone and dialled a number in Scotland.

'Hugo Moncrieff,' said a voice.

'Soon to be Sir Hugo,' said Craig.

70

'AS YOU KNOW, Nicholas, this will be our last meeting.'

'Yes, Ms Bennett.'

'We have not always seen eye to eye, but I do feel that we have both come through the experience unscathed.'

'I agree, Ms Bennett.'

'When you walk out of this building for the last time, you will be a free man, having completed your licence.'

'Yes, Ms Bennett.'

'But before I can sign you off officially, I have to ask you a few questions.'

'Of course, Ms Bennett.'

She picked up a chewed biro and looked down at the long list of questions that the Home Office requires to be answered before a prisoner can finally be discharged.

'Are you currently taking any drugs?'

'No, Ms Bennett.'

'Have you recently been tempted to commit a crime?'

'Not recently, Ms Bennett.'

'During the past year have you mixed with any known criminals?'

'Not known criminals,' said Danny. Ms Bennett looked up. 'But I've stopped mixing with them, and have no desire to meet up with them again unless it's in court.'

'I'm relieved to hear that,' said Ms Bennett as she ticked the relevant box. 'Do you still have somewhere to live?'

'Yes, but I anticipate moving quite soon.' The pen hovered. 'To a place I've been to before, which is officially sanctioned.' The biro ticked another box.

'Are you presently living with your family?'

'Yes, I am.'

Ms Bennett looked up again. 'The last time I asked you that question, Nicholas, you told me that you were living alone.'

'We've recently been reconciled.'

'I'm delighted to hear that, Nicholas,' she said, a third of the boxes ticked.

'Do you have any dependants?'

'Yes, one daughter, Christy.'

'So are you presently living with your wife and daughter?'

'Beth and I are engaged, and as soon as I've sorted out one or two problems I still have to deal with, we plan to be married.'

'I'm delighted to hear that,' said Ms Bennett. 'Might the Probation Service be able to assist you with these problems?'

'It's kind of you to ask, Ms Bennett, but I don't think so. However, I do have an appointment with my counsel tomorrow morning, and I'm rather hoping that he will be able to help me move things along.'

'I see,' said Ms Bennett, returning to her questions. 'Does your partner have a full-time job?'

'Yes she does,' said Danny. 'She is the PA to the chairman of a City insurance company.'

'So once you find a job, you'll be a two-income family.'

'Yes, but for the foreseeable future, my salary will be considerably less than hers.'

'Why? What job are you hoping to take up?'

'I'm expecting to be offered a position as the librarian in a large institution,' said Danny.

'I can't think of anything more worthwhile,' said Ms Bennett, ticking another box and moving on to the next question. 'Are you thinking of travelling abroad in the near future?'

'I have no plans to do so,' said Danny.

'And finally,' said Ms Bennett, 'are you worried that at some time in the future you might commit another crime?'

'I've made a decision that will render that option impossible for the foreseeable future,' he assured her.

'I'm delighted to hear that,' said Ms Bennett as she ticked the final box. 'That completes my questions. Thank you, Nicholas.'

'Thank you, Ms Bennett.'

'I do hope,' said Ms Bennett as she rose from behind her desk, 'that your lawyer will be able to get to grips with these problems that are troubling you.'

'That's kind of you, Ms Bennett,' said Danny as they shook hands. 'Let's hope so.'

'And should you ever feel in need of any help or assistance, don't forget that I am only a phone call away.'

'I think it's quite possible that someone will be in touch with you in the near future,' said Danny.

'I look forward to hearing from them,' said Ms Bennett, 'and I hope everything works out well for you and Beth.'

'Thank you,' said Danny.

'Goodbye, Nicholas.'

'Goodbye, Ms Bennett.'

Nicholas Moncrieff opened the door and walked out on to the street a free man. Tomorrow he would be Danny Cartwright.

—◦—

'Are you awake?'

'Yes,' said Beth.

'Are you still hoping I'll change my mind?'

'Yes, but I know it's pointless to try and persuade you, Danny. You've always been as stubborn as a mule. I only hope you realize that if it turns out to be the wrong decision, this could be our last night together.'

'But if I'm right,' said Danny, 'we'll have ten thousand nights like this.'

'But we could have a lifetime of nights like this without you having to take such a risk.'

'I've been taking that risk every day since I left prison. You have no idea, Beth, what it's like to be continually looking over your shoulder, waiting for someone to say, "The game's up, Danny boy, you're going back to jail for the rest of your life." At least this way, someone might be willing to listen to my side of the story.'

'But what convinced you that this was the only way to prove your innocence?'

'You did,' said Danny. 'When I saw you standing in the doorway – "I'm sorry to disturb you, Sir Nicholas,"' – he mimicked – 'I realized that I no longer wanted to be Sir Nicholas Moncrieff. I'm Danny Cartwright, and I'm in love with Beth Bacon of Wilson Road.'

Beth laughed. 'I can't remember when you last called me that.'

'When you were a grotty little eleven-year-old in pigtails.'

Beth fell back on the pillow and didn't speak for some time. Danny wondered if she'd fallen asleep, until she gripped his hand and said, 'But it's just as likely that you'll end up spending the rest of your life in jail.'

'I've had more than enough time to think about that,' said Danny, 'and I'm convinced that if I walk into a police station with Alex Redmayne and give myself up – along with this house, all my assets and, most important of all, you, don't you think it might cross somebody's mind that I could be innocent?'

'Most people wouldn't be willing to take that risk,' said Beth. 'They'd be quite happy to spend the rest of their lives as Sir Nicholas Moncrieff, with everything that goes with it.'

'But that's the point, Beth. I'm not Sir Nicholas Moncrieff. I'm Danny Cartwright.'

'And I'm not Beth Moncrieff, but I'd rather be that than spending the next twenty years visiting you in Belmarsh on the first Sunday of every month.'

'But not a day would go by when you weren't looking over *your* shoulder, misunderstanding the slightest innuendo, and having to avoid anyone who just might have known Danny or even Nick. And who could you share your secret with? Your mother? My mother? Your friends? The answer is, nobody. And what do we tell Christy when she's old enough to understand? Should we expect her to go on living a life of deceit, never knowing who her parents really are? No, if that's the alternative, I'd prefer to take the risk. After all, if three law lords believe my case is strong enough to consider a royal pardon, perhaps they'll feel that I have an even stronger case if I'm willing to give up so much to prove my innocence.'

'I know you're right, Danny, but the last few days have been the happiest of my life.'

'Mine too, Beth, but they'll be happier still when I'm a free man. I have enough faith in human nature to believe that Alex Redmayne, Fraser Munro, and even Sarah Davenport will not rest until they see that justice is done.'

'You rather fancy Sarah Davenport, don't you,' said Beth, running her fingers through his hair.

Danny smiled at her. 'I must admit that Sir Nicholas Moncrieff did, but Danny Cartwright? Never.'

'Why don't we spend one more day together,' she said, 'and make it something we'll never forget. And as it could be your last day of freedom, I'll let you do anything you desire.'

'Let's stay in bed,' said Danny, 'and make love all day.'

'Men,' sighed Beth with a smile.

'We could take Christy to the zoo in the morning, and then have lunch at Ramsey's fish and chip shop.'

'Then what?' asked Beth.

'I'll go to Upton Park and watch the Hammers, while you take Christy back to your mother's.'

'And in the evening?'

'You can choose whichever film you like . . . as long as it's the new James Bond.'

'And after that?'

'Same as every night this week,' he said taking her in his arms.

'In which case I think we'd better stick to plan A,' said Beth, 'and make sure you're on time for the appointment with Alex Redmayne tomorrow morning.'

'I can't wait to see his face,' said Danny. 'He thinks he has an appointment with Sir Nicholas Moncrieff to discuss the diaries and the possibility that he might get him to change his mind and agree to appear as a witness, while in fact he'll come face to face with Danny Cartwright, who wants to give himself up.'

'Alex will be delighted,' said Beth. 'He never stops saying, "If only I had a second chance".'

'Well, he's about to be given one. And I can tell you, Beth, I can't wait for that meeting, because it will make me free for the first time in years.' Danny leant across and kissed her gently on the lips. As she slipped out of her nightdress, he placed a hand on her thigh.

'This is something else you're going to have to go without for the next few months,' whispered Beth, as a noise like a clap of thunder reverberated from the floor below.

'What the hell was that?' said Danny, switching on the bedside light. He heard the sound of heavy footsteps pounding up the stairs. He swung his legs out of bed as three police officers dressed in flak jackets and carrying batons burst into the bedroom, with three more following close behind. The first three grabbed Danny and threw him to the floor, although he hadn't made any attempt to resist. Two of them pressed his face into the carpet while the third held his arms behind his back and snapped a pair of handcuffs on him. Out of the corner of his eye, he could just see a policewoman pinning a naked Beth against the wall, while another handcuffed her.

'She's done nothing!' he shouted as he broke away and began to charge towards them, but before he'd taken a second step, the full force of a baton landed on the back of his skull and he collapsed to the floor.

Two men leapt on top of him, one pressing a knee into the middle of his spine while the other sat on his legs. When Inspector Fuller walked into the room, they yanked Danny to his feet.

'Caution them,' Fuller said as he sat on the end of the bed and lit a cigarette.

Once the ritual had been completed, he stood up and strolled across to Danny.

'This time, Cartwright,' he said, their faces only inches apart, 'I'm going to make sure they throw away the key. And as for your girlfriend, no more Sunday afternoon visits, because she's going to be safely locked away in a prison of her own.'

'On what charge?' spat out Danny.

'Aiding and abetting should fit the bill. The usual tariff is about six years, if I remember correctly. Take them away.'

Danny and Beth were dragged downstairs like sacks of potatoes and out through the front door where three police cars, lights flashing, back doors open, awaited them. Bedroom lights all around the square were flicking on as neighbours whose sleep had been interrupted peered out of their windows to see what was going on at number 12.

Danny was thrown into the back of the middle car, to be sandwiched between two officers, just a towel covering him. He could see Big Al suffering the same treatment in the car in front of him. The cars drove out of the square in convoy, never breaking the speed limit, no sirens blaring. Inspector Fuller was pleased that the whole operation had taken less than ten minutes. His informer had proved reliable right down to the last detail.

Only one thought went through Danny's mind. Who would believe him when he told them that he'd had an appointment with his barrister later that morning when he had intended to give himself up before reporting to the nearest police station?

71

'YOU HAVEN'T ARRIVED a moment too soon,' she said.

'That bad?' said Alex.

'Worse,' replied his mother. 'When will the Home Office realize that when judges retire, not only are they sent home for the rest of their lives, but the only people they have left to judge are their innocent wives.'

'So what are you recommending?' asked Alex as they walked into the drawing room.

'That judges should be shot on their seventieth birthday, and their wives granted a royal pardon and given their pensions by a grateful nation.'

'I may have come up with a more acceptable solution,' suggested Alex.

'Like what? Making it legal to assist judges' wives to commit suicide?'

'Something a little less drastic,' said Alex. 'I don't know if his lordship has told you, but I sent him the details of a case I'm currently working on, and frankly I could do with his advice.'

'If he turns you down, Alex, I won't feed him again.'

'Then I must be in with a chance,' said Alex as his father strolled into the room.

'A chance of what?' the old man asked.

'A chance of some help on a case that—'

'The Cartwright case?' said his father, staring out of the window. Alex nodded. 'Yes, I've just finished reading the transcripts. As far as I can see, there aren't many more laws left for the lad to break: murder, escaping from prison, theft of fifty million dollars, cashing cheques on two bank accounts that didn't belong to him, selling a stamp collection he didn't own, travelling abroad on someone else's passport, and even claiming a baronetcy that should rightfully have been inherited by someone else. You really can't blame the police for throwing the book at him.'

'Does that mean you're not willing to help me?' asked Alex.

'I didn't say that,' said Mr Justice Redmayne, turning round to face his son. 'On the contrary. I'm at your service, because of one thing I'm absolutely certain. Danny Cartwright is innocent.'

BOOK FIVE

REDEMPTION

72

DANNY CARTWRIGHT sat on the small wooden chair in the dock and waited for the clock to strike ten so the trial could begin. He looked down into the well of the court to see his two counsel deep in conversation as they waited for the judge to appear.

Danny had spent an hour with Alex Redmayne and his junior in an interview room below the court earlier that morning. They had done their best to reassure him, but he knew all too well that although he was innocent of murdering Bernie, he had no defence to the charges of fraud, theft, deception and escaping from prison; a combined tariff of eight to ten years seemed to be the general consensus, from the barrack-room lawyers of Belmarsh to the eminent silks plying their trade at the Old Bailey.

No one needed to tell Danny that if the sentence was added to his original tariff, the next time he came out of Belmarsh would be for his own funeral.

The press benches to Danny's left were packed with reporters, notepads open, pens poised as they waited to add to the thousands of column inches they had already written over the past six months. The life story of Danny Cartwright, the only man ever to escape from Britain's top-security prison, who had stolen more than fifty million dollars from a Swiss Bank after selling a stamp collection that didn't belong to him, and had ended up being arrested in The Boltons in the early hours of the morning while in the arms of his fiancée (*The Times*), sexy childhood sweetheart (the *Sun*). The press couldn't make up their minds if Danny was the Scarlet Pimpernel or Jack the Ripper. The story had fascinated the public for months, and the first day of the trial was taking on the status of an opening night in the West End, with queues beginning to form outside the Old Bailey at 4 o'clock that morning for a theatre that seated less than a hundred and was rarely full. Most people agreed that Danny Cartwright was more likely to spend the rest of his days in Belmarsh than The Boltons.

—◁o▷—

Alex Redmayne and his junior, The Rt Hon Sir Matthew Redmayne KCMG QC, could not have done more to help Danny during the past six months, while he had been re-incarcerated in a cell little bigger than Molly's broom cupboard. They had both refused to charge a penny for their services, although Sir Matthew had warned Danny that if they were able to convince the jury that the profits he'd accrued during the past two years belonged to him and not to Hugo Moncrieff, he would be presenting a hefty bill plus expenses, for what he called refreshers. It was one of the few occasions during that time when all three of them had burst out laughing.

Beth had been released on bail the morning after she had been arrested. But no one had been surprised when neither Danny nor Big Al were granted the same latitude.

Mr Jenkins was waiting in reception at Belmarsh to greet them, and Mr Pascoe made sure that they ended up sharing a cell. Within a month Danny was back in his post as the prison librarian, just as he had told Ms Bennett he would be. Big Al was allocated a job in the kitchen, and although the cooking didn't compare to Molly's, at least they both ended up with the best of the worst.

Alex Redmayne never once reminded Danny that if he had taken his advice and pleaded guilty to manslaughter at the original trial, he would now be a free man, managing Wilson's garage, married to Beth and helping to raise their family. But a free man in what sense? Alex could hear him asking.

There had also been moments of triumph to sit alongside disaster. The gods prefer it that way. Alex Redmayne had been able to convince the court that although Beth was technically guilty of the offence she had been charged with, she had only been aware that Danny was still alive for four days, and they had already made an appointment to see Alex in his chambers on the morning she had been arrested. The judge had given Beth a six-month suspended sentence. Since then she had visited Danny at Belmarsh on the first Sunday of every month.

The judge had not taken quite as lenient a view when it came to the role Big Al had played in the conspiracy. Alex had pointed out in his opening speech that his client, Albert Crann, had made no financial gain from the Moncrieff fortune, other than to receive a salary as Danny's driver while being allowed to sleep in a small room on the top floor of his house in The Boltons. Mr Arnold Pearson QC, representing the Crown, then produced a bombshell that Alex hadn't seen coming.

'Can Mr Crann explain how the sum of ten thousand pounds was deposited in his private account only days after he'd been discharged from prison?'

Big Al had no explanation, and even if he had, he wasn't about to tell Pearson where the money had come from.

The jury were not impressed.

The judge sent Big Al back to Belmarsh to serve another five years – the rest of his original sentence. Danny made sure he quickly became enhanced, and that he behaved impeccably during his period of incarceration. Glowing reports from senior officer Ray Pascoe, confirmed by the governor, meant that Big Al would be released on a tag in less than a year. Danny would miss him, though he knew that if he even hinted as much, Big Al would cause just enough trouble to ensure that he remained at Belmarsh until Danny was finally released.

Beth had one good piece of news to tell Danny on her Sunday afternoon visit.

'I'm pregnant.'

'Christ, we only had four nights together,' said Danny as he took her in his arms.

'I don't think that was the number of times we made love,' said Beth, before adding, 'Let's hope it will be a brother for Christy.'

'If it is, we can call him Bernie.'

'No,' said Beth, 'we're going to call him—' The klaxon signalled the end of visits and drowned out her words.

'Can I ask you a question?' said Danny when Pascoe escorted him back to his cell.

'Of course,' Pascoe replied. 'Doesn't mean I'll answer it.'

'You always knew, didn't you?' Pascoe smiled, but didn't reply. 'What made you so sure that I wasn't Nick?' asked Danny as they reached his cell.

Pascoe turned the key in the lock and heaved open the heavy door. Danny walked in, assuming he wasn't going to answer his question, but then Pascoe nodded at the photograph of Beth that Danny had sellotaped back on to the wall.

'Oh my God,' said Danny, shaking his head. 'I never took her photo off the wall.'

Pascoe smiled, stepped back into the corridor and slammed the cell door shut.

◄○►

Danny looked up at the public gallery to see Beth, now six months pregnant, looking down at him with that same smile he remembered so well from their playground days at Clement Attlee comprehensive and which he knew would still be there until the end of his days, however long the judge decreed his sentence should run.

Danny's and Beth's mothers sat on either side of her, a constant support. Also seated in the gallery were many of Danny's friends and supporters from the East End who would go to their graves proclaiming his innocence. Danny's eyes settled on Professor Amirkhan Mori, a foul-weather friend, before moving on to someone seated at the end of the row, whom he hadn't expected to see again. Sarah Davenport leant over the balcony, and smiled down at him.

In the well of the court, Alex and his father were still deep in conversation. *The Times* had devoted a whole page to the father and son who would be appearing together as defence counsel in the case. It was only the second time in history that a high-court judge had returned to the role of barrister, and it was certainly the first occasion in anyone's memory that a son would lead his father.

Danny and Alex had renewed their friendship during the past six months, and he knew they would remain close for the rest of their lives. Alex's father came from the same growth as Professor Mori – a rare vintage. Both men were passionate: Professor Mori in the pursuit of learning, Sir Matthew in the pursuit of justice. The old judge's presence in the courtroom had made even practised lawyers and cynical journalists think more carefully about the case, but they remained puzzled as to what had convinced him that Danny Cartwright could possibly be innocent.

Mr Arnold Pearson QC and his junior were seated at the other end of the bench, checking over the opening for the Crown line by line and making the occasional small emendation. Danny was well prepared for the outburst of venom and bile that he was sure would come when Pearson rose from his place and told the court that not only was the defendant an evil and dangerous criminal, but that there was only one place the jury should consider despatching him for the rest of his life.

Alex Redmayne had told Danny that he only expected three witnesses to give evidence: Chief Inspector Fuller, Sir Hugo Moncrieff and Fraser Munro. But Alex and his father already had plans to ensure that a fourth witness would also be called. Alex had warned Danny that whichever judge was appointed to try the case would do everything in his power to prevent that happening.

It came as no surprise to Sir Matthew that Mr Justice Hackett had called both counsel to his chambers before proceedings began, to warn them to steer clear of any reference to the original murder trial, the verdict of which had been reached by a jury and later upheld by three judges at the court of appeal. He went on to stress that should either party attempt to place on record the contents of a particular tape as evidence, or mention the names of Spencer Craig, now an eminent QC, Gerald Payne, who had been elected to Parliament, or the well-known actor Lawrence Davenport, they could expect to face his wrath.

It was common knowledge in legal circles that Mr Justice Hackett and Sir Matthew Redmayne had not been on speaking terms for the past thirty years. Sir Matthew had won too many cases in the lower courts when they were both fledgling barristers for anyone to be left in much doubt which of them was the superior advocate. The press were hoping that their rivalry would be rekindled once the trial was under way.

The jury had been selected the previous day, and were now waiting to be called into court so that they could hear the evidence before passing a final verdict in the case of the Crown versus Daniel Arthur Cartwright.

73

MR JUSTICE HACKETT peered around the courtroom much as an opening batsman does when checking to see where the fielders have been placed to catch him out. His eyes rested on Sir Matthew Redmayne, who was at second slip, waiting for the opening ball. None of the other players caused the judge the slightest apprehension, but he knew that he wouldn't be able to relax if Sir Matthew was put on to bowl.

He turned his attention to the opening bowler for the home team, Mr Arnold Pearson QC not known for taking early wickets.

'Mr Pearson, are you ready to make your opening?'

'I am, m'lord,' replied Pearson, rising slowly from his place. He tugged on the lapels of his gown and touched the top of his ancient wig, then placed his file on a little raised stand and began to read the first page as if he had never seen it before.

'Members of the jury,' he began, beaming across at the twelve citizens who had been selected to pass judgement on this occasion. 'My name is Arnold Pearson, and I shall be leading for the Crown in this case. I will be assisted by my junior, Mr David Simms. The defence will be led by Mr Alex Redmayne, assisted by his junior, Sir Matthew Redmayne.' All eyes in the courtroom turned to look at the old man who was slouched on the corner of the bench, seemingly fast asleep.

'Members of the jury,' Pearson continued, 'the defendant is charged with five counts. The first is that he did wilfully escape from Belmarsh prison, a high-security establishment in south-east London, while in custody for a previous offence.

'The second count is that the defendant did steal from Sir Hugo Moncrieff an estate in Scotland, comprising a fourteen-bedroom mansion and twelve thousand acres of arable land.

'The third count is that he occupied a house, namely number twelve The Boltons, London SW3, which was not lawfully his.

'The fourth count relates to the theft of a unique stamp collection and the subsequent sale of that collection for the sum of over twenty-five million pounds.

'And the fifth count is that the defendant cashed cheques on a bank account at Coutts in the Strand, London, and transferred money from a private bank in Switzerland, neither of which he was entitled to do, and that he profited by so doing.

'The Crown will show that all five of these counts are inter-linked, and were committed by one person, the defendant, Daniel Cartwright, who falsely passed himself off as Sir Nicholas Moncrieff, the rightful and legal beneficiary of the late Sir Alexander Moncrieff's will. In order to prove this, members of the jury, I will first have to take you back to Belmarsh prison to show how the defendant was able to place himself in a position to commit these audacious crimes. To do that, it may be necessary for me to mention in passing the original offence of which Cartwright was convicted.'

'You will do no such thing,' interjected Mr Justice Hackett sternly. 'The original crime committed by the defendant has no bearing on the offences that are being tried in this court. You may not refer to that earlier case unless you can show a direct and relevant connection between it and this case.' Sir Matthew wrote down the words, *direct and relevant connection*. 'Do I make myself clear, Mr Pearson?'

'You most certainly do, my lord, and I apologize. It was remiss of me.'

Sir Matthew frowned. Alex would have to develop an ingenious argument to show that the two crimes were linked if he didn't want to arouse the wrath of Mr Justice Hackett and be stopped in full flow. Sir Matthew had already given the matter some considerable thought.

'I will tread more carefully in future,' Pearson added as he turned the next page of his file.

Alex wondered if Pearson had offered up this hostage at an early stage in the hope that Hackett would come down on him from a great height, as he knew only too well that the judge's ruling was far more helpful to the prosecution than to the defence.

'Members of the jury,' continued Pearson, 'I want you to keep in mind all five offences, as I am about to demonstrate how they are interwoven, and therefore could only have been committed by one person: the defendant, Daniel Cartwright.' Pearson tugged on his gown once again before proceeding. 'June seventh 2002 is a day that may well be etched on your memories, as it was the occasion on which England beat Argentina in the World Cup.' He was pleased to see how many members of the jury smiled in recollection. 'On that day, a tragedy took place at Belmarsh prison, which is the reason we are all here today. While the vast majority of the inmates were on the ground floor watching the football match on television, one prisoner chose that moment to take his own life. That man was Nicholas Moncrieff, who at approximately one fifteen that afternoon, hanged himself in the prison showers. During the previous two years, Nicholas Moncrieff had shared a cell with two other inmates, one of whom was the defendant, Daniel Cartwright.

'The two men were roughly the same height, and were only a few months apart in age. In fact, they were so similar in appearance that in prison uniform they were often mistaken for brothers. My lord, with your permission, I will at this juncture distribute, among the members of the jury, photographs of Moncrieff and Cartwright so that they may see for themselves the similarities between the two men.'

The judge nodded and the clerk of the court collected a bundle of photographs from Pearson's junior. He handed two up to the judge, before distributing the remainder among the jury. Pearson leant back and waited until he was satisfied that every member of the jury had been given time to consider the photographs. Once they had done so, he said, 'I shall now describe how Cartwright took advantage of this likeness, cutting his hair and changing his accent, to cash in on the tragic death of Nicholas Moncrieff. And cash in on it is literally what he did. However, as in all audacious crimes, a little luck was required.

'The first piece of luck was that Moncrieff asked Cartwright to take care of a silver chain and key, a signet ring bearing his family crest, and a watch inscribed with his initials that he wore at all times except when he took a shower. The second piece of luck was that Moncrieff had an accomplice who was in the right place at the right time.

'Now, members of the jury, you may well ask how it could be possible for Cartwright, who was serving a twenty-two-year sentence for—'

Alex was on his feet and about to protest when the judge said, 'Don't go any further down that road, Mr Pearson, unless you wish to try my patience.'

'I do apologize, my lord,' said Pearson, well aware that any member of the jury who hadn't followed the extensive press coverage of the case over the past six months would now be in little doubt what crime Cartwright had originally been sentenced for.

'As I was saying, you may wonder how Cartwright, who was serving a twenty-two-year sentence, was able to change identity with another prisoner who had only been sentenced to eight years, and who, more importantly, was due to be released in six weeks' time. Surely their DNA wouldn't match up, their blood groups were likely to be different, their dental records dissimilar. That's when the second piece of luck fell into place,' said Pearson, 'because none of this would have been possible if Cartwright hadn't had an accomplice who worked as an orderly in the prison hospital. That accomplice was Albert Crann, the third man who shared a cell with Moncrieff and Cartwright. When he heard about the hanging in the shower, he switched the names on the files in the hospital's medical records, so that when the doctor checked the body, he would remain under the illusion that it was Cartwright who had committed suicide, and not Moncrieff.

'A few days later the funeral took place at St Mary's church in

Bow, where even the defendant's closest family, including the mother of his child, were convinced that the body being lowered into the grave was that of Daniel Cartwright.

'What kind of man, you might ask, would be willing to deceive his own family? I'll tell you what kind of man. *This* man,' he said, pointing at Danny. 'He even had the nerve to turn up to the funeral posing as Nicholas Moncrieff so that he could witness his own burial and be certain he'd got away with it.'

Once again Pearson leant back so that the significance of his words could sink into the jury's minds. 'From the day of Moncrieff's death,' he continued, 'Cartwright always wore Moncrieff's watch, his signet ring and the silver chain and key, in order to deceive the prison staff and his fellow inmates into believing that he was in fact Nicholas Moncrieff, who only had six weeks of his sentence left to serve.'

'On July seventeenth 2002, Daniel Cartwright walked out of the front gate of Belmarsh prison a free man, despite having another twenty years of his sentence left to serve. Was it enough for him to have escaped? It was not. He immediately took the first train to Scotland so that he could lay claim to the Moncrieff family estate, and then returned to London to take up residence in Sir Nicholas Moncrieff's town house in The Boltons.

'But it didn't even end there, members of the jury. Cartwright then had the audacity to start drawing cash from Sir Nicholas Moncrieff's bank account at Coutts in The Strand. You might have felt that was enough, but no. He then flew to Geneva for an appointment with the chairman of Coubertin and Company, a leading Swiss bank, to whom he presented the silver key along with Moncrieff's passport. That gave him access to a vault which contained the fabled stamp collection of Nicholas Moncrieff's late grandfather, Sir Alexander Moncrieff. What did Cartwright do when he got his hands on this family heirloom that had taken Sir Alexander Moncrieff over seventy years to assemble? He sold it the following day to the first bidder who arrived on the scene, netting himself a cool twenty-five million pounds.'

Sir Matthew raised an eyebrow. How unlike Arnold Pearson to do cool.

'So now that Cartwright is a multimillionaire,' continued Pearson, 'you may well ask yourselves what he could possibly do next. I will tell you. He flew back to London, bought himself a top-of-the-range BMW, employed a chauffeur and a housekeeper, settled down in The Boltons and carried on the myth that he was Sir Nicholas Moncrieff. And, members of the jury, he would still be living that myth today if it were not for the sheer professionalism of Chief Inspector Fuller, the man who arrested Cartwright for his original offence in 1999, and who now single-handed' – Sir Matthew wrote down those words – 'tracked him down, arrested him and finally brought him to justice. That, members of the jury, is the case for the prosecution. But later I will produce a witness who will leave you in no doubt that the defendant, Daniel Cartwright, is guilty of all five charges on the indictment.'

As Pearson resumed his seat, Sir Matthew looked across at his old adversary and touched his forehead as if he was raising an invisible hat. 'Chapeau,' he said.

'Thank you, Matthew,' Pearson replied.

'Gentlemen,' said the judge, looking at his watch, 'I think this might be a suitable moment to break for lunch.'

'Court will rise,' shouted the usher, and all the officials immediately stood up and bowed low. Mr Justice Hackett returned their bow and left the courtroom.

'Not bad,' admitted Alex to his father.

'I agree, though dear old Arnold did make one mistake which he may live to regret.'

'And what was that?' asked Alex.

Sir Matthew passed his son the piece of paper on which he had written the word, *single-handed*.

74

'THERE'S ONLY one thing you have to get this witness to admit,' said Sir Matthew. 'But at the same time, we don't need the judge or Arnold Pearson to realize what you're up to.'

'No pressure,' said Alex with a grin as Mr Justice Hackett re-entered the courtroom and everyone rose.

The judge bowed low before resuming his place in the high-backed red leather chair. He opened his notebook to the end of his analysis of Pearson's opening, turned to a fresh page and wrote the words, *first witness*. He then nodded in the direction of Mr Pearson, who rose from his place and said, 'I call Chief Inspector Fuller.'

Alex hadn't seen Fuller since the first trial four years ago, and he was unlikely to forget that occasion, as the Chief Inspector had run circles around him. If anything, he looked even more confident than he had done then. Fuller took the oath without even glancing at the card.

'Detective Chief Inspector Fuller,' said Pearson, 'would you please begin by confirming your identity to the court.'

'My name is Rodney Fuller. I'm a serving officer with the Metropolitan Police stationed at Palace Green, Chelsea.'

'Can I also place on the record that you were the arresting officer when Daniel Cartwright committed his previous offence for which he received a prison sentence?'

'That is correct, sir.'

'How did you come to learn that Cartwright might possibly have escaped from Belmarsh prison and was passing himself off as Sir Nicholas Moncrieff?'

'On October twenty-third last year I received a telephone call from a reliable source who told me that he needed to see me on an urgent matter.'

'Did he go into any detail at that time?'

'No, sir. He's not the sort of gentleman who would commit himself over the telephone.'

Sir Matthew wrote down the word *gentleman*, not a word a policeman would normally use when referring to a snitch. His second catch in the slips on the opening morning. He wasn't expecting many of those while Arnold Pearson was on his feet bowling the Chief Inspector gentle off-breaks.

'So a meeting was arranged,' said Pearson.

'Yes, we agreed to meet the following day at a time and place of his choosing.'

'And when you met the next day he informed you that he had some information concerning Daniel Cartwright.'

'Yes. Which came as a bit of a surprise,' said Fuller, 'because I was under the misapprehension that Cartwright had hanged himself. Indeed, one of my officers attended his funeral.'

'So how did you respond to this revelation?'

'I took it seriously, because the gentleman had proved reliable in the past.'

Sir Matthew underlined the word *gentleman*.

'So what did you do next?'

'I placed a twenty-four-hour surveillance team on number twelve The Boltons, and quickly discovered that the resident who was claiming to be Sir Nicholas Moncrieff did bear a striking resemblance to Cartwright.'

'But surely that would not have been enough for you to move in and arrest him.'

'Certainly not,' replied the Chief Inspector. 'I needed more tangible proof than that.'

'And what form did this tangible proof take?'

'On the third day of surveillance, the suspect received a visit from a Miss Elizabeth Wilson, and she stayed the night.'

'Miss Elizabeth Wilson?'

'Yes. She is the mother of Cartwright's daughter, and she

visited him regularly while he was in prison. This made me confident that the information I had been given was accurate.'

'And that was when you decided to arrest him?'

'Yes, but as I knew we were dealing with a dangerous criminal who had a record of violence, I requested back-up from the riot squad. I was unwilling to take any risks when it came to the safety of the public.'

'Quite understandable,' purred Pearson. 'Would you describe to the court how you went about apprehending this violent criminal?'

'At two o'clock the following morning, we surrounded the house in The Boltons and carried out a raid. On apprehending Cartwright, I cautioned and arrested him for unlawfully escaping from one of Her Majesty's Prisons. I also charged Elizabeth Wilson with aiding and abetting a criminal. Another section of my team arrested Albert Crann, who was also living on the premises, as we had reason to believe he was an accomplice of Cartwright's.'

'And what has happened to the other two prisoners who were arrested at that time?' asked Pearson.

'Elizabeth Wilson was released on bail that morning, and was later given a six-month suspended jail sentence.'

'And Albert Crann?'

'He was on licence at the time, and was sent back to Belmarsh to complete his original sentence.'

'Thank you, chief inspector. I have no more questions for you at the present time.'

'Thank you, Mr Pearson,' said the judge. 'Do you wish to cross-examine this witness, Mr Redmayne?'

'I most certainly do, m'lord,' said Alex as he rose from his place.

'Chief inspector, you told the court that it was a member of the public who volunteered the information that made it possible for you to arrest Daniel Cartwright.'

'Yes, that is correct,' said Fuller, gripping the rail of the witness box.

'So it wasn't, as my learned friend suggested, a *single-handed* piece of police ingenuity?'

'No. But as I'm sure you appreciate, Mr Redmayne, the police rely on a network of informers, without whom half the criminals currently in jail would be on the streets committing even more crimes.'

'So this *gentleman*, as you described your informant, called you at your office?' The chief inspector nodded. 'And you arranged to meet him at a mutually convenient place the following day?'

'Yes,' replied Fuller, determined not to give anything away.

'Where did that meeting take place, chief inspector?'

Fuller turned to the judge. 'I would prefer, m'lord, not to have to identify the location.'

'Understandably,' said Mr Justice Hackett. 'Move on, Mr Redmayne.'

'So there would be no point in my asking you, chief inspector, to name your paid informant?'

'He wasn't paid,' said Fuller, regretting the words the moment he said them.

'Well, at least we now know that he was an unpaid professional gentleman.'

'Well done,' said Alex's father in a loud stage whisper. The judge frowned.

'Chief inspector, how many officers did you find it necessary to deploy in order to arrest one man and one woman who were in bed at two o'clock in the morning?' Fuller hesitated. 'How many, chief inspector?'

'Fourteen.'

'Wasn't it more like twenty?' said Alex.

'If you count the back-up team, it might have been twenty.'

'Sounds a little excessive for one man and one woman,' suggested Alex.

'He may have been armed,' said Fuller. 'That was a risk I wasn't willing to take.'

'Was he, in fact, armed?' asked Alex.

'No he was not . . .'

'Perhaps not for the first time—' began Alex.

'That's quite enough, Mr Redmayne,' said the judge, interrupting before he could finish the sentence.

'Good try,' said Alex's father, loud enough for everyone in the courtroom to hear.

'Do you wish to make a contribution, Sir Matthew?' snapped the judge.

Alex's father opened his eyes like a jungle beast that had been woken from a deep sleep. He rose slowly from his place and said, 'How kind of you to ask, my lord. But no, not at this juncture. Possibly later.' He slumped back in his place.

The press benches were suddenly jolted into action as the first boundary was scored. Alex pursed his lips for fear he would burst out laughing. Mr Justice Hackett could barely restrain himself.

'Get on with it, Redmayne,' said the judge, but before Alex could respond, his father was back on his feet. 'I do apologize, m'lord,' he said sweetly, 'but which Redmayne did you have in mind?'

This time the jury burst out laughing. The judge made no attempt to reply, and Sir Matthew sank back in his seat, closed his eyes and whispered, 'Go for the jugular, Alex.'

'Chief inspector, you told the court that it was after you had seen Miss Wilson enter the house that you became convinced that it was Daniel Cartwright and not Sir Nicholas Moncrieff who was living there.'

'Yes, that's correct,' said Fuller, still gripping the side of the witness box.

'But once you had taken my client into custody, chief inspector, didn't you have a moment's anxiety about whether you might have arrested the wrong man?'

'No, Mr Redmayne, not after I'd seen the scar on his . . .'

'Not after you'd seen the scar on his—'

' – checked his DNA on the police computer,' said the chief inspector.

'Sit down,' whispered Alex's father. 'You've got everything you need, and Hackett won't have worked out the significance of the scar.'

'Thank you, chief inspector. No more questions, m'lord.'

'Do you wish to re-examine this witness, Mr Pearson?' asked Mr Justice Hackett.

'No, thank you, m'lord,' said Pearson, who was writing down the words *not after I'd seen the scar on his* ... and trying to work out their significance.

'Thank you, chief inspector,' said the judge. 'You may leave the witness box.'

Alex leant over to his father as the chief inspector made his way out of the courtroom and whispered, 'But I didn't get him to admit that the "professional gentleman" was in fact Craig.'

'That man was never going to name his contact, but you still managed to trap him twice. And don't forget, there's another witness who must also know who reported Danny to the police, and he's certainly not going to feel at home in a courtroom, so you should be able to corner him long before Hackett works out what your real purpose is. Never forget we can't afford to make the same mistake as we did with Lord Justice Browne and the unplayed tape.'

Alex nodded as Mr Justice Hackett turned his attention to counsel's bench. 'Perhaps this would be a good time to take a break.'

'All rise.'

75

ARNOLD PEARSON was deep in conversation with his junior when Mr Justice Hackett said in a loud voice, 'Are you ready to call your next witness, Mr Pearson?'

Pearson rose from his place. 'Yes, m'lord. I call Sir Hugo Moncrieff.'

Alex watched Sir Hugo carefully as he entered the courtroom. Never prejudge a witness, his father had taught him from the cradle, but Hugo was clearly nervous. He took a handkerchief out of his top pocket and mopped his brow even before he had reached the witness box.

The usher guided Sir Hugo into the box and handed him a Bible. The witness read the oath from the card that was held up in front of him, then looked up towards the gallery, searching for the person he wished was giving evidence in his place. Mr Pearson gave him a warm smile when he looked back down.

'Sir Hugo, would you just for the record state your name and address?'

'Sir Hugo Moncrieff, the Manor House, Dunbroath in Scotland.'

'Let me begin, Sir Hugo, by asking you when you last saw your nephew, Nicholas Moncrieff.'

'On the day we both attended his father's funeral.'

'And did you have an opportunity to speak to him on that sad occasion?'

'Unhappily not,' said Hugo. 'He was accompanied by two prison officers who said that we were not to have any contact with him.'

'What sort of relationship did you have with your nephew?' asked Pearson.

'Cordial. We all loved Nick. He was a fine lad, whom the family considered had been badly treated.'

'So there was no ill feeling when you and your brother learned that he had inherited the bulk of the estate from your father.'

'Certainly not,' said Hugo. 'Nick would automatically inherit the title on his father's death, and along with it the family estate.'

'So it must have come as a terrible shock to discover that he had hanged himself in prison, and that an impostor had taken his place.'

Hugo lowered his head for a moment, before saying, 'It was a massive blow for my wife Margaret and myself, but thanks to the professionalism of the police and the rallying round of friends and family, we are slowly trying to come to terms with it.'

'Word-perfect,' whispered Sir Matthew.

'Can you confirm, Sir Hugo, that the Garter King of Arms has established your right to the family title?' asked Mr Pearson, ignoring Sir Matthew's comment.

'Yes, I can, Mr Pearson. The letters patent were sent to me some weeks ago.'

'Can you also confirm that the estate in Scotland, along with the house in London and the bank accounts in London and Switzerland are once again in the custody of the family?'

'I'm afraid I cannot, Mr Pearson.'

'And why is that?' asked Mr Justice Hackett.

Sir Hugo appeared a little flustered as he turned towards the judge. 'It's the policy of both banks concerned not to confirm ownership while a court case is still in progress, m'lord. They have assured me that legal transfer will take place to the rightful party as soon as this case is concluded, and the jury have delivered their verdict.'

'Fear not,' said the judge, giving him a warm smile. 'Your long ordeal is coming to an end.'

Sir Matthew was on his feet instantly. 'I apologize for interrupting your lordship, but does your response to this witness imply that you have already come to a decision in this case?' he asked with a warm smile.

It was the judge's turn to look flustered. 'No, of course not, Sir Matthew,' he replied. 'I was merely stating that whatever the outcome of this trial, Sir Hugo's long wait is finally coming to an end.'

'I am obliged, my lord. It comes as a great relief to discover that you have not made up your mind before the defence has been given a chance to present its case.' He settled back in his place.

Pearson glowered at Sir Matthew, but the old man's eyes were already closed. Turning back to the witness, he said, 'I am sorry, Sir Hugo, that you have had to be put through such an unpleasant ordeal, which is not of your own making. But it has been important for the jury to see what havoc and distress the defendant Daniel Cartwright has brought down on your family. As his lordship has made clear, that ordeal is finally coming to an end.'

'I wouldn't be so sure of that,' said Sir Matthew.

Pearson once again ignored the interruption. 'No more questions, my lord,' he said, before resuming his place.

'Every word of that was rehearsed,' whispered Sir Matthew, his eyes still closed. 'Lead the damn man down a long, dark path and when he least expects it, plunge a knife into his heart. I can promise you, Alex, no blood will flow, blue or red.'

'Mr Redmayne, I apologize for interrupting you,' said the judge, 'but is it your intention to cross-examine this witness?'

'Yes, m'lord.'

'Pace yourself, my boy. Don't forget that he's the one who wants to get it over with,' whispered Sir Matthew as he slumped back into his place.

'Sir Hugo,' Alex began, 'you told the court that your relationship with your nephew, Nicholas Moncrieff, was a close one – *cordial* was the word I think you used to describe it – and that you would have spoken to him at his father's funeral had the prison officers not prevented it.'

'Yes, that is correct,' said Hugo.

'Let me ask you, when was it that you first discovered that your nephew was in fact dead, and not living, as you had believed, in his home in The Boltons?'

'A few days before Cartwright was arrested,' said Hugo.

'That would have been about a year and a half after the funeral at which you were not allowed any contact with your nephew?'

'Yes, I suppose so.'

'In that case, I am bound to ask, Sir Hugo, how many times during that eighteen-month period did you and your nephew, whom you were so close to, meet up or speak on the phone?'

'But that's the point, it wasn't Nick,' said Hugo, looking pleased with himself.

'No, it wasn't,' agreed Alex. 'But you have just told the court that you didn't become aware of that fact until three days before my client was arrested.'

Hugo looked up to the gallery, hoping for inspiration. This wasn't one of the questions Margaret had anticipated and told him how to answer. 'Well, we both lead busy lives,' he said, trying to think on his feet. 'He was living in London, while I spend most of my time in Scotland.'

'I understand that they now have telephones in Scotland,' said Alex. A ripple of laughter went around the court.

'It was a Scot who invented the telephone, sir,' said Hugo sarcastically.

'All the more reason to pick one up,' suggested Alex.

'What are you implying?' asked Hugo.

'I'm not implying anything,' replied Alex. 'But can you deny that when you both attended a stamp auction at Sotheby's in London in September 2002 and spent the next few days in Geneva at the same hotel as the man you believed to be your nephew, you made no attempt to speak to him?'

'He could have spoken to me,' said Hugo, his voice rising. 'It's a two-way street, you know.'

'Perhaps my client didn't want to speak to you, as he knew only too well what sort of relationship you had with your nephew. Perhaps he knew that you had not written or spoken to him once during the past ten years. Perhaps he knew that your nephew loathed you, and that your own father – his grandfather – had cut you out of his will?'

'I see that you are determined to take the word of a criminal before that of a member of the family.'

'No, Sir Hugo. I learned all of this from a member of the family.'

'Who?' demanded Hugo defiantly.

'Your nephew, Sir Nicholas Moncrieff,' replied Alex.

'But you didn't even know him.'

'No, I didn't,' admitted Alex. 'But while he was in prison, where you never once in four years visited or wrote to him, he kept a daily diary, which has proved most revealing.'

Pearson leapt up. 'M'lord, I must protest. These diaries to which my learned friend refers were only placed in the jury bundle a week ago, and although my junior has struggled manfully to go through them line by line, they consist of over a thousand pages.'

'My lord,' said Alex, '*my* junior has read every word of those diaries, and for the convenience of the court he has highlighted any passages we might later wish to bring to the attention of the jury. There can be no doubt that they are admissible.'

'They may well be admissible,' said Mr Justice Hackett, 'but I do not consider them to be at all relevant. It is not Sir Hugo who is on trial, and his relationship with his nephew is not at the heart of this case, so I suggest you move on, Mr Redmayne.'

Sir Matthew tugged his son's gown. 'May I have a word with my junior?' Alex asked the judge.

'If you must,' replied Mr Justice Hackett, still smarting from his last encounter with Sir Matthew. 'But make it quick.'

Alex sat down. 'You've made your point, my boy,' whispered Sir Matthew, 'and in any case, the most significant line in the diaries ought to be saved for the next witness. Added to that, old man Hackett is wondering if he's gone too far and given us enough ammunition to apply for a retrial. He'll want to avoid allowing us that opportunity at all costs. This will be his last appearance in the High Court before he retires, and he wouldn't want a retrial to be the one thing he's remembered for. So when you resume, say that you accept his lordship's judgement without question, but that as you may need to refer to certain passages in the diary on some later occasion, you hope that your learned friend will find time to consider the few entries that your junior has marked for his convenience.'

Alex rose from his place and said, 'I accept your lordship's judgement without question, but as I may need to refer to certain passages in the diary at a later date, I can only hope that my learned friend will find enough time to read the few lines that have been marked up for his consideration.' Sir Matthew smiled. The judge frowned, and Sir Hugo looked mystified.

Alex turned his attention back to the witness, who was now mopping his brow every few moments.

'Sir Hugo, can I confirm that it was your father's wish, as clearly stated in his will, that the estate in Dunbroath should be handed over to the National Trust for Scotland, with a sufficient sum of money to be put aside for its upkeep.'

'That was my understanding,' admitted Hugo.

'Then can you also confirm that Daniel Cartwright abided by those wishes, and that the estate is now in the hands of the National Trust for Scotland?'

'Yes, I am able to confirm that,' replied Hugo, somewhat reluctantly.

'Have you recently found time to visit number twelve The Boltons and see what condition the property is in?'

'Yes I have. I couldn't see a great deal of difference from how it was before.'

'Sir Hugo, would you like me to call Mr Cartwright's house-keeper in order that she can tell the court in graphic detail what state she found the house in when she was first employed?'

'That won't be necessary,' said Hugo. 'It may well have been somewhat neglected, but as I have already made clear, I spend most of my time in Scotland, and rarely visit London.'

'That being the case, Sir Hugo, let us move on to your nephew's account at Coutts bank in the Strand. Are you able to tell the court how much money was in that account at the time of his tragic death?'

'How could I possibly know that?' Hugo replied sharply.

'Then allow me to enlighten you, Sir Hugo,' said Alex, extracting a bank statement from a folder. 'Just over seven thousand pounds.'

'But surely what matters is how much there is in that account at the present time?' retorted Sir Hugo triumphantly.

'I couldn't agree with you more,' said Alex, taking out a second bank statement. 'At close of business yesterday, the account stood at a little over forty-two thousand pounds.' Hugo kept glancing up at the public gallery as he mopped his brow. 'Next, we should consider the stamp collection that your father, Sir Alexander, left to his grandson, Nicholas.'

'Cartwright sold it behind my back.'

'I would suggest, Sir Hugo, that he sold it right in front of your nose.'

'I would never have agreed to part with something that the family has always regarded as a priceless heirloom.'

'I wonder if you would like a little time to reconsider that statement,' said Alex. 'I am in possession of a legal document drawn up by your solicitor, Mr Desmond Galbraith, agreeing to sell your father's stamp collection for fifty million dollars to a Mr Gene Hunsacker of Austin, Texas.'

'Even if that were true,' said Hugo, 'I never saw a penny of it, because it was Cartwright who ended up selling the collection to Hunsacker.'

'He did indeed,' said Alex, 'for a sum of fifty-seven and a half million dollars – seven and a half million more than you managed to negotiate.'

'Where is all this leading, Mr Redmayne?' asked the judge. 'However well your client has husbanded the Moncrieff legacy, it was still he who stole everything in the first place. Are you trying to suggest that it was always his intention to return the estate to its rightful owners?'

'No, my lord. However, I am attempting to demonstrate that perhaps Danny Cartwright is not quite the evil villain that the prosecution would have us believe. Indeed, thanks to his stewardship, Sir Hugo will be far better off than he could have expected to be.'

Sir Matthew offered up a silent prayer.

'That's not true!' said Sir Hugo. 'I'll be worse off.'

Sir Matthew's eyes opened and he sat bolt upright. 'There is a God in Heaven after all,' he whispered. 'Well done, my boy.'

'I am now completely at a loss,' said Mr Justice Hackett. 'If there is over seven and a half million dollars more in the bank account than you had anticipated, Sir Hugo, how can you possibly be worse off?'

'Because I recently signed a legal contract with a third party who was unwilling to reveal the details of what had happened to my nephew unless I agreed to part with twenty-five per cent of my inheritance.'

'Sit back, say nothing,' murmured Sir Matthew.

The judge called loudly for order, and Alex didn't ask his next question until silence had been restored.

'When did you sign this agreement, Sir Hugo?'

Hugo removed a small diary from an inside pocket, and flicked over the pages until he came to the entry he was looking for. 'October twenty-second last year,' he said.

Alex checked his notes. 'The day before a certain professional gentleman contacted Chief Inspector Fuller to arrange a meeting at an unknown location.'

'I have no idea what you're talking about,' said Hugo.

'Of course you don't,' said Alex. 'You had no way of knowing what was going on behind your back. But I am bound to ask, Sir Hugo, once you had signed the legal contract agreeing to part with millions of pounds should your family fortune be restored, what this professional gentleman could possibly be offering you in exchange for your signature.'

'He told me that my nephew had been dead for over a year, and that his place had been usurped by that man sitting in the dock.'

'And what was your reaction to this incredible piece of news?'

'I didn't believe it to begin with,' said Hugo, 'but then he showed me several photographs of Cartwright and Nick, and I had to admit they did look alike.'

'I find it hard to believe, Sir Hugo, that that was enough proof for a shrewd man like yourself to agree to part with twenty-five per cent of his family fortune.'

'No, it wasn't enough. He also supplied me with several other photographs to back up his claim.'

'Several other photographs?' prompted Alex hopefully.

'Yes. One of them was of the defendant's left leg, showing a scar above his knee that proved he was Cartwright, and not my nephew.'

'Change the subject,' whispered Sir Matthew.

'You have told the court, Sir Hugo, that the person who demanded twenty-five per cent of what was rightfully yours in exchange for this piece of information was a professional gentleman.'

'Yes, he most certainly was,' said Hugo.

'Perhaps the time has come, Sir Hugo, for you to name this professional gentleman.'

'I can't do that,' said Hugo.

Once again, Alex had to wait for the judge to bring the court to order before he was able to ask his next question. 'Why not?' demanded the judge.

'Let Hackett run with it,' whispered Sir Matthew. 'Just pray he doesn't work out for himself who the professional gentleman is.'

'Because one of the clauses in the agreement,' said Hugo, mopping his brow, 'was that under no circumstances would I reveal his name.'

Mr Justice Hackett placed his pen down on the desk. 'Now listen to me, Sir Hugo, and listen carefully. If you don't want a contempt-of-court order brought against you, and a night in a cell to help jog your memory, I suggest that you answer Mr Redmayne's question, and tell the court the name of this professional gentleman who demanded twenty-five per cent of your estate before he was willing to expose the defendant as a fraud. Do I make myself clear?'

Hugo began to shake uncontrollably. He peered up into the gallery, to see Margaret nodding. He turned back to the judge and said, 'Mr Spencer Craig QC.'

Everyone in the courtroom began speaking at once.

'You can sit down, my boy,' said Sir Matthew, 'because I think that's what they call in Danny's neck of the woods, a double whammy. Now our esteemed judge has no choice but to allow you to subpoena Spencer Craig, unless of course he wants a retrial.'

Sir Matthew glanced across to see Arnold Pearson looking up at his son. He was doffing an imaginary hat.

'Chapeau, Alex,' he said.

76

'HOW DO YOU IMAGINE Munro will cope when he comes up against Pearson?' asked Alex.

'An ageing bull against an ageing matador,' Sir Matthew replied. 'Experience and sheer cunning will prove more important than the charge, so I'd have to bet on Munro.'

'So when do I show the red rag to this bull?'

'You don't,' said Sir Matthew. 'You leave that pleasure to the matador. Pearson won't be able to resist the challenge, and it will make far more of an impact coming from the prosecution.'

'All rise,' announced the court usher.

Once they had all settled back in their places, the judge addressed the jury. 'Good morning, members of the jury. Yesterday you heard Mr Pearson complete the case for the prosecution, and now the defence will be given the opportunity to put its side of the argument. After a consultation with both sides, I shall be inviting you to dismiss one of the charges, namely that the defendant attempted to steal the Moncrieff family estate in Scotland. Sir Hugo Moncrieff confirmed that this was not the case, and that in accordance with his father Sir Alexander's wishes, the estate has been taken over by the National Trust for Scotland. However, the defendant still faces four other serious charges, on which you and you alone have been given the responsibility of making a judgement.'

He smiled benignly at the jury before turning his attention to Alex. 'Mr Redmayne, please call your first witness,' he said in a far more respectful tone than he had adopted the previous day.

'Thank you, m'lord,' said Alex, rising from his place. 'I call Mr Fraser Munro.'

The first thing Munro did when he entered the courtroom was to smile at Danny in the dock. He had visited him at Belmarsh on five occasions during the past six months, and Danny knew that he had also attended several consultations with Alex and Sir Matthew.

Once again no bills for services rendered had been presented. All Danny's bank accounts had been frozen, so all he had was the twelve pounds a week he was paid as the prison librarian, which wouldn't have covered Munro's taxi fare from the Caledonian Club to the Old Bailey.

Fraser Munro stepped into the witness box. He was dressed in a black tailcoat and pinstripe trousers, a white shirt with a wing collar and a black silk tie. He looked more like one of the court officials than a witness, lending him an authority that had influenced many a Scottish jury. He gave the judge a slight bow before delivering the oath.

'Would you please state your name and address for the record,' said Alex.

'My name is Fraser Munro and I live at number 49 Argyll Street, Dunbroath in Scotland.'

'And your occupation?'

'I am a solicitor of the High Court of Scotland.'

'Can I confirm that you are a past president of the Scottish Law Society?'

'I am, sir.' That was something Danny didn't know.

'And you are a freeman of the City of Edinburgh?'

'I have that honour, sir.' Something else Danny didn't know.

'Would you please explain to the court, Mr Munro, what your relationship is with the accused?'

'Certainly, Mr Redmayne. I had the privilege, as my father did before me, of representing Sir Alexander Moncrieff, the first holder of the baronetcy.'

'Did you also represent Sir Nicholas Moncrieff?'

'I did, sir.'

'And did you conduct his legal affairs while he was in the army, and later when he was in prison?'

'Yes. He would telephone me from time to time while he was in prison, but the bulk of our work was conducted by lengthy correspondence.'

'And did you visit Sir Nicholas while he was in prison?'

'No, I did not. Sir Nicholas explicitly requested me not to do so, and I adhered to his wishes.'

'When did you first meet him?' asked Alex.

'I knew him as a child when he was growing up in Scotland, but before the occasion when he returned to Dunbroath to attend his father's funeral, I had not seen him for twelve years.'

'Were you able to speak to him on that occasion?'

'Most certainly. The two prison officers who were in attendance could not have been more considerate, and they allowed me to spend an hour with Sir Nicholas in private consultation.'

'And the next time you met him was seven or eight weeks later, when he came to Scotland just after he had been released from Belmarsh prison.'

'That is correct.'

'Did you have any reason to believe that the person who visited you on that occasion was not Sir Nicholas Moncrieff?'

'No, sir. I had only seen him for one hour during the past twelve years, and the man who walked into my office not only looked like Sir Nicholas, but was wearing the same clothes as he had done on the previous occasion we'd met. He was also in possession of all the correspondence that had taken place between us over the years, and was wearing a gold ring bearing the family coat of arms as well as a silver chain and key that his grandfather had shown me some years before.'

'So he was, in every sense, Sir Nicholas Moncrieff?'

'To the naked eye, yes, sir.'

'Looking back over that time with the benefit of hindsight, did you ever suspect that the man you believed to be Sir Nicholas Moncrieff was in fact an impostor?'

'No. In all matters he conducted himself with courtesy and

charm, rare in such a young man. In truth he reminded me more of his grandfather than any other member of the family.'

'How did you eventually discover that your client was not in fact Sir Nicholas Moncrieff, but Danny Cartwright?'

'After he'd been arrested and charged with the offences that are the subject of this current trial.'

'Can I confirm for the record, Mr Munro, that since that day, the responsibility for the Moncrieff estate has returned to your stewardship?'

'That is correct, Mr Redmayne. However, I must confess that I have not conducted the day-to-day business with the flair that Danny Cartwright always displayed.'

'Would it be right to say that the estate is in a stronger financial position now than it has been for some years?'

'Without question. However, the trust has not managed to maintain the same growth since Mr Cartwright was sent back to prison.'

'I do hope,' interrupted the judge, 'that you are not suggesting, Mr Munro, that that diminishes the severity of these charges?'

'No, my lord, I am not,' said Munro. 'But I have discovered with advancing years that few things are entirely black or white, but more often different shades of grey. I can best sum it up, my lord, by saying that it was an honour to have served Sir Nicholas Moncrieff and it has been a privilege to work with Mr Cartwright. They are both oaks, even if they were planted in different forests. But then, m'lord, we all suffer in our different ways from being prisoners of birth.'

Sir Matthew opened both his eyes and stared at a man he wished he'd known for many years.

'The jury cannot have failed to notice, Mr Munro,' continued Alex, 'that you retain the greatest respect and admiration for Mr Cartwright. But with that in mind, they may find it hard to understand how the same man became involved in such a nefarious deception.'

'I have considered that question endlessly for the past six months, Mr Redmayne, and have come to the conclusion that his sole purpose must have been to fight a far bigger injustice that had—'

'Mr Munro,' interrupted the judge sternly, 'as you well know, this is neither the time nor the place to express your personal opinions.'

'I am grateful, my lord, for your guidance,' said Munro, turning to face the judge, 'but I took an oath to tell the whole truth, and I presume you would not wish me to do otherwise?'

'No, I would not, sir,' snapped the judge, 'but I repeat, this is not the appropriate place to express such views.'

'My lord, if a man cannot express his honestly held views in the Central Criminal Court, perhaps you can advise me where else he is free to state that which he believes to be the truth?'

A ripple of applause ran around the public gallery.

'I think the time has come to move on, Mr Redmayne,' said Mr Justice Hackett.

'I have no more questions for this witness, my lord,' said Alex. The judge looked relieved.

As Alex resumed his seat, Sir Matthew leant across and whispered, 'I actually feel a little sorry for dear Arnold. He must be torn between taking on this giant at the risk of being humiliated, or avoiding him altogether and leaving the jury with an impression that they will regale their grandchildren with.'

Mr Munro didn't flinch as he stared resolutely at Pearson, who was deep in conversation with his junior, both of them looking equally perplexed.

'I don't wish to hurry you, Mr Pearson,' said the judge, 'but is it your intention to cross-examine this witness?'

Pearson rose even more slowly than usual, and did not tug the lapels of his gown or touch his wig. He glanced down at the list of questions he had forfeited his weekend to prepare, and changed his mind.

'Yes, my lord, but I will not be detaining the witness for long.'

'Just long enough, I hope,' murmured Sir Matthew.

Pearson ignored the remark, and said, 'I am at pains to understand, Mr Munro, how a man as shrewd and experienced in legal matters as yourself could not have suspected even for a moment that his client was an impostor.'

Munro tapped his fingers on the side of the witness box, and waited for as long as he felt he could get away with. 'That's easy to explain, Mr Pearson,' he eventually said. 'Danny Cartwright was at all times utterly plausible, though I confess that there was a single moment in our two-year-long relationship when he lowered his guard.'

'And when was that?' Pearson asked.

'When we were discussing his grandfather's stamp collection and I had cause to remind him that he had attended the opening of an exhibition of that collection at the Smithsonian Institution in Washington DC. I was surprised that he did not appear to recollect the occasion, which I found puzzling, as he was the only member of the Moncrieff family who had received an invitation.'

'Did you not question him on the subject?' demanded Pearson.

'No,' said Munro. 'I felt that it would not have been appropriate at the time.'

'But if you suspected, even for a moment, that this man was not Sir Nicholas,' Pearson said, pointing a finger at Danny but not looking in his direction, 'surely it was your responsibility to pursue the matter?'

'I did not feel so at the time.'

'But this man was perpetuating a massive fraud on the Moncrieff family, which you had made yourself a party to.'

'I didn't see it that way,' responded Munro.

'But as you were the custodian of the Moncrieff estate, surely it was your duty to expose Cartwright for the fraud he was.'

'No, I didn't consider that to be my duty,' said Munro calmly.

'Did it not alarm you, Mr Munro, that this man had taken up residence at the Moncrieffs' London town house when he had no right to do so?'

'No, it did not alarm me,' replied Munro.

'Were you not appalled by the thought that this outsider now had control of the Moncrieff fortune which you had guarded so jealously on behalf of the family for so many years?'

'No, sir, I was not appalled by that thought.'

'But later, when your client was arrested on charges including fraud and theft, did you not feel that you had been negligent in the pursuance of your duty?' demanded Pearson.

'I do not require you to advise me whether I have or have not been negligent in my duty, Mr Pearson.'

Sir Matthew opened one eye. The judge kept his head down.

'But this man had stolen the family silver, to quote another Scot, and you had done nothing to prevent it,' said Pearson, his voice rising with every word.

'No, sir, he had not stolen the family silver and I feel confident that Harold Macmillan would have agreed with me on this occasion. The only thing Danny Cartwright had stolen, Mr Pearson, was the family name.'

'You can no doubt explain to the court,' said the judge, having sufficiently recovered from Mr Munro's previous onslaught, 'the moral dilemma I am facing with your hypothesis.'

Mr Munro turned to face the judge, aware that he had captured the attention of everyone in the court, including the policeman on the door. 'Your lordship need not trouble himself with any moral dilemma, because I was interested only in the legal niceties of the case.'

'The legal niceties?' said Mr Justice Hackett, treading carefully.

'Yes, m'lord. Mr Danny Cartwright was the sole heir to the Moncrieff fortune, so I was unable to work out what law, if any, he was breaking.'

The judge leant back, happy to allow Pearson to be the one who sank deeper and deeper into the Munro mire.

'Can you explain to the court, Mr Munro,' asked Pearson in a whisper, 'just what you mean by that?'

'It's quite simple really, Mr Pearson. The late Sir Nicholas Moncrieff made a will in which he left everything to Daniel Arthur Cartwright of twenty-six Bacon Road, London E3, with the sole exception of an annuity of ten thousand pounds, which he bequeathed to his former driver, a Mr Albert Crann.'

Sir Matthew opened his other eye, not sure whether to focus on Munro or Pearson.

'And this will was properly executed and witnessed?' asked Pearson, desperately searching for a possible escape route.

'It was signed by Sir Nicholas in my office on the afternoon of his father's funeral. Aware of the gravity of the situation and my responsibility as the legal custodian of the family estate – as you have been so keen to point out, Mr Pearson – I asked Senior Officer Ray Pascoe and Senior Officer Alan Jenkins to witness Sir Nicholas's signature in the presence of another partner of the firm.' Munro turned to the judge. 'I am in possession of the original document, m'lord, should you wish to study it.'

'No, thank you, Mr Munro. I am quite happy to take your word,' the judge replied.

Pearson collapsed on to the bench, quite forgetting to say, 'No more questions, my lord.'

'Do you wish to re-examine this witness, Mr Redmayne?' the judge enquired.

'Just one question, my lord,' said Alex. 'Mr Munro, did Sir Nicholas Moncrieff leave anything to his uncle, Hugo Moncrieff?'

'No,' said Munro. 'Not a brass farthing.'

'No more questions, m'lord.'

An outbreak of hushed whispers filled the courtroom as Munro stepped out of the witness box, walked across to the dock and shook hands with the defendant.

'My lord, I wonder if I might address you on a point of law,' enquired Alex as Munro departed from the courtroom.

'Of course, Mr Redmayne, but first I will have to release the jury. Members of the jury, as you have just heard, defence counsel has asked to discuss a point of law with me. It may not have any bearing on the case, but should it do so, I will fully brief you on your return.'

Alex looked up at the packed public gallery as the jury left. His gaze settled on an attractive young woman whom he had noticed sitting at one end of the front row every day since the trial had begun. He had meant to ask Danny who she was.

A few moments later the usher approached the bench and said, 'The court has been cleared, m'lord.'

'Thank you, Mr Hepple,' said the judge. 'How can I assist you, Mr Redmayne?'

'My lord, following the evidence given by the estimable Mr Munro, the defence would suggest that there is no case to answer on counts three, four and five, namely the occupation of the house in The Boltons, benefiting from the sale of the stamp collection, and the issuing of cheques on the Coutts bank account. We would ask that all these counts be dismissed, as it is self-evidently quite difficult to steal that which already belongs to you.'

The judge took a few minutes to consider the argument before replying, 'You make a fair point, Mr Redmayne. What is your view, Mr Pearson?'

'I feel I should point out, m'lord,' said Pearson, 'that although it may well be the case that the defendant was the beneficiary of Sir Nicholas Moncrieff's will, there is nothing to suggest that he was aware of this at the time.'

'My lord,' countered Alex immediately, 'my client was well aware of the existence of Sir Nicholas's will, and of who the beneficiaries were.'

'How is that possible, Mr Redmayne?' asked the judge.

'While he was in prison, m'lord, as I pointed out on a previous occasion, Sir Nicholas kept a daily diary. He recorded the details of his will on the day after he returned to Belmarsh following his father's funeral.'

'But that doesn't prove that Cartwright was privy to his thoughts,' pointed out the judge.

'I would agree with you, m'lord, were it not for the fact that it was the defendant himself who pointed out the relevant passage for my junior's consideration.' Sir Matthew nodded.

'That being the case,' said Pearson, coming to the judge's rescue, 'the Crown has no objection to these charges being withdrawn from the list.'

'I am grateful for your intervention, Mr Pearson,' said the judge, 'and agree that it would appear to be the proper solution. I will so inform the jury when they return.'

'Thank you, m'lord,' said Alex. 'I am obliged to Mr Pearson for his assistance in this matter.'

'However,' said the judge, 'I'm sure you don't need reminding, Mr Redmayne, that the most serious offence, that of escaping from prison while in custody, remains on the indictment.'

'I am indeed aware of that, m'lord,' said Alex.

The judge nodded. 'Then I shall ask the usher to bring back the jury so I can inform them of this development.'

'There is a related matter, my lord.'

'Yes, Mr Redmayne?' said the judge, putting down his pen.

'My lord, following Sir Hugo Moncrieff's evidence, we have subpoenaed Mr Spencer Craig QC to appear before you as a witness. He has asked for your lordship's indulgence as he is currently leading in a case taking place in another part of this building, and will not be free to appear before your lordship until tomorrow morning.'

Several members of the press rushed out of the courtroom to phone their news desks.

'Mr Pearson?' said the judge.

'We have no objection, m'lord.'

'Thank you. When the jury returns, after I have directed them on these two matters, I shall release them for the rest of the day.'

'As you wish, my lord,' said Alex, 'but before you do so, may I alert you to a slight change in tomorrow's proceedings?' Mr Justice Hackett put his pen down a second time, and nodded.

'My lord, you will be aware that it is a recognized tradition of the English Bar to allow one's junior to examine one of the witnesses in a case, in order that they may gain from the experience and indeed be given the chance to advance their career.'

'I think I can see where this is leading, Mr Redmayne.'

'Then with your permission, m'lord, my junior, Sir Matthew Redmayne, will lead for the defence when we examine the next witness, Mr Spencer Craig.'

The rest of the press corps bolted for the door.

77

DANNY SPENT another sleepless night in his cell at Belmarsh, and it wasn't just Big Al's snoring that kept him awake.

Beth sat up in bed trying to read a book, but she never turned a page as her mind was more concerned with the ending of another story.

Alex Redmayne didn't sleep, because he knew that if they failed tomorrow, he would not be given a third chance.

Sir Matthew Redmayne didn't even bother to go to bed, but went over the order of his questions again and again.

Spencer Craig tossed and turned as he tried to work out which questions Sir Matthew was most likely to ask, and how he could avoid answering them.

Arnold Pearson never slept.

Mr Justice Hackett slept soundly.

Court number four was already packed by the time Danny took his place in the dock. He glanced around the courtroom, and was surprised to see a melee of senior barristers and solicitors attempting to find vantage points from which to follow proceedings.

The press benches were filled with crime correspondents who for the past week had written hundreds of column inches, and had warned their editors to expect a lead story for tomorrow's first editions. They couldn't wait for the encounter between the greatest advocate since F. E. Smith and the most brilliant young QC of his generation (*The Times*), or the Mongoose versus the Snake (the *Sun*).

Danny looked up at the public gallery and smiled at Beth, who was sitting in her usual place next to his mother. Sarah Davenport was seated at the end of the front row, her head bowed. On counsel's bench Mr Pearson was chatting to his junior. He looked more relaxed than at any time during the trial; but then today he would only be a spectator, not a participant.

The only empty seats to be found in the well of the courtroom were at the far end of counsel's bench awaiting the entrance of Alex Redmayne and his junior. Two extra policemen had been stationed on the door to explain to latecomers that only those on official business could now be accommodated in the courtroom.

Danny sat in the centre of the dock, the best seat in the house. This was one performance for which he would like to have read the script before the curtain went up.

There was a babble of anticipation in the room as everyone awaited the four remaining participants who still had to make their entrance. At five minutes to ten, a policeman opened the court-room door and a hush fell over the assembled gathering as those who had been unable to find a seat stood aside to allow Alex Redmayne and his junior to make their way to counsel's bench.

This morning Sir Matthew made no pretence of slumping in a corner and closing his eyes. He didn't even sit down. He stood bolt upright and looked around the courtroom. It was many years since he'd appeared as an advocate in any court. Once he'd found his bearings, he unfolded a small wooden stand that his wife had retrieved from the loft the night before, and which hadn't seen service for a decade. He placed it on the desk in front of him, and from his bag he removed a sheaf of papers on which he had written in his neat hand the questions Spencer Craig had spent all night trying to anticipate. Finally he handed Alex two photographs that they both knew could decide the fate of Danny Cartwright.

Only after everything was in place did Sir Matthew turn and smile at his old adversary. 'Good morning, Arnold,' he said. 'I do hope that we won't be troubling you too much today.'

Pearson returned the smile. 'A sentiment with which I am fully able to concur,' he said. 'In fact, I'm going to break the habit of a lifetime, Matthew, and wish you luck, despite the fact I have never once during all my years at the Bar wanted my opponent to win. Today is the exception.'

Sir Matthew gave a slight bow. 'I will do my best to fulfil your wishes.' He then sat down, closed his eyes and began to compose himself.

Alex busied himself preparing documents, transcripts, photographs and other miscellaneous material in neat piles so that when his father shot out his right hand, like an Olympic relay runner, the baton would be passed instantly.

The noise of uninvolved chatter ceased when Mr Justice Hackett made his entrance. He ambled across to the three chairs on the centre of the stage, attempting to give an impression that nothing untoward was about to take place in the court that morning.

Having amply filled the centre chair, he spent longer than usual arranging his pens and checking his notebook while he waited for the jury to take their places.

'Good morning,' he said once they had settled, the tone of his voice rather avuncular. 'Members of the jury, the first witness today will be Mr Spencer Craig QC. You will recall his name being raised during the cross-examination of Sir Hugo Moncrieff. Mr Craig does not appear as a witness for either the prosecution or the defence, but has been subpoenaed to attend this court, meaning that he does not do so willingly. You must remember that your only duty is to decide if the evidence Mr Craig presents has any bearing on the case being tried in this court, namely, did the defendant unlawfully escape from custody? On that count, and that count alone, you will be asked to deliver your verdict.'

Mr Justice Hackett beamed down at the jury before turning his attention to junior counsel. 'Sir Matthew,' he said, 'are you ready to call the witness?'

Matthew Redmayne rose slowly from his place. 'I am indeed, my lord,' he responded, but did not do so. He poured himself a glass of water, then placed a pair of spectacles on the end of his nose, and finally opened his red leather folder. Having satisfied himself that he was ready for the encounter, he said, 'I call Mr Spencer Craig,' his words sounding like a death knell.

A policeman stepped out into the corridor and bellowed, 'Mr Spencer Craig!'

Everyone's attention was now focused on the courtroom door as they awaited the entrance of the final witness. A moment later, Spencer Craig, dressed in his legal garb, strode into the courtroom as if it was just another day in the life of a busy advocate.

Craig stepped into the witness box, picked up the Bible and, facing the jury, delivered the oath in a firm and confident manner. He knew that it was they, and they alone, who would decide his fate. He handed the Bible back to the usher, and turned to face Sir Matthew.

'Mr Craig,' Sir Matthew began in a quiet, lulling tone, as if it was his desire to assist the witness in every possible way. 'Would you be kind enough to state your name and address for the record?'

'Spencer Craig, forty-three Hambledon Terrace, London SW3.'

'And your occupation?'

'I am a barrister at law and a Queen's Counsel.'

'So there is no need for me to remind such an eminent member of the legal profession of the significance of the oath, or the authority of this court.'

'No need at all, Sir Matthew,' replied Craig, 'although you appear to have done so.'

'Mr Craig, when did you first discover that Sir Nicholas Moncrieff was in fact Mr Daniel Cartwright?'

'A friend of mine who had been at school with Sir Nicholas bumped into him at the Dorchester Hotel. He soon realized that the man was an impostor.'

Alex placed a tick in the first box. Craig had clearly anticipated his father's first question, and delivered a well-prepared answer.

'And why should this friend decide to inform *you*, in particular, of this remarkable discovery?'

'He didn't, Sir Matthew; it simply arose in conversation over dinner one night.'

Another tick.

'Then what was it that caused you to take a gigantic leap in the dark and come to the conclusion that the man posing as Sir Nicholas Moncrieff was in fact Daniel Cartwright?'

'I didn't for some time,' said Craig, 'not until I was introduced to the supposed Sir Nicholas at the theatre one evening and was shocked by the similarity in looks, if not in manner, between him and Cartwright.'

'Was that the moment when you decided to contact Chief Inspector Fuller and alert him to your misgivings?'

'No. I felt that would have been irresponsible, so I first made contact with a member of the Moncrieff family in case, as you have suggested, I was taking a gigantic leap in the dark.'

Alex placed another tick on the list of questions. So far, his father hadn't laid a glove on Craig.

'Which member of the family did you contact?' asked Sir Matthew, knowing only too well.

'Mr Hugo Moncrieff, Sir Nicholas's uncle, who informed me that his nephew had not been in touch with him since the day he'd been released from prison some two years before, which only added to my suspicions.'

'Was that when you reported those suspicions to Chief Inspector Fuller?'

'No, I still felt I needed more concrete evidence.'

'But the chief inspector could have relieved you of that burden, Mr Craig. I am at a loss to understand why a busy professional gentleman like yourself chose to remain involved?'

'As I've already explained, Sir Matthew, I felt it was my responsibility to make sure that I wasn't wasting the police's time.'

'How very public-spirited of you.' Craig ignored Sir Matthew's barbed comment, and smiled at the jury. 'But I'm bound to ask,' added Sir Matthew, 'who it was that alerted you to the possible advantages of being able to prove that the man posing as Sir Nicholas Moncrieff was in fact an impostor?'

'The advantages?'

'Yes, the advantages, Mr Craig.'

'I'm not sure I follow you,' said Craig. Alex placed the first cross on his list. The witness was clearly playing for time.

'Then allow me to assist you,' said Sir Matthew. He put out his right hand and Alex handed him a single sheet of paper. Sir Matthew ran his eye slowly down the page, giving Craig time to wonder just what bombshells it could possibly contain.

'Would I be right in suggesting, Mr Craig,' said Sir Matthew, 'that if you were able to prove that it was Nicholas Moncrieff and not Danny Cartwright who committed suicide while in Belmarsh prison, Mr Hugo Moncrieff would not only inherit the family title, but a vast fortune to go with it.'

'I was not aware of that at the time,' said Craig, not flinching.

'So you were acting with entirely altruistic motives?'

'Yes, I was, sir, as well as the desire to see a dangerous and violent criminal locked up.'

'I will be coming to the dangerous and violent criminal who should be locked up in a moment, Mr Craig, but before then, allow me to ask you when your acute sense of public service was overcome by the possibility of making a quick buck?'

'Sir Matthew,' interrupted the judge, 'that is hardly the sort of language I expect from junior counsel when addressing a QC.'

'I apologize, m'lord. I will rephrase my question. Mr Craig, when did you first become aware of the chance of making several million pounds from a piece of information you had picked up from a friend over dinner?'

'When Sir Hugo invited me to act on his behalf in a private capacity.'

Alex placed another tick against another anticipated question, although he knew Craig was lying.

'Mr Craig, do you consider it ethical for a QC to charge twenty-five per cent of a man's inheritance in exchange for a piece of second-hand information?'

'It is now quite common, Sir Matthew, for barristers to be paid on results,' said Craig calmly. 'I realize the practice has only been introduced since your day, so perhaps I should point out that I did not charge a fee or any expenses, and that had my suspicions been proved wrong I would have wasted a considerable amount of my time and money.'

Sir Matthew smiled at him. 'Then you will be delighted to

learn, Mr Craig, that the altruistic side of your nature has won the day.' Craig didn't rise to Sir Matthew's barb, although he was desperate to find out what he meant by it. Sir Matthew took his time before he added, 'As you may be aware, the court has recently been informed by Mr Fraser Munro, the late Sir Nicholas Moncrieff's solicitor, that his client bequeathed his entire estate to his close friend Mr Danny Cartwright. So you have, as you feared might be the case, wasted a considerable amount of your time and money. But despite my client's good fortune, let me assure you, Mr Craig, that I shall not be charging *him* twenty-five per cent of his inheritance for my services.'

'Nor should you,' snapped Craig angrily, 'as he'll be spending at least the next twenty-five years in prison, and will therefore have to wait an awfully long time before he can benefit from this unexpected windfall.'

'I may be wrong, Mr Craig,' said Sir Matthew quietly, 'but I have a feeling that it will be the jury who makes that decision, and not you.'

'I may be wrong, Sir Matthew, but I think you'll find that a jury has already made that decision some time ago.'

'Which brings me neatly on to your meeting with Chief Inspector Fuller, which you were so keen that nobody should find out about.' Craig looked as if he was about to respond, then clearly thought better of it, and allowed Sir Matthew to continue. 'The chief inspector, being a conscientious officer, informed the court that he would require a little more proof than photographs revealing a close similarity between the two men before he could consider making an arrest. In an answer to one of my leader's questions, he confirmed that you supplied him with that proof.'

Sir Matthew knew that he was taking a risk. Had Craig responded by saying that he had no idea what he was talking about, and that he had simply passed on his suspicions to the chief inspector and left him to decide if any action should be taken, Sir Matthew had no follow-up question. He would then have to move on to a different subject, and Craig would have realized that he had merely been on a fishing expedition – and had landed nothing. But Craig did not respond immediately, which gave Sir Matthew the confidence to take an even bigger risk. He turned to Alex and said, in a voice loud enough for Craig to hear, 'Let me have those photographs of Cartwright running along the Embankment, the ones that show the scar.'

Alex handed his father two large photographs.

After a long pause Craig said, 'I may have told the chief inspector that if the man living in The Boltons had a scar on his left thigh, just above the knee, that would prove that he was in fact Danny Cartwright.'

The look on Alex's face revealed nothing, although he could hear his heart beating.

'And did you then hand over some photographs to the chief inspector to prove your point?'

'I may have done,' admitted Craig.

'Perhaps if you were to see copies of the photographs they might refresh your memory?' suggested Sir Matthew, thrusting them towards him. The biggest risk of all.

'That won't be necessary,' said Craig.

'I would like to see the photographs,' said the judge, 'and I suspect the jury would as well, Sir Matthew.' Alex turned to see that several members of the jury were nodding.

'Certainly, m'lord,' said Sir Matthew. Alex handed a pile of photographs to the usher, who gave two to the judge before distributing the remainder to the jury, to Pearson and finally to the witness.

Craig stared at the photos in disbelief. They were not the ones Gerald Payne had taken when Cartwright had been out on his evening run. If he had not admitted to knowing about the scar the defence would have crumbled, and the jury would have been none the wiser. He realized that Sir Matthew had landed a blow, but he was still on his feet, and would not fall for a sucker punch a second time.

'My lord,' said Sir Matthew, 'you will see the scar that the witness referred to is on Mr Cartwright's left thigh, just above the knee. It has faded with the passing of time, but still remains clear to the naked eye.' He turned his attention back to the witness.

'You will recall, Mr Craig, that Chief Inspector Fuller stated under oath that this was the evidence on which he relied before taking the decision to arrest my client.' Craig made no attempt to contradict him. Sir Matthew didn't press him, as he felt the point had been well established. He paused, to allow the jury more time to study the photographs, as he needed the scar to be indelibly fixed in their minds before he asked a question that he was confident Craig could not have anticipated.

'When did you first phone Chief Inspector Fuller?'

Once again there was a silence, as Craig, like everyone else in the court other than Alex, tried to work out the significance of the question.

'I'm not sure I understand,' he replied eventually.

'Then allow me to refresh your memory, Mr Craig. You phoned Chief Inspector Fuller on October twenty-third last year, the day before you met him at an undisclosed location to hand over the photographs showing Danny Cartwright's scar. But when was the first occasion you came into contact with him?'

Craig tried to think of some way he could avoid answering Sir Matthew's question. He looked towards the judge, hoping for guidance. He received none.

'He was the policeman who turned up at the Dunlop Arms when I called 999 after I had witnessed Danny Cartwright stabbing his friend to death,' he eventually managed.

'His friend,' said Sir Matthew quickly, getting it on the record before the judge could intervene. Alex smiled at his father's ingenuity.

Mr Justice Hackett frowned. He knew he could no longer prevent Sir Matthew pursuing the question of the original trial now that Craig himself had unwittingly brought the subject into play. 'His friend,' repeated Sir Matthew looking at the jury. He expected Arnold Pearson to leap up and cut him short, but there was no movement from the other end of counsel's bench.

'That's how Bernard Wilson was described in the court transcript,' said Craig with confidence.

'Indeed he was,' said Sir Matthew, 'and I shall be referring to that transcript later. But for now I would like to return to Chief Inspector Fuller. On the first occasion you met him, following the death of Bernard Wilson, you made a statement.'

'Yes, I did.'

'In fact, Mr Craig, you ended up making three statements: the first, thirty-seven minutes after the stabbing had taken place; the second, which you wrote later that night because you couldn't sleep; and a third seven months later, when you appeared in the witness box at Danny Cartwright's trial. I am in possession of all three of those statements, and I must admit, Mr Craig, that they are admirably consistent.' Craig didn't comment as he waited for the sting in the tail. 'However, what I am puzzled by is the scar on Danny Cartwright's left leg because you said in your first state-ment – ' Alex handed his father a single sheet of paper, from which he read – 'I saw Cartwright pick up the knife from the bar and follow the woman and the other man out into the alley. A few moments later I heard a scream. That was when I ran out into the alley and saw Cartwright stabbing Wilson in the chest again and again. I then returned to the bar and *immediately* phoned the police.' Sir Matthew looked up. 'Do you wish to make any amend-ments to that statement?'

'No,' said Craig firmly, 'that is exactly what happened.'

'Well, not quite exactly,' said Mr Redmayne, 'because police records show that you made your call at eleven twenty-three, so one is bound to ask what you were doing between—'

'Sir Matthew,' interrupted the judge, surprised that Pearson hadn't leapt to his feet to intervene, but remained resolutely seated in his place, arms folded. 'Are you able to show that this line of questioning is relevant, remembering that the only offence left on the charge sheet concerns your client escaping from custody?'

Sir Matthew waited long enough for the jury to become curious about why he had not been allowed to finish his previous ques-tion before he responded. 'No, I am not, m'lord. However, I do wish to pursue a line of questioning that is relevant to this case, namely the scar on the defendant's left leg.' He once again made eye contact with Craig. 'Can I confirm, Mr Craig, that you did not witness Danny Cartwright being stabbed in the leg, which left him with the scar shown so clearly in the photographs which you handed over to the chief inspector and was the evidence he relied upon to arrest my client?'

Alex held his breath. It was some time before Craig eventually said, 'No, I did not.'

'So please indulge me for a moment, Mr Craig, and allow me to put forward three scenarios for your consideration. You can then tell the jury, from your vast experience of the criminal mind, which of them you consider to be the most likely.'

'If you feel a parlour game will in any way assist the jury, Sir Matthew,' sighed Craig, 'please be my guest.'

'I think you will find that it's a parlour game that will assist the jury,' said Sir Matthew. The two men stared at each other for some time before Sir Matthew added, 'Allow me to suggest the first scenario. Danny Cartwright grabs the knife from the bar just as you suggested, follows his fiancée into the alley, stabs himself in the leg, pulls out the knife, and then stabs his best friend to death.'

Laughter broke out in the court. Craig waited for it to die down before he responded.

'That's a farcical suggestion, Sir Matthew, and you know it.'

'I'm glad that we have at last found something on which we can agree, Mr Craig. Let me move on to my second scenario. It was in fact Bernie Wilson who grabbed the knife from the bar, he and Cartwright go out into the alley, he stabs Cartwright in the leg, pulls out the knife and then stabs himself to death.'

This time even the jury joined in the laughter.

'That's even more farcical,' said Craig. 'I'm not quite sure what you imagine this charade is proving.'

'This charade is proving,' said Sir Matthew, 'that the man who stabbed Danny Cartwright in the leg was the same man who stabbed Bernie Wilson in the chest, because only one knife was involved – the one picked up from the bar. So I agree with you, Mr Craig, my first two scenarios are farcical, but before I put the third one to you, allow me to ask you one final question.' Every eye in the courtroom was now on Sir Matthew. 'If you did not witness Cartwright being stabbed in the leg, how could you possibly have known about the scar?'

Everyone's gaze was transferred to Craig. He was no longer calm. His hands felt clammy as they gripped the side of the witness box.

'I must have read about it in the transcript of the trial,' said Craig, trying to sound confident.

'You know, one of the problems that an old warhorse like myself faces once he's pensioned off,' said Sir Matthew, 'is that he has nothing to do with his spare time. So for the past six months, my bedside reading has been this transcript.' He held up a five-inch-thick document, and added, 'From cover to cover. Not once, but twice. And one of the things I discovered during my years at the Bar was that often it's not what's in the evidence that gives a criminal away, but what has been left out. Let me assure you, Mr Craig, there is no mention, from the first page to the last, of a wound to Danny Cartwright's left leg.' Sir Matthew added, almost in a whisper, 'And so I come to my final scenario, Mr Craig. 'It was *you* who picked up the knife from the bar before running out into the alley. It was *you* who thrust the knife into Danny Cartwright's leg. It was *you* who stabbed Bernie Wilson in the chest and left him to die in the arms of his friend. And it will be *you* who will spend the rest of your life in prison.'

Uproar broke out in the courtroom.

Sir Matthew turned to Arnold Pearson, who still wasn't lifting a finger to assist his colleague, but remained hunched up in the corner of counsel's bench, his arms folded.

The judge waited until the usher had called for silence and order was restored before saying, 'I feel I should give Mr Craig the opportunity to answer Sir Matthew's accusations rather than leave them hanging in the air.'

'I will be only too happy to do so, m'lord,' said Craig evenly, 'but first I should like to suggest to Sir Matthew a fourth scenario, which at least has the merit of credibility.'

'I can't wait,' said Sir Matthew, leaning back.

'Given your client's background, isn't it possible that the wound to his leg was inflicted at some time before the night in question?'

'But that still doesn't explain how you could possibly have known about the scar in the first place.'

'I don't have to explain,' said Craig defiantly, 'because a jury has already decided that your client didn't have a leg to stand on.' He looked rather pleased with himself.

'I wouldn't be so sure about that,' said Sir Matthew, turning to his son, who on cue handed him a small cardboard box. Sir Matthew placed the box on the ledge in front of him, and took his time before removing a pair of jeans and holding them up in full view of the jury. 'These are the jeans that the prison service returned to Miss Elizabeth Wilson when it was thought that Danny Cartwright had hanged himself. I am sure that the jury will be interested to see that there is a bloodstained tear in the left lower thigh region, which matches up exactly with . . .'

The outburst that followed drowned out the rest of Sir Matthew's words. Everyone turned to look at Craig, wanting to find out what his answer would be, but he wasn't given the chance to reply, as Pearson finally rose to his feet.

'M'lord, I must remind Sir Matthew that it is not Mr Craig who is on trial,' Pearson declared, having to almost shout in order to make himself heard, 'and that this piece of evidence' – he pointed at the jeans which Sir Matthew was still holding up – 'has no relevance when it comes to deciding if Cartwright did or did not escape from custody.'

Mr Justice Hackett was no longer able to hide his anger. His jovial smile had been replaced by a grim visage. Once silence had returned to his court, he said, 'I couldn't agree with you more, Mr Pearson. A bloodstained tear in the defendant's jeans is certainly not relevant to this case.' He paused for a moment before looking down at the witness with disdain. 'However, I feel I have been left with no choice but to abandon this trial and dismiss the jury until all the transcripts of this and the earlier case have been sent to the DPP for his consideration, because I am of the opinion that a gross miscarriage of justice may have taken place in the case of The Crown versus Daniel Arthur Cartwright.'

This time the judge made no attempt to quell the uproar that followed as journalists bolted for the door, some of them already on their mobile phones even before they had left the courtroom.

Alex turned to congratulate his father, to find him slumped in the corner of the bench, his eyes closed. He opened an eyelid, peered up at his son and remarked, 'It's far from over yet, my boy.'

BOOK SIX

JUDGEMENT

78

Though I speak with the tongues of men and of angels, and have not . . .

Once Father Michael had blessed the bride and groom, Mr and Mrs Cartwright joined the rest of the congregation as they gathered around the grave of Danny Cartwright.

And though I have the gift of prophecy and understand all mysteries and all knowledge, and though I have all faith so that I could remove mountains, and have not . . .

It had been the bride's wish to honour Nick in this way, and Father Michael had agreed to conduct a service in memory of the man whose death had made it possible for Danny to prove his innocence.

And though I bestow all my goods to feed the poor, and though I give my body to be burned, and have not . . .

Apart from Danny, only two people present had known the man who had come to be buried in a foreign field. One of them stood upright on the far side of the grave, dressed in a black tailcoat, wing collar and black silk tie. Fraser Munro had travelled down from Dunbroath to the East End of London to represent the last in the line of Moncrieffs that he would serve. Danny had tried to thank him for his wisdom and strength at all times, but all Mr Munro had said was, 'I wish I'd had the privilege of serving you both. But that was not the Lord's will,' added the elder of the Kirk. Something else Danny hadn't known about the man.

When they had all met up at Wilson House before the marriage ceremony began, Munro took some considerable time admiring

Danny's paintings. 'I had no idea, Danny, that you were a collector of McTaggart, Peploe and Lauder.'

Danny grinned. 'I think you'll find it was Lawrence Davenport who collected them. I merely acquired them, but having lived with them I intend to add more of the Scottish school to my collection.'

'How like your grandfather,' said Munro. Danny decided not to point out to Mr Munro that he had never actually met Sir Alexander. 'By the way,' added Munro sheepishly, 'I must admit to having hit one of your adversaries below the belt while you were safely locked up in Belmarsh.'

'Which one?'

'Sir Hugo Moncrieff, no less. And what's worse, I did so without seeking your approval, most unprofessional of me. I've wanted to get it off my chest for some time.'

'Well, now's your chance, Mr Munro,' said Danny, trying to keep a straight face. 'So what have you been up to in my absence?'

'I must confess that I sent all the papers concerning the validity of Sir Alexander's second will to the Procurator Fiscal's office, alerting them to the fact that I felt an offence may have been committed.' Danny didn't speak. He had learned early on in their relationship not to interrupt Munro while he was in full flow. 'As nothing happened for several months, I assumed that Mr Galbraith had somehow managed to have the whole episode swept under the carpet.' He paused. 'That was until I read this morning's *Scotsman* on the plane down to London.' He opened his ever-present briefcase, took out a newspaper and passed it across to Danny.

Danny stared at the front page headline. *Sir Hugo Moncrieff arrested for forgery and attempted fraud.* The article was accompanied by a large photograph of Sir Nicholas Moncrieff that in Danny's opinion didn't do him justice. When Danny finished reading the article, he smiled and said to Munro, 'Well, you did say that if he caused me any further trouble, then "all bets are off".'

'Did I really utter those words?' said Munro in disgust.

For we know in part, and we prophesy in part.

Danny's eyes moved on to the only other person present who

had been a friend of Nick's, and had known him far better than either he or Munro had. Big Al stood to attention between Ray Pascoe and Alan Jenkins. The governor had granted him compassionate leave to attend the funeral of his friend. Danny smiled when their eyes met, but Big Al quickly bowed his head. He didn't want these strangers to see him weeping.

But when that which is perfect is come, then that which is in part shall be done away.

Danny turned his attention to Alex Redmayne, who hadn't been able to hide his delight when Beth had invited him to be godfather to their son, the brother of Christy. Alex stood next to his father, the man who had made it possible for Danny to be a free man.

When they had all met in Alex's chambers a few days after the trial had been abandoned, Danny had asked Sir Matthew what he'd meant when he'd said, 'It's far from over yet.' The old judge had taken Danny to one side so that Beth could not hear his words, and told him that although Craig, Payne and Davenport had all been arrested and charged with the murder of Bernie Wilson, they were still professing their innocence, and were clearly working together as a team. He warned Danny that he and Beth would be put through the ordeal of a further trial at which they would both have to testify about what had really happened that night to another friend who was buried in St Mary's churchyard. Unless, of course . . .

For now we see through a glass, darkly; but then face to face: now I know in part; but then shall I know even as also I am known.

Danny couldn't resist looking across the road, where a newly painted sign had recently been put in place: *Cartwright's Garage, Under New Management.* Once he'd completed the negotiations and agreed a price with Monty Hughes, Munro had drawn up a contract that would allow Danny to take over a business that he would be able to commute to each morning by crossing the road.

The Swiss bankers had made it clear that they considered Danny had paid far too high a price for the garage on the other side of the road. Danny didn't bother to explain to Segat the difference between the words price and value, as he doubted if either he or Bresson would have spent much time with Mr Oscar Wilde.

And now abideth faith, hope, charity, these three; but the greatest of these is charity.

Danny gripped his wife's hand. Tomorrow they would fly to Rome for a much-delayed honeymoon, during which they would try to forget that when they returned they would have to face another long trial before the ordeal would finally be over. Their ten-week-old son chose that moment to express his feelings by bursting into tears, and not in memory of Sir Nicholas Moncrieff, but simply because he felt that the service had gone on for far too long, and in any case, he was hungry.

'Shh,' said Beth soothingly. 'It won't be much longer before we can all go home,' his mother promised as she took Nick in her arms.

In the name of the father and of the son . . .

79

'BRING UP the prisoners.'

Court number four at the Old Bailey was packed long before ten o'clock in the forenoon, but then, it was not every day that a Queen's Counsel, a Member of Parliament and a popular actor were arraigned on charges of murder, affray and conspiracy to pervert the course of justice.

Counsel's bench was littered with legal luminaries who were checking files, arranging documents and in one case putting final touches to an opening speech, as they waited for the prisoners to take their place in the dock.

All three defendants were being represented by the most eminent legal minds their solicitors could instruct, and the talk in the corridors of the Old Bailey was that as long as they all stuck to their original story, it was doubtful if any twelve jurors would be able to reach a unanimous verdict. The chatter subsided when Spencer Craig, Gerald Payne and Lawrence Davenport took their places in the dock.

Craig was so conservatively dressed in a dark blue pinstriped suit, white shirt and his favourite mauve tie that it appeared as if he had entered through the wrong door, and that it should have been he who was seated on counsel's bench waiting to deliver the opening speech.

Payne was wearing a dark grey suit, college tie and cream shirt, as befitted a Member of Parliament representing a rural seat. He appeared calm.

Davenport wore faded jeans, an open-necked shirt and a blazer.

He was unshaven, which the press would describe the following morning as designer stubble; but they would also report that he looked as if he hadn't slept for several days. Davenport ignored the press benches and glanced up towards the public gallery, while Payne and Craig chatted to each other as if they were waiting to be served lunch in a busy restaurant. Once Davenport had checked to see that she was in her place, he stared blankly in front of him and waited for the judge to appear.

Everyone who had managed to secure a place in the packed courtroom rose as Mr Justice Armitage entered. He waited for them to bow before returning the compliment, taking the middle seat on the bench. He smiled down benevolently as if this was just another day at the office. He instructed the court usher to bring in the jury. The usher bowed low before disappearing through a side door, to reappear moments later followed by the twelve citizens who had been selected by rote to sit in judgement on the three defendants.

Lawrence Davenport's barrister allowed the flicker of a smile to cross his face when he saw that the jury consisted of seven women and five men. He felt confident that the worst result would now be a hung jury.

As the jury took their places in the box, Craig studied them with intense interest, aware that they and they alone would decide his fate. He'd already briefed Larry to make eye contact with the women jurors as they only needed three who couldn't bear the idea of Lawrence Davenport being sent to jail. If Larry could just manage that simple task, they would all be set free. But Craig was annoyed to see that rather than obeying his simple instruction, Davenport appeared preoccupied and just stared fixedly in front of him.

Once the jury had settled, the judge invited the associate to read out the charges.

'Will the defendants please rise.'

All three of them stood up.

'Spencer Malcolm Craig, you are charged that on the night of September eighteenth 1999 you did murder one Bernard Henry Wilson. How do you plead, guilty or not guilty?'

'Not guilty,' said Craig defiantly.

'Gerald David Payne, you are charged that on the night of September eighteenth 1999 you were involved in an affray that ended in the death of Bernard Henry Wilson. How do you plead, guilty or not guilty?'

'Not guilty,' said Payne firmly.

'Lawrence Andrew Davenport, you are charged with perverting the course of justice, in that on March twenty-third 2000, you gave evidence on oath that you knew to be false in a material particular. How do you plead, guilty or not guilty?'

Every eye in the courtroom was fixed on the actor, who found himself once again centre stage. Lawrence Davenport raised his head and looked up into the public gallery, where his sister was seated at the end of the front row.

Sarah gave her brother a reassuring smile.

Davenport lowered his head, and for a moment seemed to hesitate before saying in a whisper that was barely audible, 'Guilty.'